OUT OF TIME

OUT OF TIME

The Timeless Julieanna Scott

Book One

CHERIE BAKER

DRAGON LIME
2023

Copyright © Cherie Baker 2023

Cherie Baker asserts her moral rights to be identified as the author of this work in accordance with the Copyright, Design, and Patents act 1988.

All rights reserved. This book, or any portion thereof, may not be reproduced, stored electronically, digitally copied or used in any manner whatsoever without the express written permission of the publisher.

This book is a work of fiction. All places, characters, and events are products of the author's vivid imagination. Any resemblance to real places, events or persons, living or deceased, is purely coincidental.

First Printing: 2019

978-1-911726-00-5 e-book
978-1-911726-01-2 paperback
Dragon Lime
dragonlime.com
Cover designed by Dragon Lime.
Images by Cove 703 Designs and Novel Storm Digital Assets @ Creative Fabrica

This novel uses British spellings, such as colour, moustache, and favourite, as well as informal words specific to parts of Scotland and England.

For Wookie:
You know what you did.
This book would not have even started without you.
Thanks

ONE

The klaxon wound up to a high-pitched wail that carried on and on. I shoved my notebook in a drawer and stripped off my white lab coat. All day, all poxy day, this storm had loomed on the horizon. Of course, it came in the middle of an experiment.

Keys... I slapped my pockets. Where did they go this time? Nothing forgotten for six hundred years, yet somehow the blasted things hid every time I set them down.

After flipping a pile of papers to the side, brass glinted. Finally! I grabbed the fob and sprinted out of the lab, running down two flights of concrete steps.

My horrid mobile device jingled en route.

Whatever it was could wait, the storm would not. Heavy purple clouds obscured the sun, casting the dark-of-night across the glass foyer of my research facility.

Outside, someone fumbled at the front door. Leaves torn free by the storm pelted the figure as he slapped his badge against the console twice. The doors didn't click open. Every nerve in my body jumped to attention. My heart thumped louder. There had been no attempts on my life all year, but an innocent visitor wouldn't be out in this weather.

He flipped his badge over and slapped it against the console again, then yanked the doors open. Water poured off the white shirt plastered to his stocky frame.

Before he could get a weapon out, I shoved the man outside. He lost his balance and stumbled. The ID badge clattered to the ground. It was real.

The pieces clicked. Not an intruder, simply a new intern. I really should catch up on my emails. HR had probably sent something about him.

I helped the fellow to his feet. "Sorry, didn't see you there."

The pine trees surrounding the building swayed, their bushy green fronds bowing to the majesty of the storm.

He nodded. "Weather's a nightmare."

"Aye, you need to get inside." I nodded at the building before sprinting for my vehicle.

The moment I left the shelter of the building, a crack of thunder rolled across the concrete square. The air felt alive with electricity.

Climbing into my 1962 Ford Falcon, I put the windscreen wipers on full. The tip of the funnel cloud dangled like a babe's crib toy, slipping in and out of sight under the heavy black skies.

Even with the delay, catching up with it should be possible. I threaded through the congested city centre to the road out of town. It was barely visible through the sheets of water bucketing from the heavy skies. My motorcar sped up the hopefully empty road in pursuit.

The radio jumped and warbled, but enough got through to know the bedevilled storm was shifting west. I spun the wheel, sliding on the wet pavement, but made the turn.

Ahead of me, I caught my first glimpse of the funnel cloud. It touched down on a farm. Splinters of shattered timber pelted the nose of my vehicle. I sped closer, hoping to catch the twister as it moved across the road.

Sirens wailed to life behind me.

Were those for me? I glanced at my rearview mirror. Sure enough, blue and red lights flashed behind me. The vexing, ill-bred bonehead driving the cruiser had swung round to follow me.

I was only a few miles from the funnel cloud. He couldn't write a ticket to a mangled wreck. I floored the accelerator, but the little bird was already flying as fast as she could.

"Anna! For Christ's sake—pull over!" The PA voice was a sketchy digitised sound but clear enough to recognise Carl, a companion of thirty years.

Blasted hell. I slammed on the brakes. Tires skidded. The Falcon swerved toward the shoulder. Gravel sprayed metal.

The twister roared as loud as a steam locomotive leaving the station. It skipped the road and ploughed through an empty field. Dirt sprayed up as it moved further and further away.

Anger and frustration washed over me in a tsunami of emotion. Once again, life had ripped me from the hunt the moment before ecstasy. This had better be good.

I wrenched my door open and stomped towards the cruiser.

Carl stepped out. He hunched against the pelting rain and jogged closer. "Geoff's been shot," he shouted over the wind.

The words pierced through my anger, deflating it faster than a soufflé. "How bad?"

He swallowed and looked away.

Dead? Geoffrey was dead?

Memories of Geoffrey crowded my mind. His white moustache bobbing before he got to the punch line. Him reaching for a whisky glass. His kisses.

I sank to the ground, punching the gravel until blood ran from my split knuckles. I'd known. Some hidden part of me had, anyway. The passing of a companion always twisted my mind towards a reckless need to pursue destruction. Apparently tornadoes were my current panacea.

"Blood of my blood... aeternum vale." Farewell forever.

Tendrils of my hair waved in the wind like escaping snakes. The finality of the last goodbye bowed my head to the ground. Cold drops splatted the back of my neck, worming their way down my spine. What did it matter? I'd lost another companion. He'd been one of the best I'd ever had.

Carl coughed, shifting from one foot to the other while trying to keep his back to the wind.

The clouds may as well weep. Crying never eased this pain. Nothing brought back lost love. I stood and pulled Carl close. His breath caught a little, and he thumped my back.

"He was my friend too," he said, his voice barely audible over the storm.

"We need to know what happened. Geoffrey wasn't working on anything sensitive."

Carl nodded, but hunched further into his coat. "I can't do anything right now. As it is, I'm gonna get my balls squeezed for chasing you down. All emergency responders should be dealing with the storm."

I kicked the Falcon, leaving a dent in her fender. Confound it. There weren't any other companions close enough to help, but I couldn't call him away. His place with the police was too useful.

"Attend to your work, then meet me down-town."

I'd start the investigation on my own. This was too important to wait.

TWO

The best part of the whole depressing day was how quickly the miles disappeared on my return journey. Half an hour later, toenails clicked and muffled woofs echoed through the wall as I turned the key in my rented condo's plain white aluminium door. The same door as every other house on this street. A nice anonymous entrance in a city large enough I never needed to acknowledge my neighbours. The perfect place to exist unnoticed. I just wished it wasn't so noisy.

The door didn't budge. I leaned in and pushed harder. "Back up, silly beast."

Bouncing on his hind legs to look me in the eye, my mottled black and grey mastiff Vladimir welcomed me home with another 'arughoooo'. His vocabulary always sounded like a mix between a cow's moo and a dog's bark.

"Good evening, old cousin." Wrapping my icy fingers in his coarse neck ruff stopped the bouncing and warmed my digits. "Come, you can help me find dry garments."

My constant companion since the start of this unnatural life trotted to the closet and pulled out a pair of fifty-year-old army boots. Although scuffed and wrinkled, the brown leather pair was my favourite. He knew me so well. My shoulders eased after I slipped into the floor length wool skirt and a loose tee shirt, the only modern equivalent to a kirtle.

Tears itched at the corner of my eye. Tears I'd hidden since first learning of Geoffrey's passing. Vlad nudged me with his muzzle, bringing forth a single salty drop. Sliding to my knees, I buried my nose in his fur and let the guilt and remorse wash over me like a wave. Snuggling closer, his musky scent filled my nose and calmed the storm. "Whatever would befall me without your existence?"

He shifted around to get an itchy shoulder scratched, cooing a happy 'arughoooo'.

My melancholy broke with that silly noise. It was time to sort out what was happening. I pulled my plastic lump of technology out of my pocket. How easy was it to trace a mobile telephone signal? I didn't know enough about these monstrosities, but to understand Geoffrey's death, I needed more information so thumbed the power switch. Several minutes passed before it bleeped to indicate there were new messages.

I tapped the screen. Nothing happened. Poxy machine never recognised my fingertips. Maybe it knew something I didn't. I pulled the stylus from the case and scrolled through the emails. The in-box was full of dull but necessary correspondences about my companies. I flipped quickly through them until G_B appeared. Geoffrey had sent it three days ago. I should have known it was there—should have read it straight away.

Confound it! When I'm needed most, one obsession or another saps my attention. I promise it won't, but it keeps happening.

I scrutinised each word of the brief message.

Received a strange item this morning. Think we need to discuss. Would you be free on Monday?

Ta.

Did any of them have a second meaning? So tantalisingly close, but ultimately useless.

A nasty thought crossed my mind. It was almost thirty years ago, but some drug cartels had put out a contract to eliminate my entire troop. But surely we'd eliminated that bother….

THREE

The next morning, there was a knock just after seven. A burly man in uniform waited impatiently on the other side. Carl's short roundness was not overly intimidating but made him a formidable wrestler. He stomped in as soon as I undid the latch.

"You look tired. Let me get you a tankard."

"I have to drive. Besides, beer at seven A.M. is frowned on now-a-days. Do you have any coffee?"

He perched on my red horsehair settee while I laid another piece of wood on the glowing fire. The main reason I'd chosen this condo was the real hearth. I pulled the coffeepot away from the embers and sprinkled a dash of cold water to settle the grounds.

"I've gone through all my company records. Every one. Geoffrey has been nowhere sensitive in years. His current project was surveying trace elements in disused gravel quarries. Nobody murders for that."

"Maybe he found something. More than one man's boots ended in the air over a claim for gold."

Carl shifted his weight and squirmed to find the best placement for his tired body. The settee's stuffing had clumped into odd, uncomfortable shapes, but I loved the carved woodwork and kept moving it from house to house, anyway.

"Possibly. He hasn't submitted this month's reports yet and left a vague message asking me to review a strange item he received two days ago. I'll need to go through his desk to find it," I said.

"That may be a problem."

"What?"

"He worked from home and Tatya's not happy. When Mrs Briggs isn't happy, she makes sure everyone around knows. I can't tell if she just wants attention or there really is something going on. Every time I try to speak to her, she's blubbering, or jabbering in Russian too fast to make heads or tails of it." Carl's eyelids drooped but remained open.

He needed coffee soon, or I wouldn't get any sense out of him. I poured the rich black elixir into a porcelain cup, splashing my thumb in my haste. "Mrs Briggs could have done it. Or arranged it. Was she questioned properly?"

He squinted at me. "Anna, I'm a cop—we notice things. As far as the authorities are concerned, Geoffrey was a church mouse geologist in podunk America, with a perfect marriage. Nothing more exciting than the occasional delivery of top class pornography."

I took a breath and calmed my mind before setting the drink on the table. My worries were all circumstantial. She could be innocent. For her sake, I hoped so.

He added sugar from the silver creamer set and took a sip. "Jesus—how strong do you make this?"

"You asked for coffee. You should remember I serve coffee in the traditional manner."

Carl grimaced and put another spoon of sugar into the stout coffee, stirred and took a quick slug. "This appears to be a motiveless crime, but my gut tells me there's something missing."

"You think she destroyed evidence?"

"Possibly. Or only said what's convenient." He scowled over his steaming cup. "I could call you with updates if you ever answered your phone."

I turned away, stirring the fire. Memories of faces long gone flickered. Nothing brought back a loose word. "People might listen in. You know I do not leave trails."

"No, just complicated, boring, coded messages..." He closed his eyes and took a long gulp of his drink. "Look, I'm tired. Just call Mrs Briggs."

"For what? If there be no evidence of murder, the less she knows, the better."

Carl set his mug down, frowning. "Geoffrey was not the kind of man a burglar could sneak up on. Something's not right. For Christ's sake, he didn't even get his own weapon out. Tatya's already at risk, she just doesn't know why." He pushed his phone across the counter to me.

Scowling, I picked up the horrid thing. Telephones were awful enough, but mobile devices seemed such an unnatural way to converse.

A female voice answered on the first ring. "Hello?"

"Is that Mrs Briggs?"

"Who is this?" Her voice was rough, as if she'd been shouting or crying a lot.

"I am Dr Scott. I was your husband's... colleague. The company recently notified me of the terrible news. How fare thee?" Hopefully, my voice sounded sympathetic.

"Fare thee?"

"How is your well-being?"

"I don't need a therapist. I need answers. Who killed Geoff, and why are they following me?"

"What makes you think people are following you?"

She snorted. "You don't believe me either. Things—go missing. I know where I put them, but they're gone when I come back."

"Anything else?" I asked.

"The phone rings—I pick up, no answer."

"That's all?" I needed something more tangible. The telephone calls could be a nuisance salesmen and grief-stricken minds often mislay things.

"They shouted at Geoff before the gun went off. I tried to tell the police. They never listen."

My stomach knotted. "Do you remember the words?"

"Foreign garbage. Give us er, or a clean shirt'll do ye."

The knot seized into an iron band. It was Scottish slang for 'give it to me, or you're a dead man'. Tatya continued too fast for me to follow, but I paid little attention. My thoughts circled around, trying and failing to think of any reason Scottish robbers would be in Maple Grove. They must have traced something from my estate to Geoffrey. On the bright side, it was unlikely to be a cartel.

Mrs Briggs' high-pitched wail cut through my thoughts, jerking me back to the present. "Pardon?"

"It's my fault." She switched to Russian, but I understood. "—they said everything was clean now..." Her breath caught, and a sob started in the back of her throat.

Panic flooded me. What had this tart been involved with before she met Geoffrey?

"Stop." I bit back my shout. She probably did not understand how easily a loose word led to a trap. "Do not speak any further on this device and tell no one what you have just said. We shall finish this later today."

"But—"

I hung up the phone, dreading what would come from the decision; however, there were too many questions to ignore.

Carl frowned at me. "Think Geoff was murdered?"

"Definitely. Mrs Briggs heard the men demanded 'it' with a heavy Scottish accent. She also mentioned something about a debt she thought was cleared."

Carl's wide brow wrinkled into deep furrows. Ever since he'd lost his hair, those worry lines looked like they extended halfway across his head. He stood, picking up his cap. "Always thought Tatya was too pretty for her own good. Ever wonder how she managed to put herself through medical school?"

By the devil's toes, I should have checked. A recent immigrant wouldn't have that kind of money. It was too late now. Regret never mended a broken bone. "Can you explore that? See when and where she entered the country."

"So what's the plan?" Carl took his phone back.

"Going to need my black suit for a start." I plucked at my cheery shirt. "This isn't suitable for visiting a grieving widow."

Geoffrey's description of Maple Grove—fields, corn, and one smell did little to encouraging me to visit the place, but needs must. Blast it, it was so much harder to keep anonymous in a small town.

I followed Carl to the door. "Send me a copy of the immigration stuff when you're done."

He nodded, rubbing his head with a weak grin. "Sure, first thing this afternoon. These all-nighters get to me. Never used to be a problem when I was twenty."

I patted his arm. "Take care, my friend. I have no wish to lose more companions this season."

"You taught us well. Bastards only get one surprise." He stepped out and walked away. He'd learned long ago not to park the squad car within sight of my anonymous addresses.

Leaning my head against the door, I closed my eyes, and my fingers curled into my palms until the nails drew blood. People had used murder more than once to find the key to my immortality. All it ever gained them was a vendetta. Neither I nor my companions knew that secret.

FOUR

Maple Grove perched on top of two bluffs that were cut in half by a mighty river. The city council had made it an economic hub for the area. The place was as thriving as you could get in this part of nowhere. It had plenty of shops, three petrol stations, a fair ground arena that doubled as a hockey rink in the winter, a cinema, and a museum.

At first I drove through streets crowded with identical new houses, but that changed abruptly to a historic area where imposing homes lined up like debutantes at a ball. Each one was a showcase of wealth and grandeur from a by-gone era.

Geoffrey purchased his home in this part of town since it was too nice to lurk unnoticed for long. I'd need to speak to the neighbours. Someone must have seen something.

I turned the block before the Briggs' address and halfway along found a narrow gravel alley. The lane was a necessity for messy activities such as coal deliveries and stable sweeping in the eighteen hundreds, but a security liability now.

I let Vlad out and walked along the alley, peering between the houses to the main road. Vlad was not nearly as polite, wandering in and out of gardens and sheds with his nose pressed to the ground. It could be difficult to explain if anyone confronted us, but he often found important details.

The Briggs' dark blue Victorian building looked comfortable and loved. Yards of pristine white railing covered the porch, delicate wooden gingerbread fretwork punctuated the gables, and white lace curtains hung in the large widows overlooking the street. It was all very nice. It did not fit my memories of Geoffrey at all.

As Vlad and I got closer, a slim person in a red hooded sweatshirt and jeans emerged from a side door. They stomped toward a metallic blue WRX Impreza with gold wheel trim. A tall woman in a matching herringbone jacket and skirt trotted out the door and shouted something. The slim figure hunched into the hood further and jerked the car door open. It roared to life with a sound like pebbles rattling down a drain. Moments later, garish noise that passed for music these days blared out of the speakers. The vehicle backed up carefully, turned, and sped away. The woman shook her fist at the fancy vehicle.

The tall woman was most likely Mrs Briggs, but I'd need to find out who she was arguing with this early in the morning. Their departure was quite suspicious. Sadly, the car turned the corner before I could make out much of the licence plate.

Vlad and I made our way up the pavement to the house set on a short clipped lawn, with a perfect floral border. Geoffrey's humour had overruled good taste in one area, though. A copy of the manneken pis proudly urinated on the roses.

I glared at my hound. "No digging."

He shook his shoulders and trotted around the side of the porch, sniffing at piles of leaves.

My boots clicked on the polished wood porch. A wicker rocker and swing sat in the corner opposite the door. The furniture looked brand new.

I knocked. The curtains twitched before the door opened a crack. The subtle scent of chamomile, patchouli, and sandalwood drifted around the woman I'd seen on the drive. Slightly taller than me and on the wrong side of fifty, her hair was bright coppery red. What was she thinking, using that dye job? It looked as if she'd used her head to filter toxic waste. Obviously an attractive woman under normal circumstances, today her make-up was a poor mask. Thick concealer covered the dark circles under her eyes, but even waterproof mascara smeared if rubbed too often.

I held out my hand. "Mrs Briggs—"

"It's Doctor," she barked.

I forced a smile. "My mistake, Doctor Briggs, I called earlier. I'm from your husband's work place—Could we speak inside?"

"No."

"Excuse me? You mentioned you were having some... problems after your husband's untimely demise. I'd like to offer my assistance."

"Why?"

I paused. She was being very abrupt. What was she hiding? I forced a breath in. Calm down. Her husband was murdered in their own home. Why wouldn't she be scared?

"Let me start over. As a representative of your husband's employer, there are a few papers I need you to sign, but I can also help if you're facing difficulties at the moment." I flashed a laminated plastic badge from the head office.

She peered at the badge, comparing the face on the square to me, then nodded slightly. "I expected his manager. Why are you here?"

"I liked Mr Briggs' jokes and found his interest in Native American artefacts fascinating."

"If you found his stupid rocks appealing, you should look at that infernal museum he wasted so much time in. It doesn't explain why you're standing on my porch." She pursed her lip and stepped back.

Bloody stubborn woman would not make this easy. "Dr Briggs, your husband will be greatly missed. The company can give any financial and personal support needed. All you need to do is speak to me."

She tilted her head and looked at me with a tight, guarded face. "Just what do you actually do?"

"I'm the senior director of development." That would have to suffice, considering the enormity of what she could never know about me or my business.

"Geoffrey never mentioned you. Why would a senior director give a fig about a geologist or his widow?" She closed her eyes, her face a torrent of pain for a moment before the steel shutter fell again.

"I think of my employees as family. When something this awful occurs, it's only right to attend to the affair personally."

She snorted and crossed her arms. "I'm not buying it. Geoffrey travelled extensively for many projects within the company. I've seen nothing with your name on it."

I forced a smile. "I am the senior director. Do you think my name will be on every letter or payslip?"

She turned to shut the door.

"We studied together at Edinburgh university before our current commercial interest." I blurted it out without planning. Even with all the memories running high, that was a poor choice.

Tatya straightened her back but didn't turn. "You studied with Geoff and are a senior director now? How convenient."

"You mentioned the police won't listen to your story. If you convey the account to me, I can arrange legal aid. You won't have to soldier on alone." I knew more than most about the loneliness and confusion grief caused. Nothing mended it, but words helped some.

"What I have to do is of no concern to you. Good day!"

I shoved my foot forward as Tatya flung the door closed. Two small bones cracked, sending a lance of pain up my leg. Foul sheep harpy! I could have done without that.

"I need to collect Geoffrey's outstanding notes and reports. There is at least a month's worth of work unaccounted for."

Damn it. Her enthusiasm for getting me to leave smacked of hiding something.

She spun round. The lacquer in her hair held every single strand in the perfect coiffure. "You need your reports?" Her hands balled into fist. "You had him jumping to your tune while he was alive! No more."

"Excuse me?"

"You think I'm blind? I doubt you're a director, more likely a measly typist. All these years, I wondered who he was sneaking off with. Now that I know I'm disappointed. He could have done better—did do better. Get off my land before I call the police!" She slammed the door hard enough to leave the swing rocking.

How dare she accuse me of being a pox-ridden harlot? I marched across the worn porch planks. Sharp pain shot through my foot with each stomp. Damn it. Two cracked metatarsals. That would take at least an hour to go away.

Over-wrought, grief-stricken widows never reacted like this to a man. Shame Carl was engaged. He would have fared better. Tatya hadn't even let me into the house.

I was still as clueless about who had attacked Geoffrey as before we started. That infernal woman's jealousy, however well substantiated, was getting in the way. I have to come back. Every mortal had to sleep eventually, but since the sun was still up, I might as well visit the museum. Geoffrey might have an office or desk there.

When I whistled, Vlad galloped to me, chewing vigorously on something. He dropped his new toy, a dented orange and blue soda can. My heart sank. The soft drink was virtually unknown in America, but very popular in Scotland. Who were these spongy toad lickers, and why were they still in Maple Grove?

"Come on Vlad, it's too nice a day to drive."

FIVE

The journey to the museum was brief. Set on a manicured lawn surrounded by hedges and parking lots, the large brick mansion loomed into view after less than ten minutes walking. I would have preferred several miles to stretch my legs and take the air, but this lead was more important.

Ironically, everything about the manor's design was contrived to display wealth—the position on the hill, the pineapple motif on the gate, the use of brick when everyone else made do with timber. Now it was in public ownership. I stifled a grimace. It would be filled with the taste of death and decay, yet if Geoffrey had spent a lot of time here, so must I.

Large banners fluttered from the two-storey balcony announcing a special exhibit. The crisp canvas shone against the dark red brickwork. On the banner, three red tulips tilted over the edge of a vase. The petals brushed against the top of a decayed skull while transparent bubbles floated toward the window. I stopped. Vlad ran into the back of my leg.

Dumbstruck, I blinked and looked again. There was no mistaking that composition. I leaped the wide stone steps two at a time. Vlad caught up, thrusting his shaggy head into my hip.

"Best behaviour," I whispered.

Cocking his head to one side, his enormous amber eyes mocked me. Of course, he knew that already.

An eerie hush greeted us inside. Even though there was no one at the entrance to observe us, we moved with the careful balance of purpose and casualness that rendered us almost invisible. The only sound was Vlad's toenails clicking on the polished floor.

The signs for the exhibit led through two wide corridors filled with glass cases of junk. No matter that it was neatly labelled, it was still junk, now stored forever. What a waste.

Pausing at the final gallery, I waited for an elderly couple in the adjacent room to leave, then glided across the empty room to a bench near the painting. Vlad settled under the seat. Well, mostly under, his massive body would never fit, but he tried. Laying his head on his paws as if napping, he fell motionless. He could have been one of the statues in the gallery.

Filling the far wall was the painting I'd come to see. The tag read, 'Anonymous, eighteenth century, Flanders'.

I could almost smell the turpentine again and hear his raspy voice scolding if I tried to talk to him while he worked. His name may have been lost to history, but I knew.

Oh, Hans—so many years. Would you have believed this would fly around the world?

He was so clever and his conversation so charming. Allowing him to rearrange my clutter in exchange for his company had seemed a trifle. His long hair touched his shoulders, and he would shake his head like a horse in the field rather than let go of his brushes long enough to move it out of his way. His short nose turned up at the end, especially when he squinted for just the right light. A perfectionist to detail, but he could waste whole days forgetting larger, more important tasks like eating or getting his clothes laundered. At the time, it had upset the Brethren to bring an artist into the troop. They couldn't see any way he would prove useful, but he grounded me. Kept me sane during those dark years after the slaughter.

"Enjoying the exhibit?" asked a man as he took a seat on the bench next to me.

Startled, I jerked away. No one had managed to get that close without my knowledge in centuries. The man was thin. Painfully thin. What exactly held his bones together—skin or his suit?

His scent was strange as well. It was too generic, somehow a perfect summary of humanity without any uniqueness. It might be a new fragrance. The chemicals modern perfumers had at their disposal were truly astounding, but the effect was unsettling.

I inched further away. Hopefully, he would leave. "It's a pleasant surprise... the painting is unusual." I tried to sound uninterested.

Nodding slightly, he clasped his hands in his lap. "It is quite vibrant, especially considering its age. This is the first public display. I was lucky enough to discover it in an old barn."

I coughed to hide my smile. This was merely the most recent, not the first display, but no matter. So much faded to distant history, how could the man possibly know the truth?

The man continued without pause. "In my humble opinion, vanita's are unappreciated in modern art. Renaissance society understood the transient nature of life so much better than today's youth. You can't help admiring the way he captured the delicacy of life in the floating soap bubbles."

God, yes! I'd blown soap at the still life for hours before Hans was happy with the arrangement. He was so fussy about minutiae, but the finished work was worth it. He was particular in other ways, too. A warm flush crept up my cheeks. His bedroom antics were particularly entertaining. Creativity could be put to use in so many ways.

A young man in a Hawaiian shirt and halo of frizzy blue hair wandered into the gallery, interrupting my thoughts. The lad rummaged in his bag as he ambled toward us, continuing to walk without looking until he knocked into the corner of my bench. His sketchbook dropped with a bang. As he bent to retrieve the book, his bag crashed into my shoulder, shoving me to the side.

All I had wanted was a few moments of peace to remember my old friend before beginning the investigations, but solitude was elusive today.

The boy jumped up, patting my shoulder. "Sorry… Sorry… bit clumsy in my excitement."

"'Tis fine. Carry on with your study." I waved at the painting. At least Hans' work was getting some appreciation.

The young man's eyes glowed as he grabbed a handful of coloured pencils and turned to face the painting. "I love the way he uses texture. I wonder what his influences were?" he murmured as his hand leaped across the notebook.

He was so earnest, it did not bode well for getting rid of him quickly.

The boy bumped into Vlad. My hound had a good sniff. A gentle flip of his tail signalled his approval before he stretched his long front legs in a good impression of a yogi and emerged from under the bench. He shook himself once before sitting at my side.

My hound usually kept well out of sight while we were in public. What was he doing?

The man next to me raised an eyebrow. "Does this hound belong to you, madam?"

"I would not be so bold as to encourage that pretence, but he does tend to follow me around." I inclined my head, patting Vlad's shoulder.

"Whether he is yours or not, pets have no place in a gallery. I have to ask you to take him outside." His tone was formal and stiff.

I tapped Vlad's shoulder. "You heard the man."

Looking up at me, Vlad's expression asked if we were going to listen to the thin man.

"Don't worry, I won't be long."

He trotted across the room without a second glance.

"That was quite impressive. Does your hound always understand so much?" asked the thin man.

I fought to restrain a smirk. "Only when he wants to."

The boy flashed his notebook at us. "Not bad, eh? Doubt I could ever paint as well as those dudes, but it's fun to have a go." He stuffed the pad back into his bag.

He'd captured the essence of Hans' work is less than two minutes. "It is impressive. Is it usual for you to work so quickly?" I asked.

"Ya... well, if it's just a rough sketch, why spend too much time on it? Only has to be good enough that I can remember it later when I'm typing." He held out his hand.

"I'm Stefan, by the way. Don't think I've seen you round here before."

"Dr Scott," I said, taking his overly warm hand.

"Do you know anything about it?" He hooked his thumb over his shoulder at the painting.

"A bit." A slow smile crept across my face at the understatement of the year. I take my humour where I can. 'Tis not easy finding something to laugh at after so many centuries. "Most likely, it was painted in the sixteenth century, in the lowland countryside, not Flanders, and the master was left-handed."

Stefan tapped the page with his pen. "Wow. That is so cool. How can you tell? There isn't anything in the books about it."

The thin man tilted his head toward me. "That is because there is no documented proof."

I didn't have time to explain art history to the boy and the pedantic, flea-brained skeleton. "Simply my opinion. Look at the where the brush strokes originate from. Also, I think the scene outside the window has a canal in the distance."

Stefan stepped up to the painting and peered at the small window set in the background of the painting. He squinted, then shrugged. "Can't tell, it's tiny." Stefan spoke in a rush of words, bouncing on his toes. "Anthony travels all over the world, bringing art to places that normally wouldn't have any. There were some of Rubens' work here last month and a Goya the month before that."

Alarm bells rang in my head at the mention of a travelling exhibit. It would be the perfect cover for a covert operation.

The thin man bowed his head, hiding a smile. "As ever, your eagerness is astounding."

Stefan's face clouded over. "Sorry, but you weren't saying anything."

"So, when did this show open?" I asked.

The thin man tapped his fingers together as if counting. "Three days ago, I believe. Time passes so quickly, it's hard to keep track."

Two days ago, Geoffrey was already cold. This man couldn't have been involved. Pity, but I hadn't expected to wrap up the case that easily.

I stood up. It was time to get back to my investigations. Memories would have to wait for another day.

The thin man scrambled to stand as well, watching me with a smile that created tiny creases at the corner of his lip. Something about that smile made me want to smile back. I extended my hand. "I'm afraid I must take my leave."

He took my hand, bowing slightly. His electric blue eyes made my breath catch as he raised it to his lips. "Dr Scott, a delight to have made your acquaintance."

Outside of the Brethren, it had been centuries since anyone had used the correct way to accept a lady's hand instead of the current, vulgar shake.

Stefan froze in place for a moment, then began patting his bag and pockets frantically.

"Are you all right?" I asked. He appeared to have lost something.

"Uh... I think I've left the iron plugged in," he mumbled as he rummaged in his bag, violently pulling out books and pens, before throwing them back.

"Excuse me? There is an electrical appliance in your bag?" I may not understand all of modern technology, but I knew you needed wires for that.

"No... at home. I think I've forgotten to unplug it. The house could burn down! Um, I've got to go," he said in a rush, hurrying out of the room without looking up.

He seemed a very strange boy. Why would a house burn down from an unattended appliance? I must be unfamiliar with them.

Turning back to Anthony, I felt a faint flush rise to my cheek. "Pleasure to meet you, Anthony."

He bowed his head slightly. "It has been a delight. You must come here more often."

"As a matter of fact, I expect I will. I'm trying to catch up with a few things a friend of mine did with the archaeology department."

A loud, angry bark shattered the peace of the gallery before Anthony had a chance to reply. Breaking into a run, I raced to the entrance. That bark was never a good sign.

Outside, Stefan lay curled into a small ball on the lawn next to the front steps. Vladimir stood over him. A small crowd encircled the two, but each time someone took a step closer to Stefan, Vlad responded with a vicious bark.

Elbowing my way through the throng, I faced my hound. Two amber eyes met mine unflinching. A low growl rumbled through his chest. "Stand down, Vlad."

I took one step closer. He growled again.

Vlad had only bitten me once in our lifetime. It was not something I wanted to repeat. Without blinking, I took another step. "Psychotic beast—how can I examine him if you won't let me near?"

Vlad raised his lip, showing me his teeth.

Why was he making such a scene? I stared him in the eye. "I just want to help the boy."

Vlad blinked and dropped his gaze.

Finally, the hound had seen sense.

I dropped to my knees by the young man. Laying a hand on his shoulder to reassure him, I leaned close. "Stefan, tell me what's wrong. I am a doctor. I can help you."

"They're all dead." His body convulsed with silent tears.

"Who's dead?" I asked, looking around.

"Everyone. I've seen it in my dreams... I left the iron on... or the toaster or something. The house could be on fire." He covered his head with his hands.

Vlad walked round to Stefan's other side and sat on the grass, pressing his nose to the boy's shoulder, nudging him to turn over.

"Stefan, I want you to take a deep breath. Can you do that for me? Now count with me, in one-two, out one-two." If I could get him to calm down, perhaps some of his rambling would make sense.

Vaguely, I heard Anthony behind me. "Thank you for your help. Everything is under control. Please... back to your business." Soon he was the only one standing on the pavement and Stefan's crying calmed to soft hiccups.

"Can you sit up?" I asked.

Stefan blinked at me, but pulled himself up. Vlad hooked his head under an arm, snuffling at the flowery shirt.

Covering his face with one hand, Stefan bent forward, hugging himself tight with the other arm.

"Stefan... Could you start over and tell me what's wrong?"

He nodded, but didn't say anything.

I looked up at Anthony. "Any ideas?"

Anthony sighed. "I think he has had a fright, but I do not see any clear reason why."

Stefan tried to smile a little, but pulled Vlad close again, shoulders shaking. "I'm sorry. I hate it when those happen in public." He lifted his head and ruffled Vlad's ears. "There is no reason for the panic, but my head doesn't seem to care."

Anthony knelt at his side. "You are safe. Would a warm beverage help? There is a café here."

Stefan nodded briefly, but refused to let go of my mastiff.

"Vlad can come with us, of course." I glared at Anthony, but he simply shrugged.

Anthony led us along a garden path perfumed with hyacinth blooms to the back of the rambling manor where round tables crowded a courtyard patio. The smell of fresh bread and coffee drifted out of the open door. Inside the former kitchen, the original range hosted an array of sugar and milk options for patrons at the end of a shiny counter full of sandwiches. More tables covered with pretty embroidered linens cluster at the back of the room.

I steered Stefan to the furthest one while Anthony went to speak to the waitress. Stefan dropped into a chair and looked at the floor. Nothing could have been further from the bubbly ball of energy I'd met just a few moments ago.

"Stefan, can you speak now?" I took a seat next to him and pointed at Vlad to settle on the other side.

He shrugged. "You deserve that much. For no reason, something scares me. One thought leads to another—suddenly I'm convinced everything's screwed up. All my family will be dead because I did something wrong. I know it sounds insane

—but the feelings are so real. I can't move. Can't even tell myself to stop."

Anthony set a mug of hot chocolate in front of Stefan. "You should not feel embarrassed. Many people have trauma. I'm sure you will find a way to deal with it," Anthony said with a languid wave of his arm.

Stefan smiled ruefully. "I've tried. Nothing helps. I used to be a normal guy, starting my first year at university. It got so bad I left. I couldn't face getting out of bed. The only safe place was under my blankets." His head fell forward, blue hair covered his face, and his voice fell to a whisper.

"But you come to the gallery regularly," I said

Vlad sidled up to Stefan, resting his shaggy chin on the young man's lap.

Stefan tapped his spoon on the table, pointing at Anthony. "Cause of him. Well... his program. The shows are only here for a week. I'm trying to get my degree on-line. The new stuff he brings gives another angle on the subject. It really helps my score."

He took a sip from his mug. His face took on a thoughtful look before he blurted out. "I have a big essay due in a few days' time... I'm struggling. We're supposed to find something not on the web or in a book." The bright sparkle in his personality returned as his mind moved away from his inner demons.

"As you are my most loyal patron, there is a collection of smaller works not on public display. Would you like to see that?" Anthony said.

"That's awesome." Stefan turned to me and hesitated. "I know you just met me, but you really seem to know this stuff. If you have a few minutes, could I pick your brain?"

I wanted to say no, that I was engaged, which I was, but Vlad moved his head enough to glare at me for a long moment. The smug beast was always more sociable than me.

"Very well, a few minutes, and then I must attend to my errands."

Stefan grinned. "Thanks a mill." His face filled with the excited glow I'd seen in the gallery earlier.

Anthony nodded. "Follow me."

His calm exterior barely showed interest. Hell, it barely showed life.

How odd. He knew Stefan well enough to offer this assistance. Surely he should be pleased the lad was recovering.

We followed him out of the café to a plain white door marked No Admittance. He flipped on a light and started down a set of concrete steps. The basement of the museum was vast, but with art still wrapped in protective canvas bags leaning against the walls, boxes stacked to the ceiling, and the four of us, there was hardly any room to move. Vlad surprised me and immediately settled under a table, pretending to nap at Stefan's feet.

Anthony moved a large box with such controlled grace, it was like the coiled energy of a dancer or martial arts master. Seeing him shifting packing crates just didn't seem right.

"How did you end up working for a travelling art show?" I asked.

"I studied in Europe, learning to paint like the masters; however, photography removed any need for this kind of work. It made no economic sense, so I reverted to showing history instead."

I could understand that all too well. Modern inventions took away the enjoyment of the creative process, but human memory didn't even realise they'd lost something. Sadly, there was nothing I could do to halt progress. It simply surged along, and I had to try to remain afloat within it.

Anthony opened a simple still life arrangement and held the unfinished work at arm's length before laying the frame carefully on the table. It was obvious why these had not been shown. None were at all dramatic.

As the pile grew, so did my memories. Moving a few frames, I uncovered one of Hans. He'd begun it a few days before I had to leave, but I never saw the finished piece. It was as stunning as the star attraction in the main hall, merely on a much smaller scale. "Perchance you could start with this one."

Stefan leaned over to my side of the table. "Ooh, that is nice."

Anthony glanced over. "It appears to match the masterpiece in the gallery. The correct style and use of colour would make a good comparison for your thesis."

I lingered with it in my hand, as if holding the creative composition could bring back the person who made it, while Stefan searched through his sketchbook to find a blank page.

He settled on a wooden stool and took the painting from me, turning it to the side. He squinted and nodded, angling his pencil along with the tiny variations of brush strokes, then started making notes.

Anthony stepped back from the work table. "If these are sufficient, I must return to my work. Turn out the lights when you're finished."

Stephan nodded without listening. Anthony's slow, deliberate steps echoed into the distance.

I took the opportunity to look around. There were a few dusty boxes of rocks and pottery shards, but nothing that had

Geoffrey's name on it. I needed to explore the rest of the building.

"Stephan, I have an errance to attend to. Shall I leave Vladimir with you and return in an hour?"

He glanced up. "Sorry... just so... Uh, thanks." His gaze dropped back to the canvas, and he scribbled another note.

I remember that kind of single-minded devotion. Hans would be proud. Just like the master, his work inspired deep concentration.

The museum only had two floors of displays, so finding what I wanted didn't take long. Geoffrey's stuff was in the last room on the ground floor. Spanning the entire length of the building, eight foot tall windows let in dappled light from the river bank. An odd collection of local paintings, artefacts, and a full sized diorama made up of old shop mannequins dressed in beaded buckskin kneeling by a camp fire filled the space. There were six glass-fronted cases under the window laid out with stones of various sizes, ranging from chips of arrowheads to a chunky stone axe. Although a few pieces were quite interesting in a historical sense, nothing about them even hinted at anything sinister or Scottish. 'Twas another dead end. This lack of progress in finding Geoffrey's killers was getting old fast.

A silver-haired gentleman in a dark blue uniform pointed to a fragment of a carved bone pipe. "We're especially proud of these. Mr Briggs was very generous to donate them."

I smiled. Geoffrey had a knack for helping people without even trying. "Did you know him well?"

"Hard not to. He was here every day!"

"How interesting. Some of his papers have gone missing. Did he have a desk or anything here? We can't finish this month's accounts without his reports."

The curator tilted his head and peered at me. "He might have. Who's asking?"

I flashed my corporate badge. "I would have asked at reception, but it was unattended."

The curator hesitated.

"He was such a dear colleague. Everyone at the company is in pieces, of course," I said.

The chap nodded with a frown. "So pointless... this mess. Come with me."

We walked down a musty hall to a door signposted for staff only.

"I hear they didn't even steal anything. Who does that?" he said and took out a set of keys attached to a brass chain looped around his belt. The enormous bunch rattled as he flipped through them, looking for the right one.

I drifted closer. Gossip often held a nugget of truth. "Really? Nothing?"

He opened the door to a neat room lined with bookcases and shelves. A circular table with a few chairs took up most of the centre of the room. A card and pen lay beside today's Maple Grove Chronicle with the headline—local teen killed in tragic car accident.

"I hear Mrs Briggs' car got ransacked the night after his death—again nothing stolen, but the insides were ripped out and left on the street." He shook his head. "No respect anymore. Hope they catch the vermin."

"That's awful. It will be dark soon. Is it safe to park here?" I hunched my shoulders and clutched my arms to my side. It was over the top, but people who felt useful and appreciated were more likely to talk. No better way to discover if the criminals had caused any other mischief around town.

He shrugged. "Most likely, but the police won't say. Kids with too much energy do stupid stuff."

My fear spiked. The vandalism Mrs Briggs mentioned could have been a raccoon if the door wasn't locked. They were too clever for their own good. Or pranksters. My stomach tightened. It could also be someone else.

"Maple Grove appears so safe. Hard to believe, isn't it?" I said.

He went to a row of wooden cubicles. Each contained an assortment of personal clutter—coffee cups, magazines, notebooks, sun glasses.

"All the best towns seem like that, but this ol' place had her share of excitement over the years. Anyway…" he patted a mostly empty cubicle. "This was Geoff's."

The wooden box contained two packs of playing cards, a well-thumbed reference text of Ancient American pottery, and three small notebooks.

Not exactly earth-shattering, but the notebooks were at least a place to start. Flipping the top one open, I scanned the pages. Latin words with dates in Roman numerals spilled across the sheet written in Geoffrey's flowing script. A quick check proved the other two books to be the same coded diaries.

His flowing script was tight, with a sharp slant to the right. It made the stuff difficult to read, but I had practice. Combined with the fact that he wrote in an ancient language, the diary was secure from a casual eye.

"Thank you. These will be very useful."

The curator smiled a little. "Glad someone wanted them. Seemed a shame to throw the stuff out."

That was interesting. Why hadn't Tatya taken anything? "I wouldn't want to remove something Dr Briggs might want—"

He snorted. "Naw. She hated the museum. Didn't even look around, just collected the sympathy cards and left."

Thankfully, if there had been any clues here, they were most likely still on site. I squeezed his hand. "I'll make sure the corporation knows of Geoffrey's interest in your work. I'm sure a donation could be justified." Perhaps a small fabrication, but, as much as I didn't like actually visiting myself, museums had their uses.

The man's smile grew, and he beamed good cheer all the way back to the main hall. It never hurt to have an inside ally.

After bidding my new friend good-day, I found a cosy, wood-panelled room on the second floor of the building. Several wing-back chairs dotted around the perimeter for reading and quiet conversation.

The building was silent this late in the day, only open for a few afternoon classes really, so all the seats were empty. I settled by an empty hearth and flipped through one of the notebooks. Two were complete, the other only half full. I started reading backwards from the day of his death. It might give me a place to begin my search.

My hopes fell as I skimmed the pages. He recorded thousands of tiny details, but none seem pertinent. It really wasn't useful to know he needed to buy milk or that a grandchild's hamster expired.

I read on. Two days before his murder, someone had pushed a letter written on deerskin vellum and sealed with wax under his front door in the middle of the night. Penned in a combination of Old Scots and Gaelic, two languages he wasn't fluent in, he thought it odd, but not a threat. He intended to bring it to me for a full translation.

The diary slipped from my fingers. Real vellum was incredibly difficult to purchase; deerskin had been practically impossible to acquire for centuries. Puking hedge-born rats. It was almost certain Geoffrey's murder was connected to my lineage.

I rubbed my temple. My mind felt slow, but there didn't appear to be any other connection. I needed coffee to be sure I wasn't missing something obvious.

I set out for the café. Such a blissful discovery, the coffee bean. Much better than the fiery tonic of ginger and onion I used to drink to keep my fatigue at bay. It cleared the clutter of a thousand memories and tasted divine. True love.

"Six espresso in one, if you please." The young maid behind the counter raised an eyebrow, but poured the thick coffee into a single take away cup.

With the warm brew circulating around my system, thoughts returned to the present. Geoffrey must have a place he considered safe to leave that letter. If not here—where? It was time to collect Vlad. We had some sniffing to do.

Stefan looked up as I came back into the workroom.

"Have your studies prompted any question?" I asked.

He moved the canvas bag the painting had been wrapped in and thrust a sheet of yellowed paper into my hand.

"This is so cool!" He pulled out his sketchbook, flipping to the last page, and showed a drawing of a woman wearing a

Tudor gown with a mastiff at her side. Stefan's sketch matched a faded grey drawing on the back of the lining paper.

My legs trembled, and I spilt hot liquid down my leg. Hans—you mutton-headed clown—you promised! I set the drink onto the workbench before I spilled any more.

"Pretty cool huh, it looks just like you. How many people would be so lucky? You've got a doppelgänger. Never would have found it if the glue hadn't fallen apart," he rambled on.

Doppelgänger? Was he that thick witted?

Hans, you villainous knave. Despite explicit instructions! What had possessed the clay-headed lout to make a likeness of me? Now there was not only his portrait, but Stefan's copy I had to get rid of.

"Have you shown this to anyone else?" I asked.

"Anthony came in while I was working."

My stomach twisted. Would the flea brained lad remember if I simply destroyed the sketchbook or did I need to take more drastic steps?

It was quiet here, but it would be difficult to explain why such a young man's heart simply stopped beating.

No, the reaper had taken enough this week. It would be sufficient to destroy the drawings. A couple of sketches caught my eye while flipping through the pages. They looked similar to the archaeology collection, but were not on display. "What are these?" I asked, holding the book open to him.

He leaned over. "Those... just something Grandpa dug up. He collected arrowheads. Said those didn't fit the group. I liked the shapes, so he let me draw them."

I froze. Now that I'd been prompted, the resemblance between him, Geoffrey, and Tatya was quite easy to spot. My mind had been on other things. Even so, that was not the sort of thing I normally miss. Vlad's tail thumped against the floor as he looked over his shoulder again. The infernal hound had made the connection before I did. No wonder he wanted to protect the kid.

"It looks like quite a collection."

Stefan bounced in his seat. "You think those are neat? You should see the ones in his study."

"I'd love to."

He dropped into a slouch, unwilling to meet my eye. "I haven't been in there since... the thing last week."

Tatya's stonewall might be formidable, but any stronghold was only as stout as its weakest port.

I sat down next to Stefan. "You want to talk about it?"

He shook his head.

"Don't worry. Vlad and I knew Geoffrey. You can trust us."

Vlad leaned against Stefan's hip. The boy ruffled the dog's ears. "I miss Papa."

"We all do." The final syllable warbled. I leaned back in the chair and closed my eyes, forcing emotions into the back of my head and out of my voice. They had no place in this discussion.

"Gran's acting weird, too. Keeps pulling the curtains and shouting at us to keep out of sight," Stefan said.

Was she worried about a sharpshooter getting the rest of her family? Had the motor car destruction been a threat?

"Some people are just naturally nervous."

He shook his head. "Papa always had a stream of people to play cards with, but Gran never said much. She would read or work on her puzzles. She likes quiet." He rubbed his arms.

"There were noises that night. Odd noises, not loud but not normal house sounds."

Startled, I sat up. "You were there when Geoffrey was shot?"

He nodded.

"Did you see anything? Any people around the neighbourhood you didn't recognise?" I asked.

"I've not seen anyone, but I feel watched all the time." He hugged himself tighter.

"That must be unsettling. I'm sorry you're having such a hard time."

"Gran's got it bad too. Went mental about losing her keys today. Twenty minutes later, they were in the hall tray. She's not blind. They were not there one minute and back the next."

"That seems odd." What else could I say that didn't sound flimsy about disappearing keys? Everyone misplaces their keys. I do it regularly.

"And the tool shed was open," he said.

How could that be suspicious? "A door is easily forgotten."

"No! I always lock it. The riding mower's expensive. I'd never hear the end of it. When we came out this morning, the door was swinging in the breeze."

The opening bars of Mozart's Serenade for Strings interrupted with a cheerful but too high-pitched melody. This hollow copy completely lost the majesty of the piece.

Stefan jumped up and looked at his phone. "Gran's been trying to call for the last hour! I have to go. I'm late for Papa's visitation."

He shoved his pens and sketch book into his bag and flung it over his shoulder.

By the devil's—I had not destroyed the drawing yet. "Stefan, do you need any more help with your essay?"

He turned back, bouncing eagerly. "My head's gonna be messed up after all this funeral home stuff... Can you come back tomorrow?"

His enthusiasm was endearing. Shame his mind was not stable. "My pleasure."

Tomorrow wasn't perfect, but it would have to do. After he left, I poured my coffee over the lining paper. The beautiful charcoal sketch blurred into a smudged puddle. One down, one to go. There would be no trace of it by sundown tomorrow.

SIX

Vlad and I slipped out of the café. So far, the warehouse of decay had not been very instructive, but it would appear odd to ask further questions at the moment. I kicked at a loose stone on the path.

Where would Geoffrey store a strange package? Surely, he wouldn't leave his family at risk if it was suspect, but where else could he hide it? This mystery simply did not want to relinquish any secrets.

I should go to the visitation, but if the rest of the family were there, it was the perfect time to investigate his home. For goodness' sake, either the criminals were incredibly confident or completely inept to have left that can of soda. Should make capturing them easy, extracting information maybe less so, but for the moment restricting their free movement would be enough.

The walk was peaceful—until Vlad left off snuffling the grass and sprinted toward a nature path at the back of the gallery.

Bloody hound. Didn't he understand we had things to attend to? "Come here!"

He paid no attention, turning into a rapidly shrinking blur on the narrow path that switched back and forth down a steep limestone bluff to the river's edge.

I slipped into a steady lope. The sound of his bulk crashing through the undergrowth was easy to follow, and the path wasn't very wide. There was a pause, followed by a short, high-pitched squeal. The first of today's rabbits. He gobbled for a few moments, then took off again. All I saw were tufts of fur scattered under a raspberry thicket.

He led me over a fallen tree and under a bridge. After three more squeals, Vlad stopped running in the middle of a thick woods. I caught up to him staring at a gnarled oak. Blood matted his muzzle, but he whined and scratched at the trunk. One lucky squirrel had been faster today. Tomorrow… who knows?

I tugged at his collar. "This is simply gluttony. You have had four furry things already."

He shook, making his ears slap together like a pair of hands clapping. Blasted lucky beast. Any fresh blood infused him with energy. I had to make do with sipping from close friends or drinking strong coffee.

"I know you do not agree with me, but you have had enough."

He snorted and scratched at the tree one more time. I ruffled his ears and reached into my pocket for a dog biscuit. One of Geoffrey's notebooks fell on the gravel path.

I knelt to retrieve it and glanced up as I stood. Fancy houses lined the top of the twelve-foot cliff next to the path. Few would attempt to climb the rocky wall, but it wouldn't be that hard. A matter of courage more than skill.

We could go up that way to observe the Briggs' rear garden, but these notebooks were much too bulky to keep running around with. Besides, I did not wish to spare the time to find a laundress with the knowledge of dry chemical cleaning if I soiled these trousers.

"Come along. You need a tidy, and I need to get rid of these." I patted my bulky pocket. We trotted back up the path, arriving only slightly out of breath at the top. Thank heavens I'd been mostly healthy when my unnatural life started. As much as fresh injuries never lasted, old ones never healed. I would not have wanted centuries as an invalid.

I unlocked the car and hid the notebooks under the seat, replacing them with a set of lock picks and a short dagger. That was better. Much safer. Only fools walk about unarmed.

When I tried to wipe Vlad's face with a handkerchief, he shifted away. "Biscuits?"

He returned for the crunchy treat, chewing and dribbling while I brushed at his scruffy muzzle. The mottled brown fur didn't really need it. The blood was gone already. He'd reverted to his immutable state quite quickly today.

"That shall do." I tucked the dirty cloth into the seat pocket and pulled on a pair of skintight leather gloves. "'Tis time to find out what Tatya's hiding."

The house was quiet when we approached. The only car in the drive was Geoffrey's company issued BMW. I walked up the steps and rang the doorbell.

All remained silent.

I pressed the buzzer again and focused, straining to hear the slightest movements inside the building. All remained still.

I stepped off the porch and walked down the neat brick driveway to a smaller white door on the side of the building. It was locked. I followed the drive further to the back of the house. Someone might have left a patio entrance or window open.

As I stepped around the side of the house, a gigantic mass of grey and brown in the shape of a man startled back. Before I could get over my shock, it dropped to all four and darted across the lawn. I ran across the open lawn, but the creature leaped over the barbed wire at the end of the yard and slithered down the rocky ledge.

Damn it. What was that thing? The creature darted across the footpath at the base of the cliff in a flash of fur and leaped into the water. It was as big as a moose but moved like a cat. Vlad scratched at the limestone under three strands of barbed wire. A bit of rock broke off and somersaulted down to the water. It looked a lot steeper from this side.

I pulled Vlad away. We would not climb down after the creature. My hound trotted to the stout wood side fence with his nose pressed to the ground. There had been no wild animals that size in Maple Grove since the ice ages. Even then, nothing would have been standing on hind legs before running with such speed and grace. Could it be a bear? No, the ears and head were the wrong shape.

I walked back toward the house. Behind the garage, the door to a large tool shed swung in the breeze.

According to Stefan, that was always locked. I peered into the gloom. The dark space was quiet, nothing moved. I flicked on a light. The shed was full to overflowing with tools and equipment neatly arranged. The wall held rows of little boxes and jars filled with screws and bolts over a tidy work bench. It even had a small square of carpet with a comfortable chair near a window. A good sized coffee pot and one mug waited on the worktop. This must have been Geoffrey's oasis.

Why would a wild animal want to get inside? There did not appear to be any food. More importantly, how could it open a locked door? It was most peculiar.

Vlad returned from trotting the perimeter, whining at his loss of prey. He stood at attention, his hackles raised in a spike of anger, looking between me and the drop at the end of the garden. I patted my dagger. By the father, if that thing came back, we'd be ready. Other than a solitary lilac bush near a neglected child's sandbox, the backyard was mostly lawn. It couldn't sneak up on us.

The old screen door rattled on its hinges, but the inner door was stout, shiny, and brand new. The criminals must have come in this way when they attacked Geoffrey, yet the new lock wasn't that secure. If Tatya was truly frightened, she should have sprung for a double action dead-bolt. I pulled three ordinary blunt pins out of my hair bun and pressed into the lock, gently feeling for the clicks.

Vlad wandered around the garden while I worked. The picks took less than a minute to spring the latch. Long enough for him to cock his leg and piss on the lilac shrub as if he owned the place. When I opened the door, he galloped up with a look as if to say, 'What took so long?'

We slipped inside, closing and re-locking the door quietly.

The porch contained a collection of boots lined up like a parade and coats on a stand by the inner door.

Pulling Vlad back, I pointed at the floor. "Stay. I'll be back."

He huffed a soft puff of air before settling down by the door. Whether he was blocking or guarding our exit, I wasn't sure.

Three steps up led to a perfect kitchen. Everything had a place; there was not a speck of dust or sign of life anywhere. It could have been a photo shoot in a glossy magazine instead of a family kitchen.

Beyond the kitchen, something glinted along the hall. I moved closer. Each side of the walkway had seven sets of bladed weapons mounted in spiral shapes. Each one started with small daggers and ended with a two-handed sword from different countries. A decorative display of brutality. I had no idea Geoffrey was that interested in military artefacts.

The hall widened near the front door, and the ceiling extended all the way to the third floor to show off a grand staircase. Double oak doors led off to either side. The doors on the left side opened to a pleasant living room, while the doors on the right side were latched.

I stepped into the living room. Just inside the doorway, a potted palm hid a pistol with a silencer.

I froze. That was not something I'd given Geoffrey. Why had she put it in the plant pot? It didn't look like it'd been there long. The bruised plant leaves hadn't even turned brown. Everything else about the room simply looked like a welcoming reception room, so Geoffrey's study must be on the other side.

I crossed the hall and opened the door. The smell of wax and Geoffrey's cologne drifted into the hall. Inside, the drawn curtains left the air feeling dank. The smell of cleaning compounds stabbed my nose. Something moved. It looked like Geoffrey waving.

I snapped the lights on.

The chair behind the desk was empty.

My knees locked together to stop my trembling. It must have been a reflection off something.

The harsh lights illuminated a room of devastation. Random papers covered every flat surface, books pulled out from the shelves had been left in piles around the room, and the smooth polished wood of the grandfather clock had smudges. The work of cleaners who wanted to get the job done and be out again as soon as possible.

To put it mildly, the place was a mess. The only untidy space in the house. Geoffrey might have kept a bastion of manliness in the garden, but this looked more like the chaos that descended after crime.

The study had cream walls and plants like the lounge across the hall, but no obvious weapons. Shelves containing geodes, crystal clumps, ants in amber, and arrowheads circled the room. He loved everything made from the bones of the earth. Under the shelves hung old maps carefully mounted and framed. I peered at the closest one, a large yellowed sheet with torn and ragged edges, Portsmouth dockyard 1756.

Why did he still have that? I'd thrown it out while looking for candles in an old trunk. I shook my head. One more thing I'd not realised.

Textbooks and binders filled one wall, but the thing that caught my eye was the antique game table. Only large enough for four to play cards at, the small table tucked near the window would have received perfect light when the curtains were open.

I sat down and bitter-sweet memories flooded back. I'd scoured my collection of storage spaces to find something special for his graduation present.

It had stunned Geoffrey when the eighteenth century piece had been delivered. A warm tingle curled around me, almost like a hug from a friend.

I ran my hand over the centre square covered in green leather surrounded by intricate geometric patterns inlaid with ivory, walnut, and rosewood. It had seen so many pleasant evenings—whisky, cards, chess, and... A warm flush crept over my cheeks.

I pressed two large diamond patterns on opposite corners at the same time. There was a soft click, and the leather pad rose a fraction of an inch. Lifting gently, the musty smell of old books tickled my nose.

Inside was a collection of papers, some old coins and two small shards of a dull silver stone. They seemed to have some sort of letters carved into them, but since they were so small, nothing was complete. It certainly wasn't immediately familiar. It could be fragments of early Viking runes. I slipped them into my pocket. I'd research them further another time.

A photo from Geoffrey's graduation slipped out of a stack of letters held together with a large paper clip. I flipped through them.

Feculence—Marcus.

Why had I ever fallen for that unreliable, irresponsible twat? I am old enough to know better. Guilt twisted my stomach into a knot. It was my mistake to trust him, but they ended up paying for my weakness. The photo was of a student I did not know, but Geoffrey, Marcus, and I were clearly visible in the background. Much younger versions of them. I, however, had not aged a day since. Damn modern technology!

I'd need to feed the photo into some cleansing fire. I slipped it into my pocket to deal with this evening.

The next envelope contained a newspaper clipping: Svetlana Briggs, aged thirty, lost her fight with cancer... will be sadly missed... two children...

Geoffrey hadn't told me anything about that. No wonder Stefan was so cynical and anxious.

I jerked my mind away from the newspaper and leafed through the rest of the stack. But it was all family mementos. Nothing to do with me.

I slid the board back into place. Where else could he have hid a letter? There were over a hundred books. Geoffrey could have been slipped it into any without a trace. I didn't have that much time. I scanned the titles for a clue. After trying several random books, a booming chime tinkled through the room.

Indeed, it was obvious I should have started there. The tall bird's-eye maple clock dominated the room. Large was the wrong word for it. Vast would be better. The brash size and grandeur would be perfect for concealment. After assessing its shape, I began working through all obvious places for a hidden catch. Each piece of wood remained firmly attached, but tucked on the top of the decorative cornice was a small brass key. It most likely opened the clock face to reset the time, but I tried it anyway. The glass dome opened, allowing access to the dial. It also showed a faint sliver of light along the side panel. A brilliant artisan could build a small vertical drawer behind that decorative trim. I wedged the tip of my nail into the hairline crack and pulled. The polished wood slid forward with a squeak. Inside, a plain brown packet bulging like a tax demand, yet it had no address or postage on it. I opened the packet and pulled out a heavy cream sheet sealed with orange wax.

The vellum letter. Triumph coursed through my mind. It was here all along. Geoffrey must have believed it to be benign. Sadly, there was no imprint on the seal. I squinted at the spidery writing, in an ancient combination of Gaelic, Latin and old English. The odd mix was very difficult to work out; however, it did not appear to be a demand for anything. I read through the script a second time. It seemed to be an apology. My fingers felt numb. It was useless.

What an obscure ruse—A mea culpa from someone Geoffrey didn't know, in a language he couldn't even read. Who would murder for that?

I wanted to throw a blanket over my head. Why did every clue make this question harder? I slid the drawer back and closed the clock face. The pieces didn't fit. Tatya was angry and elusive, either could be guilt or grief. A modern letter written in forgotten languages did not point to her, yet made no connection to me either.

A few seconds later, a scraping noise at the front of the building broke my musing.

Bloody idiots. Who would try to break into the front door in broad daylight?

There was a second obvious sound of someone prying at the frame outside.

Maggot-brained fools did not even know how to break a latch properly. I turned out the study lights and lifted one of the two-handed swords off the wall. It felt sturdy. Hopefully, they were not theatre props.

Vlad paced up the hall, ears twitching. He cocked his head, letting out a soft whisper of a bark, then sat down just under the stairs and glared at the front door.

Our visitors hesitated, with the edges of a hushed argument rasping through the wall. For all that the words were lost, the guttural Glaswegian twang was unmistakable.

The tick of the long-case clock echoed through the house. A frontal assault would make my investigations so much easier; however, the duo seemed to have a crisis of bravado. After several minutes, the sound of scraping resumed, ending in a sudden snap as the old frame parted from the latch.

I flicked the lights on. "Evening, gents"

Two men stood a few feet inside the hall. Both were scruffy and unkempt. It could be by design, though I'd bet my front teeth it was due to a lack of experience. Hopefully, the incompetent criminals would crack quickly. It'd be easier than getting the story erased from a police file later.

Momentarily blinded, the taller man turned away.

Raising the sword, I slammed the pommel into the closest chap. There was an audible crack before he screamed. Blood flooded across his face. Spinning round, I kicked the other one before he could attack. The lout wobbled, bumping into his injured partner on the way down.

"Eejit." Bust nose man kicked at his partner.

"Stop your blethering." The tall man rolled over and climbed to his feet, glaring at his mate.

"Wheesht!" the smaller man hissed and held one hand over his mangled nose.

I crouched with my sword ready, moving between them and the outside door as they squabbled.

"Tell me—why are you here?"

The injured man reached under his jacket and pulled out a revolver. "Nae hen, yer dead!"

I swung the sword again. The gun boomed as my blade sliced across his hand, lopping off the tip of a finger. Brilliant—sharp edges. Never would have expected that on the display pieces.

The shot went wide, only grazing me, but it didn't matter. Even a direct hit would have limited effect. I certainly wouldn't die of it.

Before he could shoot again, I circled the blade circle round and smashed the flat into his forearm, cracking bone and leaving it in a twisted sickle shape. The gun clattered to the floor.

"You, my friend, are not very bright," I pointed the sword at his chest. "What idiot sent you?"

His companion slapped the first man on the side of the head. "Eejit! Keep the heid. Nae pistols. I telt ye to bin it after the last one!"

"Dinnae call me eejit! G told us to get it." He attempted to slap his companion, but the broken arm hung as limp as a snapped corn stalk.

Although that was going to be a problem soon if he didn't get some medical attention, it served him right for snooping around where he wasn't welcome.

I kicked the gun well out of reach. The two carried on arguing as if I wasn't in the room. My patience wore out. "You two are the worst pair of jesters I have ever laid eyes on," I said through gritted teeth. "That shot would have woken the neighbours. They shall call the constables. So you have two choices: talk to me or the authorities. Who is G and why does he think I'll allow him to murder one of Mine?"

When neither spoke, I pointed the sword directly under the chin of the fellow with a broken nose. "I don't make a habit of repeating myself."

"I'm no snitch hen!"

He spat blood. His companion nodded while looking around wildly for an exit. The taller man took a handful of his partner's jacket and pulled him toward the hall.

In an ideal world, it might have been a good choice, as it led to the side door, but they had apparently forgotten about the bark earlier. The pair got two steps into the hall when the growl became audible to human ears. I smiled. The school of hard knocks could be so cruel to the stupid.

They stumbled back, falling over each other in their haste to retreat. When they were just inside the room, I held up my hand. Vlad halted, growling louder as they edged away from him.

Resting the sword point on the floor, I leaned forward, tapping my fingers on the hilt. "Have you reconsidered my offer to chat?"

The shorter one's lips clamped together tightly, despite the glistening sheen of sweat on his brow and trembling hands. His state of shock was probably numbing the worst of the pain... for now.

A flick of my hand was all I needed to release the hound with demeanour from hell. Perchance I should enlighten the simpletons.

Feet pounded up the porch steps. "God—the door! I knew it. Why doesn't anybody ever listen? I asked if it was locked, but no…." Stefan paused and took a step inside. "Anna? What are you doing here?"

"I came by to drop off some papers for your grandfather," I said calmly over my shoulder, without taking my eyes off the criminals, "but these cretins were here. They broke in."

The smaller one shied back, but the taller flipped two fingers of defiance at me.

Stefan pointed to the blood on my arm. "You're hurt."

"'Tis nothing. Step back."

He reached for a scarf hanging by the door, crossing my line of vision. The taller criminal spied the opportunity, grabbed his partner, and sprinted out. As I leaped to block them, Stefan caught my arm, trying to wrap the scarf around the bullet hole. The criminals slipped by, thudding down the steps.

"If you want justice for your grandfather, I was never here. Understand?" Shaking free of his attempt at first aid, I stepped back and tossed the sword to him.

Out of reflex, Stefan grabbed the hilt. He blinked at me, then the bloody weapon and the fingertip on the floor.

He might have nodded, but I sprang down the steps without waiting. The criminals had a good lead already. I needed to catch Vlad. My hound dashed across the road with a beard of froth gathering on his chin. Somehow, the burglars doubled their speed and raced to the main road.

Vlad's angry baying drew people out of dark buildings, only to have them slam the door again when they saw the foam dripping off his muzzle. Pushing myself to the limit, my feet slapped the pavement in a rapid staccato. I had to catch my hound before he got his prey. Few survived when the blood-lust took over. I needed at least one of them capable of speech.

The burglars turned right to a smaller side road crossing the river on an old-fashioned bridge with a waist high decorative railing built long before safety-mad legislation. The taller man grabbed his companion's shirt and threw him over the edge. Unfortunately for tall-man, the pause was enough to let Vlad catch up.

My hound's teeth clamped down on the man's jacket. He shook hard enough to knock the criminal to the ground and kept shaking the jacket with vicious jerks. The man kicked while fumbling with the clasps. Vlad stumbled, just enough to give the Scotsman time to wiggle free. He leaped over the railing, waving two fingers as he plummeted. Although I snatched at his hand, gravity took its natural hold. All I could do was watch as he fell into the swift stream, churning with rapids. There was a blur of black beside me. I snatched Vlad's collar before he sailed over the railing as well. It was over twelve feet down to the river. I had no wish to wait for a broken leg to heal.

Holding him tightly, I patted his head. "Don't worry, we'll get them." His lunges trailed off, and I released his collar before scooping up the coat discarded by our intruders. A mobile phone clattered to the ground.

"Careless and clumsy." I shook my head and slipped the phone into my pocket.

Sirens echoed in the distance. I inspected the jacket, but there wasn't anything else hiding, and dropped it in a heap. The police deserved some kind of evidence.

SEVEN

I whistled for Vlad to follow. He looked up from his pacing along the bridge, growled his frustration one last time at his lost prey, then bounded up the street to join me. It might look bad to flee the scene of a crime, but I didn't have time to deal with bureaucrats right now.

We walked back to the museum for all intents and purpose nothing more than a woman and her pet out for an evening stroll. The sun slipped low on the horizon, leaving a beautiful clear, crisp dusk, with just a hint of a breeze. I loved this kind of evening. Shame we had business to attend to.

At the museum, we zig-zagged down to the river's edge. We met a couple on the gravel path out enjoying the weather with a little brown Pekingese. The tiny dog growled at Vlad.

"I think two guys just jumped off the bridge. Did you see anything?" I asked.

The woman gathered her pet into her arms and stepped away. "No, Chester keeps trying to escape. With all of his antics, we wouldn't have seen a blimp land."

The courageous mite barked at my brute from his safe perch. Vlad cocked his leg against the woman's shoe.

She stared at Vlad, mouth open in horror.

"Sorry, bladder infection."

I grabbed Vlad's collar, dragging him away. He shook and grinned at me. I ruffled his ears. Bloody ill-mannered beast, but I loved him for never becoming civilised. Quite a refreshing change from the modern world of rules and order.

At the bridge, two police women talked on radios, but they didn't look down. Vlad and I kept walking quickly. It felt hideously slow, but running would catch their attention.

Thirty feet downstream, Vlad stopped and scratched at the grass. Faint traces of blood showed on the bent stalks of two broad leaves. The criminals had scrambled to shore here. We walked on with Vlad's nose pressed to the ground. Their trail turned away from the river and dipped through a ditch to get into a weedy scrub forest.

Vlad sniffed all the growth and watered some, paying especially close attention to the thin paths rabbits left.

"Not those. Remember what we're looking for?" I held the phone close to his nose again.

He snorted, lowering his snout to the ground to patrol the edges of the human size paths. There was plenty of evidence of urban wildlife. The over-grown grass practically blossomed with cheap beer cans, plastic bags, and aerosol cans. Vlad surged ahead of me, then to the side, before circling behind and crashing back through the undergrowth.

"It's a good thing I'm not trying to sneak up on anything. You make more noise than a flock of geese," I scolded.

He looked at me with his head cocked, one ear up and one down as if to say, 'It's not my fault you're so slow!'

Ahead, the path widened into a clearing. There were people gathered around a bonfire in the centre.

"Time for a brief detour, cousin." I grab Vlad's collar, gently steering him off the main path to a slimmer deer track that wound through the trees. As we approached, the raucous laughter and horseplay revealed local teens blowing off steam. I turned to creep further into the forest, working my way around without drawing attention, until one reveller broke away from the group. He stumbled into the forest, fumbling at his trousers.

It was inconvenient timing. I pulled Vlad back from the path while crouching down to avoid being in direct sight.

The kid undid his fly and hummed as the unmistakable smell of impatience wafted into the forest.

A pale blur moved in the trees just before a figure appeared beside the drunken lad.

She looked sad, her small round face wrinkled in agony, as she repeatedly reached out to touch the boy; however, he zipped up and headed back to the gathering without acknowledging her at all.

The girl covered her face with her hands. Her shoulders shook as she sobbed silently.

"Come on." I shifted to resume our travel, although it was dubious we'd be able to pick up the trail now the scent was contaminated.

The pale girl looked up.

I must have spoken too loudly. She ran toward me, but her feet didn't quite touch the ground. The grass on the other side was clearly visible through them. She was less than an arm's length away, yet Vlad hadn't even glanced up. Flaring my nostrils, I heaved a breath in. Nothing. She ha no scent of any kind.

Hell's bells! Whatever this thing was, it definitely wasn't human. I dropped into a ready stance to fight or flee as needed.

Her mouth moved, but only the faintest of whispers floated out. "You can see me?" Her face lit up with a beaming smile. "You can hear me!"

A thumping race car roar of blood pumped in my ears as I slowly nodded.

"You have to tell Konner… Tell him to stop acting like an idiot," she exclaimed, but it was a faint sigh like the wind in the trees.

"I have no idea what you're talking about," I said, yet there was familiarity to her face.

"I'm Jayden, went to school with them." She waved at the crowd by the bonfire.

With each word, her features became more solid. Scrolling through the archive of my memory, the pieces clicked. I'd seen her picture on the newspaper article in the museum staff room—Local teen killed in a tragic road accident.

I forced my feet to remain in place. Death had been one constant in my long life—plague, war, and famine had seen to that. There had been none indications of an afterlife, no contact of any sort from the departed. What kind of trickery was this?

"He finally asked me out! I'd been waiting, trying to get his attention for ages." Her oval face pinched tight over her cheeks.

She did not appear threatening and might even know something useful. Speaking to the creature would only delay me a moment. "Surely you should move on as well," I said.

Who had decided that was soothing? Most likely some tired church official.

"I get pulls around my heart, but I couldn't leave with Konner so upset," she said. Her wrinkled brow smoothed some as she spoke.

"I'm no expert, but if you have a feeling, you should probably follow it." I shrugged my shoulders. "Your path has ended. You have to see where the next one goes." Even though it sounded heartless, it was the truth. Sweetness would not change the facts.

Her hand raised to cover her mouth. "I... I had plans, dreams."

I tried again, more gently this time. "Sadly, plans have very little to do with the when or where. Be brave and see where the next adventure takes you. It could be wondrous." My heart flip-flopped. Perhaps the words held truth. So many of my dear friends had gone there... I would never know.

She looked at the rough ground. "I'm scared."

I reached out to her. My fingers passed through rather than giving her a reassuring touch. Suppressing the shudder that ran through me, I let my hand fall to scratch Vlad's ears.

"All would like a companion for the final journey, yet you must walk this one alone."

Unless there be angels, guardians, or some transient being like so many religions suggested. Was there any truth to it or was it simply a way to avoid the terror? Again... it was not something I could ever verify.

There was a flicker beside her, yet the tree leaves were still. Damn it, this was a strange night. Be gone, foul demons of my mind.

"Stay with me? Please," she asked, bringing my attention back to the ghost.

I sighed softly. The kid was terrified. How many times had my own life bled out with none close to hand? More than I liked.

The scent was fouled. Vlad would have difficulty recovering the criminal's trail, with all the urine on the ground. I might as well ease her suffering if I could. With luck, this may be my opportunity to meet the elusive reaper-of-souls and learn why he'd forsaken me all these years.

"Aye mistress. 'Tis been a long day. May we sit?"

She nodded, and I settled on the ground with my back against a fallen tree. Vlad stretched out at my side, resting his chin on my knee, and the girl tucked up on my other side. She was quiet for a long time. Long enough, I thought she'd fallen asleep, yet when I looked over, her eyes were wide open, watching the forest in terror.

Could my mind be playing tricks on me? I'd been alive for almost six hundred years, yet had never seen a ghost. Was it something about Maple Grove? Stefan's panic attacks involved perceived apparitions. Perhaps there was a hallucinogen in the air or water.

My thoughts drifted. I took a deep breath, calmed my mind, and let it drift to the bottom of my deep well of consciousness. The answer must be here somewhere. All I needed to do was look.

Right before sunrise, the grass next to the ghost girl blurred into a fuzzy green grey patch. I brought my full attention back to the forest, scanning the trees. Leaf shadows cast by the moon fluttered. The girl sighed and was gone. Just like that, without fanfare or fuss, she was simply gone.

My heart sank. I'd held vigil all evening, yet discovered nothing new about my immortality. Tonight did not differ from any other battlefield. The grim reaper does not show himself for a ghost any more than when collecting a wounded man.

The pre-dawn forest was silent and still—too early for songbirds, too late for those that hunt by night.

I did not know her. She wasn't even human; however, her sudden absence made my throat tight.

I hugged Vlad close. "Just you and me again, cousin."

His tail thumped the ground while he snuggled closer to get his back scratched. I indulged him for a moment. Death's visit was as elusive as ever. Would I ever know what lay on the other side?

Vlad trotted off in search of rabbits, but I needed coffee. The stronger, the better. My dew drenched pantaloons clung to my leg as we walked back. The linen would recover, but it was not suitably respectable any longer. I needed to change and speak to my companions. Although my evening meditation had recalled no Scottish artefacts in Geoffrey's guardianship, something may have been posted to him.

When we got to the river, I nearly tripped over a column of smooth stones stacked knee-high. The top stone teetered on the haphazard pile. "Cod-brained youths. Dangerous way to mark a gathering venue."

Vlad sniffed the pile and looked at me quizzically.

The river splashed around a tight bend here. Had the teens built the tower or the criminals? The tall Scot might return to search for his missing phone, but the other chap would need a physician. Stay or go…

The emergency services would not hand names to me, but Carl would have means to find out. That was more likely to turn up one criminal than wondering in the woods.

A shiver wriggled up my body. Wet clothes were miserable this time of year, regardless of the fact that it was harmless to my health. I kicked the pile over and headed down the trail. I could contact Carl from inside the comfortable warmth of a coffeehouse.

After we climbed into the Falcon and I put the heaters on, I reached into my pocket for the burglar's mobile device. My finger brushed the lump of rock from Geoffrey's desk. Where had he dug it up? Regret tugged at my chest—I'd never know. I squeezed the bittersweet memento and pulled the phone out. It probably contained useful information, but it would take time to work out. Right now, it was more important to move my vehicle. I tucked the phone in the door pocket and started the engine. It would look suspicious to leave it parked in the same place much longer.

After ten blocks, the houses had shifted to modern family styles again. Further on, a 1930s petrol station sported signs for coffee and breakfast. The small building surrounded by concrete had obviously not sold fuel for over a decade, but looked like a pleasant eatery.

There were only two other cars. That was good, but I didn't want to be trapped, so parked facing the exit.

My mobile telephone took its time warming up, then chimed to let me know there were unread messages. Of course.

I rang Carl without checking them.

"God, Anna—where have you been? The Briggs' had another break-in."

"I know. I was there."

Carl sputtered. "What! Nobody mentioned that."

I smiled. Stefan was as smart as his grandfather. "It's a long story. Have there been any A&E admissions for amputated fingers?"

The phone went silent.

"Carl?"

"How did you know that?"

"I know a lot of things, but what I don't know is who."

"The police have an APB out to every medical centre in three states. No suspects yet. Anna, there's more. Geoffrey's designate has the private number, asked for the guardian."

Feculence. That wasn't good. A guardian enquiry required immediate response. "I need you here."

"I'm on duty until this afternoon."

That was not helpful. I pressed my lips together, taking a deep breath. Life was rarely convenient. "Very well. Is Bill on his way?"

"As far as I know."

"Fine. I shall meet the designate late this afternoon. The address will be sent to you and Bill. Be early."

He snorted. "I'll be there... the Missus' gonna be pissed. You owe me."

"Noted. To every companion I am in turns a devil and a saviour. Tonight is no different."

Carl harrumphed, and the phone went silent. Sadly, the duties of our family of odd fellows often rode rough-shod over ordinary plans.

Where could I meet the designate? Obviously not in a coffeehouse or car park, and my condo was two hours away. I needed something local, private, and anonymous.

I pressed the speed dial for the company's private database access.

"Reference number please." A slight inflection in tone was the only thing that gave away the robotic nature of the answer service.

"2006."

The phone clicked, and another rang. A sleepy voice picked up on the fifth tone. "Anna?"

"Sorry to wake you Lance, I need some discreet accommodation with the usual features in the Maple Grove area. Pay for it through one of the minor funds."

He sighed. "When—"

"Immediately."

"I'll do what I can. It's not a going to be easy… small town you know."

"I have every faith in you, young sir."

"Remember that next time I miss a target."

He chuckled, and I suppressed the comment that threatened to leap to my lips. It had been a clear shot at short range. The sort to get people killed if it were not a training procedure. Men today… So different from my early husbands. Did the fellow really feel that tongue lashing was harsh? I'd barely raised my voice.

Lance's views were a matter for another day. I pulled my focus back to the reason I'd telephoned. "Carl and Bill will need the address as well."

"Anonymous I presume."

"Indeed."

I hung up and tossed my phone into the glove box. What did the designate need the guardian for? Geoffrey had kept his choice quiet. I hadn't even met the esquire yet. It could be a hoax.

Coffee first. My mind would work better after that, but this establishment did not appear to allow pets. I stepped out, swinging the motor car door close to its frame, yet ensuring the latch did not catch. Vlad jumped up and scrambled over the seat to my spot.

"Be good—See, it's open." I tapped on the door, and it moved.

He nodded and set his snout on the dash over the steering wheel, watching the shop and drooling.

With luck, the proprietors had ginger loaf. I'd need a bribe to get back into the driver's position. Infuriating critter tore the carpets to shreds last time. Drool was an improvement.

Funny how no matter how long life is, there was never enough time. I was supposed to meet Stefan today to destroy the sketch. That would have to wait. Confound it all. I didn't have the resources to tackle everything.

I hurried through the pine door and crashed into Anthony. With the agility of a ballet master, he shifted his balance, keeping his coffee upright with only a slight rattle. A patron at the window with a smart phone, glanced over.

Embarrassment poured through me. I'd not touched anyone unintentionally for centuries. How could I have missed him? "Forgive me—"

"Not a problem, Dr Scott. All's well that ends well." Anthony said. His voice was so smooth, each word sounded like velvet. He flashed a stiff smile. "Doctor, I was wondering... Do you have plans for this evening?"

Startled, I stepped back. He glanced away, staring at the ground as if afraid to meet my eye.

"Oh, dear... I would be delighted, but I am rather occupied. Some other time, perhaps?" I smiled with a wink.

He dipped his head. "As you wish, Doctor. I will ask again—at another time."

I walked into the small shop, trying not to blush.

Feculence! He remembered me. Worse still, there was something about that man that made me want to smile. A good evening out followed by a long night in would have been fun.

My heart sped up. Pure enjoyment without attachments. No questions, no complications, no scandal. A woman's freedom in such matters was one of the slight benefits of living in this noisy, messy, modern world. Heat flashed up my neck. I ducked my head and took a deep breath. The scent of coffee and fresh bread filled my nose and calmed my mind. Life was too complicated for fun at the moment.

A gentle breeze from the ceiling fans wafted over me as I wove through a handful of round tables to the wooden counter displaying cakes. These days, my eyes enjoyed food more than my stomach, so I ordered six double espressos and leaned over the display case to appreciate the colourful iced fancies. There were no ginger cakes for my beast—doughnuts would have to do.

I handed over the magic plastic card that paid for things these days. So odd, yet easier than carting around bags of coin.

Outside, Vlad paced the car park, sniffing and pissing regularly. Obviously, sitting in the car was too much strain on his civility today.

"Not—"

He galloped to me, grabbed the paper bag out of my hand, and tore it open.

"—ginger."

Three sugary grease-cakes spilled over the tarmac. He gobbled them whole.

Was he really that hungry all the time, or was it a habit?

I held the motor-car door open. "In."

He trotted over and licked my hand, nuzzling me and wagging his tail in appreciation before hopping in and sprawling across the entire back bench. He was so cute when he wasn't being a horrid beast.

My mobile phone chirped like a trapped bird. I set the tray of coffee on the dash and retrieved the device from the glove box.

One new message gave me the address for the safe-house along with—'Sorry, best I could find.'

I took a sip of my bitter coffee. The brisk turn around was as expected, but why the apology?

EIGHT

After a forty-five-minute drive from Maple Grove, I pulled up to the rented abode with an abrupt stop. A faded for sale sign hung by the front drive of a semi-derelict house. No wonder it was available at short notice. The sad, unloved split-level home looked like a bomb had gone off on the lawn, and the wooden steps leading to the front entrance appeared ready to cave in. Hopefully, I would not need to be here long.

Around the side of the garage, there was a black lacquered box with a combination lock that contained the keys. That seemed a bit trusting. A busy property agent wouldn't want to drive forty-five minutes to retrieve keys; however, it meant the place was not very secure. No wonder Lance had apologised. Under normal circumstances, it was entirely unsuitable, however, needs must.

The heavy door swung open, and a faint scent of wood smoke drifted out. My shoulder knots eased a little. It smelled homey. The building may be better kept on the inside. The fluorescent bulbs flickered, eventually catching to illuminate a landing in between a half flight of stairs up or down.

Best to start at the top. I climbed the stairs, listening to each creak to memorise the patterns. About twenty feet away from the top step, a stone hearth took up an entire wall in a large room that combined living and dining space. Careworn furnishing cluttered the centre of the space in a jumble, but other than that, it appeared clean.

Vlad looped around the room, nose pressed to the floor like a pup. He skirted a glass patio door and leaped over a chair, knocking it over with a crash. The crazy mutt was making enough racket to wake the dead.

I clapped loud and sharp. He slid to a halt, looking over his shoulder.

"Is that the way we treat a new house?"

He sat on his haunches with his tongue out. His eyes laughed at me as he woofed once.

I threw up my hands. Yes, I suppose it was how a hound would behave in a new home. "Go outside and keep watch. There's plenty of room for all that jumping."

It was time to survey my surroundings. To be incarcerated was worse than death. My few experiences with torture had left no doubt of that in my mind. The glass patio door led to a set of steps into a fenced garden. No exits, but also more difficult to sneak up on. A utilitarian kitchen lurked next to a dark hall leading away from the living space. I flipped on another blue-white bulb. It cast eerie shadows along a narrow passage. Two stout wooden doors paired off opposite sides with a third at the end. No exits.

Inside the first room, a set of bunk beds lined one wall with a narrow window opposite. Outside included a magnificent view of the neighbourhood and a long drop to the ground. It wouldn't be easy to escape from, but possible. The other two bedrooms had a similar layout and a comforting distance to ground level.

The small wash facility had a bath, basin, and toilet in white ceramic. No area to hide, no escape.

I went downstairs. Halfway along was a door that led to an empty garage. The remaining steps ended in an echo filled vault of unfinished concrete and household mechanics—furnace, air conditioning, ducts, water heater.

Surveillance equipment became smaller and harder to detect with every generation. It would be nearly impossible to verify the area was clean, but considering Lance arranged it less than an hour ago through a corporate name, the possibility that my adversary could have installed something before my arrival was slim.

The house would do, since I had no other options. I went to the motor-car to retrieve my travel trunk, a small clothing satchel, my mobile telephone, and the device retrieved from the crooks. The wooden castors banged over each step up to the main floor. It was awkward, but smaller than my preferred portmanteau wardrobe case. A shame porters had gone the way of steam travel. Life was so much more civilised back then.

Vlad followed me inside and settled on a rug by the hearth. The wooden case had neat drawers on one side and a larger open area on the other side containing boxes. I pulled out a large steel lined tea-caddy and deposited the thieves' apparatus inside it. That was better. Radio waves could not get through the metal. It was hard to trust anything so complicated.

I turned on my phone. It blinked, reminding me of a need for additional electricity. I plugged the device in, then keyed a number stored in my memory.

"Reference number."

The robotic voice mail sounded English today. It was a pleasant change.

"1392." I spoke slowly to be certain it understood. My code accessed every file.

"Please state the nature of your emergency."

"1966's designate—name?"

"Unavailable."

"Age?"

"Unavailable."

The Liverpool accent was getting a bit irritating now. This was pretty basic information. How could the data be missing?

"Identifying features?"

"Unavailable."

This was not good. How could Geoffrey have left it in such a mess?

"Historical information."

"Geoffrey Briggs—relative—inactive."

I slammed my fist into the wall. Pain radiated up from my palm, throbbing in time to my fury.

"Please rephrase the question."

"Send message. 1966's designate. The guardian is available at three P.M. Address to follow. Use security code four."

I hung up, feeling tense. It could be a trap, but it was also a dead end. If the system considered the designate inactive, either Geoffrey had nominated an unsuitable candidate, or they had not begun training. Both would be a lead weight right now.

The whole request was questionable. It could be a set-up. Whoever called, obviously knew the phone number, but what else did he know? Hopefully, Bill could throw some light on Geoffrey's choice once he got here. My estate kept more records than the telephone system. Much harder to hack into an underground medieval vault.

An enormous clock over the hearth showed ten A.M. That gave me enough time to go to the museum, destroy Stefan's sketch and still be back before three. I took the cloth satchel to a bedroom, changed out of yesterday's soggy mess, and draped the trousers over the door. The Chanel suit would be repairable once dry.

When I headed to the door, Vlad trotted behind me. "Stay. Watch. Be Good."

He snorted, scratched at the brown carpeted landing, and nibbled a loose end.

"Fine, eat the place. Just don't complain about it later." I pulled the door closed. I never understood what happened to all the oddities he chewed up, but they never reappeared, and he never had a sore belly.

NINE

The drive to Maple Grove passed in a pleasant blur of freshly ploughed fields and budding trees. Spring was my favourite season, full of new life and fresh beginnings. The perfect time to eliminate a butcher or two. Another happy, glowing thought lifted my mood—Bill would be here soon. I don't mind doing the work myself, but it was nice to have a second pair of eyes on the ground. Even I can miss things.

The museum parking lot only had three cars. One matched a vehicle from the coffee shop this morning—Anthony. Meeting him right now would be awkward. Better to get in and out as quickly as possible.

Stefan never mentioned a time or place to rendezvous, and I didn't have time to waste wandering around. I lunged up the steps two at a time. Hopefully, someone could page the boy.

The reception hall was empty, but a light was on in the small room behind the desk. "Excuse me... Hello?"

There was no answer.

I glanced at the hall clock, and my stomach tightened. There wasn't much time before I needed to return for the meeting. I'd have to find Stephan myself.

I moved as quick as was reasonable through the displays. Not quite a run, but definitely more than the usual amble seen in these quiet halls. None of the seating areas had any visitors. I returned to the ground floor and made my way to the back of the building. The café had a few tables occupied, but not by Stefan. Where else could he be?

On a whim I tried the basement door. It was unlocked. Maybe he had gone down to view the paintings again.

A single light illuminated the concrete steps, casting a yellow pool on the dusty floor below. In the back of the room, another light shone over a hunched figure at a long table.

Working my way around boxes and canvases in the dark wasn't easy, but I avoided tripping or breaking anything in the thirty yards of gloom. The figure straightened. My heart skipped a beat. It was too tall to be Stefan.

Anthony wore a crisp linen shirt and smart trousers with a long apron over everything that almost looked like a skirt. He must be working on a restoration. I turned and caught my foot in a box. Stacks of picture frames crashed to the floor.

Anthony looked up, and his eyes twinkled. Was it mirth or just the spotlight? He tucked a pair of magnifying glasses into a pocket. I settled my face into a neutral mask. This was not the time or place to flirt.

"Have you seen Stefan?" I asked.

"No. I will have words with him when I do."

That seemed ominous. "Is there a problem?"

He frowned. "A painting has been damaged."

Guilt squeezed my chest. "Surely nothing important."

"He damaged an unknown work before we could catalogue it. That is criminal."

Only a bureaucrat would believe that, but at least it was gone. "Some things need to be left in the past."

He gestured to the table. "Not always. I lifted enough of the stain to see the original."

This wasn't good. "How? It was covered in coffee."

He studied me. "You seem to know a lot about it..."

Confound it, Anthony hadn't mentioned what made the stain. I needed to choose my words more carefully.

"Stefan showed me. It was like that when he found it." That was weak. God, what was wrong with me? I usually think quicker than this.

"Really..." Anthony moved closer. "The likeness bears a remarkable resemblance to you."

I shrugged. "Coincidence. Only so many genes in this world." Blood pounded in my ears. He was making some very alarming conclusions.

"And the hound?"

Feculence! Vlad was in the drawing. There was no way to explain that.

I struck out, slamming the heel of my hand toward his temple.

His carefree smile vanished, and he ducked while grabbing my wrist. "Stop. I'm not who you think I am."

He should not have been able to catch my hand. Few mortals moved fast enough. "So who are you?"

He was quiet for a long time. The ticking of a clock somewhere echoed through the room. He released me with a sigh.

"I'm not supposed to speak of these things, yet following the rules is only making it worse." His forehead wrinkled as the stress of an inner struggle pressed on him.

My paranoia rose. "If you weren't supposed to get to know me, why ask if I had plans?"

He leaned closer. "I'd hoped we could spend time together without it getting complicated. This isn't how I envisioned this conversation." He trailed off into silence, but his gaze locked on me.

I knew all too well about having restrictions that didn't seem obvious. "Are you pledged to the church? A member of the C.I.A.? Married?" I'd only known Anthony a short time, yet there were no indications of any such deceptions.

He stepped back with a sharp jerk. "No, of course not… I'm sorry. This must be coming out all wrong." He sighed and looked at the floor again. "The truth will sound like a fiction and once I tell you, we will both be in breach of the rules. I thought I could manage this, that we could be friendly, however my attempts are proving inept."

I was old enough it should not matter his invitation had an ulterior motive, but disappointment clawed at me. And I was angry. Angry with myself for letting him get under my skin. I'd not fallen for a flirt in centuries.

He shifted his head quickly, as if he'd heard something. I scanned the room. There didn't seem to be any movement or noises. Now was my chance. I grabbed the lining paper off the table and ran.

The gloom felt even darker after the golden glare of the work-station. My perfect memory allowed me to sprint to the stairs without a single trip. That should slow him down a bit. I raced up the steps three at a time. I heard nothing behind me. Where was he?

It didn't matter. I'd be free and clear once I got to the café. The patio garden would have plenty of places to lose him.

Why was Anthony acting so strange, anyway? Perhaps he was connected to the murder after all.

I burst through the door, shut it, and nearly crashed into Anthony in the small hall.

Foul rats of the night! How did he get up here before me? There must be a service lift. No wonder I'd heard no one behind me.

"Dr Scott—There is much we need to discuss. Come." Anthony beckoned to a room on the other side of the hall.

I backed up. He wouldn't corner me in what appeared to be a tiny and private room.

Where was the nearest exit? Anthony blocked my path through the café, and the hall leading away had glass display cases for twenty yards, no doors and no cover. Worm-infested donkey dung—neither was ideal.

I ran toward the cases. He wouldn't dare fire a weapon in such a public space and it put distance between us. The more the better.

Light, quick feet slapped the polished stone behind me. Good. That didn't sound like Anthony. I ducked into a gallery filled with modern prints. An Asian couple with a pram stood close to a Warhol image, nodding and pointing. A toddler wandered around them, his stumpy legs shaking, before he tumbled to the floor.

I leaped, narrowly missing the small body squalling on the floor. The woman scooped the infant up, and the man shouted, but I didn't stop. Damnation, it was not my fault the child was clumsy!

I passed under an archway into a gallery of sculpture. A plinth rocked. Something shattered.

Although I hadn't touched it, the crash released something deep within me. The destruction felt amazing. If only I could be rid of all my problems so easily.

The gallery ended in two rooms, both dark. I set a foot in the first. The lights flicked on. No exits. No more galleries. Odorous shite cauldrons! Would nothing proceed in my favour today?

I turned and darted toward the second room. The lights flickered to life, illuminating a sparkling sculpture of neon glass curlicues and spikes in the centre of the room. I sprinted to the side, giving the object a wide berth.

Crystal shattered behind me. My heart fluttered. Surely not—I glanced over my shoulder. Splinters of glass glittered in an arc across the floor. The chaos felt like meat for my famished soul, but how had it broken? I was five feet away.

The polished wood floor may have bounced.

Never mind, 'twas done now. The front entrance was in sight. I sprinted into the last room. The smell of patchouli and sandalwood greeted me, ratcheting my nerves up another notch. Tatya.

What was she doing here?

"Anna—Wait." Stefan shouted from a doorway.

By the Devil's toes, I needed to speak to him, but there was no way I could stop now. One more loose end. I was beginning to hate Maple Grove.

I barrelled out the door and down the steps. The parking lot was only a few yards away now. I sprinted along the tall hedge that surrounded the space. This was too exposed.

Surely Anthony would guess I'd go to my motor car. I dashed through a gap.

Tatya walked along the path on the other side.

I slid to a halt.

"You again?" She pulled something from her handbag.

Her palm hid most of it, but I recognised the taser.

"I know you were in my home yesterday," Tatya said in a very low voice.

"I think you are mistaken."

"There were paw prints in my kitchen."

That was harder to explain. "Perchance you have an infestation of vermin."

"Do it again... I'll kill you." The whisper soft words were barely audible, but the look in her eye said volumes.

Real murderous intent was rarely that blatant. Would an overwrought widow be that irrational?

She slid the weapon back into her handbag and turned away.

"What did you do to bring such rough justice to Geoffrey?"

Her shoulders convulsed. "You beast!—leave us alone." She trotted away, her heels clicking as she ran toward the museum.

Guilt squeezed my chest. If she was innocent, that was a cruel choice of words. The key question was if.

I sprinted the last few yards and leaped into my motor car just as Stefan entered the parking lot. His Grandmother trailed behind him. Luckily, the engine roared into life on the first turnover, and I was moving before they spotted me.

Stefan waved, but I didn't slow. I'd have to destroy his sketch book another day.

TEN

I drove at a steady pace. There was no rush. I'd make it back at least an hour before whoever was claiming to be Geoffrey's designate. Hopefully, the papers Bill was bringing would give a way to verify his identity.

I needed a background check on Anthony as well. He suspected something—but was he involved in Geoffrey's murder? His slight accent and study in Europe could mean he had connections. Could he be directing the yobs? Dim-witted cretins needed someone to pull their strings.

Then there was the tangled mess of Tatya. Was she simply a distraught widow, or was she involved? Tasers that small were not available on the high street. Where did she get it?

As many facts as my brain kept, there were not enough pieces to make a logical conclusion. I made the last turn leading to the split-level house.

A figure sat on the top step. I slowed the auto. Had the designate arrived early? As I neared the drive, I relaxed. The fellow seated on the porch was my companion Bill.

The tall man, with a face as weather-beaten as the crags of his homeland, stood. He was dressed casually today, almost scruffy, with the rough look of having shaved yesterday but not quite had time for it today. Loud barks echoed from inside the building.

"William, why are you sitting outside?"

"Vladimir." His lip twisted into a grimaced smile.

"He was set to guard, but I thought he'd recognise you."

Bill shrugged. "Aye, he recognised me all right. Wagged his tail hard enough to leave bruises, but would nae let me in. Here I am, thinking I was late—bloody delayed flight and the hire car's gutless—"

"And no doubt thrashed to within an inch of uselessness now." I held out my hands.

"Aye, naturally." He took one, bowing over it as gallantly as any courtier of the renaissance before kissing the fingertip.

My stomach fluttered. He could be so elegant when he wanted, and he knew I loved it. Clasping him by the shoulders, I kissed both cheeks and whispered into his ear. "Later, young sir."

The colour of his cheek reddened slightly, giving away his interest.

I opened the door, and Vlad scurried out. Finally released from his task, he circled Bill, sniffing and wagging so much his whole body shook.

Bill thumped his shoulder with affection. "Nae bother wee man. I know what she's like."

I raised an eyebrow but didn't comment. Forty and still as cheeky as a teen.

Inside, the hall carpet was little more than loose threads. Monstrous beast. Thankfully, the corporate expense account would cover the damages.

Upstairs, I righted the chair knocked over this morning. "Welcome to our encampment."

Bill tossed his heavy bag into a corner. The thud echoed through the vast room. I put my phone in the tea caddy and held the box out to Bill. It was the best way to ensure no one accidentally recorded anything they shouldn't. He winced and pulled a device from his back pocket.

"Do ya really think that is a good idea? Carl might need a wee chat."

"Better safe than sorry," I said.

Bill quickly glanced at the screen, then set it in the box with a grunt. "I assume you've swept the place?"

"Indeed, but you are welcome to scrutinise the building afresh."

He swept an arm around my waist and pulled me close. "I trust you."

Each whispered word tickled my neck, sending shivers to my core.

I slipped free and patted his cheek. "Your faith is welcome as ever."

I wish I could give him what he wanted, but that part of my life was over. A shiver swept over me, and I went to the hearth, piling kindling around a small log. A fire would lift this damp spring chill.

"Now, what do you know about Geoffrey's designate?" I asked.

He dropped into a chair. "Nae much. It's one of his grand-kids. Originally Stefan, but it's been changed to Jamie. For some reason, the change was not confirmed, probably because he's only nineteen."

Stinking cow-plop. The Stefan I'd met was definitely unsuitable. The panic attacks may have been a recent development. Could be why Geoffrey listed an alternate, yet if he was too young, it made no sense. "I've met Stefan. Not at all suitable. Jamie might be, given time, but if he's nineteen—"

"Aye, understood. Nae peep from me. He'll not know who or what you really are." Bill got up and pulled a thick manilla folder out of his bag. He removed a heavy sheet of parchment covered in spotless medieval calligraphy from the folder.

Our oath... Four hundred eighty-seven men had spoken those hallowed words pledging their life to me. Bill held it out. Nigel hadn't lost his touch. It was a spectacular piece of illumination.

"Sadly, we shall not need it today."

Bill tossed the beautiful work into the fire.

"Such a waste."

"Och, nae waste from where I'm looking."

I meant the calligraphy, but his intentions were obvious from the way his gaze lingered.

"Do you remember any Scottish correspondences sent out in the last month?" I asked.

He rubbed his chin. "Nowt from us."

Why were there never simple answers?

A motor car slowed outside. Gravel crunched in the drive.

I clenched my hand—the candidate was early.

"You take the upper floor." I pointed to my case. "Standard equipment, take your pick."

Bill flipped the trunk open and pulled out a crossbow. "Really? This is your idea of a useful urban weapon?"

"Firearms jam, powder gets wet. Solid steel rarely fails." I walked down the steps and waited just inside the door. The ebony hilt of my dagger felt heavy in my hand.

Bill crouched along the edge of the banister. It wasn't much cover, but the angle and height would give him an advantage. With luck, we would not need it.

Vlad paced down the stairs and lurked on the first step below the landing. The fur on his neck bristled like a porcupine as he growled at the door.

Feet echoed up the porch steps. A tentative knock tapped. That was not the code. My fear spiked. It was a set-up.

There was a shuffle outside. "Ugh, let me!" Three loud bangs followed by three soft taps.

That was right, but my adrenalin didn't recede. I opened the door a crack, keeping my face hidden. A pair of lanky lads stood on the top step. They wore jeans and big raincoats with the hoods pulled over their head despite the lack of any precipitation today. One shuffled back, awkwardly holding a backpack while looking over his shoulder. The second elbowed the first one. "Hurry up. It's Papa's last request."

The young man holding the bag shuffled back another step. "Um, I don't know if this is the right place. Grandpa left us some stuff... the note said to 'contact the guardian'." His voice squeaked as he spoke.

Even without seeing his face, it was obvious this was Stefan. The fear in his pose was palpable, but that he had come regardless proved something. "Please, come in." I opened the door enough to let them inside.

"Anna? What are you doing here?"

"That is a very a long story. Suffice it to say, I will ensure your message gets to the appropriate people, but why did you bring a friend? Didn't the secretary mention this meeting was by invitation only?"

Stefan glanced over his shoulder. "Papa's note was addressed to both of us. That's my twin, Jamie," he said, shaking back the hood of his jacket.

The other lad entered the room with grace. He stood behind Stefan, scanning the stairs without speaking. It was a pose full of confidence. Why had Geoffrey made a mess of nominating them both? It was obvious the second one was more suitable.

I shook my head slightly, turning my attention back to Stefan. "What did Geoffrey give you?"

He rummaged in his backpack, then drew out a wrinkled sheet of expensive paper and a blue box. "It's all Greek to me."

Paper decoupage covered the box. Its edges, crinkled with age, showed the seams of a puzzle box. Easy enough to open if you knew the sequence, but if not—simply a pretty object. Faintly written in pencil around the top were a list of runes. At least Geoffrey had left the instruction on how to open it. I'd work it out later. It would take some time and glanced at the note—

Dearest Stef and Jam,

If you're reading this, something has happened before I could give you the proper training. I'm sorry to leave you without more explanation, but there was never the right time. Please take the blue box to the Guardian. You can contact them at the phone number below. They will give you instructions you must follow to the letter. It's going to be a grand adventure. Please do your best.

Love Papa

My stomach twisted into a knot. Were they completely unaware of my nature? A blank slate can be useful, but not during a crisis.

"Pray tell, do you know why your grandfather sent you here?" I asked.

The second lad suddenly spoke. "No. Quit asking stupid questions."

The outburst was intolerable. I forced a smile, biting back the rebuke normally issued. It wasn't his fault he was too ignorant to show proper respect. "Jamie, you seem quite upset, but it would be for the best if you could remain civil."

"Not until you start making some SENSE." Jamie's voice rose to a shout, and the jacket hood fell back.

Long black hair cascaded down over eyes that blazed in anger.

I'd tried to include a woman in the Brethren once before. It had not worked out. No wonder Geoffrey had not attempted to confirm his change of designate. I would never have approved it.

Anger gave her courage enough to stare at me without flinching.

I smiled to myself. Her great-great-grandfather had a wicked temper, too. It must run in the family.

"There's someone in the bushes." Stefan craned his neck and pointed to the row of greenery huddled around the base of the building. "There."

Vlad rushed through the gap between our bodies, hackles up. I grabbed Stefan's elbow and pulled him inside, pointing to the basement stairs. "Down—Both of you."

I threw the puzzle box in a corner and stepped out. Bill leaped over the banister. I vaguely heard Jamie, her voice loud even in the confusion, "What's with the crossbow?"

"Keeping you safe. Get the fuck down," Bill shouted.

Vlad was already on the lawn, galloping toward the far corner of the building. He dived into the bushes.

A flash of grey brown fur slipped into the trees between the houses. It was the wild animal I'd seen at the Briggs'. Feculence. Was it following the twins? How? No animal would, or even could, do that.

Vlad roared a series of echoing barks, but did not pursue the animal.

"Och—you again!"

Shapes scampered through the greenery. Bill took aim, but the foliage was too dense to separate friend from foe. A soft ping sounded from the tussle. My hound screamed a wail of pain and collapsed on the grass. Two figures, one with white tape across his nose, an arm in a sling, and a silenced gun, ran across the lawn to the same row of trees the animal had fled to.

Vlad panted and whined. I leaped over the stair railing and dropped to his side, laying a hand on his wheezing chest. Poor bastard was in a world of pain. It would pass. The only question was how long. He whimpered again. Arseholes!

"Anna, we need to—"

"Hold on, let me sort Vlad."

I sliced my wrist and dribbled a thin line of blood over Vlad's lip. It usually hastened his recovery. He licked my hand between growls at the trees.

A few heartbeats later, Vlad's wounds disappeared. He stood up and shook from nose to tail, making his whole body shimmy. The gash on my arm vanished as well. It could not be called healing, simply that it was not there anymore, as if it had never happened.

"Right, now can I go get them?" Bill said.

"What's going on?" Jamie shouted from the porch.

As much as I wanted to kill those cretins, I could not. If the twins had observed Vlad's recovery, I had to ensure they would remain silent. Permanently, if necessary. The air around me felt too heavy. Everything was too tight.

"You go. Vlad's more than ready for a fight."

Bill glanced at the duo standing on the porch. "You sure you don't need us here?"

"Go—Carl should be here soon."

I tucked my dagger back in my boot and went round the bushes to the porch steps. Lovely squeaks and creaks followed each foot up the rickety stairs. Nobody could sneak up on those. It might be what had saved us.

Jamie stood on the landing with hands on her hips, blocking my path. "What's going on?"

"I'll explain inside."

She shook her head. "No way."

She had good instincts, but I could not let her walk away. "If you leave now, you will never know the truth, and you will be disobeying your grandfather."

"Come on, Stef, we don't need answers. This party's two cans short of a six-pack." She twisted and shoved, attempting to knock me away and charge down the stair.

I grabbed her hand, stepped aside, and let the momentum carry her into a wrist lock. She stumbled to a knee with her arm twisted behind her back. Her face pinched tight with the pain, but she didn't cry out.

Leaning close, I whispered in her ear, "There are only two choices here. Leaving was not one of them."

Stefan backed up, looking between his sister and me. "Come on, Jamie. Papa wouldn't send us into a trap."

"Inside. I won't ask again." I released my hold. Hopefully she'd do the smart thing—I had no wish to snuff out life barely started.

"I thought Gran was a bitch…" Jamie glared at me.

I held out a hand to help the maid up, but she slapped it away and leaped to her feet in one fluid movement.

"Shall we?" I gestured to the door like an usher at the Royal Albert Hall.

Stefan turned and scampered inside. Jamie's shoulders and back were as rigid as a soldier. "I'm only doing this cause of Papa's letter."

"That is enough." My stomach clenched. If she would not be cooperative, how much had she seen?

After locking the door and slipping the key in my pocket, I followed the twins to the lounge. "If either of you have a telephone with you, put it in here." I tapped the iron lined tea box.

Jamie snorted and crossed her arms. "No! You have no right."

"It's for your own safety. Ever wonder how those criminals found you? Phones can be traced."

Stefan put his in. "Just do it, Jam."

She scowled and set hers on top. "Whatever. You owe me a new one if it goes missing."

I smiled. The phone was not the only thing that might go missing if she could not be trusted. "Have a seat. Would you like a beverage? I am making coffee."

"WTF? Coffee? That slobber hound got shot. Then—both of you—were fine again. That's insane. It does not happen," she shouted.

Bollocks! She had seen. With any luck, she had not recorded it with her phone. Bill would need to check her log files later.

Stefan took the seat nearest the fire and peered at my face. "That drawing wasn't a coincidence, was it?"

I stirred the fire. Blessed mother—this was awkward. They knew too much, yet I could not ask them to take the oath.

"What do you think I am?"

Stefan looked at his hands. "I don't know."

Jamie flopped into a seat. "Go on—explain your way out of this."

I sighed and set the poker down. They needed more facts to make sense of this. "I shall only answer question on two conditions. Whatever I say, you tell no one outside of this room."

She nodded tersely, too quickly to have really thought about it.

I pulled the dagger out of my boot, tapping the tip against my finger. "That means if I hear you've babbled anything, ANYTHING, I will find you and shut your mouth permanently." I slammed the blade into the chair cushion a hair's breath away from her hand.

Stefan swallowed and drew back, but Jamie crossed her arms and met my gaze without flinching. Her lip curled into a half smile. "Lady, you've been watching too many Mafia movies. If it's important, my lips are sealed. You just need to convince me it's important. What's the second condition?"

I pulled a decorative pin from the neat bun coiled at the back of my head. The fiendishly clever enamel butterfly had been made by a Belgian jeweller centuries ago. When I squeezed the sparkling wings together, a razor-sharp blade, much like today's scalpels, slid out. It could be used for the tiniest nick up to severing a digit.

"You let me taste you," I said.

Jamie pushed her chair away. "What? No!"

"It's a tiny nick, hardly enough to notice."

"Fuck this."

Jamie drew the dagger from the chair cushion and threw it at me. I ducked as she grabbed Stefan's arm and tugged.

Stefan remained seated. "I want to know what's going on."

"Suit yourself."

Jamie spun and ran to the stairs. Her feet slid in her haste, thumping down three before she grasped the front doorknob and yanked. Something thumped, and the door rattled. I went to the banister railing and leaned over just as she raised her foot again to kick at the lock a second time.

"Stop. You will do yourself more injury trying to break the door down than letting me have a tiny sip."

She spun to face me. "How long are you going to hold us prisoner?"

"What happens next is entirely up to you. We can sit and be civil or continue this altercation, which you have no hope of winning." I did not mention imprisonment was the least objectionable activity that might occur to ensure her silence. Threats of that nature were rarely effective.

She returned to the lounge, but remained standing and kicked at Stefan. "Fat lot of help you've been."

Stefan kicked back. "Quit being a grump. We can't run off now."

She pointed at me. "Creepy lady just said she wants to taste us! You want to hang around after that? I don't."

Stefan jumped up. "Papa was part of this. What ever it is, there has to be a reason he sent us to her."

"I hope you enjoy black coffee." I opened my travel trunk and rummaged through the boxes, dumping out a collection of blades to find the espresso pot. It was a completely innocent thing to do, of course.

Jamie's breath caught.

"Black is the only proper style. Milk is an abhorrent practice that dilutes the brew." I closed the case and smiled at the young woman.

She pursed her lip. "Can't stand coffee. Don't suppose you have any diet soda?"

"Sadly, I have not stocked up to entertain properly."

"What a surprise."

Stefan glared at her.

She flipped her hair over her shoulder, wrinkling her nose at him while miming something.

"It's fine. I brought my own." She pulled a bottle of cola out of her pocket and took a swig. "Go on then—do your thing, so we can get out of here."

"Sit down and make yourself comfortable." I gestured at the old armchair she'd just left.

Jamie dropped to it but sat rigidly. Stefan resumed his perch on the edge of the next one.

I knelt down and removed my hair pin again. "Try to relax. A quick prick is all I need. You'll barely notice."

Stefan nodded, but turned his head away. To distract him, I pressed my nail into his palm before stabbing his index finger. Running my tongue over the tip, swirling the red drops and swallowing, locked the smell and taste into my memory forever. When he swayed, I shifted to let him lean on me.

After a moment, he raised his head. "What did you do? That felt incredible."

"I'm please you think so." I patted his cheek, then looked at his sister. "Ready?"

She pursed her lip, but held out her hand. "It's weird, but doesn't seem dangerous. Get it over with."

Again I pressed on her palm, but she didn't even look away. The blade pierced her skin without a single flinch. Blood welled up. I licked the tip, fighting my revulsion. Holding a woman's finger in my mouth was the strangest feeling I'd had in centuries; however, the taste was nearly identical to her brothers. She sagged to her left. I reached out, but she pulled herself upright.

"Whoa, that was seriously cool. Do it again."

I shook my head. "A sip is all I need."

"What do you mean?"

"I know your smell if you betray me," I said, keeping my face perfectly still. There was no need to make it sound threatening. It was a fact.

Jamie nudged her brother. "Still think that was a good idea? Now she can follow us."

He shrugged. "She must have been able to do that to Papa. He didn't seem worried."

Jamie wrinkled her nose and glared at her brother. "Whatever."

"If you do not break faith with me, you have nothing to worry about." I tapped my head. "What's in here, stays in here."

She crossed her legs and looked away. Her foot made a rhythmic snick-snick-snick noise as it tapped the chair.

Ruinous damsel. She was proving more difficult to persuade than a geriatric brigadier.

"To live with regret and self loathing for eternity, with no hope of atonement or oblivion, would be a sentence worse than the seven pits of hell. I have endured torture, been burnt, hung, and thrown off cliffs to get the names of my companions. The pain was beyond mortal comprehension, but it fades over time." I paused, focusing on my breath, forcing the agony back into the dark closets of my mind. "If you only remember one thing about me, know this—I have never turned my back on one of Mine."

Looking slightly green, Stefan's lips puckered before he blurted out. "Burned? That's grim. How come you're not a shrivelled, black mess?"

"I have no idea." I poked my finger with the scalpel blade. Blood welled up. A single drop fell and disappeared mid-fall. The skin on my finger returned to its original unblemished state. "Nothing affects me."

"What? Nothing?" Jamie snorted.

"My body may be completely broken, no pulse or breath. Sometimes it has been laid out in a crypt or even buried, then with no healing or recuperation, so to speak, I am back, exactly as you see me today."

If I truly died—my memory would be of blackness, yet if even a small amount of blood still flowed, I remembered it all, just couldn't do anything. It was not pleasant... I forced myself to feel the smooth brass pin in my hand. I was safe—for now.

Jamie held a hand over her mouth. "That's gross. I'm surprised you're not even more insane."

I suppressed a smile. "Even more insane?"

"Well, you're definitely not normal. I'm still trying to decide just how messed up you are," she stated flatly.

The courage of young people—that joyous bliss of conviction that they were right and knew everything they needed to. Sadly, life usually had a way of proving them wrong.

The front steps creaked. Adrenalin snapped through my chest. Someone was outside. I shoved the hair pin back in its place. "Stay here. Do not move. Do not speak." I pulled the dagger from my boot.

Jamie open her mouth then closed it and leaned over to pick up the fire poker.

I slipped down the steps. There were no windows to check who was outside. It could be Bill, but his steps should have been heavier, and Vlad's toe nails would have clicked.

The knob rattled. My stomach tightened. If the Scots escaped, they were more clever and fit than I'd given them credit for. I stopped with my back to the wall, not behind the door where I'd get knocked to the floor if they tried to kick it in. The feet moved again. The railings groaned. He must be leaning over it. Why? There were no entrances on that side.

The feet came back. A heavy thud landed on the door. Why were they knocking?

Another heavy thud landed. They really were idiots if they thought I'd simply open the door for a knock.

Three light quick taps followed the third thud. Warmth flooded my face. Paranoia had turned me into a simpleton. I unlocked the door.

Carl glanced over my shoulder to scan the hall. He'd exchanged his uniform for jeans and a light jacket, but still had his firearm in its holster. He gestured to the crushed shrubs. "What happened?"

I stepped out and pulled the door closed so Stefan and Jamie could not overhear. "The Scots paid a visit. Bill and Vlad are in pursuit."

He nodded. "And the extra car?"

"Designates came early."

He raised an eyebrow but didn't question the plural further. "We have another problem. I looked up Tatya's story."

"Don't tell me. She used to live in Scotland?"

He shook his head. "Worse—She doesn't exist before 1980. There are no landing papers, green cards, or documentation of any sort. Not just here. I had a friend look through the global systems. She's a ghost."

My stomach clenched. An illegal with fake papers. She wouldn't be the first to marry to get citizenship, but they had been together for over forty years. It wasn't enough to implicate her, unless Geoffrey was going to say or do something.

"Sadly, that doesn't help."

Carl picked at the splintered wood railing. "Nope. Did you know she's not just a doctor? She's a senior consultant of nuclear medicine."

Although she would have access to potent chemicals, it must be a coincidence. "Suspicious, but we need more evidence. Geoffrey wasn't poisoned. Someone shot him."

Carl nodded and kept picking at the weathered timber. "And just so you know, there were no admissions to A&E for severed fingers in the past two days."

"Of course not." Whoever G was, he had long arms and planned well. Those idiots would not have been able to keep things this quiet on their own.

"We can deal with that this evening. Right now we've got two nervous colts to tame, well one is a filly." He opened his mouth, but I carried on. "Don't ask. Keep the details light around them. Neither has pledged yet. I'm not sure if they're in danger, but I think something followed them from Maple Grove."

The wrinkles on his brow grew into a small crag of skin. He hated politics. "I'll follow your lead."

I opened the door.

Carl glanced at the bare threads that used to be carpet. "Glad I don't have to keep that critter."

"He has his charms."

Carl snorted. "The sort only a mother could love."

We returned to the lounge, but the patio door was open, and neither of the twins were in sight. Bollocks!

ELEVEN

Carl looked at the open door. "Shit—I'm too tired to chase a runner."

"The garden has a six-foot fence. How did they get over it with no sound?"

I went to the door. Stefan stood on the grass, looking bewildered. He put one foot on each side of the fence corner, trying to brace himself against it, but slid down. I coughed.

He startled and turned. "Jamie..." He cringed. "I told her not to."

"Come here."

He shuffled through the long grass, refusing to look at either of us.

"Stefan this is—"

"I know who he is. He came to the house after Papa was shot. Are you going to arrest me?"

Carl chuckled. "For what? Having blue hair?"

Stefan sagged in relief. "I thought I was in trouble. Jamie's such a pain."

"How did she get over the fence?"

Stefan sighed. "Told you she's better than me. She does parkour all the time. Little fence like that—pfttt." He mimed a jump.

"I see. Any idea where she's going?"

"Who knows? She can't handle…" He spread his hands. "She doesn't like change."

Poor darling was in for a rude awakening. "That's life I'm afraid. Now come inside."

Carl went to the tea caddy and placed his mobile device inside. "Looks like a phone warehouse in here."

I glanced over his shoulder. Jamie's bright turquoise phone case stood out among the black plastic.

"Is she in trouble?" Stefan sank into a chair. "For all that she's a pain-in-the-butt, she is my sister."

"I'm not happy with her, and she may have fallen into difficulty, but not by my hand." Not yet anyway.

Bone deep lethargy restrained my body and mind into ponderous lumps. Coffee would mend this. I went to the kitchen and filled my espresso pot with water.

Blast it. I would not waste time looking for the maid. I still had her phone, her car, and her brother. She'd come back, eventually. With no proof, few authorities would believe a rambling story about an immortal woman.

Unless… she was going back to Tatya. That could be a problem. Especially if Tatya was pulling the Scots' strings.

"Stefan, how close are your sister and Tatya?" I shouted from the kitchen.

He snorted. "Like fire and gasoline."

"So she wouldn't go back there now?"

He shook his head. "Jam's been talking 'bout moving out a lot this week. Said the house is too stuffy without Papa."

That was good. At least Jamie would not confuse that part of the problem further, yet it still left me with the question of who was responsible for Geoffrey's passing. Retribution was not coming swiftly this time.

I stirred the fire and set the little pot on a trivet over some embers. It wasn't the fastest way to make a brew, but I preferred the subtle taste of the smoke.

Carl curled his lip back in revulsion. "You can't expect the kid to drink that. It nearly killed me. You got any supplies for regular folk?"

"It was not my first priority. Perhaps you could procure some of that street food young people are so fond of."

Stefan frowned. "Street food?"

Carl rubbed his hands. "Chicken it is. The Missus' been after me to eat so much salad you'd thought I'd grown hooves."

"And don't forget, Vlad will be hungry when he gets back."

"Natch, when isn't he?"

"Stefan, go with Carl. He shall need a second pair of hands."

Stefan sat up with a jerk. "You're letting me out?"

"Of course. Unwilling accomplices are no use to me."

After they left, I stared at the embers and let my mind drift. It usually allowed the memories to sort themselves out. A jealous wife that was an illegal immigrant was not necessarily a terrorist bent on everlasting youth.

Was Tatya colluding with the Scotsmen? G could be a code name for her. Although her hair was ginger coloured, nothing else fit.

Why say anything about the demand if she was trying to cover up for them? Throw me off the trail? She did not know I would even care. Was she trying to find something sent to Geoffrey and simply using me to do her leg work? Could she be that clever?

This introspection was getting me nowhere. Whatever Geoffrey sent with the twins could be the missing piece. I went down to the front door. The pale blue Victorian floral pattern gleamed in the shadows where I'd dropped it earlier.

Paying attention to the sequence of runes, I slid each of the pieces to the correct place, but the lid remained firm. Resetting all the segments, I started again, this time listening closely to each move for the very faint click that followed. At the second to last move, there was no noise. That's where the problem lay.

A shadowy figure at the bottom of the basement stairs caught my attention. I froze, throwing out my senses. Surely the burglars had not got in.

I crouched and set the box down. The figure remained motionless. Was it a piece of furniture? Surely I would remember that.

Shifting sideways, I inched close enough to reach the light switch and flicked them on. In the brief second between dark and full light, Geoffrey stood at the base of the steps. Then nothing. The bright hall was empty. I leaped down the stairs, sliding on the carpet, but the cavernous cellar was silent and empty. No one could have moved that fast.

Damn it, that's because no one had been there. It was another apparition.

A black cloud of doubt clung to my mind. I returned to the landing and picked up the box. Was I finally losing my grasp on reality? Could I be catching Stefan's problem? That sort of thing wasn't supposed to be contagious. What a purulent mess!

I threw the puzzle to the floor and stomped on it. The thin wood shattered. The cracking noise fluttered up my spine. Good God, that felt splendid.

A sooty green-gold ball lay in the shrapnel. I picked it up. It was some sort of cracked thin metal shell, possibly copper or gold. The outer coating peeled away as I shifted the ball to my other hand, and a dull silver rock dropped into my palm. A warm tingle buzzed up my arm. How strange. There shouldn't be any heating on in May.

Along one side, there were some engravings that looked like runes but were not angular enough to be Viking. I held the stone up to the light. It glittered faintly, as if a thousand tiny points of light were hidden inside a thick fog, but I could not read the writing any better. The other side had a sharp edge, like someone had shattered it, and a worn leather thong hung from a hole near the top.

How peculiar. I'd seen nothing like it. I wrapped the stone back into its protection and spotted a letter in the wooden debris. My heart sank. I knew that handwriting. I'd not seen it for many years. To be honest, did not want to see it ever again.

Geoff, I found this last winter when I cleaned out a bothy. Looks like that stuff Anna collects. What do you think? Would she like it? Can you find out what it is? If it's any use, make sure you don't spoil it and tell the old bag. I want to break the news that Marc's not as useless as she thinks.

Cheers

Disbelief fought with anger. Marcus had lugged Geoffrey into another mess. Why had someone so intelligent remained loyal to that lemon? Blast it!

A triple knock and woof announced Bill and Vlad's return. I let the bedraggled pair in and covered my hound with a woollen cloak from the trunk before he could shake mud everywhere.

Bill leaned back in a fireside chair and pried off his hiking boots. "We had nae luck. The tracks lead to a wee burn. It's nae like they went for a swim, the water's too shallow for that. We travelled up and down the for a mile each way—naught."

I pressed my hand to my temple. "Damn, there has to be something we're missing."

"Unless those bastards can fly, they vanished."

"Could they have masked the scent in some way?"

"Nowt comes to mind."

"Jamie absconded. If those scoundrels are still here, she could be endangered."

"What did you do?"

"Me? You think I drove her out?"

He smirked. "Wouldn't be the first time."

"Not this time. She's overly sensitive."

"Aye, right. Know who else is sensitive?" Bill said with his typical grin. His eye danced. "You hide it well, but you're knackered."

I waved at the coffee bubbling away. "I shall be fine once this is ready."

He moved closer. "Would madame like something a wee bit stronger?"

I looked at the floor. The full moon was only a few days away. It should have been Geoffrey's turn. "Bill, it's not—"

He kissed me, drowning the words with the warmth of his lips.

"It'll make us both feel better." He came round to knead the back of my neck.

I leaned into him, the warmth of his fingers thawing the iron bands wrapped around my chest. "That sounds…" I pulled away and patted his hand. "Later, dear."

He bowed slightly, sadness and regret clouding his expression for a moment before he turned away.

Why did my body still crave the closeness? Could I not just wither into an old crone content with her knitting instead of the continual torment of what could never be? Once a year, he would survive. Twice would leave him feeling poorly. More than that was usually fatal. It'd taken three dead husbands to realise my lust was stalking them.

I leaned closer to the fire, stirring the embers until the smoke stung tears into my eyes. The pain was as good as any to clear my mind.

I'd come to no conclusions yet about the ghosts. A second set of ears might help. "I've witnessed something recently… yet am unsure if my observations have any logical conclusions."

Bill nodded, his face tight. "You? Unsure? You must be really knackered."

I set the coffee on the hearth, gathering my courage. "Imagine I told you I've seen a ghost?"

Silence hung in the room. The crackle of the fire was loud in the absence of voices. A minute went by before Bill coughed. "Och, did you say ghost?"

"It's worrying. Am I delusional? Is there a part of my mind that has become unhinged after all these years?" Relief poured through me at finally speaking my fears.

"If this is the first time in six hundred years, either you're grubbed, or it's real."

"I had a long conversation with a maid in the forest. I thought that was why Vlad and I lost the scent yesterday."

"Conversation? What did she say?" Bill leaned forward.

I waved my hand absently. "Nothing useful to our problem. She was dismayed at being deceased."

"So she was greetin'… Anything else?"

"I've seen a few others—most are just shadows, but one was very clear."

"Geoffrey?"

It was just one word, but Bill knew the awful reality that apparition would cause. "I don't know if it really was him. It was just a fleeting glimpse. It could be my subconscious because I've been thinking about this case so much." I didn't know what was more frightening, a genuine ghost or losing my mind.

"Just folklore, but usually people who die in violent ways need resolution. That's why they turn into ghosts. His death was pretty violent…"

That wasn't good. If Geoffrey was hanging around because of unfinished business, it was another reason to get this mess cleared up quickly.

"We need names. I hate having an anonymous, shadowy nemesis like big G. It's too theatrical," I said.

Bill laughed, a deep bass rumble shaking his whole body while slapping his leg. "Theatrical? Look around you. Your entire life is theatrical." He threw his arms wide to indicate the lounge cluttered with old weapons, clothes and cooking gear.

He was right, I suppose. All my personal gear were the oddities usually found in the back of a dusty antique shop. Things that were not nice enough to be in the front, but too good to throw away. It was not a normal life.

"Regardless, we need to deal with whoever was behind Geoffrey's death. Any idea of where to find the Rat?" I asked.

He frowned. "The Rat? He's not been in contact with us since you gave him early retirement."

"Pity. Would have been nice if something worked out easy for once," I said.

Bill's blue eyes pierced the gloom as if he could see into my soul. "How do you know he's still alive?"

"I usually feel it if one of you is ill, hurt, or deceased." I rubbed my forehead. He should know this.

Bill's bushy brows scrunched into a thick, confused caterpillar. "Aye, but you cut him loose. Dinnae that cut the tie?"

Shaking my head, the loss pinched my gut. "There's no real retirement. Nothing severs the bond. I just quit asking him to reciprocate." It was a source of continual hunger for both of us.

TWELVE

Vlad raised his head and barked before I heard anything. Seconds later, there were feet on the steps. Lots of feet, at least three people. I grabbed my dagger, but Bill beat me to the landing by the front door. A triple knock on the door ended with a giggle.

"Good 'nough?"

It was almost the right code. Vlad lifted his head, scenting the air, then turned and went back to the fire. I put my dagger away. It must be Carl, but what had happened to them? Had the Scots ambushed the party while getting supplies?

Someone stumbled. Feet shuffled on the porch. Bill opened the door and stepped back. Carl manoeuvred a very tipsy Jamie into the hall. His eye was swollen, and a purple splotch grew across his cheek.

Bill's smile grew into a wide grin, casting a mischievous twinkle into his features. "Going off-piste Carl?"

"If I ever say I'm bored—slap me." The burly cop shifted Jamie's weight to keep her upright as she swayed.

Nothing should have blackened his eye that much. He never let a foe get close enough. "Were you attacked by surprise?"

Carl glared at Jamie. "She thought I'd arrested her brother. The vodka talked her into heroics."

Jamie grinned and hugged Carl. "Dude, I said sorry like a million times already."

He stiffened but didn't release his hold lest she fall over. "Don't do it again."

She rubbed the top of his head like a lucky charm. "But it's fun."

"Is it okay for me to come in?" Stefan peered around the door with two large white plastic bags.

The smell of roast chicken followed him. I grabbed Vlad before he could vault down the steps. "One moment." I hauled the hound back to the lounge and pointed to the sofa. "Stay!"

The mastiff sat down, but his ears remained pricked, and his eyes never left the stairs. A trail of drool formed on his lower lip and dripped to the floor.

Carl struggled up the flight and deposited the maid in one of the fireside chairs.

"What's wrong with him? That's gross," she said, watching Vlad.

"Nothing, that's what he does when he's hungry," I said.

Carl snorted. "Just remember, he's always hungry, and you'll be fine. He will eat anything."

"All right lad, I'll be your blocker," Bill said.

Stefan came up the steps with the carrier bag held over his head, and Bill followed behind. Stefan hurried to the dining table, setting the bag down and backing away.

"Which one is Vlad's?" Bill asked.

Carl looked through the bags, removing two buckets of chicken and a variety of foam cartons filled with side dishes. Vlad whined and looked at me. I shook my head. He swayed from paw to paw but remained sitting.

"Makes no difference to me. You got any preferences, Stefan?" Carl said.

Stefan blanched. "Not really, Jamie doesn't like the extra crispy but…"

Carl tossed the bucket of plain chicken at Vlad. "Dig in, bud."

My hound launched himself off the seat and grabbed the bucket mid-flight. He flipped his head viciously left and right, as if he still needed to break the chicken's neck. Greasy pieces flew all over the room.

I sighed. It was his newest game, but the mess was worth it. Every minute he was hunting a stray wing from his bucket was one more minute the rest of them could eat in peace.

Bill found plates and Carl started opening containers.

"Come on. If you're hungry, now is the time," I said.

Jamie huffed a deep sigh, but staggered to the table. I took a sip of coffee. The warm elixir puddled into a golden glow in my core. Thoughts flowed smoother, quicker. Thank God that had not changed.

"Now tell me, how many pints down am I?" Bill rubbed his hands.

"Burger joints don't do booze." Carl handed him a can of cola.

"Och, juice it is then."

"Since you're all here, we should say a toast," I said.

I opened a drawer in the travel trunk and unwrapped a dusty blue bottle. It was only one hundred-year-old cognac, but was the best I could find at short notice. I took the bottle to the table and poured five glasses.

My gaze focused on the ceiling. Too many eyes would meet mine otherwise. No crying, not now. I'd done enough of that for Geoffrey.

"Brothers, please be upstanding for our Geoffrey." I paused, listening for the shuffle of feet and embarrassed coughs to fall into silence before raising my glass.

"Fare thee well, my companion. May your journey be swift and your destination peaceful." I lifted the glass to my lips. The acidic tang bit at my tongue, matching my mood. The men followed with a soft chorus of, "To Geoffrey." A stark contrast to the recent cheer.

I let the warm liquor burn its way down my throat before glancing to my side. "Stefan, Jamie, he was your patron. Would you like to start?"

The pink flush on Stefan's neck rose until his ears were bright red. "I… I don't know what to say." He paused. "I miss him? Is that what you want?"

"You can say anything you want. A memory, a story, a goodbye, or nothing at all. It's up to you," I whispered.

Jamie swallowed and looked at the floor. Her toe traced the pattern of the tiles, but her voice rang through the quiet room. "He was my Papa. He played cards with us in the evenings, took us fishing, and taught us to tell the truth." She dropped her voice to a whisper, as she raised her head and looked at me, "but I didn't know much, did I?"

After she had fallen silent for several seconds, I raised my glass. "To Geoffrey."

She shuddered as she took a sip of her glass. I clasped the girl's shoulder before nodding to Carl.

"I remember the time Geoffrey decided we didn't know enough about explosives."

I raised an eyebrow. "That story?"

Carl grinned mischievously. "The youngsters should hear it. Bout twelve years ago, he'd got some dynamite from a local construction site... We were playing around with it in the field. Well... the neighbours caught wind of it and came to check up on us." He paused, stifling a chuckle with one hand. "Geoffrey had lit the end of a stick just as the car drove up the road. Couldn't do anything with it like that, so he threw it into the scrub and walked into the house as cool as a cucumber. The stick went off just as the car passed the driveway. Left a hole six feet wide in the back forty. The car slowed, then just kept on driving. Guess they decided it was too much trouble to get out to question the fool." Carl raised his glass, his stout arm holding up his glass like a torch. "To Geoffrey, a brave S.O.B. if I ever met one."

Bill stepped forward. "Long before the two of you were even a twinkle in your mum's eye, I trained with Geoff for a year. He taught me a lot about being a good bloke." His cheeks flushed. "Taught me a lot about how to approach women." Bill tilted his head. "Sveta, your mum, bless her, was quite— Well let's just say, a young man and a pretty woman—staying in the same house. Things developed. Geoff sat me down and told me in no uncertain terms, Anna may have chosen you, but if you carry on with my daughter, you won't see your next birthday." Bill chuckled. "Got to admire that. I could kick his arse nine times out of ten, but he was nae feart of me."

I hadn't known that. Considering how rough Bill was in his twenties, it was no surprise Geoffrey had considered him unsuitable as a son-in-law. Or maybe he simply didn't want his daughter to go through the uncertainty I introduced into my companions' lives.

Bill chuckled. "Here's to you ol' man. Safe journey."

I raised my glass and took a sip.

The remainder of the meal passed with more stories and gallows humour. The laughter dispelled enough melancholy, the twins shared their own memories. It was the best way to show them the Brethren were quite simply my family. Good, bad, and ugly times were all taken in stride and held dear.

"Why don't we move to some more comfortable seats? The food's finished. It should be safe to sit near the hound again."

Bill took a stack of plates to the kitchen. Carl opened another can of cola and took a sip, then started crumpling empty food tubs and tossing the detritus back in the carrier bags in between sips.

"Don't you want help washing up?" asked Stefan.

"Next time. Today must have been a shock to your system. You two relax."

The twins picked up their glasses, and Jamie grabbed the bottle of cognac before shuffling to the sofa.

I laid a hand on Carl's arm and leaned close. "Do you remember Marcus?"

He spat out his cola. "You, for real? That muthafucka—"

"I think Geoffrey stayed in contact. Keep an eye out. He might come to town."

He slammed the tin on the table.

"And remember your oath. Do not eliminate him. He is still your brother-in-arms."

Carl's fist crashed into the table, catching the edge of a spoon. It sailed across the room.

Bill ducked it as he came around the hall. "Did I miss something?"

I glanced at Carl, but he shook his head and stalked to the kitchen.

Bill raised his eyebrow with a silent offer of help.

"Everything's fine. Carl's just received some news he didn't like."

Bill poured a cup of juice without further question and joined the twins by the fire.

I took the pot to the kitchen. "Do you wish to speak about it?" I asked as I filled the vessel with water.

Carl gripped the counter. "I know the rules, but after what he did—" He pressed his lips together and grabbed a knife, viciously scraping leftover off the dinner plates into the rubbish container.

I added coffee to the pot and set the lid in place, but Carl's knife continued its incessant screeching across the stoneware.

"Fair enough. Find me when you change your mind."

I went back to the lounge and set the coffee on the fire. The room felt tense. Too many unanswered questions, too many unfamiliar faces.

"Stefan, let me refresh your drink." I turned, shielding the cognac bottle from his sight and poured some into his glass before topping it up with cola.

"Where does this probation thing leave us?" Stefan took the drink and slumped against the futon, picking at a loose thread.

"Come to the meetings. When in doubt, ask. Nae will think less of ya. We all start as newbies," Bill said.

"But what about Jamie? She's always better than me."

I still had not decided if she was even eligible, but Stefan didn't need to know that. "Then you must work hard. What else do you wish to know?"

Stefan looked at his hands, shy again for some reason. "I don't know where to start," he mumbled, pausing for a long time before squinting up through his blue fringe. "Who... no —what is this group?"

"That is a very long story. Over six hundred years ago, I was born into an ordinary life. I grew up, got married, and struggled to survive like any in my family. Then one night, everything changed. I don't know how or why I became immortal."

He waved at Bill. "What about him and Papa? What are they?"

"After a while, I realised I needed help and gathered a group of laymen and monks since the church held all knowledge and most influence in those days. They kept me sane and assisted with my quest for answers. Hence, why my companions still call themselves Brethren."

Jamie looked away, tapping her foot on the floor. "Yeah, but how did Papa get mixed up with you? He seemed so normal."

"His grandfather nominated him. It has been passed down through your family for generations. Current members nominate most of my associates. If I find them acceptable, they take an oath of fealty and become one of my companions. Occasionally, I add new members from the populace, but not often. No amount of money, fame, or power will get you in."

She tossed back her drink and poured another. "You think we feel lucky to be here? Got the golden ticket?" She shook her head at me. "What good is it, and what does it cost? I'm old enough to know there are no free rides in this world."

Her face twisted in a snarl of rage, but I didn't think it was all about today. She had an edge in her voice, like anyone with a rough start to life. I softened my tone. "Geoffrey must have seen a great deal of courage, intelligence, and aptitude to nominate you. It should be taken as an enormous compliment. There are many things I can and will contribute to improve your life."

She wrinkled her nose. "Such as…"

"First, there is the matter of your generous compensation within one of my companies. Have no fear. I always endeavour to utilise your natural talents and interest, so you will not lead a dull life and will never have financial worries. Second, your health will be robust long beyond your years, as long as I only take occasional sips—"

"Sips? What? Like that thing earlier?"

"Much like a tree growing in the shadow of a mountain —my life without the occasional sip of human blood would not end, but would not thrive either."

Jamie wrinkled her brows. "Is that a joke? Vampires are so cliché."

"I would not use that term and cinematography is a false prophet. I do not kill, hypnotise people, have zombie slaves, fly at night, turn into a bat or any other creature. My condition is not contagious and sunlight has no effect—I neither tan nor burn."

Stefan nodded, his face tight with worry. "What do we promise in your oath?"

Jamie's nose wrinkled before I could speak.

"We both take it. I'm not a barbarian. Once you're one of Mine, I care for your well-being, and you help me with my quest."

"But Papa died... So what good is it?" Stefan's eyes locked on a speck on the floor, but his fingers never stopped picking the loose thread on the worn beige futon.

Carl came out of the kitchen. "Believe me, kid, it helps. I've survived more things than I ought because of her and that hound. Those ass-holes slipped in on Geoffrey. She can't be everywhere."

Guilt warmed my cheeks. I'd been distracted and hadn't felt the danger. I should have paid more attention, but there was so much information in the modern world. Reading those emails would have cluttered up my mind forever more. Each day, my nightly meditations took longer and became less effective in organising it all.

Carl slipped his jacket on. "I've got to go, told the Missus' I'd be back hours ago."

He clenched his hands, but said no more, just took his phone out of the tea-caddy. The ringer started chirping almost immediately. He glanced at it and his shoulders slumped. "Great, I've got to explain this—" he pointed to his black eye. "And herself is furious. Thanks for another wonderful evening, Anna."

I walked him to the door. "Your assistance was invaluable today, Carl. My apologies if its caused more strife at home." I leaned into him and kissed his lips, caressing the back of his neck.

He pressed close, clutching my body to him. Squeezing his need, frustration, anger, and shame into one tight embrace. Then he jerked back and glanced up the stairs at the new designates. "Sorry S.O.B.'s. If I'd known what you cost…" He snatched another kiss and spun away, shutting the door harder than necessary.

Guilt spread over me like treacle. None of this was fair to him or his family, yet each companion chose to follow me. It was more than I'd been given.

Many hours later, Vlad quit nuzzling the paper pail that had contained fried chicken. He had already licked every crevice enough times to turn it into paper-maché. He snorted, jumped on the sofa, and lay down. Stefan slumped on his side, cuddling into the big dog, and began to snore.

Jamie stared at the ceiling after mixing my cognac with her cola all evening. Heathen. It did not even need ice, let alone cheep soft drinks.

She raised her head a little. "I looove you guys." She tried to stand to blow a kiss, but lurched sideways and knocked me to one knee. Bill grabbed her elbow and steered her to a pile of cushions on the floor. She slumped onto her side, her snores cutting the silence of the room before her head hit the pillow.

Bill yanked me to my feet. "Serves you right," he whispered.

I blinked at him innocently.

He wrapped his arms around me, pulling me close. "I know you would, could, and do pull that trick on our young friends. Quite regularly. You pulled it on me before I grew wise to it," he murmured into my ear, running a finger down my neck.

A shudder raced down my spine, anticipating where those fingers could go next. "It's not difficult to do with the young or Scottish. You are all so eager to get drunk. Besides, it was the only way to keep them here tonight. I don't trust those wretches that disappeared. They pop up all too easily." I laid my head against his chest, savouring the warmth.

His hands played over my back, exploring the curves. A shiver followed his fingers downwards. I pulled back with a sigh. "What am I going to do with them, Bill? If I could amalgamate two into one, he would be perfect, but each is a vexing half measure."

Bill ran his hand across my cheek. "They might surprise you. Give them a chance."

"I cannot have a maid in the troop. It will not induce brotherly love."

A merry grin lit up his face. "Perhaps not, hen, but she'll break unwanted fingers right quick."

She definitely seemed confident. I patted Bill's cheek. "Now you should be in your bed as well."

"I'm not tired—jet lag." He leaned forward to wrap his arms around me again. "There are other things we could do while it's quiet."

I glanced at the drunken youth. With Vlad on watch, they were as safe as anywhere this evening.

Closing the door to the furthest bedroom, I pressed against his solid shape. My hands ran down his muscular back to trace his body. A shiver of anticipation quivered over me. I rarely let myself get this close to anyone. Good heavens, it felt marvellous.

The razor edge of my hair pin glinted in the light. A swift stab induced red drops of blood on my finger.

"My life belongs to you, my friend—freely given, freely taken, drink your fill."

His eyes never left mine as he took my hand, licking the finger slowly. Then he sucked the tip into his mouth. My knees trembled, and the room spun. Bill quickly slipped an arm around my waist to catch me.

He took the pin and pressed it into his exposed flesh. I ran my tongue around the puncture. He gasped and clasped the back of my head, pressing me closer. Drinking in the warm salty elixir, I licked and sucked until I felt him sway. Slowly nudging him back toward the bed, I shifted my weight.

He sat down abruptly, laughing as he held up his hands. "You've got me. Now what are you gonna to do with me?"

"I think you have an excellent idea of what I shall do." I murmured, sliding my leg across to straddle him.

Hours later, he sank back to the bed with a sigh. I lay at his side and wrapped an arm over his languid form. The strongest of my companions reduced to a kitten.

"Well done, sir."

His groggy smile only lasted seconds before he drifted into a deep slumber. I rested my head alongside his. For a moment, I allowed myself the luxury of feeling and ignored the fact that he would pass in a blink of an eye. It was too harsh to consider while basking in the warmth and comfort of holding him.

When his breath echoed with a nasal hum, I disentangled myself and slipped from the bed. I needed a quiet place to think.

Padding out into the stillness of the lounge, Vlad raised his head when I slid the patio door open, then flopped back as I stepped out into the cool night air. On the side of the house, there was a crooked chimney made of stones worn smooth by the weather. It towered above the roof by ten feet.

Perfect.

THIRTEEN

The next morning, amaranthine skies shifted from crimson to gold to aqua as the sun rose. Pity the grandeur of the vista did not match my day. Jamie would not be any more cooperative with a sore head, and Stefan's courage would not have blossomed overnight. On the other hand, the stillness of the night had restored my memories and clarity of thought.

Since Vlad needed to hunt, it was time to leave. I shifted my weight. Tiny bits of sand cascaded over the edge of the roof and bounced on the patio twenty feet below. Not enough for a fatal fall, but broken legs hurt. I did not need to start my day with that. Hugging the chimney stones, the smell of coffee mixed with wood smoke drifted across my nose. I let my toe explore crevices until it found purchase. One after another, hand and feet worked blindly to reverse my climb.

"Were you on the roof all night?" Jamie's voice dripped with scepticism.

Startled by the sound, my toe slipped. My heart hammered in my chest as I scrabbled to clutch anything. One finger wedged into a tiny crevice, stabilising my balance. That was close.

"What are you doing outside?" I said.

"Thought I heard something too big to be a bird."

My foot touched the ground, and I let go of the stones. The smell of shingle tar lingered on my hands. "It is a quiet place to think."

She snorted. "It's weird. What's wrong with the library, or a pair of headphones? That's what normal people do."

"I see nothing wrong with the roof. It's… adventurous."

She shrugged. "Adventure—seems overrated to me. Never understood why Stef used to read all Papa's travel books."

"Used to?"

Her cheeks flushed. "I shouldn't say."

"I will find out sooner or later."

"After Mom—he got into… stuff. Took an awful trip. Didn't even want to get out of bed after that."

So that explained his paranoia and panics. LSD could do terrible things. "Was your Mother's death what made you an alcoholic?"

Her mouth dropped open. "Excuse me?"

"I know the smell of vodka mixed with soda. It was on you yesterday. That is not a typical beverage for mid-afternoon."

She swallowed. "A little nip now and then's not a problem."

"No, but it's not just a little, is it?"

"What would you know?" She crossed her arms and leaned against the porch railing.

I sighed. Arguing would not solve this. "I know what it is like to wake up feeling miserable so often it becomes normal. I'm sorry life gave you a rough start."

She sagged. "What differences does it make? I'm a mess, and my life is a mess. The bottle makes it fun again."

"The decision is yours, but I can help."

"How?" She flipped her hair over her shoulder and glared at me.

Guilt twisted my gut. One taste should be enough to kick the habit, but... she was too young... unaffiliated and... female. Damnation Geoffrey, why did you give me this burden? "Do you want relief?"

She snorted. "You sound like Stef's pal. He had all sorts that would help for a price."

"I won't lie. My cure is addictive in its own way, but you will feel on top of the world for months. Long enough to sort out your life and say goodbye to the bottle."

"Maybe I don't want to change."

I patted her arm. "It is your choice. Just remember, I have an obligation to help should you alter your opinion."

Her lip twisted into a half smile. It might be the start of a truce. Time would tell.

We went into the house. Stefan sat up and slumped back to the futon with an arm over his face. Vlad sidled up to me, looking between the patio door and the empty food containers.

"Come, you can catch more creatures by the stream." I took him down the stairs to the front door.

A cream coloured packet lay on the shredded carpet. Bloody Hell. Where had that come from? Nothing should have got past Vlad last night.

I picked it up and cracked the wax seal. It was all written in the same spidery mix of archaic languages as the one delivered to Geoffrey last week.

M'lady. Forgive my trespass. I was unaware this was your abode. It will not happen again.

Another apology, but from whom? Were the Scots conflicted? Did one of them know me? I recognised neither of them, unless... I tried to picture their faces as children, but nothing fit. Confound it!

Vlad scratched at the door. I let him out and returned to the top of the stairs as Bill came down the hall looking bleary and washed out. Taking a comfortable seat, he sat for several minutes, just looking blankly at the wall. I hid my smile. Poor dear, staying up half the night trying to keep up with me will do that to a man.

"Once I manage to find my arse with both hands, I'll take Vlad and head downstream further. See if we've missed anything," Bill said.

"I don't think we should split up today. Something is still stalking the house." I handed him the letter.

Jamie snorted. "The four of us are gonna look strange at Papa's funeral. Besides, I am not going dressed like this."

"That's today? Why did you not mention it earlier?"

She wrinkled her nose. "Oh, great and wise guru—I thought you knew everything."

Stefan pulled a blanket over his head. "Shush..."

I clapped my hands. "Right, new plan. Step one—industrial coffee. Step two—Jamie takes Stefan home. Bill and I will follow you to watch for any stalkers. The funeral will be harder to stay close, but there won't be many hiding places, so you two should be safe. I want both of you to rendezvous here after the event."

"Whatever. I think you're getting excited about nothing."

Two men followed them here yesterday, then shot Vlad before disappearing. And she didn't feel there was any danger? What was wrong with her?

Bill set the letter down. "Another apology?"

"I think so, but who sent it?"

He chuckled. "Clowns hired to do a job over their head. One of them is scared."

"It could be a ruse. Something to get us to let our guard down. They shot Geoffrey after he got one." I crushed the paper into a loose ball and nestled it in the embers. There wouldn't be any further clues from the script, might as well be useful in other ways.

Jamie looked at her watch. "Hope that coffee's quicker than yesterday. We're late already."

"How long?"

She frowned. "Bout two hours."

I'd have to make do with conventional cooking methods.

Bill shuffled over to his bag and pulled out some clothes and a razor. "Best get tidied up."

I took the pot to the kitchen, then went to change. Electric heat was faster, and the lack of flavour would not matter to Stefan and Bill. They needed it more than I did this morning.

My Channel suit still had mud up the trousers. I'd have to wear the only black dress I had with me for the funeral. Feculence. The fifties swing skirt gave me enough room to run if I had to, but I hated the thing. It was so immodest.

I shimmied out of my long skirt, and the rock from the puzzle box fell out of my pocket. The two pieces from Geoffrey's desk had fused to the broken side with no obvious crack or seam.

How odd.

The new pieces turned the lumpy rock into a pleasing oblong egg. I pulled, but nothing shifted. Very odd indeed, it must be magnetic. I set it on the dresser and slipped on the simple black house dress. Bloody thing was so plain compared to the designer suit. It needed jewellery, which in my haste to pack, I had not included.

I looked at the rock amulet. He may be a bloody, clay-brained fool, but Marcus was correct about the stone. It was pretty... similar to the meteorites I collected.

I picked it up, holding the rock up to the light. It shimmered slightly. The dark silver colour would set off the neckline of the dress. It was better than nothing.

A sense of rightness clicked as the leather thong slipped over my head. Warmth radiated from the stone nestled just over my sternum.

I pulled on a pair of short suede boots. Flexible enough for running and not too unusual with the skirt, but they did not have space to hide my dagger. By the Father, I'd have to carry a handbag. With any luck, there wouldn't be much fighting.

When I returned to the lounge, Bill and Jamie stood by the patio door with mugs of coffee deep in murmured conversation. He'd put on smart trousers, a shirt that was not too wrinkled from travelling, and a dark tweed jacket. A warm tingle shivered up my spine. Menace—even when carefully contained in pretty packaging—was still dangerous.

He glanced at me, and his eyebrows went up. A smile lit his face. "You should wear that more often. Nice to see you have knees."

I flushed. I was still not comfortable showing any leg, let alone knees. "Get your fill now. It shall not become a habit."

"Shame, you carry it well."

I knelt by Stefan. "Come on lad, coffee's ready."

He peeled the blanket back from his head. "I can't go."

I stood, yanking him up with me. "Rubbish. It's Geoffrey's funeral. We're going."

He stumbled a few steps and plopped back to the floor. "My head's ready to explode."

Blast it. Maybe his addled brain hadn't reacted well to the drink. What did I have with me? Willow bark tea was not strong enough. I opened a few drawers in my travel trunk filled with small packets of herbs and dusty containers. A dark blue bottle caught my attention. Theriac. That would do nicely.

In the kitchen, I poured a shot into a mug of black coffee and returned to Stefan. "Coffee and a pain reliever."

He took a sip and made a face.

My version of the Roman cure-for-all-poisons had never failed to revive my companions after overindulgence, but it wouldn't win any flavour contests. I stood over him. "Good start, now finish it."

Bill opened the tea-caddy. The box started pinging and chirping as soon as he lifted the lid. He took out his phone and passed the box to Jamie.

She took out two, handed Stefan his and started scrolling through hers. "Gran's been trying to call since yesterday. She's reported us missing."

Confound it. They were nineteen. Surely they had stayed out overnight before. "Tell her you're on your way."

She scowled, then looked at Stefan. "You do it. Tell her we went to a party, and you were sick again. She'll believe that."

His shoulders slumped. He got up and shuffled into the kitchen.

"Here—Jamie—put my number on your phone," Bill said.

While they sorted out the digital contacts, I went to the front door and whistled through two fingers. The ear spitting noise could carry for miles. Hopefully, it wouldn't need to.

A few moments later, my mastiff galloped across the lawn and leaped over the steps. He licked my hands and snuffled my skirts, looking for a treat.

"Stop, I need to look respectable." I gave him a small piece of dried meat. "The rest is for later."

He sighed.

"On guard." I pointed to the house.

Vlad pushed around Bill with a snort. The twins came out.

Stefan didn't even look up as he shuffled past me. "Gran's furious, but glad to know we're on our way."

Jamie moved her vehicle quickly, but surprisingly precisely, for such a young driver. I had to concentrate to keep my old Falcon in sight of her Impreza.

"I've been thinking," Bill said.

"No comment."

He chuckled. "Seriously, when I was a boy in Glasgow, there were rumours on the street about a nasty piece of work that went by the name 'G'."

"That was nearly forty years ago… but it could be the same character. What did you hear?"

He tapped the dash a few times. "It's been a while. Mostly things to scare kids. Stories you tell your buddies, or make a dare about. Like don't let G catch you. So-and-so did and was never seen again."

"A bit vague, but thanks, Bill." It was another dead end. Not a surprise, really.

He shook his head. "They persisted longer than most school-boy stories. I'll look into it tonight. See if any of my mates remember more." He paused. "Bollocks! Bloody time zones. It'll have to be tomorrow morning. If it's the same geezer, I want to know. Glasgow's my patch."

Jamie pulled into their drive. I drove around the block and parked facing the house. Close enough to watch without being obvious. A big black car arrived twenty minutes later. The chauffeur walked to the house, removed his hat, and tapped on the front door. Tatya came out wearing a smart black dress with a slim line pencil skirt. Her bright red face almost matched her hair, but even dressed for a funeral, she carried herself with a regal dignity as she stalked to the car with the driver. Stefan followed in a dark suit a few steps behind. Somehow, his blue hair had been tamed by enough styling product to look conservative.

The front door hung open.

Jamie did not appear.

After five minutes, the black car drove away.

Bedevilled, bone-headed damsel. I told them to stay together.

Bill unfastened his seat belt. "You follow the funeral party. I'll check on Jamie."

"No, the car will go straight to the church. They shall have plenty of witnesses. We'll both go in."

The maid came out just as I twisted to open my door. She looked stunning, all-be-it unconventional, in a fitted charcoal grey blazer over skinny black jeans. The outfit could have been why Tatya was so angry and left without her.

Jamie locked the door, then turned and scanned the block. She tilted her head in an acknowledgement to us before donning an enormous pair of glamour girl sunglasses and went to her own car. The Impreza rumbled to life and backed out of the drive.

FOURTEEN

The parking lot at Holy Trinity was full by the time we arrived. A bittersweet problem. Geoffrey was such a warm and funny chap. He'd touched a lot of lives. I'd been lucky to have him in my troop.

Jamie drove by the church and found a spot on the street a half block down. I had to go another two blocks to find a space.

By the time Bill and I walked back, she'd already disappeared inside the brick building. We climbed the wide stone steps in front of the curved dome. Inside, soft organ music played in a minor key. All the pews were full to the point that people stood in the side corridors.

"Can you see them?" I whispered.

Bill was at least a half head taller than most people. He nodded. "Front row. All three of them."

As far as I knew, Geoffrey was not very religious. All this pomp was for Tatya's benefit. The only good thing about it was that nothing could happen to them in front of so many witnesses.

The music changed. A man with a long black beard walked down the centre aisle waving a brass incense burner.

Behind him came four men carrying a simple oak casket. The smell of myrrh filled the room. I had to force my feet to stay put. Why did the church still use it? It never masked the stench of rotting corpses.

It was a long ceremony. Long enough, I itched to leave. Four hundred and eighty-seven times I'd had to say goodbye. We were barely inside the vestibule. It would be easy to step out. What Geoffrey was to me, to all the Brethren, could never be spoken here. My throat pinched. The same farewell all my beloved received—hidden in the shadows, trying to stay out of sight, trying to remain calm.

After what felt like an eternity, Geoffrey's casket left the building by a side door for cremation. The procession of clergy and family made their way back down the centre aisle. Perhaps in shock, perhaps too angry to cry, Tatya scanned the rows of people as she walked. I stepped back. Bill's shadow was all I had to obscure my form. We were too close to the door.

Tatya's eyes locked on mine. She stopped. Stefan bumped into her. Jamie waved at the door, looking impatient. Tatya shook her head, her face contorting into a pinched mask.

She said something to the twins.

"She's not a whore, AND she's paid more attention to us in the last two days than you have in ten years!" Jamie's outburst echoed through the silent church nave.

Over two hundred heads turned to look at us. Stinking cesspools. What was wrong with that maid?

Tatya's hand whipped up to slap, but Jamie caught it and twisted. "Not this time, Gran. Never again. I'm out." She pushed the older woman aside and stomped out of the building.

Stefan darted after Jamie.

Tatya glared at me. "Haven't you done enough?"

I stepped away from Bill. No use trying to stay inconspicuous now. "I will take the blame for many things, but this situation is nothing to do with me."

"Nothing? Nothing? You ruined my marriage, plotted to kill my husband, stalked me and twisted my grandchildren into your puppets. How could it be any more yours?"

I met her glare without flinching. "Those are some very strong accusations. Do you have any proof?" What did she actually know, and what had her imagination conjured up?

"No." Her lip twisted into a tight sneer. "But, I will. You won't get away with destroying everything I've worked so hard for."

I leaned close and whispered. "And what did you do before 1980?"

The colour drained out of her face.

I tapped my head and walked away. Hopefully, that was the end of it, but I could have done without such a public outburst.

There was a gap along the parked cars where the Impreza should have been. The devil take them! Jamie and Stefan had left already.

Bill waved at me to slow down.

"I got a text from Stefan. They're heading back."

About time that girl used some common sense. Vlad was as good a bodyguard as anyone. I slipped my arm through Bill's elbow. "Best news I've had all day."

He squeezed my hand. "Did I miss something? What was the 1980s reference?"

"Tatya didn't exist before that."

Bill raised an eyebrow. "Been one hell of a roller coaster day. Hope the troubled two-some get the kettle on. I could do with a cuppa."

"I liked it when the British remedy for everything was a pint."

He chuckled. "That has its appeal, too."

The sunshine warmed my face as we walked the extra block to my Falcon. It would have been a lovely spring day without the stench of death on my clothes. Thankfully, I'd not seen any more ghosts at the funeral. The idea of a conscious Geoffrey going to the crematorium was intolerable.

"Dr Scott, I am so pleased to have found you. We must speak."

I jumped sideways, knocking into Bill. How did Anthony keep doing that?

"Now is not a good time."

Anthony bowed his head. "My condolences for your friend's passing, but this matter must be addressed immediately."

Bill assessed the stick figure. Although Anthony was a couple of inches taller, he looked like a strong wind would blow him away. Bill rolled his shoulder and shifted in front of me. "Sorry mate. She said no."

Anthony tilted his head. "I understand it is not ideal, but I must insist."

Bill shoved Anthony. The stick man bent at the waist, but his feet did not budge.

Anthony had moved like lightning in the basement yesterday. I could not afford to have Bill laid up just now. I pulled my companion back.

"We're late for a meeting. If you need to speak, do so quickly."

My phone started chirping. Bloody thing. I really must take the time to learn how to set automatic voice mail.

Anthony glanced at the crowd coming out of the church. "There are too many people here. Please, join me at the coffeehouse."

"What part of 'we're in a hurry' didn't register?" Bill bristled.

I fished through my handbag and took out a business card. "The company will reimburse the breakages."

Anthony shook his head. "I have managed to..." He paused as if searching for the correct word.

Bill's phone jingled.

Bloody modern conveniences. So much noise pollution nowadays.

Anthony smiled and continued his ramble. "Ah yes—I have restored the damage."

Bill nudged me. "We've got trouble."

"—but I would like to—" Anthony continued his monologue.

I spun into a sidekick that thumped on Anthony's hip mid sentence. He flew backwards, landing in a crumpled heap on the grass. Without waiting to see if he got up, Bill and I sprinted to my car.

I started the engine and pulled away while Bill thumbed his phone to return the missed call. Anthony walked into the road, watching us leave.

His face was blank. No anger, frustration, or disappointment registered. I wouldn't want to play poker with that man. He also didn't seem to have a firearm. I let out my breath. That was too close.

"Stefan, sorry mate... What?" Bill's face twisted.

I didn't need to hear. My gut told me something was wrong with Jamie. I swung the car around the block and put my foot down.

"Easy lad... keep your heid... we'll be there in five." He put the phone down.

"Where."

"Geoff's place."

Fecking small town. I'd had enough of Maple Grove for a lifetime.

I pulled up to the front of the Briggs' and jumped out. Why had the idiots come back here? They were supposed to go straight to the safe-house.

Stefan opened the door with half his buttons undone and his navy blue tie dangling from one hand. "I heard Scottish but—" His cheeks flushed. "I looked everywhere. Her car's here, all her stuffs here—"

"Take a breath, then start over, nice and slow," I said.

He gulped a breath of air. "I needed the bathroom and Jamie wanted her bag, so we came back. While I was doing my business, I heard that Scottish stuff, then a whoosh-bang noise."

Bill rubbed his chin, scratching at this morning's stubble. "Remember what they said?"

Stefan wrinkled his brow. "Something like 'That's what G's after. She can tell us how to find 'em'. Then Jamie shouted —'Give it back!' I came out as quick as I could, but they were gone."

"What did Jamie want back?" Bill asked.

Stefan wrinkled his brow. "My notebook... Don't know why they'd want that. It's just full of doodles and sketches."

Donkey-brained imbecile! They were after my immortality. I should have burnt the book when I had the chance. The only good thing about it was that it proved Tatya was just a jealous widow, not a scheming criminal.

I looked away and took a breath. Getting angry wouldn't mend this. With only a tiny sip from the girl, my internal compass was going to take a bit of time to orientate.

I forced a smile. "We shall find her."

Stefan's worry lines grew deeper on his brow.

Bill tapped Stefan on the shoulder. "You and your sister on the same mobile contract?"

Stefan nodded.

"Try one of the phone finding apps," Bill said.

Stefan fished in his pocket, pulled out his device, and tapped a rapid sequence. "Bingo." He smiled and turned the speakers up.

The static hum of the road under tires echoed from the thing. My chest tightened—they'd taken her to a car or van. It could be headed anywhere by now.

Bill gave Stefan a thumbs up. "Impressive. Think you could do the camera as well?"

Stefan frowned. "Probably. Let me get my laptop." He ran back into the house.

I followed him into the gloomy front hall. With all the curtains pull down, I never saw the figure on the stairs.

A flash and pinging noise were my only warning before pain exploded through my chest. I crumpled to the parquet floor tiles. Blood pooled from my chest wound.

"I warned you not to come back," Tatya said in a low, tight voice.

Bill grabbed something off the wall. "Put the gun down."

Tatya gasped. "Bill? It's been so long."

Pain seared through my chest. Every internal organ gasped for blood, for oxygen, for life. Damn, this was going to take a lot of coffee to repair.

"Hands where I can see them," Bill snarled.

High heels clicked on the stairs. "At first I thought it was government men... then she visited." Tatya spat the words out in a hiss of fury.

I wheezed in a shallow breath and coughed a puddle of blood. A far away ting-a-ling of a phone rang. The infernal devices even interrupted death. Blackness wavered over my mind. By the devil's tail. I did not have time for a full regeneration now. Horrific, ill-bred wench, shooting in the dark. There's no honour in this world anymore.

Tatya's feet moved down the stairs again. "Why did she need to gloat? I knew—"

Light steps ran from the kitchen, tapping at the keyboard as they came. "I got it. Easy once you're in one, the others are just a click away!" Stefan stopped and plastic clattered on the floor. "Oh god, what happened?"

Heel's clicked, Tatya stumbled. Noises confused my tracking of movement.

"Stop it Gran—they're here to help!" Stefan shouted.

Glass cracked. Feet scuffled. Something heavy fell and shattered.

Confound it. I did not know what was going on and couldn't do anything like this. Thrice-damned swamp-rats.

Stefan tried to roll me over and press his hands around the gushing wound. Pain blossomed and grew roots with every tiny movement. Shame death would not hurry and end this agony.

Suddenly the pain was gone, thank the heavens, but my body had never responded to my pleas before. Wonder why now?

Shaking my head, I climbed to my feet. Now was not the time or place to mull it over. As soon as this was finished, I would need to find out.

There was no blood on me or the floor. Never was after one of my episodes. The only evidence of my injury was a small tear in the bodice of my dress. Stefan swallowed and scooted away.

Bill picked a firearm out of pieces of shattered pottery and pointed it at Tatya.

I stalked up to her.

She screamed, backing into the sitting room until she fell into a floral arm chair. "How... What..."

"It is a long story I do not wish to discuss at the moment. Do not test my patience further. Sit and do not speak."

Bill stood guard with the pistol pointed at her head.

"You were such a nice boy. What did I do to deserve this?"

Bill flashed a tight I-hate-you smile. "You blasted a hole in Anna."

"Stefan, show me the computer," I said.

He blinked, then crawled across the hall to pick up the laptop and brought it to me. His eyes darted between Bill and his Gran, then he leaned close and whispered, "Are you really okay?"

"As good as I ever am."

The cracked computer screen showed a grey mist hanging outside a wind shield plastered with rain.

Jamie's phone must have been thrown on the dash of the getaway car. An icy shiver ran down my spine despite the bright sunshine in Maple Grove. Where the hell had they gone that was raining so heavily? While I tried to picture the morning's weather report, a statue came into view in the camera's corner.

I stared at the enormous horse's heads made of silver plates—one flung back to glare into the murky sky, with eyes wide in defiance. It summed up my feelings exactly. "Is that… what I think it is?" Shock made it difficult to speak.

Bill shifted closer to peer over my shoulder while keeping the pistol focused on Tatya. "Aye, it's the Kelpies."

Stefan bit his lower lip, chewing at the corner. "Is that a problem?"

"This can't be Jamie. You must have got the wrong phone. Those statues are in Scotland," I said.

Stefan shook his head. "It is hers. That's the id number, same as on my contract." He pointed to a number in the lower corner of the screen.

"Well, there's no way it could travel across the Atlantic ocean in ten minutes." I drew out the words as my mind scrolled through all the methods of modern travel I was familiar with.

One occupant of the getaway car coughed, interrupting the road noise. "Sick of jump'en. Pull in the services. I fancy a cuppa."

"G dinnae want any stops."

The same voices I'd heard yesterday. A chill swept over my limbs, rooting me in place.

"It's only a cuppa, two-minute job."

"Get a grip. We hand over the girl and get a real bevy."

"That's not possible," I whispered. My head spun. "They can't be in Scotland."

"Nae impossible, just dinnae know how... yet," Bill said.

His calm cut through my stupor. "We need to be on the next plane out of here. Ring corporate shipping—charter the first flight out of here. Then call Carl. Tell him to put everyone who is able to stand by. We might need a bigger task force."

"You're coming?" he asked.

"No matter how much I hate flying, Jamie's in captivity because her grandfather knew me. That requires my personal attention."

"We'll get her out." Bill handed me the firearm and clasped my shoulder, then pulled out his phone and left the room to make the arrangements.

Stefan moved to sit on the arm of Tatya's chair and squeezed her hand.

"Who are they?" Tatya whispered.

Road noise shifted to scraping and rock crunching. My attention snapped to the laptop. The vehicle rolled into a fenced parking lot with several large dirty white buildings covered in sooty black mould. Images jiggled, then went shadowy as the phone went in a pocket.

The buildings looked like bonded warehouses. Although not great as far as clues go. There are about a thousand of them in Scotland. I had tasted a tiny drop of Jamie's blood. She was a needle in a slightly smaller haystack now.

"Fetch the girl... Ya! She's pretty... very pretty."

A slapping noise, followed by a thud and soft moaning, echoed from the laptop. Without a picture, it was impossible to tell who or what had been hit. Detestable, yellow-livered churls.

"Ya! She's got spirit... Give me her phone."

The phone came out of the pocket, and the picture flickered to life again. It bounced and tilted. Rain drops splatted the display, showing flashes of Jamie held by one of the Scots. She had tape over her mouth and looked furious, but otherwise appeared to be in good health.

The phone changed handlers, flashing an image of the shorter burglar laying on the floor holding his injured arm. A large round face framed with thick black hair loomed into view. Everything in me seized into a ball of loathing.

Layers of flesh settled around the man's chin, obscuring any definition of neck. His bulbous round nose perched between thick cheeks like a wayward roast potato.

I stopped breathing. Of all the impossibles, this was a step too far. I must have lost my mind—first ghosts, now that monster.

"Ya, how's this work?... Bloody thing... Fingers like sausages—You—Open it." The fiend, with a voice like gravel, stopped speaking and shoved the phone back to the first man.

The lackey tapped a few times, then the picture tilted and returned to G.

He held the phone close, obscuring everything other than the slight sheen of sweat glimmering on his ear. Which was a better view than that. His bloated face was etched in my mind. I didn't need any reminders.

A musical piece I didn't recognise, something with a thumping beat, played.

A pale cream land-line phone on a circular end table rang. Stefan twitched but remained sitting, eyes glued to the laptop. The phone rang again, then switched to an answering machine.

"Give back my goods—I let your girl go." The voice echoed in slightly delayed double time as the authentic voice and the feed on the laptop clashed.

Tatya leaped up, her heels slipping on the polished parquet floor, and sprinted to the phone. "Who is this?"

"The package. I want it. Two days or I start chopping." He grunted a throaty noise that could have been a laugh. "Not so easy to do things without hands."

"What package? Describe it," Tatya said, despair making her voice waver.

A heavy laugh boomed over the line. "I know you have it. We've seen the pictures. Two days. My associates will be along to collect."

"I really don't know what you want…" Tatya's voice broke into a sob.

The phone clicked off. Tatya dropped the earpiece and stumbled away, staring at it until she tripped on a small rug, falling to her knees.

"Och—Bugger. That's upped the ante," Bill said from the doorway.

Although G's face was fatter now, it hadn't changed in any other way. *That monster should have been buried a long time ago. How could he still be alive and why did he want to find me after all these years?*

Perchance the Gods were playing a cruel joke.

Stefan knelt down, draping an arm over his Gran. "What was that about? We have nothing worth stealing."

I stared at the floor. It was happening again. I'd brought another nightmare to my loved ones.

Tatya leaned into the lad and shuddered.

Nausea washed through me. Jamie was tough, but nothing could have prepared her for this.

"I would hazard the reference was to hand me over." I clenched my fist to stop them shaking in fury, but the desire to cut that bastard's balls off would not leave me!

Bill frowned. "What's got into you? We've had ransom threats before."

I grounded myself, anchoring that anger to the back of my mind. "I saw something. Something that shouldn't exist. It brought back things best left buried."

"That's not very helpful," Stefan muttered.

The iron shutters slammed around that memory. I straightened, pasting on a calm facade, and looked at Bill. "It is ancient history, but Jamie's nightmare has only started. When's our flight?"

Stefan leaped up to stand in front of me. "You can't go now! What about us?"

"Your sister is in danger. The sooner I can get to Scotland, the sooner I can help her," I said in slow, measured words. What did he think I could do from here?

Stefan shook his head and planted his hands on his hips. The first act of direct defiance I'd seen in him. "We shouldn't split up. What if they come back? What then?"

I glanced at Tatya, then glared straight at Stefan to see who would blink first. To give him credit, he didn't flinch.

Tatya buried her head in her hands and rocked back and forth. "They said we would be safe... they said... no one... could..."

Alarm rang through me. "Who?" I clenched my jaw to halt the torrent of abuse I wanted to hurl at the woman.

Tatya flung up her head. Mascara ran down her cheeks, turning her face into a grotesque Gothic icon. "Take your pick Mafia, KGB, FBI, MI6..."

I knelt down and grabbed both her shoulders like a child, forcing her to look at me. "WHAT—Did—You—Do!"

She closed her eyes, trembling in my grasp like a cornered vixen. "I... I played them..." Her voice fell to a whisper. "The Americans..." She swallowed. "They promised I'd be safe. But I'm not and never will be!"

Military grade tech might have a way of getting Jamie to the other side of the world in an eye blink. That kind of discovery would be kept very hush-hush. Since no government had shown interest in me for decades. Her actions had led to this. Her's—not mine. Images of Geoffrey's casket flashed through my head.

She must hold the blame. I wanted to shake the pathetic woman until her head flopped like a wet rag. "Did you even love Geoffrey?"

"What!" Sobs racked her body again. "What's that got to do with this? They sent me to find medical advancements."

Was she fibbing? A plant would be very good at spinning a story on the spot. I didn't need this extra loose end.

"That... that man said he will start chopping in two days." Her breath drew in sharply. "I don't even know what they want. How can I find it in two days?" Her voice climbed to a fever pitch.

Stefan interrupted her. "Easy Gran, Anna can help." He stared at me as if daring me to refuse.

"How? What can any of you do?" Tatya's voice barely contained her contempt.

I move away from Tatya. Geoffrey had loved the woman. I wouldn't dishonour his memory by harming the wretch.

"Stefan, I shall have Carl send a bodyguard to the house. Until then, stay here and keep her quiet. Do not speak to anyone other than Carl. Do not report Jamie's absence. Do not leave this house. Do not even answer the door."

His chin dipped, only a small, crisp nod, but enough. He might make a competent companion after all.

"We have an idea where they took Jamie and will do our best to free her, but if we fail, give them any and everything you have that is Scottish." Hopefully, it would not be necessary.

"I don't know if I should thank you or damn you—but may the Lord speed your way," Tatya said, her voice breaking.

"We'll take every help we can get," Bill said with a loose grin.

A soft sob caught in her throat.

Bill clasped Stefan's shoulder, his cheeky grin growing wider. "Trust me. We've done this before. Anna's got a knack for getting our people out of sticky spots."

"Only because you continuously insist on getting into trouble," I said as we walked to the door. Pity I did not have more mature friends.

FIFTEEN

I stopped for six double espressos while Bill called Carl and arranged for two of the Brethren to guard the Briggs' house. No doubt I'd get an earful from the lucky chaps later, but I wanted to know Tatya was not plotting further bother. The rest of the drive back passed in silence. Although my fatigue had lifted some, my mood was still as black as coal when I pulled into the gravel drive of the rented house.

Bill's hand settled on my shoulder. "Anna, you're with me now. Whatever happened is long gone. It cannae hurt you."

"Would that it were true…"

Bill hadn't asked for clarification on this situation, but what would cause him more danger—knowing my secret or working blind? I sighed. For good or for bad, it was time to talk. I settled my shoulders. Bill's clear blue eyes locked on me.

"When I was a young woman—well compared to what I am now, they considered me an old dame then—a stranger came to my shop. He demanded money and shoes. I refused, more because we had none than bravado. He pawed at my bodice, saying that if I didn't have any coin, he would take his payment in other ways. When he covered my mouth to stop me from shouting, I bit him and ran to the door. The monster was fast and strong. He flung me to the floor and kicked hard enough to break a rib." I took a deep breath. It was a long time ago. I'd had far worse since.

"But I had managed to pull the door latch. As the wind swept the door open, Vladimir came in. He lunged at the stranger, taking a chunk of his hide before the man disappeared. Neither Vlad nor myself were ever the same after that night."

Bill squeezed my hand. "What does that have to do with today?"

"He has Jamie." Silence stretched out. The clinking of the cooling motor echoed around us.

Bill took a long, shuddering breath. "Anna, I know you are rarely wrong, but are you sure?"

"Unfortunately, I will never forget the sound of his voice or the way he walked. His body is fatter but, other than that, he has not changed." My voice was flat, drained of emotion, only logic left for now.

"Och Anna…" Bill put his arms around me, pulling me close, and kissed the top of my head.

I leaned against him, savouring the warmth before drawing away. As much as I wanted it, he could never understand what this meant. I wasn't sure I did.

When I stepped out of the vehicle, my one point of reference, the only anchor in my chaotic life, bounded down the steps to greet me. I gathered Vlad to my chest, burying my nose in his neck ruff.

He wiggled and woofed, then snuffled me for a treat. I tossed three from my handbag in the air. It would keep him occupied for a few seconds.

Inside, shredded hall carpet extended all the way to the lounge. Every last thread was mangled. Bloody beast.

I wiggled out of my dress as I walked. It wasn't wearable anymore, but the cloth might be useful later. After slipping into a long skirt, tee-shirt, boots and jacket, my shoulders relaxed. These had pockets and places to hide weapons. Thankfully, we were flying private charter. There was no need to be defenceless. I tucked a knife into my boot and another one in the bodice of my jacket. My hand lingered on the glittering stone hung around my neck. I liked it, but jewellery would only get in the way and tucked it into a pocket. Everything else in the bedroom got rolled into my satchel, ready to travel.

I pulled the door closed and walked down the hall to the lounge. Bill's back was to me. Clad only in a pair of worn jeans, muscles flexed and rippled as he waded clothes into a ball and stuffed them in his duffel bag. Good God, I wish we were not in a hurry.

Bill slipped a black shirt over his head and broke the spell.

"Ready?" he asked as he tucked his shirt in.

"Nearly." I quickly gathered the few possessions in this room. Everything in my travel trunk had a specific location. I merely had to return them to their rightful place. Centuries of evading pursuit made that habit stick.

Bill flung his duffel over his shoulder and took the awkward wooden trunk from my hand. "You have nothing to prove, hen."

Although perfectly capable of lifting it, why dispute with a gentleman? I locked the door, then slipped the keys back into the box on the side of the garage. It would be ready if anyone else needed the safe-house.

The hire car's boot only had enough room for Bill's bag and my satchel. The trunk had to sit upright next to Vlad on the back seat.

Laptop keys clicked while I backed out of the drive accompanied by Vlad's growling his displeasure at having to share the space.

"Hush, you have plenty of room," I said.

Bill didn't glance up from manufacturing the documents for our flight. He knew who I was scolding.

Half an hour later, the hire car tootled up the ramp to the interstate. I pressed the accelerator harder to no effect. Barnacle-butts, Bill was right. This thing was gutless. Shame I'd had to leave my Falcon behind.

"Did we really have time for all that nonsense at the Briggs?"

"It'll be close," Bill muttered over the keyboard clicks.

"How close?" I asked, gripping the steering wheel.

He shrugged. "You said first flight. I'd say the speed limits might need to apply to other people today."

I glanced over to see an enormous grin.

"You cheeky scoundrel." I switched to the outside lane. Tatya's blessing had better hold; we had no time for constables.

The miles passed in a blur. It normally takes two hours to get to Minneapolis; we did it in one-fifteen. Even gutless vehicles can make up time if flogged hard enough.

I pulled up to the company warehouse and got out with Vlad and the luggage. I hated airports. So much chaos, delay, and bureaucracy. Flying was worse, though. A shiver ran down my neck. It was the quickest way to get to Scotland and the ransom demand had not given us any time to loiter. Besides, week-long boat voyages were no picnic, either.

While Bill took the hired vehicle back to the return depot, I showed a member of the ground crew my corporate badge. He pointed to a small private jet.

My stomach did a somersault looking at the tin can that would prevent us from falling thousands of feet into the ocean. There were things worse than death. All the plush seating and fancy lights did not hide the fact it weighed too much. The contraption should not be able to leave the ground.

I took Vlad to a large wooden packing crate next to the plane. "Vlad, get in." All he had to do was sit quietly for a few hours. He wouldn't even need to be in the box if he could behave. Was that too much to ask?

He retreated, ears flat back, growling louder. The fact he was wasting the precious extra minutes by refusing to get in did not concern my stubborn hound.

"I don't like flying either, cousin," I said, ruffling his ears. He lunged forward, licking my face. Although I detested the slimy feel, I let him. It was the least I could do if he would cooperate. "Now, get in."

I pointed to the box with a bed and chew bone. He flopped on his side and whined.

"Vlad, there is no time for this."

Bill sauntered across the echoing warehouse carrying a steaming tray of bacon sandwiches and two cups of coffee. Vlad sat up and licked his lips. I grimaced. Bill had remembered Vlad's weakness.

The crew seemed to be occupied doing mechanical things. I flipped open my travel trunk, took out a packet of dried chamomile root, and doused the food with it. Vlad jigged from side to side, drool forming a puddle under his chin.

I threw the sandwiches into the back of the crate. Vlad dived over the bed and pounced on them. When he lay down and closed his eyes, I fastened the side panel in place. Festering pox crypts! I hated tricking him like that. At least he would sleep from most of the flight.

I wheeled him onto the aircraft. If he would behave, there were more comfortable ways to travel, but this was the only way to get him to Britain without destroying the aircraft.

Bill handed me a coffee before sprawling across a leather seat. Wrapping my hands around the steaming cup hid the shaking. It had begun earlier this time. The engines had not even started.

Smartly dressed air crew checked our papers and indicated where the safety belts were on our seats. I sat down.

Bill pulled a magazine out of his back pocket and flipped through it. His casual pose in the face of the impending miracle of hurling through the air without dying was astounding.

Focusing on the steam coming off my beverage, I counted the seconds until the pilot announced the departure of our mobile prison.

The engines rumbled to life. The body of the craft vibrated in time to the noise. I set the cup aside and curled my nails into my palm. Blood trickled down my wrist. It gave me something to think about. Anything was better than dwelling on the forced enclosure we were about to endure for the next nine hours.

Bill patted my leg. "Don't you worry. We'll be in dreary old blighty before you know it."

I tried to put on a calm smile, but was not sure it worked. The plane taxied down the bumpy runway, bouncing my head against the back of my seat. Each thump sent waves of panic through my veins. Think of something else.

How was Vlad? I heard nothing from the box in the corner. That was good. At least he was in the cabin. We'd tried to fly as cargo once. Since the cold and low oxygen wouldn't kill us, I thought it would be a good way to avoid the bureaucrats.

Never again… When my lungs screamed for oxygen, pure reflexive panic had set in. Then the body shut down, blacking out, only to reanimate a few moments later and live it all over anew until we finally landed.

I swore I would never set foot on an aeroplane after that. Life doesn't let you keep some promises, though.

Bill dropped the criminal's phone in my lap. "Get your head round that. It'll help pass the time."

"And what are you going to be doing?"

He held up a hip flask. "I intend to get myself round this, then catch a few zeds."

"Charming. Going to leave me to my own amusements the whole way?"

"Hopefully." He took a swig.

As much as I fiddled with the phone, all the buttons seemed to do the same thing. Eventually, the plane settled into a steady cruise, and the cabin lights dimmed. Bill's snores took on the monotonous rhythm of deep sleep.

I set the phone aside and closed my eyes, letting my mind drift free.

When I'd first heard of astral projection, I believed it to be another falsehood. I could never thank the old yogi on the banks of the Ganges, who took the time to speak to me about it properly. His teaching gave me a way to see what was going on in other parts of the world long before digital technology.

Marcus... Marcus—my dear... Where are you?

Nothing happened. My mind floated in a land of mist. It had been quite a few years since I'd tried to track this errant fellow. I focused on a combination of memories—sandalwood incense, sea salt, climbing chalk, dusty libraries, love, and betrayal. It gelled into a beacon I followed like a name tag.

Zooming through the sky, I plunged into awareness of Marcus knee-deep in an icy burn. Older than I remembered... of course, but the years had not been kind. His brown locks, now matted to his head, were thin across the top and streaked with silver. His skin had been weather-whipped to a ruddy glow and lined with enough creases to look like he'd slept on a fishing net.

Heather and bracken covered the land on either side of the sloped bank. Marcus scrambled up the muddy edge to some rocks and stood still for a moment. The base of a mountain was visible, but the clouds were too low to distinguish any features.

"I know you're there, Anna. It's no use trying to hide," he shouted. "Why? After you forsake me for all these years? Why Now!"

Damn, a mobile speaking device would have been better right now. Astral projection was all one way. I could hear and see him, but he would only have a vague sensation of being watched.

"You'll not find me." He spun around, his hands waving at the mist. "There's nothing here. You can't trace hundreds of miles of emptiness." He tapped his feet in a square jig, dancing around like a manic squirrel hiding nuts. "It finally paid off." He waved two fingers at the sky. "How do you like it!" he shouted, shaking his fist instead of repeating the rude gesture. "Think about that next time you want to expel one of us."

He hummed loudly, hurrying along a faint path.

It was an excellent tactic. One I'd taught him. With his mind filled with the dull repetition of 'Mary had a little lamb' I couldn't pick up any conscious thoughts about his location.

He might lose his concentration if I followed long enough. After a few hours, it was obvious he'd been practising, yet I needed to know if he was involved with the kidnapping. I'd have to track down the infernal mutton-head. Another thing I didn't need.

An Essex voice scratched through the aircraft speakers, indicating we should prepare for landing. Fear spiked through me. Landing was as hazardous as taking off. Each only slightly less than flying…

Physical reality crashed into my awareness with that thought. Astral projection depended on complete relaxation. Fear short circuited it.

Bill yawned, twisting to the side to stretch his six-foot frame. "So, was it worth it? Did you find Rattie?"

"I saw him, but not enough to pinpoint his current location. He's being particularly unhelpful."

"He was always petty. If it'd been anyone else killed, I'd have thought he set us up, but he wouldn't do that to

Geoffrey." Bill gazed at the wall. "You remember how Geoff tried to take the blame for Marcus after Columbia? Always wondered why he did that."

I stayed silent. Columbia was hard on all of us. Discouraging the interest of a drug gang that didn't fear anyone was no laughing matter, but apparently, their friendship survived the crisis.

Vlad whined inside his crate.

"Just a few more feet," I whispered, but he scratched and woofed loud enough to draw stares from the crew.

The plane landed with a jolt. Tires squealed as the pilot braked. Grey tarmac raced by. I released my death grip from the armrest. We were safe.

"After you snored the entire way here, I should make you open Vlad's crate," I said.

"Nae my fault I can sleep. Best way to travel."

I snorted, but couldn't help smiling. "While you were so blissfully unaware, I was working on the extraction. All that phone had on it were a few photos and a dire music collection. How can people listen to that noise?"

I got up and undid the latches on Vlad's crate. The hound bolted out, knocking me backwards, even though I was expecting it. He licked my ears and anything he could reach while bouncing on the spot.

"Enough already. Yes, I love you too. Now go tell Bill how much you missed him," I said, pushing the big dog off me as I sat back up.

Bill poked buttons and patted Vlad's head absent-mindedly before a big smile lit up his face. "The biggest bunch of idiots I've ever seen. Why would anyone send them after you? You'd make mince out of 'em."

"How does the phone tell you that?"

"They've locked none of it. Didn't even put password protection on the emails. Means I can get everything off this as easily as the owner."

I nodded. "Fools are easier to bin."

"Aye, cannon fodder if I ever saw it."

"Bastard."

"Aye, but you knew that already."

The crew opened the hatch, and an airport official entered with a hand-held scanner and stack of paperwork. The stout woman waved the scanner over Vlad's neck. He jigged side to side, licking at her and knocking the device out of her hand.

She forced a smile. "Madam, would you be so kind as to restrain your… pet?"

I waved a bacon strip under his nose. He sneezed on me and raised a lip, but stopped jumping on the customs' official.

Fifteen minutes later, I took my first breath of fresh air on our walk to the car park. For all that it cost my company to charter those tin cans, you would have thought they could improve the smell.

We stopped at the estate's old Land Rover. Bill unlocked it and I tapped the back seat. Vlad stopped savaging the outside of my luggage and jumped, his tongue hanging out in a comic dog grin. He knew he'd made his point. Insufferable beast.

Plastic crates of outdoor equipment and supplies to make stalking expeditions comfortable filled the boot of the Rover. Bill shifted a few and made enough room for all our luggage.

"Two routes on this phone's local map are new. There could be bonded warehouses in the area. I'd say it's as good a place to start as any," Bill said as he slammed the tailgate.

"Do you wish to drive or shall I?"

SIXTEEN

I drove. It'd been a while, but I had learned in Britain. The left never felt like the wrong side of the road to me.

Scottish countryside zipped past the windows. The plains around Edinburgh gave way to gentle rolling hills that were cheerfully green and delightfully free of rain this morning. It was a nice welcome home. With luck, the rest of the trip would prove as accommodating.

We stopped at the first location Bill had found on the criminal's phone. An open field with a small stream running through it.

"This?" I said. It could be a spot to pick up or leave messages, yet there was no evidence of any such activity.

Bill frowned. "It's the right coordinates, but looks like a dead end. Turn round and head back toward the city."

I swung the Rover in a tight U and headed back the way we'd just came. Ten minutes later, we pulled into a car park in town.

"Hopefully, we'll have more luck here. There's nothing else of any use on this. Lots of personal rubbish, but suspiciously absent of any info about a trip abroad." Bill tossed the phone into the glove box and climbed out.

"Maybe the lout is less of an idiot than we're giving him credit for," I said.

"Or maybe his boss sent nothing important that could be traced," Bill said.

So much had changed over the centuries. Smooth paving had replaced the cobblestones, and the shops were much shinier, but church spires didn't move. I could still find my way around. Odd to hide Jamie in such a public place. It looked nothing like the deserted warehouses on the camera yesterday.

"The gods must be smiling at us today." I pointed across the street to a run down chip shop.

The slouchy burglar shuffled along with his arm bent at a funny angle under his coat. He kept his head tucked into his collar while his taller companion reached for the door.

"There are days I wonder who is watching you up there." Bill nudged his head skyward.

"Do not ask." I shuddered. Too many stories of demonic possession had ruled my childhood. It was still hard to shake the belief.

I slipped into the crowd, effortlessly merging with the bustle to get closer to the shop while Bill leaned against the wall and casually leafed through his magazine. On the pavement across from the shop, I stopped and randomly pressed buttons on a phone that wasn't even turned on.

Our quarry left the diner a few minutes later with white paper bags stained with grease.

Bill stood up and sauntered along behind them. I put my phone away and hurried forward as if late for an appointment. They didn't even notice the tail. Was it incompetence or arrogance?

They stopped a few blocks away in a small gravel parking lot and got into a battered white van. Vlad bunched up his legs, preparing to corner the men, but I snared his collar before he could leap.

I wanted those men wriggling. Corpses offered no answers. Vlad's shoulders tensed, and the fur on the back of his neck stood on end.

"Wait. Just a few more minutes, cousin," I murmured, stroking his ears.

The wide open lot did not offer any cover, but the two men seem more concerned with lunch and the football on the radio than going anywhere. I tossed a sharp nod at Bill. He gave me a thumbs up before turning to fetch our Rover. I looked at my watch. The damn thing was parked on the other side of the busy precinct.

If they drove away before Bill got back, it would be problematic, but getting them into our vehicle would equal the playing field quite a bit. Life was so much simpler when the only getaway was on horseback.

I leaned against a protective railing erected to force people to walk the few extra feet to the crossing lights and pretended to be absorbed in checking my inanimate phone while watching the van out of the corner of my eye.

The footie droned on. The passenger threw sloppy punches in the air each time his team scored. After a few minutes, a chirping ring-tone caused the driver to drop his pie in his haste to answer. The conversation was too far away to hear. After a few minutes, the driver turned the phone off and flung it across the dash in disgust. The van engine roared to life. The driver gunned the accelerator, scattering gravel as the vehicle tore out of the parking space.

I let go of Vlad's collar and sprinted across the car park. They were already at the exit but had to wait for space in the traffic to pull out. I sprang, landing on the back bumper with a loud thud.

Hoping no—expecting—they would stop to check the noise. The sudden lurch of acceleration almost made me lose my grip on the door frame. Vlad galloped behind the van. Tongue out, his huge strides matched the pace of the vehicle.

At the next corner, the van lurched to the left on two wheels, almost as if they had made the turn at the last minute. The sudden change of direction, combined with the acute angle, broke my grip on the thin frame. Scrabbling at the smooth metal didn't help. Falling backwards, my shoulder exploded in agony when I met tarmac and rolled across two lanes of traffic.

Sitting up, my right arm flopped limply against my leg. Definitely dislocated, maybe broken as well.

A hatchback from the other direction slid to a halt, horn blaring in my face as I climbed to my feet. Vlad galloped after the quickly shrinking van.

The young man behind the wheel leaned out, waving his hands at me. "Get out of the road, eejit. You got a death wish?"

Having fulfilled his civic duty, the driver weaved around me and floored the accelerator. Our Rover slid round the far side of the car park and swerved to avoid the boy racer. I jogged toward Bill. He veered and flung the passenger door open. I jumped in without letting him come to a stop.

"That way."

Bill sped up, turning the corner with precision. "You going to be okay?"

"Hurts like hell." I shrugged and tensed to conceal my cringe as the movement jostled the break. "We both know that will not last. I shall just have to let you and Vlad do the persuading once we catch up with the scoundrels."

"Happy to."

His set jaw and sparkling eyes made a chilling combination. Two blocks down, a car swerved. Vlad galloped down the middle of the road, but the van was not in front of him anymore. Bill pulled up next to the hound, and I opened the door. He leaped over me into the back seat, bumping my arm in the process. I took a deep breath to bite back a squeal and isolated the pain away from my conscious thoughts.

Vlad nudged the back of my neck, whining slightly.

"I know. 'Twas an accident." I patted him with my good hand while he licked my ear.

"Lovely reunion, but we're blocking traffic. Where next?" Bill kept his eyes on the road.

In the distance, something caused horns to blare.

"That could be them."

The Overfinch conversion proved it was worth every penny. Bill wove around the traffic with a surprising delicacy for such a bulky vehicle. I only had to close my eyes once before we caught up with the van.

It was indeed our boys. Bill followed, keeping one car between us and them. Eventually, they turned down a lane with no other traffic. It was the road to the empty field. Bill dropped back further to avoid being seen. The van pulled onto a grassy lay-by. We drove by as they both got out and walked toward the stream. Although I turned to watch, all they appeared to be doing was standing around. Why all the precarious driving to get here?

Bill parked on the far side of a small hill to conceal our vehicle. Fresh agony raced up my arm as I pushed my door open.

"You got a scarf or anything in here?"

He passed me a white linen tablecloth and grabbed a pair of binoculars from the boot. Fashioning a sling from the cloth reduced the continual jabs of pain to minor annoyances.

"You sure you're up for this? Vlad and I can handle it if you want to rest." His brow wrinkled with concern.

"Come on. Quit wasting time asking if I'm well. A bit of pain has never stopped me before and will not do so now."

Crouching to keep a low profile, we scurried up the grassy slope. At the top, Bill lay on his belly and scanned the field with the binoculars. He swore softly. "Where the hell did those shites go?"

"Let me have a look." The van was still parked in the field, but the only movement was dry bracken nodding in the breeze. "Damn! We only took our eyes off them for a minute."

"Could have been a pickup. Maybe they went back up the way we came?"

I sat up and leaned my head on my good hand. "We don't have time for this. I should have jumped them in the parking lot."

Bill rolled over. "Too many witnesses. You would get nae sense out of them."

"Perhaps, but the plan to follow them to the warehouse seems really foolish now they've disappeared, and we're no closer to freeing Jamie." I picked a piece of grass, rolling it into a small ball in my hand. "These chaps are dangerous, if nothing else, because they are completely invisible."

"Takes one to know one, eh?" He leaned against me, his grin infectious.

I grinned back, my black mood lifting. "Takes a thief to catch a thief. You may be onto something there."

Vlad wiggled under my good arm to get between Bill and me.

"Jealous devil, I had not forgotten you were there." I rubbed his ears, making his tail thump against the ground.

"No, leave him," screeched a high-pitched voice below us.

My head snapped up. I grabbed the binoculars and scanned the field. Tatya rolled over, spitting out grass, and struggled to her feet. The tall man stomped out from the stream, dragging Stefan.

I passed the glasses to Bill.

"That's not possible," he said.

"What ever happened to two days?" I mumbled.

The shorter one pushed Tatya into the van, standing guard, until his companion shoved Stefan in and slammed the panel closed.

Bill shoved the glasses into his pocket and sprinted for our Rover.

SEVENTEEN

I hitched up my skirt and caught up with Bill. He'd parked the Rover facing the way we'd come, allowing us to get over the hill in time to see the van before it disappeared down the lane. Bill hung back enough to keep them in view and followed without being obvious.

My stomach twisted into a knot. They were far enough away, we could lose them again. "Would they notice if we got closer?"

He shrugged. "No reason for me to get sloppy, just because they are."

I nodded and let him concentrate. There was too much at stake to lose sight of them now. How had they captured Stefan and Tatya? I'd set guards on the house. A chill swept over me. Had these bastards killed more of my men?

After a short drive through the countryside, the van pulled up to a ten-foot tall chain-link gate. The shorter burglar slid out of his seat and shuffled around the front of the van to wrestle one handed with a large lock.

Bill turned down a side lane, and I opened my door a crack to slip out with Vlad. We scuttled into the foliage, squeezing through thick greenery for a better view of the warehouses.

Pain stabbed through my shoulder, and I dropped the binoculars. Damn joint was taking its time to heal. I shifted my weight to scan the compound without bumping the injury.

The chain-link gate swung open, and the crook waved the van into the compound with an exaggerated flourish. The driver stepped out of the van, holding a plain brown box. From the largest building, a fat man in faded jeans and a rugby top came out with four bulky men behind him. My stomach lurched. The waxy complexion and lumbering step hadn't changed at all.

Vlad tensed, the bristles on his back confirming my suspicions; it was the same ogre.

Holding a cigarette with two fingers, he leaned forward and cupped his other hand around it. "You get it this time?" he mumbled around the paper.

The driver thrust the box at him. The big man pawed through it and held up a bottle of whisky. "Nice! Very nice…" G passed it to the nearest flunky and continued to sift through the box. "Ya! That's a kick to the bollocks. Where's the rest of it?"

He lifted something too small to see, even with the binoculars, and glared at the driver. With a sigh, G thrust the box at the closest henchman.

"Fuck sake! Do I have to do every fucking thing myself? Fetch me the granny."

The driver's colour fell. He snapped his finger at his buddy, who trotted up to the van. The short guy leaned back to slide the door open one handed and righted himself too slowly to see Tatya.

She leaned out of the vehicle and braced against the edge to kick as though her life depended on it. The man twisted in on himself, knees tight together before falling to the side.

"Would you look at that? Now THAT is funny." The fat man nodded with appreciation and shoved the driver in the van's direction. "Hold on to her better than your mate."

"Nae problem." The tall one nodded, as if to convince himself this would be easy, and circled Tatya.

She matched his movements, then let out a string of Russian so fast I could not catch the words, but the tone was unmistakable.

The tall man lunged. She danced back and Stefan leaped out of the van onto the man's back. He pulled the criminal's shirt up to cover his face and held on tight. Tatya spun and kicked a hard round house into the man's knees. He screamed, lurching to the side. Stefan rolled off, landed unbalanced, but jumped back up with the athleticism of youth. He grabbed his Gran's hand and ran for the gate.

She shook him off and planted her feet in the gravel. "They have Jamie!"

The fat man sauntered up to Tatya. "Ya, and there's nothing you can do about it." He opened his hand. "Where's the rest of it?"

Tatya furrowed her brow but didn't speak.

G slapped Tatya's face with a crack. "Bitch."

Her head whipped back, and she landed in a sprawl. A small red blotch welled up on her lip. Stefan jumped at the big man, but one guard grabbed his shoulders before he could get close.

G waved his open hand under Tatya's nose again. "This! Your bastard husband broke it!"

Her lip twisted into a sneer. "It was like that when he found it."

"Doubt it." G yanked Tatya up by the arm, then shoved her at the closest guard. "Fun's over, lock 'em up. You!"

He snapped his fingers while pointing at the man on the ground. He curled into a ball, wilting under G's scrutiny.

"Not very good at this, are you? Dropped by a granny." G strode over to them and kicked the driver in the ribs. "Get me the Rat."

I flinched. Did G say the Rat?

"He's hard to find, boss." The flunky muttered.

"Don't care. He's the man with the juice. Do it or you vanish."

G sauntered into the building. Two of the guards frog marched Tatya and Stefan behind him and two stayed outside to keep watch. One of them knelt down to examine the whimpering driver. Eventually, the driver stood up, leaning heavily on his mate, and hopped like a drunken rabbit inside the warehouse, leaving a single man on watch.

"One guard—" Bill mumbled in my ear as he dropped to the ground next to me. He propped the crossbow against his knee. "Want to take 'em?"

I tried to flex my arm and pain shot through my shoulder. Damn thing was taking its sweet time to regenerate. "No, we're outnumbered. We need a plan."

He raked his finger through the fallen twigs, snapping them into little pieces. "Fair do's…, but it gets under my skin seeing our folk get roughed up and just sit on my arse."

He was right. There was nothing worse. Blast it. The sooner we could get them out, the better.

"We need to locate Marcus before G. Theres no telling what juice G's after, but it won't be pleasant." I should have taken care of that loose end years ago. I'd foolishly thought—what? That he'd apologise? The man's pride would never allow him to admit his error.

"Good luck finding him."

"Might your uncle be able to help?"

Bill dropped the twigs and patted his pockets until he found his phone.

"Nigel—yes I'm fine... no I won't... Got a question for you—any idea where to find the Rat?... Anna tells me he's still alive... Aye she's here... Aye she's fine—Look, Uncle, we're pressed for time. Get yourself down to Stirling... Two hours?! You don't need to... Drive safe, old man." Bill slipped the phone into his pocket. "He's on his way and sends his regards."

"Very kind of him." I smiled, remembering the way Bill's uncle liked to drive. Two hours was being careful. "You able to keep watch on your own?"

"Nae bother, you do what you need to." He picked up the binoculars again. "Nowt going on at the moment."

I settled down, and Vlad lay his head and shoulders across my lap. Over three hundred years ago, I'd taught him to keep watch for me like this. I scratched his ears. It was a minuscule payment for my safety.

I closed my eyes and let my spirit flow toward the anger and confusion Marcus had thrown at me the last time I'd tracked him. It followed the gentle pull until I landed on a sandy beach.

Marcus blinked and looked at me. Or where I would have been if a body accompanied this form of travel.

"DAMNATION, woman. You left me. Can't you just bugger off and be done with it?" He stomped, and his boot sank into the sand up to his ankle.

I wanted to explain what I needed, yet the best I could hope for was a flicker of intuition might get my meaning across. I focused on thoughts of Geoffrey and peril.

"Just go. I'm not interested. WHATEVER it is, I'm not interested. You hear me?" He shook his hand at the sky. A family setting up a picnic startled. The mother drew her babe close as the apparent nutter raving at thin air stomped around their blanket.

Marcus clomped along the beach with his shoulders hunched. Clearly, he would not be helpful; however, he would get tired eventually. I would not. I drifted along with him.

Following him into the forest, he continued up a muddy path, cursing. "You may be older than me, but I'll lay a trail even you can't keep up with."

He giggled, leaving the main path to follow a deer track further into the bracken. Splashing across a fast-moving stream, he came out the other side, dripping. "Aye, looney, old-rats don't mind swimming. I'll be doing a lot of that, Anna. Maybe I'll get pneumonia and die. That would be jolly good. You can't follow us there, can you?" He shouted, but his body slumped as he made his way along the track, weaving around fallen timbers. He continued up the hill to a clearing on the top of a small ridge.

The shape of the hill and lochs in the distance confirmed my original guess about his location. "Got you," I whispered.

He slumped. "I know…" he muttered so quietly, I almost missed it. Dark brooding replaced the manic gleam in his expression.

I woke with a jump. Vlad sat back, cocking his head questioningly.

He'd heard me! How had Marcus heard me?

I rubbed Vlad's ears. Although tormented, Marcus might have enough heart left to be useful. I would prefer not to end his days just yet.

Vlad mooed his strange appreciation noise and wiggled to get his belly in on the action. I removed the sling and stretched, reaching up with both arms. There wasn't any pain. I swung it in a small circle just to be sure, then crawled back under the hedge to where Bill was watching the warehouses.

"Did you find him?" he asked without looking up from the binoculars.

"Glenmore."

"Close to civilization for him. How's the arm?"

I settled under the scrub next to him. "Was slow but 'tis mended now. Still quiet?"

"A car went out, short guy driving this time, no passengers unless they were in the boot." He passed me the glasses. "You look knackered."

I shrugged. Bone deep weariness had been building for days and coffee seemed to have less effect than it usually did. I'd deal with it when I had more time.

He shook his head, delicately stroking the side of my cheek before removing one of my hairpins.

I laid a hand on his. "'Tis fine, truly."

"Damn, you're stubborn, but you're no superwoman, despite what you think." He flicked out the scalpel tip, drawing it firmly across the length of his finger.

Bright red blood welled up along his finger. He held it to my lips. I licked the cut, swallowing each crimson drop before any could fall. He shivered, moaning softly with his eyes half closed. It was only a moment until the flow stopped; a moment was all I needed.

I kissed him. "My thanks, but are you trying to follow Karen? You know how dangerous too many feeds are in such a short time."

He raised his head with a weak grin on his face. "Aye, it'd be a good way to go, but no… I'm not chasin' her." He twisted around as best he could in the thick hedge growth and picked up the binoculars. "You worry too much."

It was a few years ago, but the despair I'd seen in his eyes while his wife's coffin sank into the ground wouldn't let me believe him. The car accident had been so sudden. Perhaps I should have stayed in Scotland longer…

Bill twitched sharply, grabbing his back pocket.

"You all right?"

"Och—that tickles—Phone's on vibrate." He grinned, pulling out the offending item. "Nigel, where you?… you know the A91, well take that out of town, turn onto the wee lane just after the warehouses, you'll see our wagon… park up further down… We'll send Vlad out…yes she's here." He turned off the screen and tucked it into his jacket pocket.

I tapped Vlad on the shoulder. "Remember Nigel?"

Vlad sat up with his ears perked and his tail thumping against the ground.

"Yes, the one with the bacon. Go find him."

Vlad wiggled under the hedge and bounded across the open field, a streak of black and grey parting the rapeseed like an ocean liner at full steam. Luckily, the hedge blocked the sight of the field if the guards bothered to look.

A little while later, rustling announced Vlad's return, walking instead of bouncing this time. A medium-sized man trotted stiffly behind him, his face alert despite his stiff joints.

"Anna, been a while. Good to see you again, Pet." He winced as he bent down.

"Do not trouble yourself," I called, squirming out from under the bush.

I pulled him close to kiss each cheek of his solid, weathered face. There were more lines than the last time. "'Tis good to see you." I met his eye. No matter what else time withered, they remained the same.

Nigel turned and grabbed Bill in a bear hug.

"Hey, I'm no poof." Bill's gruff tone contradicted his huge grin as he slapped his uncle on the back.

"Right then, wee bawbag here wouldn't have called for a jolly. What's the problem?" Nigel asked, his worry added extra lines to his face.

"Outnumbered and ill-informed, we're at an impasse here. I need you to monitor these poxy miscreants. If they move the prisoners, try to follow."

Bill passed him the crossbow. Nigel frowned, but took the weapon.

"I'm all right for watching, but my fighting days are over."

I squeezed Nigel's arm. "Fear not, I shall leave Vlad. Let him do the rough stuff. He's good at it."

Nigel patted the hound's shoulder. "Shame there are no bacon sarnies. Bribery works a treat with this fella."

EIGHTEEN

The sun had set by the time we finally pulled into the gravel parking lot on the shores of Loch Morlich. The moon peeked out between heavy clouds, only casting a dim glow on the sandy trail. Feculence, the lack of light, would encumber us.

Bill packed a rucksack with a few things, and we set off. Owl hoots drifted through the night air. It made a welcome change from the rattle of the Land Rover. The accursed thing was slightly more comfortable than a wooden carriage, but only slightly.

Bill whistled a tune that blended into the bird calls. It was second nature to him after leading so many stalking parties on the estate.

I squeezed his arm. "It does my heart good to have you along for this." I would have gladly consigned Marcus to the earth rather than speak with the spoilt brat again. He had better know something useful.

Bill winked at me. "Would nae miss it for the world. End of the month reports are due—this beats flying a desk any day."

Would he still say that if Marcus proved uncooperative? I glanced over and chuckled. He would probably enjoy the excuse to pummel the creep even more than a cosy chat by the fire.

Familiar peaks made a fortress of muted earth tones that rose to the murky sky all around us. I breathed a deep lung full of pine scent. The highlands were the only place I still recognised. The only place I could escape the noise and congestion of the modern world. Would that I had visited under better circumstances.

We started up a steep rock-strewn path. At the last rise before the bothy, I stepped behind a boulder to shelter from the wind. A splatter of chilly rain struck my cheek. Brilliant.

"You sure he's here?" Bill asked, peering over the edge to get a better view of the small stone hut.

Smoke clung to the roof line, but it was a public space. Anyone could be inside. I closed my eyes for a moment and let my senses stretch out. Moments ticked by. Anger as sullen as the dreich weather rolled out from the cramped building. It boiled and ebbed, but never faded.

Bill nudged me. "Anna, I cannae feel my feet."

"Forgive me Bill. He's there and practically shouting his anxiety, resignation, and anger."

"How you want to do this?" asked Bill quietly. "If he's worked up for a fight, stomping in's gonna make him kick off."

"I'll go. Give me a few minutes, then join us."

"Och, I can dae that."

Bill laughed without mirth and followed me soundlessly to the stout wooden door. I strained my ears.

Inside, someone paced in front of the fire. "Devil spawn... Lurking in the dark... She likes that... I'm not her toy

—No sir-ere… How many?… How many does it take… Kill a rat?… Not a lot."

Marcus rambled on, answering his own questions as he shuffled from side to side. His tone snapped, harsh and brittle.

I threw back my shoulders. Marcus was not the first angry man I'd had to face, and he wouldn't be the last. The door creaked on its hinges as I stepped into the sparse room.

Marcus had his back to me for a fraction of a second before he spun round. He pulled off a dirty cap and threw it at me. "I knew you were out there. Why? WHY!"

"Marcus," I kept my voice soft. With luck, it would calm him. "I have questions."

"I am done answering to you. You—You turned your back. I owe you nothing! You promised a family. A bond stronger than any love. Bollocks! One little mistake, and I was chucked out like last week's rubbish." His skin flushed red purple under his dark beard.

I sat down on a wooden bench near the door. "I asked you to take some time to ponder your actions."

"It wasn't that polite, was it?"

He stared at me like an entomologist examining a maggot ridden corpse—with unflinching focus. His wide eyes seemed to pierce my soul, attempting to drag out an apology or some form of remorse. He would not be so fortunate.

Pain shot through me. I could still smell the blood and bile around bones laid bare on the desert floor twenty-two years ago. "Marcus, it was not a small misstep. People died. People who trusted you," I said.

"That was not my FAULT." He shouted the last word and twisted away to look at the fire. "You never listened. You'd already made up your mind."

"I lead, you follow—those are my terms. You knew that when you pledged."

"Well, you can take your oath and poke it. I am not your lap dog anymore."

Bill stepped in, his six-foot frame effectively blocking the doorway.

"You know there's only one way she can release you, mate." His words came out measured and as cold as the Arctic. The blue of his laughing eyes frozen into grey steel. "Do you really want to go there?"

If Marcus was suicidal, it would be difficult to get any answers from him. Bloody impertinent child.

"It is rather permanent," I whispered. "If it is your wish for this evening, I shall make it quick." I let the words hang in the air for a moment before continuing. "Or we could sit down like civilised folk and speak."

There was no escape.

Marcus' shoulders sagged. "Damn you to hell." He dropped onto a bench on the far side of the room.

"Thank you, but I believe someone has beaten you to it."

Bill hung up his dripping wax jacket, then wandered over to sit next to the fire. "Got a brew on?"

"You'll have to boil it again." Marcus pointed to the kettle with shaking hands.

"Calm yourself Marcus. I have simply come for a chat." The man was not a complete fool. Surely he must realise that if he behaved, my visit would use nothing sharper than words.

"Really? I'm being stalked by a monster, and you think I should be calm about it?"

He slammed his boots against the floor and jumped up, throwing his hands over his head. "You smashed my life into tiny, unrecognisable shards. Twenty-two years... TWENTY TWO... A quarter of a century! And what do I have to show? Naught! Just drifted between huts, worked now and then before drifting into oblivion again."

"Perhaps you uncovered an interesting thing or two? Met some unsavoury characters? Spoken when you should not have?"

He sat down again with an ugly grimace pasted across his lip, more feral beast than human. "I've done a lot of cleaning, shifting, and doing-shit-no-one-else-wanted. That's not a life, it's an existence."

I looked at the man. Really looked at what he had become—a rusted out Maserati with two flat tires and no petrol. "Marcus, being the Rat was your choice. This is self-imposed exile."

He clenched his fist and stared at the fire. "Pretty words now you want something. Where were they when I needed you?"

I drummed my fingers from largest to smallest against the rough bench. The steady rhythm defused my annoyance. Every second I sat here, the fat one could gut an innocent. "Marcus, quit wasting my time. When was the last time you heard from Geoffrey?"

At the mention of Geoffrey, Marcus' head snapped up. "What's he got to do with this?"

Hot cinders lodged under my rib. Was he really that ignorant? "'Tis sombre tidings."

His already weary face took on an ashen tone. "No— How?"

"Do not ask me more. I have no wish to influence your words."

Marcus clenched his fist again. His beard doing little to hide his scowl. "Harsh mistress—expecting me to swallow that without a question."

"If you confess all you know truthfully, I will answer your questions until sunrise."

He looked at his watch and nodded, folding his arms. "Geoff and I wrote letters occasionally. The post office in town kept them until I could collect 'em."

"When?"

"Last one was just before the mudslide closed the pass, probably was written a month or more before that. Said little... I used it for kindling."

"Seems a lot of trouble just to comment on the weather."

He leaned forward while jabbing a finger at me. "He was the only one who even tried to keep in contact, tried to keep me sane..."

I felt a sense of unease in his mind. "Did you send a reply?" His fear spiked, but outwardly his face remained impassive.

"I think I mentioned cleaning a chimney for some snobby fat cat. Bought an estate up here, but can't be bothered to do anything useful with it. Just wanted a holiday home."

"Anything else?" I knew full well what the letter said, but why was he avoiding the amulet?

"The salmon are up, and it's been a good year for poaching. You want to report me?" His lip pulled into a sneer.

This time I did not need any of my extra senses. His whole body tensed. What was he hiding?

"When?"

"I don't use calendars. The days run together out here... maybe a month ago?" He said, shrinking inward, letting his shoulders hunch into a protective cave.

A vague answer. "How about his work? Did Geoffrey mention anything controversial?"

"Nothing ground breaking." Marcus looked down at his hands. "Nothing to get him killed. He was a genuinely nice guy," he whispered and bowed his head.

I heard the unspoken part 'not like me. I'm such a screwup.' Its clarity and vehemence surprised me. Previously, my senses had been basic intuition and empathy, not telepathy. I peered at Marcus.

Every taut muscle screamed his misery.

Just behind him, in the wavering light of the fire, a shadowy figure approached his shoulder with a hand outstretched to comfort. I shifted in my seat. It was unmistakably Geoffrey. Heavenly Father, why do you torment me with these visions?

The grief-stricken figure looked at me imploringly. His expression begged me to forgive this poor wretch. This urchin who may very well have known what trouble he sent his friend.

I shook my head. God Geoffrey, how could you ask me to forgive such a sin?

"Anna, are you all right?" Bill asked.

I sucked a breath in. Only abstract shadows from the fire danced on the wall. Was it real or had my mind finally snapped?

I flashed a glimpse of a smile at Bill. He nodded and remained by the fire, but set his mug down and shifted enough to have room to move quickly if he needed to.

I tried to pick up my line of questions, but my thoughts refused to stop playing back Geoffrey's distraught image. Blast it. "I am finished, Marcus."

Without looking up, his voice soft as if afraid of the answer, Marcus asked, "Tell me how it happened."

"While working late one night, two men broke into Geoffrey's home and shot point-blank range. Even if he'd been wearing a bullet-proof vest, it would not have been survivable." I felt nothing reciting the words. The tale had become an automated response. It kept the sharpness isolated away in a safe compartment at the back of my mind. Shame the bloody ghost would not stay there.

Marcus didn't reply, instead stared at the floor for a long time. The silence stretched into a half hour. Had he lost some of his mental faculties during his prolonged solitude?

Then, quite suddenly, he slammed his fist onto the bench. "Foul dogs need to be taught a lesson! No one messes with the Brethren. If the compadres in Columbia could learn, so can these scum."

For the first time since speaking to him, his face burned with the passion I'd fallen in love with 40 years ago. There might be enough steel left to forge a new blade.

"I want a part of this arse kicking," he said, each word clipped and precise.

"Who? Who shall we kick?"

He continued to stare at me without speaking. Would he tell me if he was colluding with G? Only when the guilt overwhelmed him. "You know retribution must be strategic. I cannot avenge Geoffrey without a target."

Marcus jumped up with his finger anchored on me like the barrel of a gun. "He loved you more than anything in this world, and you're betraying him just like you did me," he shouted. "Spineless bitch."

Bill shifted in his seat. "Mar—"

I shook my head a fraction. Bill leaned back, but his attention never left the Rat.

"You know who did this," I said it quietly, as if asking for a packet of cheese at the market.

Marcus paced the room before turning on me and leaned close, seething through closed teeth.

"NO. I. DON'T."

My stomach recoiled. The man had obviously not made the acquaintance of a toothbrush in a very long time. I raised my head, holding his gaze unflinching before speaking in a low tone.

"Do not believe—for even one moment—Geoffrey is forgotten because I take time to THINK before I act."

"Words! You're full of 'em, but some of us don't have a century to mull it over, dearie." He spat at me while backing away. "If you won't do anything about it, I will."

Stubborn cur, why was he being so obstinate? I brought my hands together to tap each nail one at a time against its opposite. "What will you do, Marcus? Have you forgotten to mention something?"

He backed up further and bumped against a wall, then began pacing the room again. "I don't know yet, but anything is better than waiting for you to decide."

"Marcus, I need to know who did this."

"Really? Those of us who only live in one lifetime would make a leap of faith and jump in."

The critter was no use to any of us if we couldn't trust him. I stood up and walked to the bags by the door. "Bill, where did you pack the rope?"

Bill pointed to the bulging rucksack leaning against the wall. "Lower left pocket."

Marcus' panic-stricken eyes snapped to me. "What are you doing?"

"It's time to take a leap of faith," I said, holding the bundle of climbing rope. "Do you still trust me?"

Marcus looked at the rope and stepped back. "Depends on what you're planning."

"A simple procedure. There's a small crag near here; trust your partner or fall. Are you game?"

Marcus pointed at Bill. "Is he coming?"

"I only need one to belay."

Bill arranged his feet on a stool and waved. "Aye, you two have fun. I've had enough dreich for one day." His eyes closed and gentle snores started before we even got to the door.

A tremor rippled through my belly. Was I being foolhardy? Marcus had been raving like the village idiot all evening. Did I really want to dangle at the end of the rope he held?

I steeled myself and strode into the night air. At least I would survive it. If he was untrustworthy, I needed to know before he damaged any more lives.

Out at the crag, the rock shone in the moonlight, slimy from the evening's rain. It was not a hard climb; however, the consequences of slipping were formidable. The damp conditions would make this a test of finesse as much as courage.

I dumped the bag of climbing gear into a mess of twisted rope and metal. The equipment had tangled, yet the frayed green canvas of my harness stood out against the bright orange and yellow ropes.

Old phobias snapped at me like a terrier, biting my ankles when I dropped my skirt into a rumpled heap. I clamped down on the shiver. No one cared in this century. I slipped the climbing harness over naked legs... and stiffened as another tremor shivered down my back. Stop worrying. Contemporary people showed more skin than this food shopping. I must learn to accept... these standards.

I checked my buckles and loops while Marcus' deft fingers sorted his own apparatus to finish a few seconds before me.

"You kept your speed."

"I live on the mountains, every inch of the mountain." He looked me over. "People don't need to be in your special club to climb. There are plenty of folks who want a weekend in the hills and will pay for a guide that knows how to get them back safely."

"So let's see how well you manage getting us home, shall we?" I looked down at the cavernous drop next to the sheer face we were about to embark on. "I have no wish to see the bottom of that."

"Nor I, lassie. I'll not drop you, no matter how much you deserve it."

"Enjoy the novelty, Marcus. It's rare I let someone get away with calling me Lassie." I turned to the cliff. "You can stay on safe ground until I get to the anchor. I'll be stranded up there if you walk away."

He checked his equipment and tugged the end of his belt to make sure it was doubled back before nodding at me. "When you're ready then."

Stepping out onto the first rock ledge, the tingle in my stomach shot through my legs. The old adage of 'just look at the next move' was the only thought in my mind when I placed my hand to test a hold before committing myself. After a few feet, a crack wide enough to secure the first nut appeared.

The repetition of hand and foot, hand and foot, put me into a Zen state of mind. Any time I couldn't reach anything secure, I searched for a way to get my feet higher.

Shifting my weight to a small ledge, I wedged my toe into a crack. My arm arched over head then fumbled for another grip hidden from view. With my weight poised over my knees, only the precarious feel of air swirled under my feet. The next move would take me to a safe zone, but only if I didn't swing off this rock like a shutter blown wide by the wind.

I pulled up and rolled over the ledge to the security of solid ground firmly under both feet again. The tension held for the climb rushed out in a surge. My legs trembled while I crouched to catch my breath.

I tied into a secure anchor and braced myself before shouting to Marcus. "On belay, climb when you're ready."

The overhanging wall blocked my view of him. The rope remained slack in my hand. Minutes ticked by. Had he untied and walked away? Steaming excrement—I could get back down, but Bill was on his own. He was perfectly capable, but tired. He may not hear the arse coming.

Was there a decent anchor to abseil from? I could do without another broken bone. I untied my knot when the rope pulled taut in my hand, accompanied by one word.

"Climbing."

I yanked my end tight. At least he was not so crazed as to abandon my trust. Eventually Marcus' hand reached over the cliff. It grabbed the same root of heather I had used and heaved himself up.

"What took so long?" I said.

He grimaced. "I was deciding if I really could just walk away and leave you to the fates the way you left me."

That was good. If he really was thinking, he would make the right choice. "Are you ready to come back?" Either he would follow me again, or I needed to get rid of him. Whatever the juice was, I could not let G have it.

"Do you really want me?" He kicked at the ground.

I hesitated for a second. Could I ever love him again? The cliff was inches away. It would be the simple answer. "Marcus, when I chose you, I saw a quick-witted chap with good intentions and the heart of a lion. Has that changed?" Sadly, his behaviour this evening did little to remind me of his merit.

"Of course I've changed. You make us all into simpering fools!" He turned his head away. "You look innocent, but wolf's teeth hide under the fluff, ready to devour our souls."

I paused. My affections required unwavering obedience. Was that a bad thing? I understood the world so much more than their simple minds ever could. It kept us all safe.

I also knew every blemish in his armour, every gap in his defences.

My hand ran up the front of his jacket, then toyed with the toggle dangling at his throat. The hiss of the zip echoed in the early morning stillness. "It's not all bad, you know." I reached under the layers of fleece to stroke his skin. "You remember how it... feels."

He closed his eyes. A shiver racked his body. "Yes... but..." His shoulders slumped as he studied the ground.

He was nearly there. It would not take much for lust to overtake anger. I leaned close, lips to his ear. "No one is stopping you now. Say the word, and I can be yours again."

He sucked his breath in and threw his arms around me. "You always knew... my life belongs to you. Damn it."

I locked my gaze on his. Clear, strong brown eyes. Deeply troubled poetic eyes. Warmth surrounded me. Eyes that I loved. "Welcome back, Marcus."

I raised my hand to the back of my head and pulled a hairpin from the coiled hair. He tracked the movement, as if counting the seconds, inches, moments until... the blade sliced along the palm of my hand. Red blood seeped from the gash. "Drink, my beloved."

He grabbed my hand in a bear's paw grip, then latched his lips around the wound, sucking in the red fluid with crazed eagerness. My knees trembled, and the ground swayed. I motioned toward a flat space further away from the cliff. He tossed his fleece behind him, took the enamel butterfly and cut through leather like skin on his palm.

"For you... only for you..." Marcus said.

I licked the gash. Warmth trickled down my throat, building in my belly to spread throughout my limbs.

I slid the zip of his fly down. We'd waited decades to satisfy this hunger. Dirt made no difference to me now. Our lust was as frantic as a starved wolf tracking a lone rabbit.

Afterwards, I curled into the crook of his arm. He had been a good man at one time. Could we rebuild his courage? His confidence? His judgement? Could I let him back into my confidence?

I shifted my position to watch the dawn chorus as they swooped over the valley below. The feel of his skin close to mine was very pleasant, and I could not continue to let him drift. That loose end needed a permanent solution.

Marcus snorted. After a moment, he asked, "Do you love him?"

Confused, I lifted my head. He was staring at the crimson sky.

"Who?"

He nodded toward the valley below. "Him, Bill." Shrugging, he continued, "or Geoffrey, or me even. Do you love any of us?" he asked bitterly.

I rolled away and pulled on my blouse. "Marcus, there is no word for what I feel for you and the rest of the companions. Love does not do it justice. I rely on you for my very existence. I share the closest parts of myself with you. You are all very dear to me."

He nodded. "So you don't. That is what my Nan always told me. Any girl won't say it, is just after yer pocketbook." His heavy canvas trousers rustled as he yanked them to where he sat and shimmed into them.

I scowled. I'd lost count of the number of women I'd watched bed their way to wealth and power. For centuries, it was the only way a woman could secure her future in this wretched world. "That's not true. Your Nan gave you inferior advice."

"No, I reckon we're just tools to you. Something to be trotted out when you've got a use for us or left in the cupboard if one becomes awkward."

I turned to face the sun. I didn't want to look at him anymore. "You are not tools. You are my companions. Do you have any idea how lonely my existence is?" Why was he picking fault now? Did he not realise how close I was to ending our contract?

"Why did you hunt me out? Was it a case of last resort, use up the leftovers?"

I spun round, anger making me say more than I had planned. "Geoffrey's killers have taken hostages! If you can think about something outside your own interest for one moment, you can come with me and dish out your proverbial arse kicking."

"Oh, I'll do my bit," he said, zipping his jacket sharply as he strode over to the climbing anchor to check the rope. "There will be retribution for this."

What did that mean?

We spent the rest of the climb down in silence. Marcus would only answer direct questions with a grunt and offered no fresh discussion of any sort. Perhaps I was being the biggest fool of us of all. His mood swings had become more erratic during his solitude. Was his mind broken beyond repair? Bloody arse, I did not have time to mollycoddle a toddler.

Back at the bothy, Bill was still stretched out by the fire. The fellow deserved it. He had driven hours to get here.

Marcus slammed the door. Bill twitched, then opened one eye.

"Nice climb?" he asked.

I glanced at the sullen Marcus and shrugged.

Bill sat up, yawning. "So we all set?"

Marcus snorted and grabbed his rucksack, packing cooking gear and clothing with the efficiency of extended practice.

I peered at Marcus. "I want all your recreational herbs before we go."

He looked up, startled. "What?"

"I'm not stupid. Indeed, the habit was plain for as long as I have known you. Also, you were unsettled during my inquisition. Whoever you're supplying is no concern of mine, but I require you to focus on my task." I held out my hand. If Marcus did nothing else of any use, this minor act was worth my trip.

"Know-it-all-control-freak." He yanked his rucksack open and fished around, handing over a green and yellow tobacco tin.

I peeked inside. The little blocks that resembled stock cubes were familiar. Plenty of folks had enjoyed them in the sixties, but it wasn't enough to have a party with. "Where's the rest?"

He held up his hands. "That's it."

Was he deliberately trying to hide something for G, or was this pure selfishness? I tapped my foot. "We don't have time for this. I can tell when you're lying."

He rummaged some more, then slapped a plastic bag of dried mushrooms and a small vial of some brown liquid into my hand.

I sniffed the bottle. Oddly aromatic. It reminded me of something I'd caught a whiff of after a particularly strange party years ago. "This is…?"

He bowed. "My special brew. Makes for one hell of a shindig but wicked fat head in the morning."

I tucked all the items into my bag. Hopefully, that potion was the juice G was after.

Marcus threw his bag over his shoulder and set off on the trek back to the Land Rover quickly to discourage any pleasantries on the walk. Bill shrugged and resumed his whistle practice.

That was good. The two of them had declared a rough truce. How the rest of the troop would take Marcus' return was another day's problem.

The dark blue Rover was the only vehicle in the gravel lot. Dawn was too early for even the most enthusiastic athletes.

Marcus stepped back from the vehicle, wincing. "Bugger that. It stinks of wet dog. I'll make my own way down."

"Get in, we have time issues." I said. Nigel had been on a solo watch all night. He was too old for that. Anything could have happened.

Bill looked at Marcus. It wasn't a friendly look, then threw his bag in the boot.

Marcus brushed at the seat, then slid across it. "Foul beast needs a bath and breath mints."

"So do you Marcus," I muttered.

Bill chuckled, slamming the boot. "He's right about Vlad, especially when you give him liver."

"Modern divas do not know the meaning of stench if you find Vlad's breath objectionable."

Bill held up a hand in defence. "I cannae help I was born after the introduction of indoor cludgies."

Bill started the Rover and pulled out to the mountain road, shifting through the gears quickly. He slid around the first bend.

Marcus braced a hand against the roof. "Where did you learn to drive—"

"Shut it. We're in a hurry."

Bill flung the Rover around another curve in the mountain road, crossing the centre line slightly and sped up, then slew sideways into the next bend.

Marcus turned away from the window.

We were too far out. The road was damp, but should not be that slippery. What was Bill trying to do?

The dizzying drop over the side of the road rushed up. Bill yanked the hand brake. The rear end of the car snapped around to where it needed to be. He accelerated again.

Marcus leaned over. Heaving noises accompanied by the smell of sour bile and tinned chilli wafted from the rear seat.

"You're going to clean that!" Bill shouted.

"I want out!" Marcus snapped the door latch.

"Fuck off. We're not stopping."

Marcus leaned over again and wretched a second time.

"You're wrecking it!"

"You should have thought of..."

I slapped my hands together in a loud clap. "Boys! That is —Enough."

They both stiffened, but stopped arguing.

"Bill, slow down to normal road speeds. Marcus, hang your head out the window if you're going to be ill again."

Marcus harrumphed. "You are trying to kill me."

Bloody arse was back to his pity parties. "No, that would be the easy option. I'm trying to keep this vehicle usable."

The Rover swerved and corrected as a gust of wind slammed into the side of the boxy craft.

Marcus leaned over toward the open window, but slime still spewed down the glass and dripped over the door frame. "Think that was tidier?"

I glared at Bill.

He gripped the steering wheel tighter. "That—was nae me. But if he cannae keep his dinner…"

"Not my fault! Your driving is crap!" Marcus pulled a maroon coloured hat out of his jacket pocket and wiped his beard.

Was he faking his illness? If so, it was pretty convincing. "I don't remember you having such a sensitive stomach, Marcus."

He scowled at me. "Don't ride in cars much. Maybe lost fortitude—Maybe some arse is driving like a circus clown."

We were in the middle of the Cairngorms. There were not a lot of ways to get to Stirling other than by motor car.

I scanned through my mental maps. The answer jumped out like a shining silver snake.

"Bill, take the exit for Dalwhinnie."

Bill frowned. "There's nothing there. Even the petrol station closed up."

"It still has a train station. Marcus, I shall purchase a one-way ticket to Stirling. We'll pick you up once you arrive. I do hope you can accommodate that much travel."

He crossed his arms. "Not as if I have any choice, is there?"

Did he realise how close the axe was to his neck? It should make him more compliant, but I would rather have him where I could reach out and slap him if he needed it. However, I could not afford to keep stopping because of his illness.

The town had no bus, shops, hotels, or any reason someone would stop to give him a lift. There was only one proper road through this section of the mountains, and considering how ill he'd just been, G should have no way to transport him out of here.

I could not lift the sinking sensation rolling through my gut. G should not have been able to fetch Jamie, Stephan, and Tatya so easily, either.

Bill pulled into a wide open parking area in front of a small white building huddled on the edge of two train tracks. It was deserted. No tremendous surprise there. I opened the glove box and removed the heavy leather pouch I perpetually kept there. Plastic money was convenient, but it was good to have hard currency in my hand again. The rattle of coins felt more real.

I climbed out of the Rover and walked through the open gate to the concrete platform. My footsteps echoed back to me. No other sounds, no movement. A single set of metal stairs climbed over the tracks to a plinth of concrete on the other side with a bare bench. It sat forlornly on the bleak hard standing, offering nothing to keep out the weather. I peaked inside the building on this side, but it was just a small waiting area. Poxy cutbacks. Network no longer staffed the station. It did not even have a ticket machine. This was execrable poor fortune. I would have to give Marcus cash to purchase a ticket.

The station did not have any electronic information signs, just a printed schedule in a chipped Plexiglas case. I read down the columns to find the time of the next departure and estimated arrival in Stirling. My stomach sank. What I remembered as a straightforward journey, with no changes and few stops, was no longer offered. Marcus would have to switch services in Perth.

There were too many options in such a large station. He could easily contact G. I clenched my hands into fists. Why were none of my plans proving to be simple? Should we simply find a bucket for the arse?

Marcus nudged me. "Got the ticket?" He pointed to a small train of three carriages approaching from the north.

The next one would be a three hours wait. I'd have to trust him.

"Do not make me regret this." I handed him a ten-pound note.

He raised an eyebrow. "Do you expect me to pay the rest? Trip to Stirling's gonna be a lot more than that."

I doled out notes until he nodded. Fifty pounds seemed an extortionate amount of money for such a brief journey, but I'd quit arguing about the cost of things a long time ago. The price of everything made my eyes bulge.

"You will have to change at Perth," I said.

"Yes, Mum." He snapped his feet together.

I didn't bother acknowledging the snipe. "One of us will be at the station to collect you. Would you like a contact telephone number?"

"No! I don't have a fancy-pants-mobile! I've been living in the wilderness."

Marcus spun on his heel and went to the carriages. The blue and silver doors slid open, and he shuffled inside. I didn't want to let the man out of my sight, but circumstances were forcing me to trust him again. He flopped down on a seat and waved through the glass, then turned it into a rude finger gesture as the train pulled away from the station.

Jerk. I couldn't help smiling. His rebellious nature had been half of what had turned my head all those years ago. I don't know why it had never dawned on me what it would feel like to be on the receiving end.

I walked back to the Rover. Overhead, the skies were heavy with black clouds scuttling across the horizon, but the rain was only a threat at the moment. Bill tilted a bottle of orange soda to his lips. His eyes drooped, unfocused and distant. Everything about this week had been more effort than it should be. He must be tired.

"I can drive if you need to rest," I said.

"Nae problem driving. Got plenty of sleep." He glanced at me with his lopsided grin. "How 'bout you after all that bollocks with the Rat?"

"It was what I expected." I turned to stare out the side window.

He drained the last of the fizzy drink and threw the empty bottle into the back seat. "Well, nae of you dropped off a cliff, so I assume it's not all bad?" He pulled out of the station.

"We don't have time for his tantrums. Hopefully, he shall be more amenable when he arrives in Stirling."

Bill shrugged his shoulder. "If..."

I forced the uncertainty into the back of my mind. Even if Marcus betrayed us, he wouldn't be much use to G. He didn't have his potion anymore.

"Now, can we get back to the task at hand? We need weapons and a way inside the compound." The twisted gleam in G's eye when he slapped Tatya brought back too many uncomfortable memories. I needed to get them out quickly.

"Got a few crow scares in the back of this old beast. You got any specifics?"

"I'd rather keep things quiet, with as low a body count as feasible. Everyone's snapping pictures and posting on the web these days. Staying anonymous is getting harder by the minute."

"Quiet, uh, crossbows are quiet but difficult on the body count." Bill tapped the steering wheel as he thought.

"Paint balls," I said, drawing the word out as my plan formed. "Yes, I think that will do nicely."

"Paint balls?" Bill glanced over with a pained expression. "Not exactly known as a deterrent, Anna."

"Trust me. When I get done with them, they will be."

He shrugged but didn't ask, concentrating on the drive. The countryside passed in a blur of green, leaving me to make plans until my head bounced roughly against the door frame. Bill pulled off the tarmac. The Land Rover lurched over another hole before finally grinding to a stop on the steep grassy verge.

"Good work horses these machines." I tapped the dash. "And they never bite."

Bill laughed. "You try to change a drive belt. They bite plenty. I've got the scarred knuckles to prove it."

"I'll take your word on that."

NINETEEN

The hedgerow embraced the edge of the crops, making the field feel secure despite the menace that lurked a few yards away. Walking along the edge of the golden field, my nose twitched. The smell of rapeseed invariably made me want to sneeze. Shame oats were not profitable enough now. They never bothered me.

Spikes of fur undulated over the yellow blossoms, and the foliage parted with an explosion of movement. Vlad burst into our path, thrusting his head into my hip, while his tail whipped the petals off the nearest blossoms. I loved the way he wiggled and hopped on his back feet with the vigour of a pup.

"Does he ever tire of seeing you?" Bill asked.

"Hasn't yet, six hundred years and counting." I slipped Vlad a treat from my pocket before resuming our walk.

Rounding the corner of the field, brown boots kicked fruitlessly from under the hedge. The heavy soles dug up loose grass, but Nigel still couldn't get enough leverage to wiggle out with his stiff joints.

Bill strode over in two long strides. "Hey old boy, you need a hand?" His smile broke into a huge grin as he practically lifted his uncle off the ground.

"We miss anything?" I asked, brushing leaves off Nigel's jacket.

Resting his hands on his waist for a moment to catch his breath, he planted his feet firmly, eyes scanning the horizon before speaking. Old habits die hard.

"Naw. Quiet mostly. A fat guy went out around seven last night. The rest got a take away about that same time. Guards change on the front gate about once every two hours. Last night's chap came back this morning with a couple of new goons."

I nodded. "I can use that. Nigel—I want you to get some rest. Bill—get him settled, then try to secure those things we talked about on the drive. I'll keep watch."

Nigel turned to his nephew. "Don't envy you, son. Glad my messenger days are long gone. Fancy a brew before her errands?"

Bill shoved his hands into his pockets, leaning back on his heels. "Nae bother, always time for a cuppa. Seen a café on the way into town."

"Let's not forget what we're here for." I shooed them toward the vehicles.

Bill saluted sharply, with a grin so wide it tickled his ears. "Understood ma'am." He turned in a smooth arch, taking his uncle's elbow on the pivot.

"When was the last time you had a proper meal?" Nigel asked, trotting to keep up with Bill.

Bill shrugged. "Couple of days. I'll get me by."

Nigel shook his head. "Quick cuppa, my arse. You're having a cooked breakfast. Armies run on their stomach."

A twinge of guilt pinged in me. I had to be more mindful of human needs. While Vlad unceasingly caught his own food when he felt peckish, polite folk didn't.

I set my rucksack down next to the hedge and squirmed into the small clearing in the centre of the old growth. Vlad scratched and dug at the roots to clear a bit more space before snuggling up to my side. He lay his chin on my knee and huffed a soft snort before closing his eyes. His musky fragrance was reassuringly familiar. I was as safe as I ever was. I picked up the binoculars and turned my attention to the chain-link fence on the other side of the road.

The guard at the gate typed something into his phone. Perhaps this wasn't a very well-trained group? The chap didn't even look up as Bill and Nigel drove by. Maybe I was being overly cautious? What if we could bluff our way in without firing a shot? It would certainly solve the problem quicker.

Unfortunately, bluffs relied on all the guards being stupid or cowardly, with no respect for, or fear of, the Boss. It might apply to one or two, but unlikely all of them. As I watched the guard listlessly tap at his phone, more realistic plans crystallised in my head.

Marcus' recreational substances would even the odds. We might even free our associates with no one getting hurt.

A few hours later, two men came out the front door of the warehouse and started loading the white van with small unmarked brown packages. Minutes ticked by, the repetitive thumps counting the time as boxes landed in the back of the vehicle. They slammed the doors closed while a beige saloon drove up to the gate. The guard shoved his phone in a pocket and let the new vehicle in.

The saloon pulled up to the van, and the driver stomped over to the men. After a lot of posturing, voices rose enough to catch snippets of conversation.

"—no baby sitter… pain in the arse." The lead packer threw a box on the ground. Glass crashed.

"Do… they're paying…" the driver countered.

A man walked around the edge of the warehouse. His long legs stretching out like a spider on patrol. A chill seized me. Anthony!

He walked up to the men and muttered something. I shifted the focus of the binoculars enough to read their lips, but then it was impossible to keep track of who was speaking.

One packer stomped his foot. "My crew look after merchandise, stuff in boxes. You want them in boxes, we can arrange that." He shouted and leaned closer to Anthony.

Anthony straightened up and looked down at the muscular man with no expression. His face could have been a plastic mask. He spoke again, but frustratingly, I missed most of it. Something about 'abundantly clear, comfortable and personally'. He looked at the saloon driver, then the two men packing the van.

Heads bobbed slowly, vaguely. Was it an acknowledgement or agreement? Or even an unspoken argument they knew they could not win? It was hard to tell.

Anthony spoke some more, but I made out even less this time. He stood with his arms hanging loosely at his side. At ease with the world. A stance of comfort, superiority, and authority. Who was in charge, him or G?

The man that had packed the van nodded brusquely, then two of them drove off with more haste than was prudent on the small lanes.

Anthony clasped his hands behind his back, watching the van careen down the lane, and shook his head before turning to the buildings.

Obviously not sure what to do next, the driver of the car watched the gate close as if he was made of board. When it re-locked, he snapped his head sideways, as if hearing it for the first time, then fished some keys out of his pocket. He gestured to the entrance. Anthony followed him inside the building. As soon as he was alone again, the guard at the gate grabbed his phone out and started tapping.

My heart hammered like a lead pendulum in my chest. Scoundrel had his camouflage well rehearsed. I'd been fooled into believing that Anthony hadn't even been in town long enough to be involved in the murder. If I'd only followed that lead, I could have saved Jamie from this grief.

A faint scuff of feet announced Bill's return. Vlad wriggled round before I could, bounding out to mob Bill with all the canine enthusiasm of not seeing a favourite person for a whole three hours.

Bill pushed Vlad to one side and leaned down to kiss my cheek.

"Where's Marcus?" I asked.

He winced. "I counted every slob off the Perth, he wasn't one of 'em."

Pin-headed, chicken-livered imbecile. I snapped a handful of twigs out of my face and stood up. How could Marcus be so juvenile? I kicked at the yellow rapeseed blossoms nodding cheerfully to the sky. Bloody bat-brained jackanapes! People were going to die! People he should give a damn about!

I sucked a breath in. This fury would not remedy the issue. I needed to focus on the hostages.

"We can't waste time looking for him. He may have wanted to stretch his legs and alighted at Bridge of Allan." Not a likely scenario, but it helped calm the screaming banshees in my head. "If he arrives late, do not shoot him."

Wherever he was, at least he had not arrived at the compound in that saloon. Could he really betray me again so easily?

Bill shrugged. "If he turns up, I'll let him live." He handed me a small bag from the chemist and poured a large black sack out with a grin. Florescent balls spilled onto the ground like giant sweets.

Vlad sniffed, pouncing on one and snapping as it rolled away. The gelatine burst, coating his muzzle with bright paint as he jumped back in surprise. He woofed loudly at the offending item and batted the shell in his paw. I pointed a finger at his nose, warning him to behave. Hopefully, our neighbours had paid no more attention to that noise than anything else we'd done.

I found the bottle I'd confiscated from Marcus in the side pocked of my rucksack and filled a small syringe with the golden liqueur. Please let this work.

Selecting a random bubble-gum pink ball, I pierced the gelatine skin and administered a small dose of Marcus' special brew into the paint. A small drop of the drug welled up, seeping over the sphere. It glistened for a few seconds before being absorbed back into the shell.

The ball didn't burst or leak. Thank the heavens. The idea was not completely ludicrous.

"So that's it? We're trusting our lives to that?" Bill asked, pointing to the quivering pink sphere.

"If this is the same brew Marcus used to make, it will kick in about 30 seconds after contact. The more that is absorbed, the greater the effect."

"Aye, but it's not exactly going to stop them from shooting at us, is it?" Bill wrinkled his brow, sitting down next to me.

"They won't be able to see straight. All logic and motivation will evaporate. Usually hallucinations start within five minutes. At that point, primeval terror inherited from our cave ancestors will do the rest."

He shook his head. "Sounds like a recipe for accidents. What happens when they decide to shoot the green lobster running down the wall? Wish we had time to get the flak jackets."

Guilt squeezed my guts. He had a good point. "Nigel could have brought them down yesterday. I must be getting senile." I shook my head with a weak grin. "If it's any consolation, I'll take point. A few stray bullets will not do a lot to this old beast." I tapped my chest softly.

"Och, seeing you full of holes isn't what I meant." He grimaced and looked away. "Why don't we find a better way? Something not doomed to fail?"

"That's harsh. I expect we have at least a fifty-fifty chance of success," I said, bumping my shoulder into his. "Come on now? Who wouldn't want odds like that?" My voice dripped with sarcasm, but he continued to stare at the ground.

"This feels like the most risky operation I've ever seen you plan. There are too many unknowns, too few options, not enough bodies on the ground. We could sit tight for a few more days, let Carl round up the boys and take them on properly with proper equipment."

Shock washed over me. Bill was asking to wait? "Are you feeling unwell?" I asked, dropping more acid into a third ball of paint.

"I'm fine." He didn't look up.

It'd been days since he'd had a night's rest, and he'd donated blood twice this week. He was not a machine.

I put the ball down, carefully wiping my hands on the grass before taking his in mine. "Anthony arrived while you were out. Our colleagues know nothing and did not volunteer for this. Every minute could be a step closer to death. They cannot be left to the fates. I shall go on my own."

He closed his eyes for a long moment, then shook his head and started picking at tufts of grass. "I never said I wouldn't go." He squeezed my hand. "I just hope your guardian angel has big wings. They're going to need 'em to shield the idiots that rush in with you." He tossed a handful of grass at Vlad. "What the hell? Anything's better than sitting under this bush another night."

The clouds still hadn't burst, but they had been gathering all afternoon; it was no longer a question of if it would rain, more like when.

Vlad snapped at the grass, then jumped up to sniff the air, drool gathering on his lower lip. A few minutes later, Nigel strolled up the path carrying a white plastic bag. The hound ran up to him, trying to nip the edge of the bag as it swung at his side, growling softly.

I stifled a giggle. As much as it might encourage his destructive behaviour, it was impossible not to laugh. The pink paint on Vlad's muzzle ruined his attempt to be intimidating.

Nigel simply lifted the bag higher and carried on walking. He made no eye contact as he purposefully strolled toward us. Nigel had learned well. Vladimir would steal food from anyone he saw as weaker than himself.

"Hungry?" Nigel asked quietly as he sat across from us.

Bill shrugged. "I could eat."

I picked up another paintball. "I'm a bit engaged. You two carry on."

Vlad continued to circle, trying every angle possible to get his nose into the bag now in Nigel's lap.

I snapped my fingers, then pointed to the ground by my side. "Manners."

With a growl, he flattened back his ears, but sank to the ground—all the while his eyes never left Nigel's bag.

Nigel took out a large kebab and passed it to Bill before opening the lid on a second one. He set the foil tray in front of my hound.

"I didn't forget you."

The large dog sprang up and thrust his muzzle into the tin, knocking it to the ground. Tendrils of greasy meat hung from his lips in between bites.

Nigel snatched his hand back. "You sure he's immortal? Seems awful hungry."

I shrugged, not taking my eye off the needle. Several paint-balls had exploded at this point if the angle was wrong. "I think it's a habit from his youth, but hard to tell."

"This the same take away G's crew uses?" Bill asked as he made a sandwich with his pitta bread.

Nigel tilted his head sideways, raising his eyes to the sky with a cheeky grin. "Well, as it happens, that very thing came up while the lads got our order sorted." He winked at me before carrying on. "Had a little chat with the driver—as they were mentioning it anyway—promised to make it worth his while to give us the heads up next time they got an order."

I pulled the older man into a tight embrace to kiss him full on the lips. "You cheeky, sneaky, clever man."

Cheeks glowing, he squeezed my hand. "You can tell me just how perfect it was later. Maybe a little reward could be negotiated?" he suggested with a raised eyebrow.

A warm glow deep within me stirred, and I patted his leg with a smile. "Mercenary to the core. When this is over, I'm sure we can come to some sort of arrangement."

Vlad finished his meal and pushed the empty tin across the path. It clattered each time it hit a stone. The noise twisted my nerves tighter. I peered through the hedge; the last thing we needed was to attract attention.

I snatched the tray. He growled and showed his long canines. A minor tremor ran through my stomach. I'd seen him take fingers off for less, but stood up, staring at the dog and growled back until he lowered his eyes. You'd have thought he might have given that up, yet even after six hundred years, he still wasn't convinced who was alpha.

A ring tone I didn't recognise jingled merrily.

Nigel slapped a hand over his jacket, a blush rising on his cheek. "Sorry, forgot to turn that down," he mumbled and read the message. "Got an order for the warehouse. What you want to do with it?"

"Request they drop the package off here. Offer whatever bribe is necessary. I have some special spices to add." I tapped Marcus' box of drugs.

He dialled the number back and spoke in a hushed whisper, then smiled at us. "He'll meet me at the end of the lane. Said it'd be bout thirty minutes."

"Perfect. Just enough time to make one last munition." If G was anything like me, hallucinogenics were unlikely to have any effect on him.

"Ready?" I asked.

Bill wiped crumbs off his trousers and looked up. "Always ready for some of that." He leaned over to pinch my bottom.

I slapped his hand away and kicked one of the paint balls at him.

"I'll take that as a no." His sarcastic smirk somehow looked disappointed.

"While it's good to see your vigour restored, we have some rescuing to do."

Nigel climbed to his feet and helped me gather the doctored balls into a pouch. Saints protect us. There had been no time to test them in the air rifles. With any luck, they would not jam.

I gave Nigel the box of resin as we walked. "Crumble some of this into each portion. Seal them back up and take it inside."

Nigel took a cautious sniff from one corner. "Pot? That's it? I was expecting something more lethal."

"Sleep is enough for simple guards." The idiots were not well-trained enough to qualify as enemy combatants.

Nigel hesitated, as if on the verge of saying something, but shook his head and tucked the box into a pocket.

Bill tapped his uncle's cheek. "Cannae go anywhere looking like a Jakey. Get it sorted, old man," Bill said.

Nigel drew himself up. "Och, the Herbert, he speaks…"

The two of them continued the gentle ribbing all the way across the field. Nothing about this plan felt right, but their casual banter helped cut some tension. They knew what I needed. Talking about anything now was simply a distraction.

We stopped at the side of the two vehicles. Bill unpacked a long handled bolt cutter from a toolbox.

"Do you have any of those stretchy head tubes in here?" I tapped the plastic crates.

He turned with a pained expression. "Stretchy head tube? Anna, they're called buffs and yes, there should be a couple."

I let the annoyance pass. One word lost amid hundreds of thousands was not worth an argument now. "Locate the darkest coloured ones please."

I went round to the back seat, found the empty soda bottle and made two light scores along the length with one of my butterfly scalpel-pins. Enough to weaken but not puncture the material, then found the spare petrol canister in the Rover's boot and poured the fuel in. I was quickly running out of pockets, so slipped it into the pouch with the paint balls.

Bill recoiled. "Fire bombs? I thought you wanted to keep the body count low?"

"This is for G. He has survived as long as I have for a reason. Regular weapons will have limited effect. Fire invariably takes me the longest to recover from. We should be well away before he can take any action to stop us."

Bill pursed his lip. "You may have a point, but I don't like it. Too hard to control."

He was right. Once lit, fire had a mind of its own. Hopefully, we would be well out of the way.

"Nigel, after you deliver the food, come back here and keep Vlad occupied. He's too bulky to smuggle in."

He nodded, holding his chin. "I'll try, but if Vlad gets it into his head, that fence will not stop him."

"Do your best. And keep the motor running. You know the stakes… if any of Geoff's family use the code, take them to the estate. Bill and I will make our own way there."

He nodded with a face set like stone. All mirth had evaporated from his eyes. He clapped his nephew on the back while reciting my companion's traditional farewell. "May fate smile on you—I'll see you when I see you."

Bill grabbed his uncle's shoulder. "Course you'll see me again, old man. You still owe me a pint."

Adrenaline had washed away his fatigue. Someone was going to get a kicking before the day was out.

The older man nodded, but didn't look at either of us as he climbed into his Mercedes and drove off to intercept the food. I opened the door of the Rover, tapped on the seat, and motioned for Vlad to jump. He reluctantly put one foot on the frame, then glanced over his shoulder with wide eyes.

I leaned down. "No tricks! You must stay here!" I pointed to the back seat, giving no room for argument from the beast.

He stepped into the Rover slowly, turned around and sunk to his belly, giving me a doggy look of disgust. I rubbed his ear, but he shifted his head, avoiding my hand.

"We'll be back soon. With Jamie. Remember, Jamie?" The tip of his tail wagged once, then settled limply on the seat.

He'd show me later. I closed the door gently. Angry hellhound or not, I felt better knowing he was safe.

Bill and I pulled the buffs over our heads, mostly covering pale flesh, then scuttled through an overgrown derelict site behind the warehouse compound with a bulky backpack. Leggy hazel bushes grew betwixt the bramble and bracken. Moving through it was neither quick nor quiet, yet none of the guards paid the slightest attention. Was it supreme confidence or ignorance? Thick coils of uncertainty wrapped around my heart and lungs, making it difficult to breathe. We stopped at the fence. Razor sharp barbed wire jutted over our heads to discourage entry, but bramble vines grew through, merging it into the foliage. It was entirely possible I was leading Bill into a trap.

Nigel's Merc rolled into the compound. Focus. Letting my mind wander down the path of conjecture now would lead to the very thing I wished to avoid.

Grabbing a handful of the fence, Bill positioned the bolt cutters. Metal clinked. The shrubbery moved but silenced the metallic ring. The guard on duty looked at Nigel and shouted something. Nigel patted the bag and held up four fingers. The guard turned back to his phone. Bill worked up the fence in a quick succession. Leaning on the handles of the cutter for each link, he put his entire weight behind the action. It was good to have him here. That would have taken me hours. One of those times when having a second, larger pair of hands made all the difference.

A few heartbeats later, Nigel drove out. He was safe.

Bill cut a few more links, enough to crawl through. I pushed the backpack in front of me as I shimmied through, holding my breath and sliding on my belly. Gravel bit into my elbows and knees, but the only sound in the compound was the beating of my heart. I waved at Bill to follow.

He thrust his shoulders into the gap with a loud rattle. The guard didn't even look up from his phone.

Then the clouds burst. Icy rain sluiced down. The guard shoved his phone into a pocket and pulled up his hood, hunching over and staring at the road. Bill and I made our way around the large warehouse through the unrelenting downpour unchallenged. Was it good luck? Everything would be slippery now, but it was nearly impossible to see us. Water ran off the hood of my coat in a steady stream.

We slid along the wall, mincing around gravel and staying in shadows. It made for painstakingly sluggish progress, but the drugs would not take immediate effect. We could not be in any haste, yet I would rather do anything than lurk like a cat in the gloom, waiting for a mouse to scurry out.

A yard light illuminated the parking spaces in the warehouse's front. It cast enough light, we halted five feet short of the end of the building. It gave Bill a clear shot of the front gate and the pitiful creature on watch there. Any guard as careless as that lad deserved what befell him. Real games had consequences.

Loud voices erupted from the other side of the corner. I clutched the rifle closer and leaned, but could not see any reason for the commotion. If we moved, we'd be in the light.

The voices continued shouting and footsteps approached our end of the building.

"If they're so useful, you bloody well look after 'em!"

"Ya! I don't care! You do as I tell you!"

I didn't need to see G to know who that was. My spirits lifted. Indeed, this was a lucky day if I could finish him as well as free Tatya and the twins. The steps continued along the front of the building.

Two men rounded the corner, but they continued to shout at each other and neither looked into the shadows where Bill and I lurked. I froze. Could we shrink into the ground?

The man who had driven the Saloon earlier today stabbed a finger into G's chest. "You aren't paying us enough for this shit. We watch bottles of whisky, not people!"

G's skin glistened in the lights, a combination of perspiration from the short walk around the building and the rain. Grabbing the man's finger, a vein at the edge of his temple throbbed under red skin. He twisted the digit backwards with a grin.

Bone cracked, and the colour drained from the man's face. He tried to jerk his hand back, but G held firm.

G's nose hovered an angel's breath from the poor fellow's face. "Ya! This is the problem! People don't shut up and do!"

A small spark of blue snapped from G's hand to the worker's. The guy's eyes rolled up, and his body collapsed to the ground like an empty sack.

G turned back into the warehouse, chuckling to himself. "Rory, get the girl! We have to go!"

Bill stared at the man on the ground. "He's not breathing, is he?"

I shook my head.

"Oh, fuck."

Confound it all. Where were they taking Jamie? Execrable muck-weasels! Were any of the captives even alive still?

TWENTY

Bloody perverse minded fates.

I nodded at Bill.

He took careful aim at the front gate. When the chap turned away slightly, Bill shot three times, hitting him in the back of the head, neck, and shoulder. The guard spun round off balance, fumbling for his weapon. Private security agents were not supposed to carry firearms, but he pulled a revolver out, pointing it randomly in the dark.

By the time I had counted to fifteen, he was stumbling with wide eyes, jerking left and right at the slightest noise. He fired at the sound of rain hitting the stones.

Bill had been right about that problem. The protection of the shadows was too flimsy for comfort.

G slammed the steel door of the warehouse against the wall. "Ya! What's wrong!"

The guard shot at G.

A blue spark jumped from G's hand and hit the man. The guard's eyes rolled up. He fell backwards.

"Ya! Rory, move!" G shouted, stomping over to the saloon parked by the front door.

A thin man in ripped jeans emerged from the building with Jamie. Her hands were bound, and the man stumbled every other step, dragging her to the vehicle. Either her legs didn't work, or she wasn't cooperating. It was now or never.

I ran from behind the building, firing a string of shots at the flunky. Fluorescent paint splotches blossomed on the car. Rory's body twitched each time he was hit, but he pushed Jamie into the back seat and slammed the door.

G gunned the engine, reversing at speed. Rory ran alongside, trying to get the passenger door open, but G pulled a sharp J-turn, flattening him to the ground before revving the engine again. He floored the accelerator and drove full tilt into the gate, then sped down the country lane.

I stomped my boot into the gravel, flinging a cloud of useless pebbles at the disappearing vehicle. G had driven right in front of me. I must be getting thick-witted—How had I missed?

Bill stalked up to the guard at the front gate before trotting over to check the guy in the driveway. What the hell had G been throwing at them? Some kind of taser? I met Bill by the front door.

"You spoil me with all these grand outings." He grimaced. "Fellow on the gate seems to have had a heart attack. Nae marks on him. Not a great way to start. Getting messy already." He nodded toward the corpses. "Best get a move on before anyone investigates all this bother."

We crept closer to the open doorway. Laughter rolled out. A small, brightly lit office to the left had all the indications of a party in full swing. Good to see Marcus' brew had not lost its traditional potency.

Bill and I crept into the main warehouse, a long room lit with a few single bulbs high overhead. It was full of rows and rows of wooden barrels stacked six high on steel racks.

Staring at the whisky, Bill lifted his nose and inhaled deeply. "Think they would notice if a few drams went missing?"

"Yes. Duty-men are notoriously keen."

We shifted by the first row of barrel with soft silent footwork. Even intoxicated men could get curious. No point giving them a reason to look about.

Turning to go down the second row, a sticky brown pool covered the floor. Possibly blood, maybe industrial chemicals. Either way, I did not want to step into the mess and leaped across.

A soft wooden thump echoed from behind the second row of barrels. My heart sped up. It came again tentatively, almost like an apology. It could be more guards. I inched around the corner with my weapon ready.

I let out a sigh as the worry lifted from my shoulders. Tatya had wriggled enough, her supermodel-length leg could reach a barrel even though she and Stefan were tied together. Duct tape covered their mouths.

I waved to Bill, then quickly glanced round the next alley to see if there were any more guards. It appeared deserted.

Bill flicked out his pocket knife, snapping a wrist tie with one sharp twist, before doing the same for the other arm. Tatya immediately pulled off the tape, her face contorting into a tragic comedy mask as she did. She opened and closed her jaw to stretch her cheeks.

I kept an eye on the corridor. "Can you walk?"

"I'm not a babushka." She snapped and scrambled to her feet. Her knees wobbled, and she stumbled.

Stefan grabbed her elbow. "Careful."

She smiled, wrapping her fingers around his tightly.

The older woman's will was unbowed, but her body looked tired. Laying a hand on her shoulder, I leaned close to meet her eyes. "There's a black Mercedes AMG on the little lane across the road from these warehouses. Older gentleman at the wheel, but he can move like a rally driver. Bill and I will take care of things in here. You need to get to that vehicle. He will take you to a safe house. When you see him, use the code 'take us home, Uncle'. Do you understand?"

Tatya nodded, her face tight. "I thought my running days were over."

"This way."

There had to be a fire escape. Even secure buildings had to follow safety codes. It would be the best way out without a fight. I took the lead, followed by Tatya and Stefan with Bill on rear guard. I listened for any movement in the large room as we inched along. Stefan caught my heel in his eagerness to leave. I stumbled and fell against a half empty barrel. The boom reverberated back, echoing off the concrete floor and steel shelves.

He was as clumsy as a new born donkey. "Steady." I whispered while waving him back.

At the end of the row of barrels, I paused and gazed up and down the gloomy alley. It was empty. The only sound was the raucous laughter from the front hall. About thirty feet away, a green exit sign illuminated a door. Brilliant.

I increased my stride. The sooner I got Tatya and Stefan out, the sooner Bill and I could question G's goons and find out where he'd taken Jamie.

Ten feet from the door, a man with more muscle in his neck than I had in my whole body stepped out of from the last row of barrels. The nose of his gun lined up with my eye. I jerked to a halt. Stefan bumped my right shoulder and stepped back with a squeak. Tatya wheezed a breath in but didn't speak.

The gunman sneered and called down the row of barrels. "Pussy. Don't know what you were so worried about…"

"Come closer and find out." I tensed, looking for the best opening to kick his weapon out of harm's way.

Marcus stepped around the end of the row of barrels behind Bill. That double-crossing pedant! My heart felt as if caught betwixt a blacksmith's hammer and anvil. Trapped with no room to move, the loud thump echoed in my ears. How had he sneaked in here?

Marcus looked daggers at the body-builder. "You lose your sights on her for a second, and we're both dead." He pointed a rifle at Bill. "Put your toy down, nice and easy."

A hollow, metallic clang rang out as Bill dropped his weapon on the concrete.

Marcus waved at me. "You too."

I threw it carelessly toward the arse. If I was lucky, the thing would go off on impact. It landed with a clatter and slid along the floor until Marcus stopped it with his toe.

Glancing down, Marcus snickered. "Paint balls? Interesting choice. Could be fun."

"Doubt you'll have time to find out, mate," Bill said, flexing his fist.

"We'll have to agree to disagree on that." Marcus chuckled with a gleam in his eye.

I shifted my stance, edging toward the end of the row. Stefan and Tatya followed my lead, inching slightly closer to the door. The body builder glowered. I could have reached out and grabbed his weapon now, but he didn't shoot. He shifted back a fraction of an inch, relying on his superior size to stay safe.

"So last night meant nothing to you?" I asked, trying to distract Marcus. If I could get him to look at me, Bill could jump him.

Marcus' eyes never left Bill. "Course not. Meant exactly as much as you intended. I've decided to stop pretending it was more than a business transaction."

A small, sad grin crept up the side of my lip. "Last night wasn't a pretence." I shook my head. "You are a member of my troop, for good or bad. I meant it when I said you could have a second chance."

Marcus spat on the floor. "That's what I think of you and your companions."

The hammer fell. My heart clenched tight. Arse! Venomous, Boil-brained, Arse! "Resignation accepted." I kept the fury and devastation out of my tone. He did not deserve to know how much his death would pain me. "Remember, you chose this."

He laughed, a hollow sound that echoed off the walls of the large space. "How much in life is choice? I didn't ask you to make me a companion all those years ago. Things simply happened and now I've got to get on with my shit."

Bill's nose flared, and his fingers twitched to make a fist again. "What do you have time for, Marcus? Cuddling up with the highest bidder? What did G promise?"

"Didn't have to buy me anything. I finally saw through all her fabrications. God," he waved the rifle at Bill. "You're the biggest loser of them all. You simper after her. Anything she asks, no matter how big a ball ache, you do it. No questions." He laughed. "I'm doing you a favour."

That putrid arse knew my weakness. There was no way to protect everyone with us spread out like this. I had to keep Marcus talking. A few more inches would give the Briggs' a clear run for the door, and I could jump the body builder. That should distract Marcus enough to let Bill get his weapon. I shifted my weight again, inching along the alley.

"You remember Colombia, Marcus? It took nine months, but in the end they all atoned, didn't they?" I called softly through gritted teeth. "You know I never forget... I never give up... and I never forgive." I shifted my weight again. The body builder unconsciously shifted back an inch. It was like boiling a frog. Turn up the heat so gradually they never notice.

"Unless you are trying to commit suicide, I suggest you put your weapon aside," I said.

Marcus squinted and brushed his shoulder across his cheek, wiping at perspiration beading up on his brow without losing sight of his target. "I'm not afraid of you anymore Anna." He twitched, then smiled. "It all makes sense now."

Adrenalin flooded me; I leaped into a flying sidekick that snapped the body-builder's head over his shoulder. He crumpled to the floor. I didn't waste time checking if he was still breathing before spinning toward Marcus.

"Out! Now!" I shouted over my shoulder.

Marcus fired two random shots in my direction. Both flew off target as he kept ducking and dodging Bill's fist.

Tatya lunged toward the fire door, dragging Stefan after her. Out of the corner of my eye, I saw her thrust the door open with her shoulder before sprinting out accompanied by the sound of the fire klaxon.

A third round from Marcus hit my shoulder. I stumbled. He swung the stock of the rifle into Bill's temple. Bill staggered back, shaking blood out of his eye. The barrel of Marcus' gun swung round to point directly at my face. I leaped at him. The matt black reflected the sick green of the fire exit as the index finger squeezed.

The barrel bucked, and pain shattered everything. Although the bullet took my cheek and left eye, my body was already in the air. The velocity of a small missile would not change that.

I fell into Marcus. My hands contracted around his throat, but had no strength. I slid to the floor as he stepped back and turned on Bill. Damn that man.

Pain thumped each time my heart tried to contract. The dull thwack of my head on concrete was barely noticeable over the rest of my agony. My vision narrowed into a small pinpoint framing Bill grappling with Marcus for control of the rifle.

Bill stumbled.

Cold crept up my limbs, entombing them in an icy sarcophagus. No—I promised I be the one to take the bullet—I promised I'd keep him safe…

The gun boomed as darkness closed in around me. A wet thump hit the concrete.

That repugnant knave! That thrice damned minion of Hades…

Easy, precise steps stopped at my side. Anthony's cultured voice spoke. "We could have avoided this trouble simply by conversing."

My guts twisted and flopped like a drowning rat.

Guilt and regret pulled me into their familiar embrace as blood drained from my body, and the welcome nothingness of death finally took over.

TWENTY-ONE

Thoughts returned before movement or sight. Black unpleasant thoughts.

I wanted to retch. First Geoffrey, now Bill. Heaven above, unless I could find his body, I could not even give him a decent burial. The bitter taste of bile rose. I'd have to tell Nigel—see the heart-break in his eyes. Stinking canker-blossoms! Another companion laid to dust.

Hell must have a special abode for oath-breakers. Why had I trusted Marcus? I had to find him before he killed again. Damned Rat, there was enough going on without this.

A flicker of an image waved at me, but my eyes were not open. It... It looked like Geoffrey?

That's just what I needed, another hallucination.

Jamie might still be alive. I had to focus on that, not what was beyond help.

I set the ghost firmly in the back of my thoughts, then relaxed my mind and let it drift free. The surface under me was too soft to be the ground or a casket and too firm to be a bed. I should be able to see more with my mind's eye in the astral plane, yet everything around me was shrouded in a soft velvety black. I could not even make out the shape of the room. That was odd. I reached out for Nigel's life-essence. I needed to know if Tatya and Stefan were safe.

The ghostly image flickered again, waving faster this time and jerking me back to the warehouse.

I started on my astral journey again, but my mind filled with a dim static hiss. I attempted to feel any of the companions, not just Nigel, but perceived the same noise.

My gut twisted into a lump. How could there be no one? Was I losing my intellect? I had died more times than I would have liked this week. Had it sapped my strength too much to travel in the unseen realms? I needed to get out of here. Why was my restoration taking so long?

Marcus was still free. Who knew what havoc that cretin was bestowing on my clan? Fear stoked a fire in my mind. I reached out again, trying to sense anything, see anything, but the cosmic flow I usually followed was absent.

Ghost Geoffrey jumped up and down, waving frantically a few feet away. His white moustache bounced like a moth trapped in a snowy bush. I snapped back into my inert body.

Hell, maybe I was losing my mind if an apparition was more real than the astral plane.

"I'm sorry—you must continue your journey," I said.

The shadowy figure shook his head from side to side, a slow methodical no.

Now even my hallucinations were being unhelpful. Marvellous.

I needed a plan. How many guards were in the building? Was I even in the same warehouse? "Can you see Bill? Tell me where his body is?"

The ghost shook his head again.

"Regrettable. He died a hero. I won't leave him behind."

The shadow figure shook his head again, but the image faded with the sound of feet in the hall. The steps came into the room. Someone lifted my arm with fingers firmly on the base of my wrist, checking for a pulse. Whoever it was set my arm back down, then gently tucked a blanket around my body.

Time passed, but I had little way of telling how much. Geoffrey did not return, and it would do little good to make plans until I knew where I was.

I replayed the Canterbury Tales in my mind to pass the time until I could open my eyes, move my head—do anything.

Half way through the third chapter, light seeped through my eyelids. I fluttered them open.

The room was dim. The watery light obscured by the overcast day more than any window dressing. I was on a lumpy couch in the break room of the warehouse. An odour of stale chip grease lingered in the fabric. What idiot put a dead body on a sofa?

Summoning all my energy, I took a breath, then turned my head an inch. I was alone. Where was Bill? Had they dumped him in a ditch?

My fingers dug into the cushions and the weight of my body made my arms tremble, but I sat up. The place looked like there had been quite a party. Half-eaten foil trays littered the table and floor, mixed with a liberal helping of beer cans and liquor bottles. Where was everyone? A return to life when my body was still intact usually took less than twelve hours. Surely a few of the idiot gangsters would still be sleeping off the party.

There was a knock, followed by Anthony's voice. "Please, put the blade down."

My hand had fallen to my dagger hilt. They let me keep a weapon? I suppose there would be no reason to remove it from a corpse. "Very polite manners for a bandit," I sneered.

"Please, we need to speak before you attempt more rash actions."

No. I needed to escape, not chat with a gangster. I kept the dagger in my hand. "Enter and be done with it if that is your intention."

Anthony pushed the door open enough to slide in and block any thought of escape. The hall behind him seemed empty. That was good. This man moved fast and would not be easy to take down. I didn't want to deal with any more guards helping once things got noisy.

"I'm sorry. Truly. I had no wish to entangle you in this," he said.

I clenched my jaw, fighting the urge to throw a bottle at him. "Sorry? One of my best friends was murdered in front of my eyes, and that is all you can say?"

Anthony lifted one of the tin trays from a chair with two stiff fingers, as if he was afraid it might bite him, and dropped it on the table, then moved the chair closer to me.

"There is much more going on than you realise. However, I believe you have been keeping secrets as well. How have come back from the dead?"

He held his hands together, fingers pointing up to make a steeple shape, and gazed at me over it. I'd had a guardsman peer at me like that once. I broke all ten fingers soon after.

I lifted my head, trying to look imposing, or at least not as pathetic as I felt, and glared at him. "You speak plainly and so shall I."

Anthony simply watched me for several minutes, letting the silence stretch out between us. Finally, he sighed. "As I have stated previously, there are rules I must follow."

I leaned back against the sofa. A less threatening pose might encourage him to speak, but I could not bring myself to sheath the only weapon I had. "Tell me what you think you know about me. What has that Rat been spewing?"

"Marcus has been secretive. All he would say is that you claim to be older than humanly possible, that you are potentially very dangerous and would not help us."

I had to smile. Even as a turncoat, Marcus had revealed little. Then fury boiled up. Why? Why had he turned on us yet kept my secret? Arsehole. Could he not simply be a villain? My fingers curled into a tight fist around the dagger hilt.

I forced them to release and shifted my gaze to watch the flies scuttling across the murky light fitting overhead. It helped order my thoughts. Blind rage would only distract me from what I needed to do—escape and bin my rubbish—not necessarily in that order.

I glanced back. Anthony's eyes were a paler shade of blue today. For all that they had once captivated me, the only thing I wanted now was to see them lifeless. I was too weak to jump him, wrestle with him, or force him out of my way. Yet my small blade only needed a small target. I hurled the dagger with a flip of the wrist. My aim was true. It flipped end over end directly at his eye. He did not move, did not even blink as silver flashed and spun. When he should have jerked in pain—nothing happened. The knife fell on the floor behind him.

Every muscle in me jerked to attention. He was less than five feet away. I could not miss, and he was not another apparition. He brushed some empty food tins out of the way and moved a chair closer. Was the blade defective?

Fear threatened to override logic, and the cave-ape in my soul wanted to hide. The man standing in front of me perpetually appeared perfect, as if carved from stone. He must have a new form of armour. If his minions could teleport between countries, something that would disrupt a simple blade would not be difficult to manufacture.

Blast it. The modern world moved too fast to monitor every invention.

Anthony stood up with a gentle smile, as if indulging a small child asking for sweets, and retrieved the blade. "You should not rely on circumstantial evidence. What makes you think my colleague and I are a threat?"

"Your colleague's habit of robbing and raping. Feels pretty coercive to me."

Anthony stopped. "Geoffrey's death and the subsequent kidnapping were Glenn's unsavoury associates' choice of action—I have dealt with them." He turned to face me. "What other misdemeanours have you witnessed?"

I pulled myself up as tall as I could with the scant strength in my limbs. "My assault. Yorkshire England… Thirteen ninety-two." I let the words drop. After all these years, it was hard to hold back once I'd started.

"Fourteenth century England? Glenn was in a new body." Anthony's eyes closed, as if afraid of seeing the truth in my anger.

"You appear surprised your treasured rules may not mean much to him," I teased.

"What did he do?"

"That thug came to my shop late one evening demanding money and shoes, of all things. We were barber surgeons—Why would we have shoes!" I took a breath and forced my fist to relax. It was a long time ago. "We had nothing—townsfolk paid us in apples for heaven's sake—but that fiend grabbed me, declaring a goodly wife would know how to give payment other ways."

I looked away, fighting the flush growing on my cheeks. It was not my fault. I focused on my breath, counting each lungful until my legs stopped quaking enough to speak without my teeth chattering. "I'm still not sure if it was luck, but our bond dog intervened before the monster could kill me."

"You are sure it was Glenn?"

"That bastard ruined my life. I will never forget his baritone. The sound of it grates on my bones."

Anthony tilted his head. "Ruined your life? Was it that traumatic?"

"Everything changed after that night." I shouted. "For hundreds of years, I have searched for the cause—there are no answers."

Anthony pursed his lip and peered at me closer. "You are not a witch or fairy?"

Was he serious? I had not been accused of witchcraft in two hundred years. "Those creatures are myth. I am very much real."

"He has not just bent the rules, but…" Anthony stumbled back, sank to the floor, and stared at me with wide eyes. "I thought he had taken liberties. This is beyond excusable."

I stared at him, open-mouthed. He was not surprised by my age, immortality, or the time frame of my story, simply that Glenn had broken whatever this rule was. "Liberties? What did you do about it?"

"After Glenn shattered his device, I hid the pieces rather than restore the enabler. I thought it was enough. I was wrong."

What was an enabler? My breath caught. "What, in heaven's name, are you?"

He looked at the floor. "I cannot answer that. Yet in all my years on this planet, I have never had such a desire to break the rules. What is different about you?" He lifted his head. Stress pulled his face tight, forcing his eyes to bulge like a gargoyle on Notre-Dame. "Why have you had this effect on me?"

"I wish I knew."

"I am sorry." Anthony looked as deflated as a beach toy after the crowds had gone home. "Glenn does not know who you are or what he's done. If he finds out, he will panic. You must leave, NOW."

"No argument about that, but where is Bill? He's coming with me even if it's in a bag."

"You are very brave, but foolhardy."

Anthony laid a hand on my arm. Pain shot through me at the touch of cold, deeper than any winter. The room faded into a translucent grey, then everything shifted, blurred and re-aliened. Colour returned and with it cool, damp air.

We stood on the edge of the road outside the mangled chain-link fence.

I locked my knees to stop the tremble. This was beyond strange. Had demons finally come to drag me into hell or just turn my earthly existence into eternal purgatory? I backed away from the thing but fought the urge to run. Whatever was left of Bill was somewhere inside the warehouse. I owed him that much.

Anthony dropped his hand. His face returned to looking like impassive alabaster, showing no emotion, no life. "I will acquire Bill and meet you at the Cairn-of-the-People after the rise of the moon. I presume you know where that is?"

I knew of the old stone monument, but did not trust this thing. Why would he need to find Bill? Was someone selling his body? A shiver ran through me. I would not have him chopped up like the grotesque saintly talismans the church used to pedal to the desperate. "You want me out of here? I go with my companion or not at all."

Anthony glanced at the building. "I'm surprised you survived this long with such an attitude. We don't have time to argue."

"No matter how many times I have prayed for death, the reaper was eternally oblivious to my pain. My companions are not. Loyalty must be reciprocated."

He tilted his head, mulling over the words. "Bill is not here. I have him in safekeeping. Trust me—We will meet you this evening." Anthony pointed at the road.

My heart leaped. Could Bill have survived? With all the oddities today, what was one more miracle?

My breath caught almost as soon as the joy surged. What had Anthony done to merit my trust? Hundreds of years' worth of treachery crowded into my mind. I'd lost count of the number of times some stranger promised me salvation, only to yank it away after they received my cooperation. Most likely, this was merely another ruse, but to what aim? What did he really want?

With my link to the companions severed, I had no way to tell. My throat constricted. Strength had not returned with my consciousness. I did not know who was inside the warehouse and had no actual weapons. To charge back in now would accomplish nothing, but Jamie may be alive. I should focus on her.

I turned away, walking with limbs that were dead weight. Each footstep shredded my gut further. If Bill was dead, he wouldn't know I'd abandoned him, but I could never forget.

After crossing the road, I stumbled down the country lane and nipped under the hedge when it thinned, so I could continue along the field instead of the road. My mind replayed the last time my feet had passed these plants. Bill's banter about Nigel's about his five o'clock shadow echoed in my mind. I shoved it firmly out of my attention. Whatever lay ahead would not be helped by those memories.

Vlad jumped up on the seat of the Rover, planting his nose on the glass, and woofed when he saw me approach. His shoulders moved in a rapid shimmy as he tried to dig his way out of the vehicle. Tufts of expensive upholstery flew by his ears. I grimaced. Bill would have been furious.

I opened the door and Vlad bound out, knocking me to the ground and wetting my face with his tongue. Although I hated doggie kisses, I pulled him close. His joy was something that still made sense.

The vehicle shielded me from casual observation while I sat on the ground, thoughts teetering on the impulse to going back, but each time I tried to get up, my limbs refused. The sun broke through the heavy cloud, warming my face, and my focus drifted upwards.

Free of that twisted demon's clutches, the gentle ebb and flow of life flowed around me again. Thank the heavens.

I reached out to find my companions.

Marcus was near, but his mind was completely addled. All images blurred and jumped randomly, giving me no sign of where exactly. Arse must be on something again.

Nigel and Stefan appeared to be at the estate. Relief warmed my belly. At least Bill had not perished in vain. They were safe.

With our limited link, all I could perceive of Jamie was pain so pervasive it clouded her thoughts like sticky black tar. None of which would help me locate her. Confound it!

I reached out to check the rest. Fourteen familiar forces and two vague notions accounted for all of my companions except for Bill. His space was blank, not dead—which left a residual smudge for weeks—just absence where his life force should be.

My heart squeezed into a lump. I could help none of them like this and lurched to my feet to get in the Rover. If I had to proceed into the lion's den, I wanted to get there first. Much harder to fall into a trap if the hunter had no time to set one.

"Vlad, get in." I tapped the seat.

Vlad growled and backed up, his ears flat against his skull.

I started the engine. "Fine, stay here."

Vlad ducked his head as I started inching the truck down the lane, then ran across the ditch and compressed his haunches into one giant leap that landed on the passenger seat, still growling.

"Big baby," I muttered, leaning over to shut the door behind him.

TWENTY-TWO

An hour later, we arrived in Linlithgowshire. Much had changed since my last visit. New housing estates and vast supermarkets obscured some landmarks, but elevation didn't change. I went up. Buildings became recognisable. The twelfth century preceptory in Torphichen, hidden behind a few younger structures, had aged. A lump stuck in the back of my throat. Moss covered the stonework. Poor thing. Were the sanctuary stones still in place? Would it make any difference to these devils?

Turning left, I started up the last hill on a steep, twisting road. On my last journey, it had been a narrow farm track lined with rock, but it'd been a muddy footpath long before that.

I followed the undulating road through woods and farm fields for half a mile, then turned off at a small lay-by. Although it was still more than a mile to Cairnpapple Hill, I'd walk the rest of the way. Anyone with half a brain would see the Rover approaching otherwise.

Vlad launched himself out of the vehicle as soon as I opened the door, scurrying by me to sniff the wind. I went to the boot and rummaged through the storage compartments.

The only weapon in the Rover was the crossbow. Not ideal for close quarters, but I did not intend to get near the demon again. I opened my travel trunk, reviewing the small collections of poison. Rosemary, garlic, and frankincense stood out as the most potent banishment tools, but would any of them be suitable for this demon? Just to be sure, I dipped the tip of the cross-bolts in belladonna and arsenic as well, then loaded one in the bow and slipped two more in my pocket. My fingers brushed Geoffrey's metal wrapped stone. Thank heavens I'd not lost that in all the chaos. I'd grown rather fond of the odd thing.

The long, damp grass brushed against my ankles as I marched to the top of a small rise. Vlad trotted ahead of me, anxiously looking over his shoulder. He obviously wanted to chase rabbits, but didn't want to get left behind again. Across a deep ravine was an unpretentious earth mound on the top of a lonely hill. The humble site, with a history that stretched back to the stone age, had a radio mast and tin hut huddled off to one side like distant cousins at a wedding. As good a place as any for the ugly things. For centuries, this position had been a beacon for communication. Why should digital be any different to the old fires?

My resources were limited, but not exhausted. I scanned the horizon while scratching Vlad's ear. There were no obvious places for an ambush. My heart rasped a loud clattered thump followed by a pause in between each beat. That was not a good sign.

I pushed my senses out of my body and into the astral copy of the field. There was no one else here. Anthony had not arrived.

I settled on my belly to watch and wait for the moon to rise.

Futile as it was, I shifted my focus to Bill's image again. There was no trace of it. It was as if someone had erased him from existence. The lump in my throat climbed higher. Had the demon taken him to Hades?

The bracken in the valley below me rustled. My stomach clenched. Cows don't creep. I inched down the steep slope on my belly and elbows, pushing the primed crossbow in front. It was tortuously slow, but there wasn't enough cover to stand up.

While curled behind the ruin of a barn at the base of the hill, my mind roamed free to search the area again. The only traces of life were too small to have made the noise. I slapped the ground. My fist only made a pathetic splat of noise. Feculence. Not even the ground would give me satisfaction today.

"I thought we would meet in the circle. Why are you down here?" Anthony asked.

Although rocketing to my feet, I stopped a hair's breath from pulling the trigger on the bow. Anthony stood silhouetted by moonlight two feet away. Alone. He had lied.

Cold seeped into my body, threatening to freeze me to the spot. I thought I'd moved beyond the superstitions of my youth, yet when facing spawn from hell, I might as well have been a toddler. I crossed myself, even though The Church and I had parted ways long ago.

Suddenly, it was plain why he'd surprised me so many times. It was my inability to see reality instead of an assumption. Anthony was not human; therefore, would not have a heartbeat, breath, or warmth.

I backed away with jerky spasms.

Anthony stepped forward like liquid mercury. "Anna, you appear frightened. Are you unwell?"

The tip of the crossbow bolt trembled but remained pointing at his throat. "Stay where you are. You tricked me into coming here tonight. More fool me. There was no proof of your good will. Yet however much I have prayed for death, I'll not go with you."

I pulled the trigger. The steel bolt hit him square between the eyes, embedding into his forehead like a horn. It should have been a killing blow.

He paused, then pulled the bolt from its resting place. Not a drop of blood came with it, just a shimmering energy haze for a moment. His face was still, its heart breaking beauty remaining smooth and clean under the curling locks, but his eyes had lost their merry glow. The cheerful crinkles erased into an unreadable perfection as he regarded me intently. Measured me.

He set the bolt down. "Interesting. That should not have touched me. I would appreciate it if you would refrain from attempting to harm me further. It was not very sociable."

I needed holy water, a cross, or even a four-leaf clover, anything that might have some effect against this creature. My feet stumbled backward, but I didn't take my eyes off the thing.

"Truly, I intended to return your partner this evening." He took another step closer.

"I'll have no more of your lies. Bill is dead and now you've come to take me to the fiery underworld."

Anthony paused and looked away. "No, I have lost him." He held out a small clear stone. "But I believe you can help me trace him. Hold this. It is like a window—he should be able to hear you and you to see him."

Deep within the stone, there was a flash of light. It could have been the moon's reflection. It could have been movement.

I hesitated with my hand outstretched. Could I really see Bill again? There was no reason to believe Anthony. Touching it could capture me as well. I snapped my hand back to my side.

No, I would not fall for any more of this thing's trickery.

Pain rocketed through my shoulder, quickly followed by the pinging noise of a handgun. Numbness followed, slowly radiating toward my chest and arm.

Anthony stumbled, disbelief on his face as he looked down.

A large black space appeared where a bullet must have passed through me and entered his chest. His hand dropped limply to his side, and the picture stone tumbled to the ground.

He stumbled back and sank to his knees, open-mouthed. "What have they done?"

Indeed, what and who could have such an effect on the devil? The black space spread further. Anthony pressed one hand to it as if trying to catch the fragments that were quickly melting into nothingness.

I spun round. Marcus stood silhouetted against the moon on the hill above us. Wretched churl.

Was he a traitorous murderer again? Or had he stopped these devils? I had to know.

Vlad snarled a vicious series of barks, then sprang through the deep grass. Marcus spun around and disappeared down the other side of the hill. I may not have the speed to catch up, but Vlad did. If he tore Marcus' throat out before I got there, I would never know what was on that bullet.

"Vladimir—Hold."

The hound stopped halfway up the hill, one paw in the air, quivering in anticipation of the chase. I hitched up my skirt to follow.

Anthony's free hand darted out and grabbed a handful of fabric. "They have disrupted my containment shield," he said weakly, his voice reduced to a soft whisper.

I shook my skirt. Anthony's hand fell to the ground.

"Back to hell with you."

"This is not a superstitious frivolity." He shifted, bracing himself as if trying to remain upright in a hurricane. There was no wind. "This amount of dark matter will disrupt gravity and destroy everything. If you do not assist me, all life here perishes." Anthony sagged, his image growing fainter. "Glenn is a fool to play with your world like this."

Damn it. Did he really expect me to believe the world hung on his shoulders? Marcus was slipping away.

"You are both fools." I called over my shoulder and moved toward Vlad.

"Stupid ape! I cannot repair this on my own. You remember how the allies ended World War II? That was a firefly in the dark compared to what I'm holding in."

Anthony made a strange motion with his hand, pulling at the sky. Starlight unravelled like a ball of string, then wrapped around him tightly until he looked like a mummy made of night sky.

Vlad whined and trotted back, leaning against me. I wrapped a hand in his coarse fur. The monster before us could control the heavens, yet begged for my assistance. That was not good. "What do you expect me to do?"

"Use the amulet."

The stone Geoffrey left me warmed in my pocket. My stomach sank. "No." I remained absolutely still to avoid giving any indications where it was.

"Your planet is about to implode, and you refuse to do anything?"

"I have no proof that is true."

Anthony fumbled in the grass, found the picture stone, and held it up. A small human shape huddled in a foetal position inside the misty depths.

"He will remain in stasis for millennia if I dissolve. Will you condemn him to that?"

My gut seized as if fiery brands had been wrapped around my torso. What was the truth? There was no way to tell. Damn it! I had to trust this thing.

The amulet glowed warmly in my fingers as I took it out of the deep pocket and held it out to him. His hand twitched, then flopped like a dead mackerel. I pressed my stone into his palm. The two rocks glowed, pulsating through a rainbow of colours.

His fingers snapped closed, holding me like a Siberian shackle. Each finger was as cold and solid as blocks of ice. I jerked back with no effect. His fingers remained clamped around mine.

"I can't do this alone," he whispered.

Frost crept up my fingers. My heart pounded as fast as if I'd run a marathon, but I could not move. The monster had me. "What do you need me for?"

"I must restore order, balance. Once that is correct, I can weave the loose ends together, knitting them into a Möbius loop that is self-containing."

Ice formed on my wrist. "I cannot fathom how to do that."

"You don't need to understand. You just need to anchor me."

White haze grew on grassy stalks as the surrounding plants froze.

What was I agreeing to? Vlad nuzzled my hip. I knelt and threw my free arm around his neck. The stone glowed brighter.

Anthony sighed. "The dog is ensnared as well? I had not realised the depths of Glenn's depravity."

I ruffled Vlad's ears, making his tail thump on the frost covered ground. "I think Vlad was infected by biting the misbegotten cur during my assault." Bolstered by my hound's bravado, I steeled myself. "But today, we will follow your lead."

Anthony smiled. "Fortuna favours the bold. From now on, I want you to feel this world, every inch of grass, every insect, the wind on your face, the damp ground under your fingers. Secure it firmly in your mind. Balance must be maintained. Your impressions will keep everything as it is, as it should be, rather than chaos. You mustn't be distracted by any other thoughts, doubts, or judgements."

"I'm not sure I understand."

"I want you to live fully in the moment, experiencing your environment with no appraisal. Second by second, feel the world around you and your place in it."

Anthony's eyes faded into the colour of pale opals. He looked even more like a possessed statue. My stomach twisted. I'd tried to master this technique years ago at a Buddhist monastery. I had failed. Judgements, interpretations of some sort, often crept in.

Hopefully, one distraction would not lead to dishevelment of the entire world.

Anthony squeezed my hand. "You just had a doubt, did you not? Notice how the air grew colder?"

It was only a passing thought, but he was right—somehow it had changed things.

I focused my attention on the coarseness of Vlad's fur and the feel of the ground under my knees, leaving no room for anything else.

"Excellent, I will begin." Anthony's fingers twitched and danced like he was leading an invisible orchestra. His outline stabilised, and the hole receded a little.

A misty fog of rain dripped on my head and froze on my face.

I wish that had waited till we'd finished.

The ground underneath me swelled and dipped.

Mustn't let myself be distracted!

It heaved again.

Oh... I'm making a shamble of this!

It heaved a third time more violently than before. Vlad pressed against me, whining.

"Focus on breathing—in, one, two—out, one, two." I mumbled to myself.

The ground stopped moving. Stars faded as the sun climbed over the horizon. The sky brightened into brilliant blues, oranges, and pinks.

It's beautiful.

The ground bucked and heaved again. I pulled my mind back to the mantra:—in—one—two, out—one—two. Three birds, one cloud, some trees—I noticed each thing as it came into the light and continued to breathe.

Through it all, Anthony's form gradually returned to solidity. His hair became blond instead of translucent, and his eyes brightened to electric blue. His tailored shirt returned to crisp white instead of midnight sky. The ice on my wrist thawed, dripping to the ground in steady wet plinks.

Finally, he sat up and cast his eye around the valley floor. A slow steady circuit that neither paused nor blinked. A mechanical movement. Then the edges of his lips lifted. His smile was tiny, but more warmth flowed from it than I'd ever seen from him.

"Thank you. I must apologise. That was a most unacceptable loss of control. I never should have allowed myself to become so distracted. I… the fabric of your world unravelled too much for comfort."

I shifted backward, rubbing warmth into my fingers and putting enough space between us, so the monster could not grab me again. "Give me your name, demon. Who are you?"

"There is no word for us in your language, which is how it should be. We are not meant to interact with your species closely enough to leave any trace."

"The original eco-tourist—leave nothing but footprints." It wasn't an excellent joke, but I laughed until tears ran down my face.

Anthony grimaced. "Especially, we should not leave footprints. I'm sorry—I do not see the humour."

I waved one hand, blinking back tears. "It's not that funny. Stress does that to humans." After taking a deep breath, I forced the hysteria into behaving. "If you're not supposed to interact with humans, why did you seek me out?"

He held the amulet up to the light. The dull grey stone flashed brightly, transforming into a sparkling opal. While watching the stone, his eyes shimmered, reflecting the iridescent colour. "You had this. Glenn is my other half and apparently he is part of you now. I need your assistance."

He blinked without haste, then lowered the stone. The silver grey colour returned. He held it out to me.

Hesitantly, I took the thong, careful not to touch the stone. "What is it?"

Anthony smiled faintly. "A tool to control particles. There are only two in this dimension. Glenn will do anything to get it back."

I dropped it on the ground and scooted away. "I don't want it. You keep it, or give it to someone else, or hide it under a rock for all I care. I do not wish to draw that monster's attentions any further."

Anthony gently picked it up, holding it out again. "You must. At first, I could not fathom why Glenn was having such difficulty tracking it. Then I realised you, and I suspect to a small extent your companions, share some of his essence. Therefore, the stone is concealed within his own shadow as long as you hold it."

If I kept this thing, the nightmare of running from Glenn would continue and if I left it—he might recover it. Of the two, letting that ogre have any extra power was unacceptable. Anthony's attempts to keep him on a leash may have failed, but everything had a weakness. I simply need to find his.

"If I'm part of him, can I influence him?" I asked.

"That remains to be seen. None of our species have been so incompetent before, so brash, to have made a half-breed like you," he said with a small smile.

I jerked upright, every muscle pulled tight like the string of a bow. Surely I was still human? Perhaps older than average, but... I felt the same as before. How could I be anything else? "You are mistaken!"

Anthony tilted his head. "It was not an insult, just a fact."

No, I did not have to be a hybrid. If it had never been done before, Anthony could not understand what Glenn's attack may have changed any more than I did. It was just one more piece in the gigantic puzzle I called life. My search for the truth was far from over.

"Whatever the core of my existence may be... I would have preferred to skip the grey hair." It was a small thing, but the only change that had occurred in my appearance in six hundred and twenty-seven years. It was hard not to feel a little aggrieved.

Anthony sat up sharply. "Grey hair? That's a sign of ageing for your species, is it not?"

I looked away, ashamed to have mentioned it. "Of course it is, and it's the first I've ever had, so do not harp on it."

"I'm afraid it's more than upsetting." He looked closely at the amulet. "I will have to study this, but it would appear you are accessing the dimension of time by touching the device. That would mean you are ageing again."

If I was becoming older, could I die? I sat down with a thump as my legs crumpled under me. I didn't really know what to think. Death hadn't been a possibility for so long. I was numb.

"Is change such a bad thing? I have always envied the human capacity for diversity." He reached out to touch me, but let his hand drop an inch from my arm. "My species perpetually exist without variation."

"So why is Glenn fatter now?"

Anthony looked away. "I do not know. He should not be."

That wasn't much help. My stomach clenched. He could simply not wish to share the information. There was no reason to count Anthony as my ally, was there?

"I am rather fond of the absence of aches, grey hair and death. Until you figure out how to control this rogue, perhaps you should keep it." I tossed the stone at him.

"No," he replied, catching the thong without looking. "There is much you need to learn. Knowledge should stop the unwanted side effects. Or at least give you the ability to choose how and why you hand over some of your precious minutes." Anthony held it out to me. The colours swirled briefly, then settled into dull, mottled grey.

How could such a small thing have such a huge effect on me? Reluctantly, I took it back.

"When can we start? I wish to be rid of that bastard in short order."

"Sadly, you are mistaken. You can't just chop him up and be done with it."

A chill settled over me with those words. "What are you talking about?"

Leaning his head in his hand, Anthony sagged. "I must not be explaining this clearly. It's not a tough concept." With a heavy sigh, he wrinkled his brow, pinching his nose. "Think of a glass of water. If someone smashes the glass, what happens to the water?"

"It would spill, obviously," I said.

"You, my dear, your unnaturally long life, are in fact the water. You only exist because of your accidental contact with Glenn, i.e., the glass."

"Oh." Not a brilliant articulation, but I was speechless. Every angle, every way I turned it, the realisation of the truth was awful. Glenn couldn't be killed, banished, or locked up physically. He was too arrogant, stubborn, and cruel to leave on the loose. And to top it all off, apparently I was a parasite on the dung beetle. How revolting.

TWENTY-THREE

"If my limited comprehension is correct, the issues at hand are: one—we are sitting in the middle of a field getting rained on; two—you want me to keep this thing away from your incompetent partner; three—by doing that, myself and all of my companions will be in jeopardy; and four—being near it will cause me to age and die... Sounds great." My mouth went dry. Words wouldn't continue even if I had known what to say.

Anthony nodded. "Correct. I'm glad you have grasped the situation so quickly."

Obviously, sarcasm was another thing he was blind to. "I seem to have little choice. Even if I ignore this device, Glenn will treat my companions as fair targets." I slipped the stone into my pocket and warmth radiated across my leg. "What can it do?"

He opened his palm. Nestled on his smooth white skin was another amulet alike to mine as a sister, except that his was the colour of clouds. It glowed and shifted tones like a kaleidoscope. When held together, the two would make a complete sphere.

"In the right hands, these tools can do almost anything. We will need to test each application to see how fully you can access the capabilities." He closed his hand, and the amulet disappeared. "This is not the right time or place to begin such an arduous task. I suggest you get some rest. We will continue this evening."

I nodded an agreement. The pain in my shoulder had been growing by the minute, as well as an aching thirst and bone deep weariness I'd not felt in hundreds of years. I could never concentrate until I had some coffee. Turning to slog back up the hill, I remembered the reason for coming out here in the first place.

"And what about Bill? You said there were complications finding him."

There was no answer. I looked over my shoulder. Anthony was gone.

I'd not just had a massive hallucination. There was matted grass the size of a tall human by the ruined barn. Where the hell had he gone? The arrogant tosser had not mentioned where he wanted to meet for his test. Idiot had better not expect me to wait for him here.

I climbed over a wire fence and trudged up the road to where I'd left the Rover. I wasn't sure if Marcus was still nearby, but there was little point in trying to track him now.

I didn't want Anthony back at my estate. A coffee shop was too public, but a hotel or a dark pub were possible meeting sites. Vlad jigged at my feet as I paused with my hand on the door handle. He needed to hunt. There would not be any prey in a city, but Bangour village was just two miles away. That would be perfect.

The whole place had been abandoned in favour of a more modern building when it proved too costly to treat mental illness with fresh air and compassion. Most of the site had rotten floors, leaky roofs and a security team watching by CCTV, but Vlad and I had made do with far worse.

After parking a short distance from the back entrance, I retrieved a small emergency packet of instant coffee from my travel trunk. I hadn't thought to bring any water, so tipped the dry contents directly into my mouth.

The bitter tart crystals tried to draw every drop of moisture from my tongue. I gagged, gulped, and poured the rest in, coughing and swallowing quickly. It was nothing like real coffee but would have to do. I called Vlad back from his exploration of the weeds and set off.

The sun tried to peek out from the grey clouds, and we strolled along the road looking like any other middle age woman out exercising her pet. It felt odd to walk surrounded by derelict buildings encased in chain-link fences, but we were not the only ones perambulating in the abandoned town. We passed a shop, two churches, a cricket pitch, bowling green, and countless residential hospital buildings. All stared back at us, unloved and decrepit in the eerily silent place.

At the back of the acreage, a small cottage almost completely obscured by rhododendron growth caught my eye. It was dark and damp but quiet, set well off the best paths. Although heavy plywood covered the doors and windows, it had been left for years, so the edges curled upward.

I tapped Vlad's shoulder. He sniffed the door and sneezed, then bound away into the trees. He'd come back once he'd had enough chasing.

After a sharp shove with my shoulder, the wood screeched and cracked away from the frame enough to slip inside sideways. It wasn't the Hilton, but I only needed a quiet place to meditate. Thankfully, the gloom obscured the worst of the dirt. Fatigue pulled at my legs, and I settled down with my back to the wall opposite the door. My head drifted toward my chest. I'd only close my eyes for a moment.

Ice brushed my lip, jerking me awake.

Feculence. I'd fallen asleep! I never sleep.

Something brushed my cheek. My arm flew out, knocking into cold rock with a thump. I leaped up with my fist poised for the next strike and peered into the gloom.

Vlad lifted his head, questioning what I was jumping around for, but did not get to his feet. Surely he could hear our visitor? Why hadn't he barked?

"Anna, do you always welcome guests with violence?" Anthony whispered in my ear. "If so, I will greet you from a distance in the future."

I whirled to face him. "By my father's honour, why do you delight in alarming me?"

A small sliver of moonlight peeked through a crack in the boarded-up window, illuminating small creases on edges of Anthony's eyes and a wide smile.

"I wanted to see if the fairy tales were true," he said.

"Fairy tales?" I raised my fist. "For someone who cannot grasp sarcasm, you've come up with a fine jest. I am no princess."

"I disagree. I have looked at your history," he whispered.

"What? How?"

"I am a dimensional being. I have existed and can exist in any place in time. All that was required was the desire."

Hell's bells, these dimensional being made evading the Spanish inquisitors look like a picnic, but the deluded imp was mistaken. My upbringing was not royal. "One afternoon could hardly scratch the surface of my life."

"I know this must be hard to grasp, but the time that passes here has no relation to the amount of time I can exist in. You are a most remarkable woman. I look forward to having you as an ally."

Flattery was such an old ruse. Did he really think I could be conquered that easily? "So, how does my story end?"

"I can only look back at what has happened. The path ahead is opaque. It exists, but I cannot travel there. Your premonitions baffle me. You could not have inherited them from Glenn."

Joy coursed through me. If I had one ability they didn't, there might be others.

"Very well. Now about tell me about Bill. You keep hinting he's alive, but I see no evidence of it."

Anthony waved at the crack in the window board. "Come into the next room. I will need light and do not wish to expose your resting place."

I motioned Vlad to stay and followed Anthony through the shadowy twilight.

In the next room, Anthony held out his stone, the mirror shape of the one I carried. An image projected in the air above it. Bill's muscular body lay on his side, curled into a foetal position as if he were sleeping or frozen in ice. There was nothing else around him, simply various shades of white, grey, and blue with no form or substance, shifting like tissue in a heavy breeze. It could have been an abstract painting.

"You have an image of him. What good is that?" I asked, exasperated.

"It is not a picture. It is this moment in time. He is in a dimension that has a similar time stream to yours, but there is no substance."

I shook my head. "Isn't all time the same?"

"Surely you have heard the legends about travelling to fairy kingdoms. The voyager would only be away for a day, but the villagers had aged and did not remember them?"

I snorted. "They made those stories up to scare children or entertain the idle. Are you implying myth was based on dimensional travel?"

"Of course. I'm surprised humans have taken so long to perceive it."

I pursed my lips, grinding my anger into a ball at the back of my head and kicked at the dust covered floor. The way he said human implied we were pets. What an execrable puttock.

"You appear to know where Bill is, so why do you fail to return him?"

Anthony dipped his head. "I am loath to admit this, but I made a mistake. I bounced Bill into the first dimension, moderately suitable. Unfortunately, I did not know about your altered state or how he had been affected by it." He paused. "I have attempted many times to bring him back, but cannot locate his essence."

My frustration exploded. In a flash, I had my dagger pressed to his throat. "You did not just tell me you've lost my best companion—did you?"

He smiled, a thin turn of his lip while looking down at me without flinching. "Yes, I have misplaced your friend."

"Is that bravery or ignorance?" I said, pressing the tip of the knife against his skin. The edge dipped into his translucent flesh, disappearing from view.

He hissed a sharp breath, but his voice remained calm. "Anna, that is uncomfortable. I would appreciate it if you would remove your weapon. Bill's misplacement was an honest mistake. Do not forget, I kept him from being shot."

I removed the knife from his neck, but kept it pointed at him. "You may have saved him from a bullet, but all you seem to have accomplished is to prolong his death."

"I'm confident you will be able to retrieve him."

I jerked. "Me? How would I do that?"

"The enabler appears to work with you; therefore, you should be able to travel there."

"Either this is elementary, or you think highly of me."

Anthony shrugged. "There is no empirical evidence you should fail any more than why you should succeed. I choose to believe the latter. Let us begin."

TWENTY-FOUR

I settled my shoulders and looked around the bare room. Amongst the junk and detritus, I found two cheap kitchen chairs with plastic seats covered in mould not worth the bother of packing. The frames were still square. When perching gingerly on the edge of one, it creaked but held my weight.

Anthony tilting his head. "You don't appear relaxed. Is that comfortable?"

"I won't relax until you and Glenn are out of my life. This will do. As you said, I am not a human anymore. The discomfort shall not be a distraction."

"As you wish." He brought the other chair to sit facing me. "Please retrieve your amulet."

Tremors squeezed my stomach. I hadn't touched the thing since yesterday, but I looped a finger through the leather lace and pulled it out of my pocket. I peeled back the foil and held it against my bare skin. Electric tingles ran up my arm.

Anthony's stone shifted colours in a pleasant rainbow effect that cast a warm glow over his face. Mine was dull grey and looked like a piece of gravel.

"Why does yours change colour when you touch it?"

"You are not coexistent yet. It is only because you have some of Glenn's essence that you can touch it at all. Now... we will start with a relatively simple task."

A small crease wrinkled his brow for a second, and a white candle in a brass holder appeared on the floor between us. "Light the candle."

I jerked my foot away from it. "That should be in my hall cupboard."

"I wanted something familiar to you. Now, please, light the candle."

I glanced at the amulet. It didn't look like flint, and I had no steel. "How?"

"Not with mechanical means. Feel warmth, picture light, contain them both into a point within the candle wick."

How ridiculous. I tried to picture the bright flare just as a spark caught light, combined it with the feeling of warmth of the summer sun on my skin, and stared at the top of the candle.

Nothing happened.

After a few minutes, I mumbled, "This is silly."

"You are not getting the power balance right. Try to change your thoughts about the heat."

Bloody idiot, asking me to play picture games while Bill withered. The suffocating intensity of being surrounded with flames on a funeral pyre flashed into my mind, complete with fear and pain. All fresh and perfect in my infallible memory.

Suddenly, our little room was incandescent. The clutter, although damp, smouldered. Smoke filled my nose.

I leaped to my feet, bolting toward the door. No death was pleasant, but burning was my least favourite.

Anthony flicked his wrist. The heat vanished, along with the smoke. "That was a more vigorous than I had expected. Again, humans surprise me. What did you do differently?"

Panic rippled through me still, but I stepped away from the door. "As suggested, I recalled something hotter."

"That's it? Just thinking about something a bit warmer should not have had the exponential increase in energy." He leaned forward, gazing intently at me. "Tell me what you pictured."

"The first time was the sun on a summer's day. Then you asked me to increase the energy. It sparked a memory of the hottest thing I've ever felt." I paused. "A funeral pyre."

Anthony was silent for a few minutes. "You went from zero to one hundred with nothing in-between. That could have accounted for the disproportionate difference, but you also changed your attitude. You went into the second attempt angry and scared."

"Well, this whole thing is a waste of time. I need to rescue Jamie and find where you hid Bill. What good is lighting a candle going to be for either of those?"

Anthony crossed his long arms as he regarded me for several minutes. "Indeed. You are now an expert?"

"No, but why are we wasting time trying out parlour tricks?" I kicked the candle holder across the room.

He folded his hands in his lap, his long legs sticking straight out in front of him like an oversized doll on a toy chair while he considered his next word. Why couldn't he carry on a normal conversation? Time ticked by with the slowness of molasses until he lifted his hand suddenly, drawing the shape of a building in the air.

"Would you ask a child to build a cathedral? We all start with minor tasks if we want to master the larger ones."

I stalked across the room, clenching my hands in time with each step. By the devils, I'd trained enough impudent boys, I should know that lesson. I retrieved the brass stand and sat opposite him. "Again."

Anthony waved his hand, and the candle reappeared. It had melted along one side and leaned heavily.

"I want you to think of a time when you were happy. Picture it clearly in your mind. Remember every detail," Anthony said.

"How is that relevant?"

"It has everything to do with success. Humans are filled with emotion. If you begin these activities with anger, doubt, or sadness clouding your mind, it appears to alter the results."

"Very well, a happy memory. A bit of amusement or ecstatic?"

"Why is everything one extreme or the other? Do you have a middle?"

I recalled the smell of charcoal and burgers at a gather last summer when all the companions had assembled. The combination of good food, good weather, and camaraderie had added up to a glorious day.

I took the warm glow in my heart and pictured the brightness of the day, anchoring it firmly into one point, and pushed that at the candle.

There was a spark, but it didn't take. I held the feeling of warmth and light, focusing all my attention on that one thing. The flicker came again. The wick blossomed into a soft flame that gradually grew, gently illuminating the dark room.

"Well done. That showed much better control." Anthony leaned forward to snuff out the candle with a flick of his finger.

I stared at him, confusion boiling my thoughts in a cauldron of fury. On any other day, with any other person, I would have chopped at least one of his fingers off for such insolence. "I finally lit the infernal thing. Why did you extinguish it immediately?"

He waved a finger at me. "The lesson was not to illuminate the room. The point was to teach you how to move energy. Now try again."

I was not an infant and should not have needed a reminder of our purpose. I bit my lip and focused on igniting the candle. Nothing happened.

My pleasant mood had evaporated and, with it, my success. Good Gods, this was difficult.

I returned my mind to the summer's day, remembering the friendship and frivolity. The warmth I felt returned, but not as intense as the first time. I combined it with the brightness of a car headlamp and pushed that at the candle. The taper flared, burning brightly from the start.

I snuffed it out before Anthony could, smiling to myself as I settled back in my chair and pictured the warmth of a warm fire after a wintry day out in the rain. The candle glowed dimly, shakily gaining strength. After several more combinations, I began to feel the pattern of images that would work, getting the strength combinations right more times than not.

Anthony nodded encouragement. "Much better. Now feel the particles in the air. Notice how they react when you work with the candle. Work with this until you can illuminate the room with no heat."

Particles? Did he mean the dust motes? More concentration was needed to get a reaction, but it worked.

"Now warm the air."

Soon I could shift between light and heat by focusing on moving tiny pieces of air. Although odd, it was reassuring. It wasn't magic or demonic forces; it was physics. The principles fit with the laws of motion and energy.

The sun brightened the front room. Night had passed without rescuing anyone. I needed to speed this up.

"I have grasped the candle trick. May we do something more constructive now?"

Anthony flicked his wrist, and a peace lily in a blue ceramic urn replaced the candle.

"What kind of practical skill requires a houseplant?"

"Move it."

As I leaned forward, he held up one finger.

"Without touching it."

Of course. This was another variation on the candle procedure. I pictured running through a field, felt the exhilaration, and the wind on my face, then pushed that toward the plant. It toppled over, spilling dirt on the floor.

"Not quite what I had in mind, but it's a start." Anthony righted the plant. "Try to lift, then slide."

I calmed my mind, focusing on the idea of lifting, remembering what it felt like to pick up heavy sacks of grain. The plant shot up, hitting the ceiling, then hovered above our heads unsteadily. The wobble grew. I focused my mind around the shape of the pot, feeling for the empty spaces of particles, matching the spin of each until the wobble stabilised. Suddenly, the plant disappeared.

I slapped the chair. "What did you do that for? I finally got it stable. That was the point, wasn't it?"

Anthony raised his eyebrow. "I did not remove it." He closed his eyes, tilting his head like he was listening for a faint sound. When he opened them, he was smiling. "You sent it to the crossroads."

"What are you talking about?" I asked.

His eyes had a merry twinkle again, the one he had when he knew something I didn't.

"You have moved it to the between-zone. The crossroads is not a place, more like a convergence of all dimensions. It is like an inter-dimensional grand central station. You can jump off one dimension and into another with a single step in the right place."

I'd only been trying to keep it from wobbling, but had changed it at a subatomic level. That sounded useful.

"How do I get it back?"

"Listen for it. Once you have located it, pull it back into this room," he said, as if it was the sort of thing every child would know.

I wrinkled my nose. "What do you mean, listen for it? Plants don't make noise."

"It is elementary. Surely you know how to listen to the essence of a thing?"

That made no more sense than what he said the first time. Dimensional beings must have more than five senses. I recalled what the plant particles had looked like before it disappeared, then pulled that toward me.

The pot arrived as it had before, but the plant had wilted with greyish green leaves that flopped over the side of the container.

Anthony touched a leaf. "You used too much energy. The life force has not come back with it."

My stomach dropped into my shoes. I'd killed it with my incompetence. I was going to have to get a lot better, or the odds of rescuing Bill alive were slim.

After a few more attempts, a collection of dead houseplants surrounded my feet. Anthony held up his hand, stopping me from condemning another to certain death.

"Perhaps if you see and feel the crossroads, you will bring things back better." He took my hand, and the world fell out from under my feet with a sickening lurch.

We stood in a grey mist. Faint lights flickered in the distance like headlamps turning on and off in a heavy fog. Green peace lily shapes fluttered at our feet. Anthony's shoes were clearly visible through the transparent leaves.

"Can I bring them back now?"

He touched a leaf, and it disappeared. "No." He paused and turned his piercing stare at me. "Corporeal beings are, without exception, at risk of slipping into the valley of death when travelling here. Movement to that realm only occurs in one direction."

It was only a lily, but I still felt guilty. I would have to be more mindful.

A flickering light on the horizon blazed again, grabbing my attention.

"What are those?" I asked, pointing to the flashes.

Anthony glanced over his shoulder. "Travellers. Each time a dimensional door opens, it expends energy. That makes the flash."

"Can I do that?"

He shrugged. "Let's find out. Think of a place you would like to visit on earth. Then step toward it."

I tried to hide my giggle. This felt like a silly game, but I pictured the wardrobe I'd left half open after throwing things into my travel trunk before the dash to Maple Grove and stepped forward. The ground dropped away with a sickening lurch, and my foot landed on thick, brown carpet. I pulled out a favourite scarf, letting the smooth silk slide between my fingers. It really was my closet.

At least the amulet had one good use. This would certainly cut down on my need for that dreadful aeroplane travel.

I thought of Anthony and stepped backward, landing in the grey zone, but didn't stop there. A picture of Vlad came to mind, and I stepped to the side, landing back at the boarded-up house with a scarf wrapped around my hand.

Anthony appeared next to me. "That was much better than I had expected. You should rest now. That much travelling so early in your training is hazardous. Time in the sunshine will refresh you."

I felt tired, but I also had an idea and nothing invigorated better than hope.

TWENTY-FIVE

I waved at the exit. Vladimir was on his feet in a single bound, dashing to the door and back three times before I could push the wood panel to the side.

Anthony followed me, slipping sideways through the overgrown doorway. Outside, Vlad trotted up and down the lane, easily walking twice the distance necessary. His tail wagged furiously with each new shrub he investigated. The sun was out for once. It felt marvellous.

"I have an idea to locate Bill." Anthony laid a hand on Vlad. "There is something special about dogs. A dog is a dog in every dimension, and this one is more so than most. He should be able to locate Bill if he accompanies me on a tour of the dimensional crossroads."

A spike of fear rammed its way down my spine, and I stumbled on a crack in the pavement. First, he misplaced Bill and now he wanted to take my most loyal supporter away. Was he trying to remove all my kin?

I tapped my leg, and Vlad's head jerked up. He bounded over to sit on the edge of the pavement. His amber eyes locked on mine, waiting for my next word. His judgement of character was better than most, and he was old enough to look after himself. He could make his own choice.

I nodded toward Anthony. "Do you have faith in him? He seeks your help to locate Bill?"

At the sound of Bill's name, Vlad jumped up on his back feet, bounced twice, then trotted over to sit by Anthony. Vlad leaned against his leg, looking back at me with his tongue hanging out.

I had to laugh at his comic expression. That dog could do sarcasm better than some people. Of course, he wanted to help find Bill.

"Very well." I glared at Anthony. "Come back with Vlad in once piece or by my ancestors valour I swear I shall send you to a dimension worse than hell." I fingered my knife. It had made little of an impression on him before, but he had felt it. I would find a way.

"I will ensure Vlad remains safe and, if all goes well, you will have Bill back before sunset."

After kneeling down to rub Vlad's neck, I leaned close to whisper in his ear. "If this loon gets you into trouble, I WILL find you."

Vlad wrinkled his nose. It was hard to tell just how much he understood. It could have been a sneeze or an agreement. I rose to meet Anthony's eyes, holding them without blinking. "Sunset. I'll be waiting."

Anthony nodded, then placed a hand on Vlad's shoulder. The two of them disappeared.

I waved at the empty space, and the iron weight draped over my shoulders eased for the first time in days. Without Anthony observing my every move, I could finally free Jamie.

Glenn's image flashed through my mind. My stomach back flipped. It was a good thing I didn't need to eat anymore. The memory made the hair on the back of my neck stand up, but an image of neon lights flashed through my head. The bastard was in the centre of Glasgow.

I'd only had a tiny sip of Jamie, but it should be enough to trace her now I knew where to start. I could jump there through the dimensions.

A picture of grey green wilted leaves wrapped around her lifeless corpse flashed through my head. A shudder rocked my whole body. That was much too risky. There was no way I could bring Jamie back like that. If I drove, I would have to watch the images in my head as well as the traffic, but I'd have an escape vehicle at my disposal. Not really much of a contest. I set off at a run for the Rover.

The traffic through town was heavy and following the picture in my head proved to be a bigger challenge than I'd expected. Thankfully, I blinked when a lorry blared its horn, swerving back into my lane before the collision.

Confound this! I parked up. Or more accurately, abandoned the vehicle in the first place it would fit and set out, following the images deeper into the city on foot. Each step boasted more money and influence; the buildings got taller and the signs glossier. The stream of morning commuters grew. I slipped along with the tide until a traffic light stopped me.

As I waited, a woman in a long purple coat cleared her throat. "Do you need any help?" she asked.

I glanced down and wanted the ground to open up. A sea of smart suits surrounded me whilst I looked like I'd been in a traffic accident, then slept in the ditch.

"I'm fine," I mumbled.

The light turned green, and I sprang off the edge of the kerb to duck down the first side street. Turning again into a back alley, I crouched behind the row of bins. Thankfully, the smell of yesterday's curry overwhelmed the less savoury taint of urine. I pictured my wardrobe at home, locking the image of its big brown doors in my mind, and stepped forward. With a lurch and falling sensation, my foot came down on thick wool carpet.

It'd worked. This was going to be very useful. No more tin-can air for me.

After jerking my mind back to my task, I stripped off the muddy tunic and skirt, leaving them in a heap before hurrying to the washroom to splash away the worst of the crud.

Then I opened the wardrobe and grabbed a knee-length skirt out. It showed much more skin than I liked, but needs must. I shimmied into it on one leg while flipping through items in the wardrobe. It had to be something that would get Glenn's attention. My hand slid across a corset.

A lump rose in my throat, but I pulled the black satin garment out. While scandalously brief, it was acceptable attire in this century. I wrapped it around my chest. The laces never needed adjusting and did up the hooks. Although Victorian corsets were better than the Elizabethan monsters, it still took a moment for my lungs to adjust to the restricted movement.

I slipped two throwing daggers into the discreet pockets sewn into the lining next to the boning before pulling on a short velvet jacket that neatly obscured the slim bulge. A pair of knee-high boots completed the outfit.

The reflection in the hall mirror didn't show any bumps other than the ones I was trying to display. Brilliant, I'd be able to move, defend myself, and still seduce that oaf.

Bracing for the lurch, I held the amulet lightly in one hand and pictured the alley I'd left a few minutes ago. Lifting my foot brought the grey space and the falling sensation before I set it down on broken concrete. The damp spring chill wormed through my bare skin. How did modern women cope with these scant things?

I focused my mind on Glenn's image and started walking. Eventually I came to a tall building with an ultra modern steel and glass foyer where his likeness faded out.

The rest of the buildings in the square were stone or brick and had a grandeur of age. This thing was all flash, a monolith of bling. Probably cost a fortune to live in, but wouldn't last. Behind the revolving door, a bored security man sat at a desk in front of a wall of marble, flipping through a newspaper. He diligently looked up from his paper each time the door moved, proving he was bored but not negligent. That was going to make getting inside more difficult.

I crossed the open plaza in front of the building to a stone bench on the opposite side. A shiver shuddered through my posterior. The seat felt like ice, but was the perfect place to watch the steady stream of people passing by. A thin man with a moustache did a double take as he marched by. I fought the urge to pull at my hem. However much the purpose of my clothes was to get attention, I didn't like it.

Hopefully Glenn would pass this way soon. I could feel him, but not enough to measure the distance.

A moment later, I spotted him heading straight up the plaza.

I waited until he was a few feet away, then stood and strolled in front of him with a rolling gait that made my hips sway, stopping at another bench. Sitting down slowly, I stretched out a foot while crossing my legs. A moment later I shifted again, as if my back was too tight, arching a bit, before leaning forward to adjust my boot.

Although he was watching, he remained on the other side of the square. Damn it. What was he waiting for? Casually, I checked my watch as if I had a place to be.

Footsteps scuffed, then the gravelly voice chuckled. "Ya! What's a looker like ye doing out here? It's freezing!"

My stomach clenched involuntarily, but I forced a smile across my lip before looking up.

He leaned against a streetlight, leering. His eyes never met mine. They were too busy tracing curves. He shifted closer, offering his hand. "Mah name's Glenn."

My smile felt tight against my cheeks as I shook his overly warm, soft and unused-to-doing-anything-useful hand. "We have met. Surely you remember?"

He frowned, the annoyance at being corrected tightening the skin around his eyes, but he leaned forward squeezing my hand. "No. I would remember a cutie like you."

The words oozed out like worms to me, making my gut revolt again. Bloody arrogant idiot needed to think harder.

Most powerful men had the same weakness, though. I cast my eye down, looking away, giving him the victory… for now. Biting my lip, I shifted forward. It was only an inch, but his eyes locked just below the satin ribbon dangling from my corset. "Never mind, first impressions are seldom correct any way. Call me Amber."

"Ya! Excellent name. Now—how about I make an impression?" His too perfect teeth gleamed through his smile.

"What are you proposing?" I asked with a wink.

"You come to my place. We have a good time."

My legs uncrossed, leisurely sliding to the ground. "Fun—I could do with some of that."

He swung an arm around me, leading me to the glass doors. "Ya! Good-time girls. Always fun."

One pudgy hand slid down, squeezing my bottom as we walked. A ball of iron knotted in my chest. Any other day, I'd break that finger, but today was about Jamie. His penance would have to wait until she was safe.

We crossed into the glass foyer, and a high pitch siren screamed. My feet froze in place. They had metal detectors on the door!

From behind the desk, the elderly guard sighed and heaved himself to his feet. "Need to check you out, miss."

The beige uniformed man rummaged around the desk, then approached with a slight limp carrying a small wand, like the ones used in airports.

I ducked my head, fluttering one hand down the bones of my corset. "It's just these," I replied, looking up through my lashes. He needed to take the hint… it wasn't fair to break the guy's nose just for doing his job.

Glenn snorted and waved the guard away. "For Christ's sake! Sit down. She's with me."

The security man shrugged. "Your building boss. You wanna let armed folk in, be my guest."

Glenn chuckled, then snorted, then roared a laugh so hard tears formed in his eyes. "Armed? My arse." He slapped the guard on the back. "Ya! Stuart, keep that suspicious mind. Makes you good at the job."

TWENTY-SIX

Many shots of whisky, rum, and tequila later, I realised my plan had a major flaw in it. Whether it was the Scottish influence, or that he was an inter-dimensional being, I'd met my match. Neither of us was even slightly drunk, although I was playing the part as best I could.

The wall of glass opposite my seat showed a panorama of the city. There was a lot of activity on the streets, so I probably had about three hours left before sunset. Confound it, all day with the cretin had not revealed a single clue where Jamie was.

Giggling, I leaned over Glenn's chest and pointed to the large aquarium by the small modern kitchen on the left side of the room. Although beautiful to look at, it'd be a nightmare to clean. "Tell me again how you dived to the bottom of the ocean for those things." I hung onto my seat, as if I was afraid I'd fall at any moment. Unfortunately, while the pose gave me a better view of the hall, it was dark.

He chuckled and stroked one hand down my back. "Ya... Was difficult. Those buggers bite back."

He launched into another long-winded rant. He never tired of the nauseating sound of his own voice. With drooping lashes, I swept my eye over the luxury flat. He definitely had a god like opinion of himself. Everything in the place was an extravagance. The couch wasn't just a seat. It was an upholstered pit in the centre of the room. A continuous cushioned oval, all in white, surrounded by a sea of gold carpet.

The unlit hall was a mystery. I'd rather not get too close to a bed, but where else could Jamie be?

I laid a hand on his thigh. "G, I've had too many of these." I held up my glass. "Where's the powder room?"

He stroked a hand down my neck and shoulder, lingering on the bare skin. "Ya, is on the left," he whispered in my ear.

Perfect. I stood up, weaving slightly, and took a tottering step. His hand shot out, but I avoided it and minced my way over the sofa to the main floor with exaggerated care. Once in the hall, there were three doors, unfortunately, all closed. I turned the handle of the first one.

"Toilet left... bedroom right. You want to skip straight to..." Glenn got up from his seat.

I dashed across the hall, closing the door behind me, and leaned against it. Damn it, now what? I couldn't check any more rooms without him seeing and there were no windows here.

The stone in my pocket shifted. It could solve everything, but was it worth the risk? I slipped it out. If I did this wrong, he'd probably know I had it and wasted all of Anthony's effort to keep me concealed.

A light blinked off the rock. My heart lurched. Was it trying to reach Glenn? I wrapped the foil around it again and shoved the stone to the bottom of my pocket. Foil was a good insulator, hopefully good enough. I'd have to find another way to locate Jamie.

The main door in the flat opened and slammed, rattling the wash room fittings.

"How's the girl?" Marcus shouted.

Girl? This was too good to be true. They could be talking about another girl, but most likely, it was Jamie.

"Sleeping! You gave her too much," G said with disgust. "No fun. No use."

"Well, your fun left her screaming loud enough to have the plod round if I hadn't given her something."

Glass tinkled as something clinked against the table. "Ya... Calm the fuck down. Have some juice."

"What are you doing with that?" Marcus' voice rose to a shrill squeak.

Glenn chuckled. "I wanted some fun."

"You gave it... to a random tart?" Marcus' voice had an edge of panic to it.

The sneak had been trying to drug me as well as get me drunk. Probably the only way he could get a leg over. Anyone conscious would run a mile at the sight of the sweat covered behemoth naked.

"Ya! Drink not fast enough."

"What?! This is a specific formula for Jamie. It'll make that slapper miserable. Don't let her go. I'll get something for her stomach," Marcus shouted. Footsteps marched down the hall, and a door slammed. It sounded like it was the one on the right.

I lurched out of the powder room and over to the couch, falling into a heap on the sofa.

"Ya Cutie… you can't be like that." Glenn pulled me close and kissed my neck. "We were just getting started," he murmured in my ear.

I forced myself to remain limp instead of pulling away. A few minutes of this pawing would allow me to kill Marcus and free Jamie, but the shivers running through my gut boiled up another wave of nausea.

Heavy footsteps marched back from the hall to the sofa.

"Ya! Mark, this is Amber," Glenn shouted. His ham-hock of a hand landed on my knee and travelled north.

I bit back bile and opened my eyes, raising a finger to my brow in a mock salute.

Marcus was only standing a foot away. His eyes widened.

"You idiot! You brought the devil straight to us!" he blurted, before shuffling back.

Glenn chuckled, squeezing my thigh before running his hand further up my leg. "Devil? Na—she's fun. Not what you described."

"I KNOW her!"

"Ya! Quiet… She's no threat," Glenn snickered, pointing to the collection of empties at our feet. "She's pissed. Can't even stand."

My acting skill must be better than I thought.

"Damn it, alcohol doesn't affect her!" Marcus shouted.

I closed my eyes and lurched heavily to the side, landing on the floor.

Glenn grabbed my arm, propping me back up, then ran his hand down my neck. "Ya… must have the wrong girl. Look at her."

Marcus shuffled back and forth. His rapid pace crunched through the plush carpet. He was close. There was a slight shift of the rug fibres when he turned. I lashed out, hooking my hand around his wrist. As I stood up, I twisted the digits.

Marcus' face crumpled when his thumb bent over the back of his hand. Pain and fear took control of his mind, and his knees buckled.

I leaned close so that only he could hear. "Time's up, Marcus."

Marcus glanced at Glenn. "Do something…" His voice cut off into a screech as I snapped the bone in his thumb.

Glenn sat on the couch dumbstruck for a second, then leaned back, folding his arms with a satisfied grin. "Not my problem. You fucked her off." He waved his hand at me. "Carry on—" Nodding with contented arrogance, he took another slug of his whisky. "We can have our fun later."

The gleam in his eye revolted me more than Marcus' betrayal. I'd had enough of his slime. "You really should have attempted to remember me." I smiled sweetly. "You'd know I'm not just a carnal muffin-pot."

"Ya! What you going to do?" He waved his drink, and a golden spot blossomed on the white couch as he spilled half of it. "My guards, my keys, my building. You go nowhere until I'm done—if you can still walk."

I leaned to the side, kicking Marcus in the solar plexus hard enough to knock the wind out of him. Sputtering, he slid backwards along the floor, hitting the bottom of the stairs.

Powered by the momentum of the kick, I flowed into a leap and pulled the daggers out of my bodice. The blades crashed down as I landed on top of Glenn. One slammed into the folds of his trousers, pinning his crotch to the cushion, while the other pierced his hand, driving the blade through flesh and bone to the wooden armrest underneath. His bloated face drained of all colour, frozen in place from the shock.

"I'm nobody's plaything. Remember that if you recall nothing else." I shoved my weight against the blades, locking them into the wooden sofa frame, then turned back to Marcus. He'd struggled onto one knee, though still gasping for breath, when I wrapped my fingers into his hair and dragged him up until his eyes were an inch from mine.

The cloying scent of incense caught on the back of my throat. Memories flashed through my head. Some good, some awful, but all distracting. I held my breath and pulled a pin from the knot at the back of my head, twisting it so the light glinted off the polished enamel butterfly down to the razor tip.

"Remember these?"

He nodded imperceptibly, trembling slightly, as I traced the blade from his ear to collar.

"Where's Jamie?"

He put a foot on the steps just as Glenn regained his faculties.

"FUCK SAKE—FUCK SAKE—FUCK SAKE!" Glenn thundered, tripping as the daggers caught his attempt to stand.

"Blast it all, MOVE," I shouted, shoving Marcus. He ducked his head and ran to the hall opposite the sofa pit.

"I'll peel you alive!" Glenn screamed. "Strip the meat from your scrawny bones and feed it to my pets."

My skin crawled as if it was trying to make sure it was still attached. Execrable malt-worm knew a good threat.

One of my own daggers whistled by my ear and thunked into the hall door frame.

I pulled the blade out, tucked it into my bodice, and wrapped my finger around the stone amulet. Thinking of the intensity of funeral fires combined with blinding light, I aimed my thought at the sofa. Please let it be right.

A wave of heat knocked Marcus and me to the floor, but also blocked the entrance.

More than half the main room was alight. The flames spread along the carpet, catching furnishings and draperies in the main room.

"Guards!" Glenn roared from on the other side, while batting at the flames with his bare hands.

The blaze raced along the shag pile. Feather pillows exploded, raining flaming tufts, which ignited more carpet. The bonfire turned, bolting straight toward us!

TWENTY-SEVEN

"Right Marcus, where is Jamie?" I demanded.

He nodded his chin to the left.

Dragging him by his broken thumb, I jerked the last door open. A flight of stairs led into darkness. It might be a trap, but there was nowhere else to go. I leaped up half a dozen in double quick time. Smoke filled the stairway. Marcus' foot tangled under mine. I slammed into him, and we slid into a twisted heap back at the bottom.

Confound it! His stumbling might be clumsiness, but I had no time to put up with it. I cracked his head against the floor hard with a hollow thump. "Do that again, and I'll skewer you right here. Now get up and stay up!" I shouted.

He blinked, scrambling shakily to his feet, nearly running up the stairs ahead of me. He fumbled to get a key into the slim lock with shaking fingers. I tapped my foot twice, but he flung the door open before the third.

I waved the dagger at him. "You first."

He backed away from the blade, pushing the door open further, shaking even harder. "It wasn't my idea. You have to believe me," Marcus pleaded as he stepped backwards.

Windows made up all sides of the small room. Originally, it must have been a conservatory, but there weren't any plants. Now all it held was an enormous bed. I suppose you didn't need much for Glenn's type of party.

When I stepped into the room, the sharp scent of disinfectant cut at my nose. Stefan's sketch book lay open next to a box of metal instruments on the floor. The surgical steel gleamed in the light. They could have been medical… could have been… My fist clenched.

Jamie's pale naked form lay across the bed with one wrist cuffed to the headboard. The faint rise and fall of her chest was the only sign she was still alive underneath the bruises and blood.

At that moment, the fury twisting in my stomach clouded out any rational words. I took one step forward, my whole body tense. "Unlock those cuffs."

Marcus blanched, edging away. "I don't have that key. Glenn allowed me to sedate her when the screams got too loud, that's all."

"Then get out of the way, you useless toe rag." I pushed him to one side and knelt down to inspect the lock.

Jamie murmured in her drug induced sleep and rolled away from me. The maid did not know who was touching her, but knew enough to get away. There were so many bruises on her arm, it looked like snakeskin. My teeth ground together as my jaw clenched. The lock snapped. Jamie pulled her arm to her chest, curling into a ball.

What had fractured the lock? I hadn't even touched the amulet. I'd have to contemplate it after getting Jamie out of this cesspit.

I eased her upright. She whimpered as her weight shifted and shivers shuddered through her body. The poor maid was freezing. There was nothing to wrap around her in the room, not even a sheet.

I snapped my fingers at Marcus. "Your fleece. It's the least you can do after involving her in this."

Marcus pulled off his top, holding it out with a shaking hand. "How's it my fault? I've never even seen her before yesterday," he shouted back.

"That package you sent Geoffrey, the one you didn't think I knew about. That egomaniac wants her to tell him where it is."

I lifted the shirt over Jamie's head, but she pushed me away. Her eyes rolled back, showing a ghastly amount of white.

"Shh, I'm simply trying to clothe you." I held the shirt out.

She pulled it on and hugged herself tightly with unfocused eyes, still rocking in place.

Marcus shook his head. "How did she know Geoffrey?"

"Look closer. Notice anything familiar?" I asked.

Jamie had her mother's complexion, but her grandfather's blue eyes.

The realisation dawned on him. The colour bleached out of Marcus' weathered face, but he remained staring at Jamie.

I ran a hand over the box of instruments. "Fine way to pay back your best friend. Drug his granddaughter to the eyeballs, so a sadist can torment her without the neighbours complaining."

He spun to the corner and bent double with a horrible retching sound as his body heaved, ejecting his last meal onto the floor. Leaning his head against the wall, he closed his eyes and pounded his fist.

I slipped Stefan's book into my coat pocket. Although it nearly tore the lining, I didn't want to leave any evidence for that creep. "Come Jamie, it is time to leave." I leaned forward, but she didn't even look at me.

Marcus turned back, wiping his mouth and dabbing at a thin trail of blood running down from his nose. "I'll carry her. She obviously can't walk."

I didn't have time to negotiate with a spineless turncoat. In my opinion, Marcus should be dropped into the deepest pit of filth for his acceptance of this. The sooner I was rid of him, the better.

"So now you've developed a sense of morality?" I snorted, lifting Jamie to her feet.

She swayed, lurching to the side, and I stumbled to hold her up. He leaped forward, steadying Jamie before we toppled. By God's toes, he was right. The maid could not even stand, let alone walk.

"Let me do one thing right today?" he said, holding Jamie's elbow with his good hand, as if she were made of glass, afraid to touch any part of her lest she wince again.

"You know this changes nothing. You're scum and a dead man walking either way."

He flinched but didn't move.

I shifted my weight, bringing my knee up to my waist. It wasn't the easiest thing to do in a skirt, but I wasn't concerned about modesty anymore. Flexing my foot, I tested the distance twice, then slammed it into the lock on the door that led to the rooftop.

It burst open, slamming into the wall. Glass shattered with a loud crack. Crystalline shrapnel fell to the ground with a roar that was quickly over. Luckily, the boot protected my foot from the falling razors.

Cold air slapped me in the face, and my teeth chattered like a wind-up toy. Marcus passed Jamie to me. Her half-closed eyes never even blinked. Although she was wearing less than me, the poor kid was so drugged she didn't even notice the temperature.

A seven-foot tall brick wall enclosed the edge of the rooftop space. Calling it a garden would have been too generous a description of the wilted dry foliage condemned to eternal thirst. Rows of the poor things led to a small patio laid out with a fire pit and dining table. By the size of the safety wall, the architect must have been more worried about suicide than an inferno, but there had to be a way down.

"Glenn's going to get around my diversion soon. Where's the fire escape?"

Marcus climbed over the broken frame one handed and flung an elbow at a shadowy corner of the roof. "Over there."

My stomach sank. The furthest corner. Sixty feet. Not far usually, but today it felt like the ground stretched out to infinity. Jamie hung between us with an arm over our shoulders. Her head never lifted, and her feet barely shuffled.

We inched closer. Agonizing minutes ticked by. This had to be the slowest escape ever. Scourge and pestilence—my blaze could not have been that good. We were going to get caught.

We entered the shadows. A steel gate interrupted the brickwork, showing tantalising glimpses of the city below. The escape looked ancient. Hopefully Jamie could negotiate the narrow treads. There was no handle. Instead, a keypad beside the frame glowed faintly in the dim light.

I glanced at Marcus. "What's the code?"

A whistling rasp came from behind us. I pushed Jamie at Marcus and dived the other way. A large terracotta pot flew over my head, smashing into the locked gate, and spilled a sad geranium on the ground.

"Humans can't throw fire. What are you?" Glenn shouted.

I rolled to the side and sat up as Glenn stormed out of the conservatory. Sweat gleamed off his brow and tiny tendrils of steam encircled his head. His trousers split open from zip to mid-thigh, but he walked with no sign of discomfort. Damn, the blade must have missed.

Marcus eased Jamie down the wall and crouched at her side with his head down, eyes tightly squeezed shut. Pointless fool-born yokel.

I moved between Glenn and Jamie. "Shame, you're not the kind to remember. Age must be getting the better of you."

He frowned but kept advancing with the methodical plod of a lion, sure his prey could not escape. The beast was intent on playing now.

I inched away from Jamie and Marcus until my back pressed against the exit. With my mind, I reached out and felt the four pairs of bolts securing it to the wall. Please let this work.

The sun gleamed off Glenn's eye as he looked around the roof. Two opaque orbs with all the warmth of a dead eel. A hollow, manic chuckle, entirely without mirth, rippled from him.

Gently nudging the spin on the particles. I felt the first bolt move. I pushed a bit more and heard a faint tinkle as it fell to the ground.

Glenn stopped, crossing his arms and thrusting his chin at the gate. "Ten blokes can't move it, you ain't."

I didn't have time to waste on a retort to his monologue and closed my eyes to focus on the second bolt.

He chuckled again, a noise like gravel in a bucket. "Ya! Close your eyes. Wish you were somewhere else!" He tapped his foot on the roof and shouted at Marcus. "Ya! Get off your arse! Frightened of a girl?"

The second and third bolts slid free. Nearly there. One more and Jamie would never have to see that thug again.

Glenn chuckled, and pain exploded in my chest. My eyes flew open. Six inches of window glass protruded just above my corset, and a thin trail of blood trickled down the hollow between my breast. By the devils—that hurt. Arse.

I plucked the glass out and pressed a hand over the wound.

Glenn's face was tinged with purple as he waved at Marcus. "She got you by the balls? Grab her for fuck's sake."

Marcus stood up, looked at Glenn, then at me. The untrustworthy curmudgeon turned toward me. I steadied myself, blocking out the pain of the laceration, and slid one hand down to the hilt of a dagger.

Marcus didn't grab me, he just stood there with his face calm. For the first time since Colombia, all his worry lines were gone.

"Anna, you may be a bitch, but you at least have honour. Get Jamie out of here." He spun and threw himself at the brute.

The surprise of the attack won him a minor victory. Glenn's back slammed into the floor of the terrace. The overgrown man roared with incoherent fury.

For the love of all that's holy, how could he show valour now? Damned man.

A bolt of blue electricity sparked from Glenn, sending Marcus flying across the roof. He hit a satellite dish with a clang, sliding to the floor in a crumpled mess.

"You must be a good shag to inspire that kind of loyalty." Glenn smirked and advanced on me quickly this time.

Knife in hand, I circled, watching for a weakness. Pity there was no way to hide anything useful in modern clothes. I would have preferred a sword, or any proper weapon, for that matter. Two daggers and a shaky understanding of astral manipulations to fend off a beast with electric hands, and a company of guards were not great odds.

He puffed out his chest and swaggered as only a fat man could.

The lumbering sway looked like a duck waddling. Despite the tension building in my belly, the silliness of it cut through everything. I giggled.

"Pathetic monkey's gone nuts." Glenn hitched his trousers up.

While he was distracted, I struck a fast sidekick to his knee and leaped back again before he could reach me. Bone and cartilage cracked. The joint severed. He wavered, lurched to the left, then hopped on one leg, but kept his balance.

"Ya! Bendy. I got a use for that," he muttered, rubbing at the injury.

He hadn't cried out—hadn't shown the slightest sign of pain. Heavens above, that was not good. Would any of my defences make an impact?

The misaligned joint knitted back into a straight line. He stood upright.

It usually took me a few hours to restore a broken bone.

Glenn flung his arm out. Blue lightning raced from his fingertips.

The force of it slammed into me like a cannonball. My body went rigid, every muscle trying to contract at once, before crashing to the floor, locked in an agonizing spasm. The force tore me apart from the inside out. All neural messages scrambled. Convulsions racked my body, followed by the coppery taste of blood when I bit my tongue.

Footsteps plodded over to me. His boot smashed into my rib, just like he had six hundred years ago. Hadn't this man learned any new tricks?

Another kick landed on my shoulder with a crack and a fresh wave of pain. I had to get up. The only good thing about a lifetime of torment—it didn't take long to separate my logic from the agony. To get control back, I followed the energy particles with my mind's eye.

Blue lightning darted through the microscopic landscape of my neural system like a game of ping-pong ball. I reached out to one, but it bounced off a bone to shoot away in a new direction. Thousands of them zipped back and forth through muscle tissue, like a miniature firework display.

I could not grasp them without impeding the electrons. I pictured a slug crawling up my garden fence. It'd been a hot summer's day; the thing had taken all day to move three feet. The blue flashes stopped bouncing off bone, but still buzzed through enough cells I couldn't move. Slow thoughts, slow, slow. What was slower than a slug?

Another boot crashed into my kidney; the wave of agony knocked me out of my trance.

Mewling, rump-fed, rough-hewn, canker-blossomed, arsehole. May you die a thousand deaths! My muscles locked tighter.

That wasn't helping. I was better than him. I needed to focus on slow thoughts. Slow… like icicles melting, mould growing on cheese, a tortoise eating a leaf. The blue lightning turned into a blue fog that hung stationary in my cells. I nudging the lightening with my mind and it rolled away from the muscles. I gathered it into one arm, then one hand. The boot pulled back to kick again with a satisfied chuckle.

Foul beast deserved to be drawn and quartered. I shifted, grabbing his foot just before contact and used his momentum to roll onto my back while letting all the energy stored in my hand run up his leg.

He buckled, flailing wildly before crashing backwards. A wet crack echoed as he landed. With any luck, it was his head.

After pushing his flailing foot out of my way, I rolled to my knees and crawled up to his head. His eyes followed, but his tongue seem to be paralysed.

I leaned over him, tracing the tip of my dagger over the outline of his nose. My hands trembled—he needed to be hurt. He needed to feel as much as his victims.

Feet thundered inside the flat. The way the sounds overlapped made it impossible to tell how many. My heart launched at my throat. Bloody reinforcements.

I cut Glenn's throat. The six-inch knife half severed his head from his neck, slicing through the layers of fat like butchering a pig. Lord knows I had done enough of those, but they squealed louder. It wasn't as good as a full decapitation and Glenn hadn't bled, so he may not stay down for very long, but it was all I had time for. The boots were getting louder.

Shoving the dagger back into my bodice, I scrambled up. Cruddy luck, but revenge was not sweet enough to be captured again.

Marcus roused enough to push himself upright, but his leg buckled as soon as he put weight on it. Bloody waste of space. Why had he just shown a backbone? I could have left him with a clear conscience without that. Hell fire! I'd have left a corpse here with a clear head and light heart before he tried to attack Glenn so Jamie and I could escape.

I dragged him toward the gate. It felt like I was sinking into the floor, each boot thud hammering me further in to the quicksand. There was no way I could run with them both like this. I set his leaden weight down next to Jamie.

Two men in suits stepped out of the conservatory, glass crunching with each stride. Good god, they were big. Nearly as wide as Glenn, but it was all muscle.

Glenn's nearly headless torso quivered and raised an arm. A snicker tickled the back of my throat. I couldn't help it. He looked like a low budget theatre prop.

Then he pointed at me, and the guards started running.

Damn! I should have known better than to find life amusing.

The amulet's metallic surface shimmered in my hand, not reflecting light, though. If anything, it pulled light towards in. I slipped the thong over my neck and pictured the alley with skips full of the stale smell of curry, sweat, and piss. Jamie and Marcus had better be more robust than peace lilies.

With all the feelings from that place filling my mind, I took their hands and stepped forward... toward the guards.

One more leap of faith.

TWENTY-EIGHT

I stumbled off balance into the side of a rusty skip surrounded by squashed cardboard. By luck, the alley was empty. I released Marcus and Jamie, letting their dead weight slide to the ground.

Jamie seemed to doze with a calm, regular, rise-and-fall of her chest. Marcus, on the other hand, was a problem. Although he hadn't turned into a brittle grey husk like the potted plants earlier, he showed no signs of life.

I sunk to my knees. Should I let fate have its way this time? If he hadn't just shown a glimmer of goodness, I'd thank God for doing the job for me. My head sank into my hands, blotting out the sight of his dark curls. Who failed who? The question circled my head over and over. Did he deserve to die? What made me a worthy judge?

OH, hell! I should at least attempt to revive him. A silly staying alive CPR advertisement flashed through my head.

The goons in the poster had grinned, but nothing changed in Marcus as I pumped my palms over his chest. If anything, his waxy skin stuck to my hands, making it harder to do compression; perhaps his heart was a rigid mass already.

I could stop and say I'd done my best. It would be perfectly reasonable. Jamie and I had a better chance of escape if I wasted no more time.

His head flopped to one side, and dark hair fluttered in the breeze. Wherever death takes people, it can't be instant. How else would I have spoken to the ghost in the forest? I could probably bring him back if I crossed into the grey zone.

The image of Bill falling into the dark flashed through my mind in nearly the same instant as Anthony's impassive face watching the peace lily fade. Was Marcus worth the risk? I did not know what lay outside our own dimension.

Mary, mother of mercy, take this choice away from me.

My life belongs to you, freely given, freely taken, till death do us part... My life belongs to you, in times of need I will offer my aid, freely given, freely taken... My life belongs to you, freely given, freely taken—The sound of his voice the day we'd both sworn the oath echoed in my mind.

I stared at the grimy alley wall, my breath escaping in a long, heavy sigh. Damn, man, there was little choice. I was not an oath breaker.

What would happen if I travelled to the land of the shades? A shiver crawled up my spine. I wouldn't go that far.

Marcus' nasal voice was the perfect focal point to aid my journey. I held it in my mind and stepped forward. Although a murky grey fog enveloped me instantly, Marcus' form hovered an inch from my face. It was all I could see in the shifting haze.

"What are you doing here?" I shouted, relieved and annoyed to find him so easily.

"You move fast! I fell, or you dropped me—I don't know. When I looked up, you were gone."

I shook away his excuses like an annoying mosquito and grabbed his wrist. "For the love of Joseph… We don't have time for this." Stepping back to the alley, I threw his shade at the body next to me.

After a moment, he took a huge gasping breath, coughed, and sat up. His unwavering stare locked on the wall as if he was afraid to turn his head. "I've had some wicked trips, but nothing like that. Did we…?" he asked with a voice barely loud enough to hear over the city traffic.

"If you mean, did we just visit the valley of death? Perhaps." I got to my feet even though fatigue pulled at me, begging me to sit down again. This was no place to rest. We needed to put as much distance between us and that monster as possible.

"Thank you for coming back," he said, the tension still holding him rigid.

My teeth clamped together tight enough to crack walnuts. I didn't want his thanks. Having him around caused more problems than it solved. "Just help me get Jamie up. We need to move."

Although Marcus climbed to his feet with a lurched and a wince, he slid Jamie's arm over his shoulder.

Damn man. Damn him to hell. He shot Bill. Why couldn't he just be useless? Why did he have to keep showing virtue?

We limped three abreast, bloody and dishevelled. Our awkward pace should have prompted questions, but it didn't. What did it take to make people raise an eyebrow these days? Marcus' fleece barely covered Jamie like a poorly made mini dress. We must have looked like two tarts and their dealer after a nasty night out.

After a few blocks, Marcus coughed but didn't look at me. "Tell everyone you pushed me off the roof. I'll do whatever you need from the shadows. I'm good at stuff nobody else wants." He rambled on, shrinking in on himself like a cat left out on the doorstep in a downpour.

It was tempting, but exile had caused this mess. I wouldn't make the same mistake twice. "You don't deserve such an easy reprieve."

He snorted. "If you think I was asking for an easy way out, you really don't understand what it feels like to live as an outcast."

I raised an eyebrow, but left that argument for another day. "You must answer to Bill."

Marcus stopped cold. "He's not dead?"

"I don't think so, not yet anyway."

"OH shi…" The colour drained out of his face. "I never wanted to have a reason to fear him, but it doesn't get much bigger than shooting in cold blood." He hung his head. "I've been a prize twat, haven't I?"

"You are vile."

He looked sidelong at me. "As long as you don't agree, he can't kill me… can he?"

Infernal, fen-sucked simpleton. I wanted the arse dead, yet could not justify it at the moment. It was another mess I'd rather not have right now.

"He has free will, just like you, Marcus. How he behaves is not under my control."

He took a deep breath, looking up at the grey sky. "I can explain—"

"That is more than you allowed him."

Marcus flinched as the words cut through his hope, but I didn't feel inclined to dance around the ugliness. My eyes kept drifting shut, and my body felt like it was made of lead.

The Rover was still exactly where I had abandoned it. There were three paper tickets fluttering under the windscreen wipers, but at least it hadn't been clamped. After opening the back door, I helped Jamie slide onto the bench. She slumped to her side as soon as she was in.

"Marcus, go around to the other side. I cannot fasten the safety belt from here."

He climbed into the passenger side, crawling across the seat like a toddler before lifting Jamie's body as I slid the nylon belt over her shoulder.

"Nooo. NO! NO!"

Her fist lashed out, catching me off guard, and split my lip. A trickle of blood ran down my chin.

"Jamie, shush, you are safe. We're taking you home," I said in my best matron tone, but she kept pounding me with her fist while twisting to the side. There was no way to attach the clasp.

"Anna, she can't recognise you. That drug makes everything fuzzy. I'd hoped it would help if the memories were blurry." Marcus ducked one of Jamie's wild swings.

"Damn it, how long before it wears off?" I asked, trying to hold both her wrists without squeezing.

"She's going to be in a hell of a lot of pain. What's your hurry?"

"At least she wouldn't be fighting her own rescue." My tone was sharp. Everything had been more difficult than it needed to be today. If this was some kind of cosmic joke, I'd missed the punch line.

Marcus pointed to fresh blood oozing from one of Jamie's lacerations. "She was quiet walking here. Let her sleep on the seat."

He was right. "Very well. It may not be the safest, but staying here is more dangerous."

I released the maid. Jamie curled up like a cat and closed her eyes. She looked contented. Marcus' cocktail must blur more than just the pain. Perhaps the mutton-head had given her a blessing.

I tossed the keys at Marcus. "You remember how to drive, don't you?"

He caught them, his mouth opening and closing like a fish on dry land. I climbed into the passenger seat, fighting to keep my eyes open.

"You're trusting me?"

"Never again, but..." I blinked and forced my eyes open. "Needs must."

"Do you think those bastards know where we are?" Marcus asked, starting the engine.

"No idea." I slumped into my seat. In all my years, I'd never faced so many problems all at once. There had to be a way to make sense of it all and plan our next move, but my eyes drifted shut again.

"Where are we going?" Marcus ground a gear and the Rover lurched forward.

"Just get us out of the city, Marcus," I mumbled.

My eyes refused to stay open, so I sank into the welcome blackness. A heavy weight lurched into my lap like someone was sitting on me. Who the hell was that? Also, why didn't they just get their own seat? Perhaps opening my eyes would be useful, but they felt too heavy.

"Ye should know the signs!" said a thick voice.

That voice felt familiar, but where had I heard it before?

"She ain't supposed to be here. How do we send her back?" said an American.

"She's not dying, she's just taken a bad turn," said the first voice.

Who was arguing? Why did I feel I should know them?

Had Marcus turned on the radio?

I tried to open my eyes again, but they were so heavy they didn't even flutter. More noises scraped and scuffled near me, followed by weight on my arms.

Blast it, were they trying to rearrange the car while I slept? Someone was in for an earful. I pushed against the seat, but there was no strength in my arm. It didn't even twitch.

The blackness pulled on my mind, dragging it deeper into the darkness. It didn't matter who was arguing. I'd rest for now and deal with it tomorrow.

Inside the darkness, waves of warmth enfolded me like sinking into a hot bath after a winter storm. The tensions I'd held all week unravelled, melting into the warmth. Nothing mattered anymore.

A hand tapped my cheek. It shifted to the other side, gently tapping again.

Refreshed, I opened my eyes to see Geoffrey in his perfectly pressed blue suit—the one they had buried him in—sat next to me with one hand on my shoulder. Outside the Rover's windows, a colourless copy of Rannoch moor drifted by. Buchaille Etive Mór's sharp crags erupted from the featureless plain like jagged horns guarding the entrance to Glen Coe. I hated that valley. Too many souls had died here.

"Finally," he said. It was one of voices I'd heard a few moments ago. Why had I not recognised him?

I coughed and got my voice to work. "Dreams, I'm out of practice…"

"Anna, don't be so stubborn." Geoffrey tapped the floor with his toe.

I looked down. How had he touched the vehicle? "I'm losing my mind. You can't be real."

His eyes twinkled. "You think you know what's real?"

After six hundred years on this earth, I should, but this week had changed everything. "I've had that stupid rock in my pocket all week. You didn't speak to me once. Why now?"

Geoffrey frowned, tapping his toe harder. "You've been mighty hard of hearing. I've been trying to get your attention for days… And you shouldn't be here. What were you thinking?"

Damn it. Geoffrey should know I didn't need or want a nanny. "What else could I do? You must have seen the state Jamie was in."

"Anthony told you to recharge, but no—you think you're invincible." He wagged a finger in front of my nose. "I've got news for you, Missy; this time you can die and if you're not careful, it's going to be sooner than you realise. Too soon to have done anything useful."

The words shot through me like an arrow. Bottomless dung pits—that would leave Glenn free to torment the world. Anthony had hinted, but nothing was ever clear in his explanations. I slumped.

"I don't even know what to avoid. It's not like I have an instruction book. Any suggestion?"

He shook his head. "We've already crossed over. Our experience will be no use to you."

Puzzled, I studied his familiar face. The moustache twitched as he nibbled a corner. I missed seeing that. "Who's we? You become royalty after dying?"

Smiling with wicked glee, he touched my hand, but all I felt was a breeze over damp skin. "Seeing as how you're so close, you might as well look. Shouldn't make you any worse."

He stood, and my spirit body floated up with him, leaving behind an empty husk that shuddered once, then fell still.

We left the vehicle and stepped into the highland mountains, but further north. It looked like the hills around my estate to be precise, but the muted, subtle shades of yellow green had fuzzy edges like an unfocused camera. Geoffrey waved his hand at a deep glen, then stepped to the side. "We—are those who followed you."

The mist shifted to show legion upon legion of men standing shoulder to shoulder on the hillside. Each face was familiar and dear to me. My knees trembled. I tried to grab Geoffrey's arm to keep upright, but passed through, and I stumbled forward.

"You are ALL here?" My voice faltered as I pointed at the valley. My translucent hand only filtered the army instead of obscuring them.

"All four hundred, eighty-seven," he said.

As I savoured faces I thought I'd lost long ago, dizziness threatened to overwhelm me. "There's a Valhalla for my fallen warriors?" I didn't smile. The joke was too thin to be amusing.

"Well… we don't have the bottomless horns of mead. Maybe you could sort that out for us," he said, his eyes glowing with mirth.

"Oh Gods, what have I done?" I whispered, covering my face with my hands. My trembling legs finally gave way. I collapsed to the ground.

Geoffrey knelt at my side. "You did what you had to with good intentions and integrity. There are plenty that have done worse, for a lot less."

"I've played with your souls without knowing." The horror of it gnawed at my gut. I hung my head, squeezing my eyes shut. "But I released you. It's part of the last rites. Why are you still together?"

He shrugged. "We're not like the other shades. It's more comfortable."

What an idiot I'd been. How could I have tangled the afterlife of these men so badly? I'd infected them with a curse worse than mine. I had never even considered that the oath could last after the grave.

Memories flashed through my head. The earth under my feet felt firmer. Suddenly fatigue crashed onto me as if roots were growing into my legs and sucking all the energy out.

"I've had more than my fair share of time on the other side. Maybe it's time I find you that mead?" I said without looking up. There was nothing I could offer that would heal this.

Geoffrey's slap sliced across my cheek like the frozen sting of a winter gale. "Damn it Anna, this is no time for pity! Remember Glenn? What he's just done to my granddaughter! How about Stefan and Tatya? What about Bill?"

I jumped up, shaking with rage. 'Twas all too apparent how many people had been hurt already and that it had been my fault. Why did he need to point it out?

"Desist, I…"

His eyes flared. "Good! There is still life in you."

I missed the meaning of it though, too angry to listen. "I know what's at stake. Do not dare to presume I am indifferent to their suffering."

"Even when the ACTION is inappropriate?" asked Anthony's soft, lilting voice.

I spun around. Anthony and Vlad stood in a dimensional door behind me.

"You are right, Mr Geoffrey. There is much business left undone." Anthony said without moving.

Geoffrey stepped closer to scratch Vlad's ears, but his fingers did not stir a single hair. "Her spirit was roaming." He leaned closer to Anthony. "Can she still go back?"

Anthony nodded. "Humans cannot live in the valley of shades, but she has not strayed completely into the valley, has she?"

Geoffrey's moustache twitched, hiding his smile, and the worry lines on his forehead smoothed out. "Ah, that's good."

Anthony frowned. "However, only those who have lived can enter. She will need to find her own way home."

I threw up my hands. "So why did you come?"

Anthony tilted his head. "We could not find you at sunset. Vladimir was worried."

"And how did you know that?"

"He told me."

Vlad looked up with eyes that pulled at my soul. "Home now. Dinner time."

His lips didn't move, but a voice had come from the dog's body. Maybe it was a hallucination from whatever Glenn had been trying to drug me with. I knelt down to study the hound. He looked the same as usual.

"Since when can you speak?"

"I always talk, you don't always listen." He licked my face and jiggled in place. "Now come on. Dinner time."

He was right, as usual. We had work to do and people who needed us.

Anthony clasped his hands behind his back. "Your body is dangerously low on energy. If you bring your spirit close enough, it will find the way back. Use the stone."

It wasn't very precise instructions, but dimensional travel was natural for him. I'd have equal difficulty attempting to teach a fish to breathe.

I rubbed Vlad's ears one last time before standing and clasped the stone around my neck. Geoffrey had said four hundred and eighty-seven. That meant Bill was still between the realms. My feet lifted. I thought of all the problems ahead, all the people counting on me, and flew higher.

The valley of shadows faded, and the hills receded into soft marshmallow shapes. They reminded me of Glenn.

That arse needed punishment. Earth would be better off without him. Medieval retributions shifted through my thoughts. None of them were horrendous enough for that vile rat-footed-toad-licker.

A hard jerk, reminiscent of falling off a runaway horse, pulled me back into my body.

TWENTY-NINE

A soft hand on my neck tilted my head, and warm salty flesh pressed against my lips. I licked once, swallowing the trickle of blood. I licked again. Ravenous, I pressed the skin to my mouth, drinking in the vitality. Icy spikes slammed into my belly.

I didn't know that taste.

I pushed the arm away. What was going on?

My eyes snapped open. Tatya met mine a few inches away. She drew back and held her bleeding wrist to her chest with a wince, then stroked Jamie's back. The maid lifted her head from her grandmother's shoulder with a weak smile.

Jerking upright, I glanced around. I was home... as much as I could call anything that—I'd lived in the gamekeeper's cottage off and on for over five centuries—, but it was not a relief. Never had so many unpledged souls fed me. What had I condemned them to?

A fire burned in the grate, keeping off the worst of the Scottish chill. Nigel, Stefan, and Marcus, all very pale and quiet, sat around the small lounge on my mismatched, careworn furniture. Memories flooded back—Men long gone to dust, naked and warm, bearded and close shorn, tall, short, all held close under blankets by the fire. Nigel's tender kisses on his first night. The many late night trysts with Marcus. Bill being carried out by his collar and belt loop after he got too drunk to stand at his first gather… The tiny building invariably felt safe and comfortable, much more so than the manor, but would it be enough this time?

Marcus lifted his head. "Good—you're awake. We were about out of donors." His words dribbled out.

I wiped my mouth, conscious of my dishevelled hair, clothes that revealed too much skin, and face smeared with blood.

"Marcus told us about your anaemia, that you needed more blood urgently," Tatya said through pursed lips. "It seemed a minor exchange for returning Jamie."

I turned my gaze on Marcus again. "Do you have any idea what you've just done?"

He exploded out of his chair, waving his bandaged hand. "You fainted. For all I knew, you were knocking on death's door! Anna, you've never been that still before! Ever! It scared the crap out of me. You needed blood, but God knows I didn't have enough. What else did you think I could have done? Even if I had called every companion, it would have been days before they could arrive. Do we have that much time?"

We didn't, but I never fed without the oath. He knew that. Bastard was causing more trouble than he was worth. "You have made another grievous error in judgement," I croaked, looking pointedly at Marcus.

He turned away from me to stare at the wall. "That's gratitude for you."

Nigel coughed. "Marcus asked my advice, Anna. You looked awful when he dragged you in. Blood was all I could think of. We all agreed to it."

I wiped my mouth with the back of my hand. "Forgive me, you should not have been asked to do this."

"Anna, you got me away from that scum bag. No biggie," Jamie said, trying to smile through her swollen lip.

I laid a hand lightly on her arm. She never would have been there if I had kept a better watch on my fellows. "You owe me nothing. This really is too much so soon after your ordeal."

I struggled to my feet, and the fresh blood pounded around my head, then worked its way to all my limbs. I held my hand out to help Tatya to her feet. Frustratingly, I was in her debt. "My thanks, it was very generous," I murmured softly, not looking at her.

She snorted, not acknowledging my words, and got to her feet by putting a hand on her knee. "It is a very archaic way to deal with anaemia," she said, holding Jamie's elbow as the girl stood up, wincing. "Why did that monster do this? Why her? Why all of us?" She stared at me, not blinking, as if her dark eyes could dig the answers out of my soul.

I could not tell her. I was not even certain I understood Glenn's reasons. "The cause is not your concern. What's happened cannot be undone, but..." What? What could I promise her? I wanted to say Glenn was a walking corpse. That was how I normally settled a vendetta. How could I make an immortal atone for his sins?

"Does this mean we're oath bound?" asked Stefan miserably from the other side of the room.

Tatya stiffened and threw a protective glance at Stefan. "This was a medical emergency. Since when did that require an oath?"

"Stefan, you have not uttered the words, so have pledged nothing." At least I hoped they hadn't. Who knew what changed my companions into ghosts?

Tatya turned to me, her voice dripping with acid. "I knew Geoffrey was in some secret club, and I am not fool enough to think it was all fun. This mess is connected."

"He was one of my donors long before he met you."

She crossed her arms, glaring at me. "No wonder I could never satisfy him."

"Tatya, it wasn't a competition. There are things I could never give Geoffrey. Marrying you was the happiest day of his life."

"Of course he was happy. He had someone at home to cook, clean, and raise the kids while going off to play with you. Like a pig in muck, he had the best of everything!"

"Not quite, I cannot… No, will not, dote on one person ever again. You shared a special place in his heart that was never in any jeopardy from me. I'm a demanding, harsh taskmistress. If you have any doubt about how difficult it is living with my rules, just ask Marcus."

"Oh, so I'm useful again, am I?" he mocked without turning to face me.

"You're a royal pain," I said through clenched teeth.

"Pot, kettle, black," remarked Tatya sarcastically.

Nigel held up a hand. "Please, there's no need for bickering."

He had a point. Everyone was on edge. A break might calm some of these frayed nerves. "Most of you are dressed in your nightclothes. Please, return to your beds. I do not wish to disturb your rest any further. We can discuss this in the morning."

"That's not good enough. I want my family safe. You tell me how you're going to do that," Tatya said.

My shoulders sagged. "I don't know. What I can tell you is that as long as you stay here, I and all my companions will protect you with our lives."

Tatya snorted. "I may not, but Jamie needs rest." She wrapped her arms around her granddaughter and arched her brows, looking between me and the men in the room. "And what about you?"

"I have some work to do, unless you would like me to assess Jamie's injuries."

"I have done that already. Although my specialism is in research, I am a fully qualified doctor. If you can be bothered to recall." She held her body rigid as she spoke, every muscle shouting 'we don't need you', but at least she was polite enough not to say it as she left.

Marcus waved. "Sleep well Tatya."

"I would sleep better with a lock on my door," she replied with a glare over her shoulder.

THIRTY

"Well, are you going to your slumber?" I asked Stefan after Tatya and Jamie retreated.

Stefan stood by the wing back armchair, shifting from one foot to the other, looking at Marcus, then me with uncertainty in his eyes. "You really OK?"

"My body is revived, and I have declared a truce with my associate, if that is what concerns you," I replied.

He finally blurted out, "What happened? Last I knew, that ass-hole had you and Bill cornered. We heard shots." He waved his arm at Marcus. "Then he turns up in the middle of the night with you half dead on his shoulder, Bill is nowhere in sight, Jamie's covered in blood, mumbling like a zombie. For all we knew, this was some kind of trick to finish us once and for all." His lower lip trembled slightly, but he threw back his head, brushing his fringe at the same time to hide it.

I draped an arm around Stefan's shoulder. "Bill and I encountered difficulty, but the situation is improving. Sometimes action must wait until explanations are complete." I glanced at the two older men. "This is not one of those times. All I can say for now is that I recovered your sister. I intend to do the same for Bill."

He shook his head once, still looking uneasy. "And what about Vlad? Where's he?"

"He'll be here soon."

Marcus rolled his eyes, flopping into his chair again. "I should have known the hound would turn up like a bad penny."

How could I explain a relationship that had lasted for six hundred years? Even if it was with a dog, that was commitment on a level mortals would never understand.

Stefan fidgeted, but he must have realised that even if he asked more questions, they wouldn't be answered. "You'll not disappear before morning, will you?"

I pulled him into a bear hug. "If I go anywhere, I'll be back before you wake."

After he had gone to bed, the habit of a lifetime reared its head. "Shall we have some coffee?" I asked Marcus and Nigel, heading for the kettle on the range.

"You got anything stronger?" asked Nigel.

I paused and veered to the solid oak cabinet in the corner. "We're in Scotland. Do you really have to ask?" I selected a one hundred-year-old whisky and three glasses before returning to the seats. "You feeling well enough for this after tonight's feed?" I held up the bottle.

Marcus' eyes lit up when he saw the label. "Ooh, certainly. Never pass up a taste of the good stuff."

"Might as well have a toast," I quipped without mirth. Light danced off the golden liquid, casting miniature rainbows on my hand. At least something looked cheerful in the room tonight.

"What happened to Bill?" Nigel frowned as he stared at the glass. "I hope this isn't a farewell drink."

I raised mine. "To hope." After taking a sip, which didn't help the pain, I met Nigel's eyes. "Bill's not dead yet, but I've no idea how to recover him."

Nigel lifted his glass. "To hope." A slight smile passed his lip, then he shook his head and downed the drink in one swallow. "I trust you. Bill trusts you. You'll find a way," he said, laying a hand on my arm and standing up. "But if you don't mind, I've had enough for one day. I'll see you in the morning." His steps fell flat; a man who had lost too many friends to force cheer in the dark.

Marcus shifted in his seat with a flush growing on his cheek. "I'd like to help get Bill back."

"Marcus, until a few hours ago, I was going to cut you into tiny pieces and have fun doing it. Do you really think I'm going to take you into my confidence now? You aligned yourself with that bastard. You turned on a brother in cold blood and generally have proved yourself to be despicable." I tapped his chest with my fingernail. "I still don't know what caused your change of heart on the rooftop, but you made a choice. That is the only reason you're still breathing now."

He set his untouched glass on the table. "Oh… I thought we had come to an understanding?"

"I've given you a momentary reprieve. IF you're trustworthy, it might be extended."

"And saving your life twice today isn't proof?" he demanded.

"It's a start."

"God, you're a hard arse," he muttered. "If you must know, I'm not sure how I hooked up with Glenn. I was en route to Stirling—as requested—when one of his cronies tapped me up in Perth and offered me a ride. Thought I'd save a few quid, so agreed. Before today, it was the oddest trip I'd ever made." He wrinkled his nose and took a sip of whisky. "They stopped the van at a stream, shoved me into the water, and I rolled out in the warehouse soaking wet, smelling of wet dog, and feeling sick. No idea what drugs they were using, but it was fast acting."

I pressed my lips together. The guards must move between the dimensions. Anthony implied Glenn wasn't supposed to be able to do that without the stone, so how had he managed? Damn it, he had too much power still.

Marcus set his glass down and looked at his hands. "Being around G felt familiar, sort of like you, but not entirely." He shrugged. "We had a few drinks, talked about life. Everything seemed to make sense. He said he could mend things." Marcus sagged.

Nausea rose as the words wormed into my belly. It never crossed my mind Glenn could appeal to my companions, but if his contamination gave me this long life, I probably had more in common with the cretin than I realised. Feculence. Was I a monster like him?

"Does not explain why you shot Bill or why you suddenly helped me. Makes you look unstable and likely to still be a traitorous bastard," I said, looking at him over the top of my glass. Conflicting emotions played across his face like a film on fast-forward.

"The day I had the two of you cornered was odd. I was so angry—furious. It was like someone had flipped a switch. I pulled that trigger, feeling I had nothing left to lose—I was the pathetic wretch you'd thrown out. There would never be a way back, and standing in front of me was this golden boy. The man who had all the luck—that life went smoothly for—

that you loved." He hung his head, then took a swig of his whisky. "I decided if I couldn't hurt you, I'd take away something that would."

My heart clenched into a lump of lead. He'd intended to use my affection against me. Arse.

"More fool you. Bill is hereditary. Your membership was my choice."

He glared at me. "I know that NOW! But that day… the world was sliding sideways. NOTHING made sense."

"You know what else makes no sense? Why you stayed with Glenn!"

"And go where? I'd wandered around on my own for the last twenty-two years. Nobody wanted me or would notice if I didn't come back."

"All I said was that you shouldn't be an active companion until you apologised. Not that you couldn't have a life and family of your own."

"You do not know what it's like being thrown out. To be told you're not needed or wanted. Being on my own made sure it wouldn't happen again."

"So what was yesterday all about? The sudden heroics."

"You're a scary bitch. You wanted me dead, and not in a pleasant way. I was too terrified to think. The smell of that place…" He looked at his glass for a long time. "When I worked in hospital, the place stank of chemicals. Smelled a whiff of that in Jamie's room…"

I shuddered, remembering the box next to the bed.

Marcus' gaze remained anchored on the liquor in his hand. "The smell brought back the day I woke up without pain. I knew I should have died of that overdose, but I was alive. Your hair brushed my face as you leaned over to say I had something better now." He paused, downing his measure of whisky for courage. "Turned out to be a curse, but I didn't know it then, and despite what's happened, you saved my life. Opportunity to do something useful came up so, I took it. I wasn't planning. Sometime it takes a few knocks on the head to let the sense in," he said, staring into his empty tumbler.

It didn't atone for his actions or explain everything, but it was enough for now. I needed to find out what was on the bullet he shot Anthony with. If keeping Marcus close gave me an advantage against those two, it was worth the discomfort.

I refilled our glasses and clinked mine against his. "Here's to good sense. May you continue to use it without further knocks to your cranium."

"I'll drink to that. You kick harder than an angry Clydesdale madam." After saluting me with his glass, he downed the dram in a single swallow.

Skritch, Skritch, scratch.

A black nose pressed against the side window. I jumped up and hurried across the room, banging my ankle on route through the crowd of furniture, then flung open the casement. If I didn't open it before he got too excited, he usually broke them.

One hundred and fifty pounds of doggy muscle bounded through the opening and into my arms, wiggling and bouncing excitedly before leaning his whole body against me in adoration, toppling us both to the floor.

I loved the way he forever acted, as if being with me was the most delightful experience in his whole canine existence. "Well done, but am I really more exciting than bacon snacks?"

"It would appear so," answered a calm voice as Anthony's long leg slid over the ledge of the window. "He is a most interesting guide. I would never have thought to smell all those lamp post without his tutelage," Anthony replied drily.

Had he finally grasped the fine art of sarcasm? I peered at his face, but it was as unreadable as ever.

"I'm sure that was most informative," I replied, attempting to match his deadpan, "but did you find Bill?"

"I have more information, but not a precise location."

Marcus regained his tongue and blurted out. "You know who that is, don't you? Why on earth is he following Vlad?"

Anthony raised an eyebrow and turned to me. "I had not expected to see Mr Marcus again."

"He made himself useful, so we have a truce. For now."

"I assume you realise your rash choice to interact with Glenn did not work out well?" Anthony said.

"It was not entirely successful."

"An understatement, from my perspective. I see no advantage gained from your action."

I counted to ten. How could he be so apathetic? "Jamie will not be harmed further. That is advantage enough."

Marcus set his glass down heavily. "God! Do the two of you ever get to the point? What the hell are you playing at, Anna?"

"Marcus, I'm going to take my visitor on a nice little walk. While I do that, I'd like to know the guests are safe. You think you're up to keeping watch while I'm out?"

"Oh, so now you trust me with babysitting?" he said through a clenched jaw.

"Between you and Vlad, I'm sure no one will come to harm."

Vladimir's ears perked up at the sound of his name. I tilted my head at Marcus. My hound trotted over and sat next to the sofa with one paw on the seat. Marcus' face drained of colour, and he swallowed hard.

"Nice to see you again, Vlad." His hand lifted, but a very soft growl caused it to drop into his lap. His shoulders slumped. "Great, now I'm under house arrest by a dog."

"You two have a delightful time," I called and pulled a long, waxed jacket out of the hall closet. I would have rather changed clothes entirely, but comfort would have to wait.

Marcus pulled a blanket off the back of the sofa, careful not to disturb my hound, and flashed a feral I-hate-you smile at me.

THIRTY-ONE

Anthony and I walked along a rough dirt path. Dozens of them criss-crossed my estate so the staff could check the sheep and coos out in the fields. It was too early to even be called morning. We were alone and, other than the trees rustling, the air was silent. I didn't want to shatter the pre-dawn illusion of peace with words, but the weight of uncertainty wouldn't rest. "How much danger are they in?"

Anthony sighed. "You have outdone yourself. I've never seen Glenn so agitated before."

"Oh, that good is it?"

"You have completely ruined our chances of concealment. Your impetuous act has left him in no doubt that you are dangerous and most likely in possession of the amulet he so desperately seeks."

"Aye, thought it might have."

"He is quizzing me closely. You made your point about not being remembered so strongly that he is literally tearing the flat to pieces to find any record of when he would have met you."

"Well, when you've got an angry wasp, why not kick the nest a few times?" It seemed I had a talent for pissing off powerful people.

"Indeed. You tell your companions to think before they act. What, if anything, were you thinking?"

There appeared to be a bit of sadness in his voice. It might have been the habits of centuries talking, but I could not help thinking he was jealous.

"My thoughts were about Jamie's abduction. That was something I would not allow any longer." I kicked at a loose stone. "Although I failed to account for exactly how different Glenn was from the average human male and ended up backed into a corner."

"You have left me in an impossible situation."

"You're not the only one. Did it ever occur to you he would just track your movements?"

Anthony waved the thought away. "He cannot travel between dimensions, and I have asked him not to send any of his associates out."

I threw up my arms in disbelief. "That's like painting a bright red X on something and saying, now don't open this box."

Anthony tilted his head, looking at me sideways. "It's against the rules."

"And from what I've seen, you're the only one playing to them. Did you see the state I found Jamie in? How could you let him do that?" I scoffed.

Anthony was quiet for several minutes as the horizon brightened with the dim glow of morning light. Sun rises were impossibly early this time of year.

"You might have a point," he replied with his head bowed. "Glenn has not shown appropriate respect for our duties."

Once again, I detected the suspicion of sadness in his voice, a slight lowering of the tone, but his face showed nothing.

"We really can't carry on meeting. I'll figure out how to get Bill back on my own."

"That is not wise. I would prefer to be able to contact you."

I raised my eyebrows. "Did you just say you would miss me?"

"I do not know what it means to miss someone, but I believe it would be beneficial to continue our conversations."

"To what purpose? You continually fail to return my companion and refuse to give me any useful way to restrain or evade Glenn."

"My original plan was that he would be ignorant of your existence. As long as the amulet was in your hands, it was hidden from him. Your anonymity was your safety. You have negated that plan. I did not have an alternative."

"Well, genius, there must be some weakness your kind suffers from."

"We have the rules that protect us from the hazards of the job," he replied with his voice trailing off as the puzzle pieces dropped into place.

"But Glenn doesn't follow the rules," I finished for him. "So what does that expose him to?"

He shook his head. "I was taught these things so long ago... Depending on his level of contamination, he could be captured for a short time, but ultimately, if he is completely saturated, he could be disassociated."

"What is disassociated? That doesn't even sound like a word to me."

"His essence would be separated from his corporeal form and then could be scattered into thousands of pieces."

"I like the sound of that. How do we go about it?"

"I do not know if it is a real consequence, or a tale to scare new officers."

I stopped, grabbing Anthony's arm. Cold seared my fingers. "Why would you need to be scared into following the rules?"

"Because breaking them is so much more enjoyable," he replied impassively, not meeting my eyes.

I shook his arm, making his teeth rattle. "How do you know it's more enjoyable? You're not willing to experience anything!"

"Glenn and I patrol the inter-dimensional borders and keep out unauthorised visitors. Your world was a holiday destination until the council became dissatisfied with outsiders interfering in your development."

I rubbed my brow. "That makes little sense. There is no evidence of activity."

He smiled at me gently. "The records are everywhere. Giants, elves, gods, goddess—nearly every creature you call myth once roamed this land, having travelled here from another dimension. They came because you can feel here. You can eat, fornicate, build, create, destroy, laugh, cry. We don't have any of that. It can be intoxicating. Some became drunk on it and caused problems. The council limited the number coming across, but that did not solve the problems. After the last prophet, which is still causing strife across your world, they halted all travel. They sent us as guardians to keep the borders safe."

"Myth and legend came to life?"

"In its simplest explanation, yes."

"This amulet you've told me to keep—that's what it's really meant for, isn't it?"

He nodded, hanging his head. "I'm an oath breaker now. We were sworn to never reveal our true nature to any native."

"That is debatable. You said I'm not a human anymore. I may not be one of yours, but I'm not necessarily a native either. Besides, you have not shown me, just mentioned it as a possibility."

"A technicality, true; however, I'm sure it counts."

I grinned, tapping him lightly on the cheek. "Well, if you're an oath breaker already, you might as well have some fun with it. Want to try anything else you're not supposed to do?" I asked, running my hand down his chest.

He jerked back, stumbling on a fallen branch. "No."

"Spoil sport. If I can't tempt you into some fun, shall we get on with the training?"

He nodded, turning to walk along the path again. "Can I assume you used the amulet during your escapade?"

I hid my smile, dropping into step with him. "I'm improving. My fireballs have more finesse, but manipulation of physical matter takes concentration. Also, I made a successful jump across space carrying two lives."

Anthony appraised me silently. "Is that all?"

"Isn't that enough? It got me out of Glenn's lair and threw him off my trail for a little while."

"So your trip into the valley of shadows didn't prove noteworthy enough to remember?"

"Oh... It went so quickly. I didn't think I needed to mention them."

"You realise there are consequences for visiting that realm?"

"I didn't make the choice lightly."

"Of course not. Just remember, you were warned."

"You're making a rather big deal about it. I only lost about a half hour of my life. That seemed a fair trade."

"Time is not a constant across the dimensions. More troublesome, you may have left a trail for something else to follow you back from the crossroads. Patrolling the borders can be problematic. Unless you erase your path, it leave a faint doorway open. I will increase my surveillance of the area."

My throat tightened. I was desperately trying to tread water in a stormy sea, but it felt as if massive waves were crashing over my head randomly. There was so much I didn't know. When would I make the mistake that dragged me under for good?

Anthony touched my shoulder. "Do not be overly alarmed. Most of the things that find a way across simply keep the tabloids in publication."

"If it's so benign, why did you bring it up?"

He shrugged. "Occasionally it isn't. I thought you might as well know that there are reasons to follow my suggestions."

I shivered, remembering the ghost stories my Nana told me as a girl. Horrible things that would eat up naughty youngsters, usually. I'd assumed they were just told to make children behave, but how much truth did they contain? My body trembled despite my warm jacket. "I won't make it a habit." Shame, it would have been nice to catch up with my companions again.

"Aside from your unapproved detours, your work with the talisman seems to be improving. Your control has developed enough, it's worth attempting to retrieve Bill now." Anthony stopped by a clearing along the track. "Ground yourself and step out of this space."

That was not a straightforward task here in the forest, but I picked a tree with a solid trunk that was mostly straight. With the amulet in my hand, I leaned my back against it, feeling the surrounding life, noting the dawn chorus as the birds woke, the sogginess of the ground seeping through my shoes, the smell of moss and pine. I let all these feelings settle firmly in my mind before stepping across the dimensions.

Anthony greeted me at the crossroads, looking exactly as he had in the natural world. Dimensional travel never took the colour or solidity away from his body.

He directed me to a pale violet-white patch of mist about six feet high. "This is the dimension where Vladimir sensed Bill, yet we could not pinpoint his location."

"What do you want me to do?"

"Picture Bill, draw all the details of his form, all the features of his face. The way he talks, the way he moves. Feel your longing to speak to him again. Put all your desires into it."

That was easy to do. The past few days had been nothing but angst and regret. I poured it into my amulet, and a faint thread grew in the grey world.

"Picture his smile, the way he tells a joke," Anthony prompted.

The line became a solid, sparkly blue colour that shimmered and bounced, reaching into the glowing mist like a demonic squash vine.

"Good, you retrieved his lifeline. I was hoping you could."

I jerked back, nearly falling over my own feet. "Hoping? You didn't know this would work?"

"I am not infallible, my dear." He looked at the ground for several minutes.

I shifted my weight. Was he being unhelpful on purpose? "What's the problem?"

Anthony shook his head and started walking. "This will lead us to Bill."

That sounded too good to be true. I stepped into the violet white mist after Anthony. We walked for a long time, what felt like hours, with nothing changing. There were no sounds. My feet did not even slap against whatever was underneath us. The mist never parted or showed any landmarks.

There was no way to tell how far we had travelled or if we had even left where we started from. The only thing I could do was count my steps—thousands of them.

"Anthony... how can we tell where we are?"

He wrinkled his brow as if it was a strange question. "We are following the thread."

I gritted my teeth at the useless explanation, but carried on walking instead of asking anything again.

After a few hundred more steps, there was a change on the horizon. A bluish glow filled the sky like a bizarre sunrise. The thread, now a ball of blue in my hands, led straight to it.

As we got closer, the glow became Bill curled up on his side as if having a nap, but made of blue light. There was no substance to him.

His skin appeared similar to Anthony's, so smooth it could have been carved from stone. My throat felt too dry. Bill looked even less real than the ghosts. "Is he asleep?"

"No, he is in stasis. There is nothing here to support his body." Anthony held out a hand. "Please, may I have the lifeline? I will keep it safe."

If this was Bill, handing something called a lifeline to a near stranger could be the end of a cherished companion. I hesitated. The ball of light pulsated in my hands, steady and rhythmic, like a beating heart. I thought of home, but the amulet did not respond and no doorways opened. Of course, it would not be that simple.

I kissed the warm ball before passing it to Anthony.

The glow skipped a pulse, then resumed its rhythmic cycle as Anthony tucked it into a pocket. I let out a sigh. Bill was still alive-ish.

Anthony stepped forward, picking up the large man without the slightest sign of effort.

A loud metallic rattle echoed through the silent fog. I leaped sideways and pulled out a dagger. My heart hammered in my chest as I scanned the mist for the source of the sound. Who knew what kind of demon might hide in the fog?

Anthony paused, then shifted Bill's weight in his arms and turned him over. A heavy iron chain looped around my companion's torso and down one leg, disappearing into the mist. Anthony set the big man down and laid a hand on the chain.

Anthony grimaced. "Glenn has found the stone."

Terror shot through me. I slapped my hands over my pockets in panic, but the amulet was still secure. I held it out to Anthony. "No, I have it here."

He smiled at me. "I should have been more precise. The picture stone. Glenn must have found it. Bill will have to remain here until I can retrieve the stone."

I sagged, the amulet dangling from my fingers. "Surely you jest?"

Anthony stood up with his head bowed. "I'm afraid we cannot return with your companion at this moment. It was not a complete waste of time, though. I will be able to come here directly next time."

Damn! Double Damned Crud Buckets. I dropped to my knees, running a hand over Bill's form. I did not know how light had substance here, but it did not matter. He was warm. I would not abandon him again.

"Leaving him here is not an option." My finger brushed the chain as I stroked Bill's back.

The links rattled. Frost formed on my hand. Bill flinched. I jerked away.

Anthony sighed. "Glenn has placed a custody band on his essence. Until that's removed, any change in his status will kill him. We can leave with a shell if that is what you desire."

Bill was motionless again; however, it was not the stillness of death, not yet anyway. "How long can he last like this?"

Anthony laid a gentle hand on Bill's shoulder. "We still have time. Do not despair until all hope truly is lost."

I started to get up when Bill's fingers twitched. He cracked open one eye. His terror dilated pupil stared at me.

My gut twisted like bait on a fish-hook. I'd have been ill if I still had food in my system.

Brushing his forehead, I leaned forward and kissed his cheek. "I'm sorry. This will end soon. I promise!"

He blinked, then closed his eye.

I got to my feet and turned to Anthony. "The sooner we get started, the sooner we free him."

Nodding in agreement, he walked away. Three steps later, we were back in the forest.

I turned in a small circle. "How did we return so quickly?"

Anthony smiled, bowing his head and looked at me through his lashes. "I told you I would be able to travel directly. It is simply a matter of knowing where."

"Very well. There are no excuses for further delays. Where do you think Glenn's hidden the picture stone?"

"Do not rush into the lion's den again, my little fox. Let me find the stone."

"You have until sunset."

He peered at me, then the sky. "It baffles me why you constantly set a deadline correlating with the actions of the solar system. Nevertheless, I shall either have success or report its lack by the setting of the sun." He disappeared.

"Damnation, I'll not trust that thing with my companion's life." However much any phrase that started with damnation would probably not end well, I didn't care anymore. It was high time for action.

I set off back to the cottage at a run. Hopefully, Stefan had slept late. I hated breaking a promise.

THIRTY-TWO

The strangest sight greeted me when I jogged up to the cottage. Tatya and Marcas sat at the wrought-iron patio table having what appeared to be a very civilised breakfast, complete with china plates, coffee in a pot, and toast racks.

I was too far away to overhear, but Tatya gestured and Marcus threw back his head, laughing. A smile lit up her face as he roared. I'd never seen her so happy.

Vladimir lay by the garden wall a few feet from Marcus' chair. Although he was stretched out in the sun with his eyes closed, the massive hound jumped up and trotted over before I even said hello.

"You hadn't fooled me, mate. I knew you weren't asleep," Marcus grizzled.

Vlad just thumped his tail against my leg, tongue out, giving me his best doggie grin, obviously enormously pleased with himself for the joke.

"Isn't it a bit early for a run?" Tatya asked.

"I could ask the same of you? I would have thought the late night warranted more sleep, not a dawn breakfast."

"We thought we would make the most of the weather. Since the rain had stopped, I suggested breakfast alfresco," Marcus interrupted.

Tatya waved at the table. "Yes, the youngsters seem to be perfectly capable of sleeping after all of last night's commotion. It would be rude to wake them, so I agreed to this nonsense."

Relief swept through me. I hadn't broken my promise to Stefan. "Impressive achievement cooking anything edible with my antiques. A lot of folk struggle with it."

Marcus wrinkled his nose. "Anna, I've spent the last twenty-some years scratching my dinner out of anything even remotely warm. That stove is the height of luxury for me."

"Well, don't let me disturb you."

"Don't be ridiculous! Surely you would like some coffee?" Tatya lifted the pot.

I fought from tapping my foot. Why was she attempting to be social? I did not have time for breakfast with my two least favourite people. I had plans that needed action.

Marcus tilted his head and looked pointedly at the cottage. Realisation dawned about why he had made such an effort preparing Tatya's breakfast.

"Enjoy your meal. I need to find more appropriate attire."

I turned and strode into the cottage without another glance at the odd couple. I needed to ring Carl. Although it was the middle of the night in the States, the sooner I spoke with him, the better. We needed reinforcements here.

In the hall, I hung up the jacket and wiggled out of yesterday's tramp clothes before pulling on an old linen dress I kept there for work in the gardens. I tucked my daggers into the belt where they belonged, then slipped the amulet around my neck. The faded, mud-encrusted, red fabric wasn't pretty, but I could move without embarrassment. Anything was better than bare arms and legs.

I tapped the keypad on the wall phone hung in the hall. Clicks echoed after each number. It might be time to update the device to something that could store recipients automatically. Dialling the long series of digits for an international call took too much time in an emergency.

The phone rang several times before it connected, clattered to the floor, and scraped. A groggy voice coughed, "Hello?"

"Carl, wake up," I said.

"Just finished a late one... Can this wait?" His words slurred as if even his voice was tired.

"I'm afraid not. We have a man down."

"Ah, it's not one of the newbies, is it?" he asked, snapping into full alertness.

"No."

"Damn... How many do you need?"

"Everyone."

"That's going to take a few days to organise."

"Get as many as you can here by tomorrow. Charter whatever you need. I'll arrange payment."

"Tomorrow? Shit, wife's gonna slit my throat. That's our anniversary."

My stomach clenched. Another life I'd screwed up. "Granted, 'tis poor timing, but Bill's life may depend on it."

Stoneware crashed in the kitchen. I gripped the phone receiver and pulled the cord as far as it would go to peer around the corner, but could not see what had made the noise.

"Coordinate with Nigel to arrange transport on this side. I have to go." I hung up on Carl. He wouldn't be happy no matter how I phrased it, so there was no point in wasting time. Someone was attacking the kitchen.

I hurried down the corridor with a blade in my hand, pushing open the heavy oak door to the large room at the back of the cottage. Stefan jumped and shoved a pile of mixing bowls back into a cupboard.

"Sorry, bit clumsy this morning."

I relaxed and eased the dagger back into my belt. He filled the smallest mixing bowl to the top with cereal, topping it with a pint of UHT milk.

"Are you planning on eating me out of house and home?" I teased, ruffling his hair as I walked by.

He ducked his head. "I really like cereal." He rattled the silverware in the drawer, looking for a spoon.

"Surprised it's still edible."

Nigel must have done some shopping. All the food I'd left would be well out of date by now. I went to the old iron range, stirred the fire, and set a kettle on top. The urge for coffee had almost made me take up Tatya's invitation. Stefan sat down at the round table in the centre of the room, crunching huge spoonfuls.

"What's the plan for today?" He tilted his head to the window. "You gonna get rid of the weirdo?"

"No. I want to keep him where I can see what he's up to. Besides, your Gran seems to be rather partial to him."

Stefan wrinkled his nose. "Ya, I don't like that much either. She should have a bit more respect. Papa's funeral was only a few days ago."

"Stef, life's too short to worry about what's proper. Trust me, it's not hurting your grandfather any."

"He's odd. Don't like him and don't like him talking to her." He stared at his bowl.

"That's the most relaxed I've ever seen her. Besides, at the moment, all they're doing is talking."

"Fine." He drew the word out and left it hang in the air for a moment as he watched the two chat animatedly outside, before turning his attention back to his cereal. "We gonna try to find Bill then?" he asked around another mouthful.

"I've already found him." I poured the steaming kettle into a cafetière.

Stefan dropped his spoon and set his bowl down with a thump. "You found him?" He craned his head to look down the hall.

"Sadly, I've not been able to free him." I wrapped my hands around the steaming jug. It might return feeling to my fingers after this morning's dew covered adventure.

Stefan slumped. "Why is this so hard?"

My thoughts circled that exact question, but it would do no good to reinforce his despair.

"I saw Bill last night. For the moment, he is alive. We must take comfort in that."

Stefan stirred absently at the last of his breakfast. "So what now?" he asked without looking up.

"Yes, what now?" asked his sister as she limped into the kitchen. Large purple bruises swelled on her cheeks and arms. She eased into the wooden seat opposite her brother, fidgeting as the hard slats caught sore flesh.

"Morning Jamie. Do you have any preferences for breakfast?"

She snorted. "Preferences? Um… kill one sick bastard, take a long bath, and drink a barrel of tequila. Maybe not in that order," she said with little energy in her voice.

My gut twisted. Torture would leave more than scarred skin on the lass. "Not surprising after what you've been through, but since all of you have come on this impromptu trip without luggage, perhaps some shopping would be useful."

She nodded, but her eyes looked vacant, as if she wasn't really listening.

Vlad trotted into the room. A large hare hung from his jaw. He dropped it to the floor, and his golden brown eyes peered into me.

"Well done. Do you want me to have it, or are you just showing off?" I rubbed his ears.

He snorted and snatched the rabbit back, throwing it in the air and catching it before giving it a good shake, then thrusting it into Jamie's lap.

Jamie slid off her chair to sit next to Vlad on the floor, stroking his back, then leaning into his side, grabbing a big handful of fur to hold him close. I think she said "Morning Vlad", but his fur muffled the words. It could have been a sob or sigh just as easily.

His tail thumped enthusiastically against the back of my chair as he lapped up the attention. She stayed like that for several minutes. When she finally let him go, a glimmer of hope glowed in her eyes again. She returned to her chair, stroking his head still.

"There are some nice shops in town. Nigel will show you. The estate has an account with all of them. Put anything you want on the tab." I didn't have time or inclination to play tour guide, but Marcus and Nigel knew the local area better than me anyway and had time to spare.

Jamie looked up as if surprised I was still speaking. "I don't care about clothes. Don't want to look good." She mumbled. "That thing... He kept pointing to Stefan's sketchbook and..."

"Clothing may seem trivial at the moment, but even in your darkest hour, it helps to cover your ass."

Her eyes dimmed again as the words brought back memories.

"I have something for you." I went to the hall and searched the pockets of my jacket, returning with the sketchbook, minus one page, and handed it to Jamie.

Her eyes grew twice their normal size as she took the worn paperback, staring at it as if it were made of toxic waste. "Why did you bring THAT back?"

I took a sip of coffee. "I assumed Stefan would want it, but I think it might be better if you direct your rage at it. Get the poison out now, rather than let it fester."

Jamie took the book, turning it over a few times. She held her hand out without looking away from the pages. "Give me your knife."

I slipped one of my daggers free and passed it over.

Jamie flipped the book onto the table and carved a stick man on the cover. She stabbed straight down several times. Precise and vicious. Five holes formed on the stick figure. Head, heart, hands, and groin.

Silent sobs shook her body.

Patting her arm, I wasn't sure what to say. Most of the people I'd helped out of a sticky situation had been men. They didn't cry on your shoulder at the end.

After what seemed like an eternity, I had the house to myself again. Getting everyone assembled had been like herding cats. I'd no sooner send one to the vehicle when another wandered off in search of god-knows-what.

Sitting down by the hearth, I poked at the fire. The morning was too warm to need it, but I liked the cosy glow. Pushing the coals around, I tried to make a pattern. Where could Glenn have hidden the picture stone? Last I'd seen, it'd rolled under a bush at the foot of the Cairnpapple. That was several hours' drive south. Glenn would not have left it there.

Had he taken it to his flat or the warehouse? He probably had other hideouts I didn't even know about. It was a lot of ground to cover, even with the help of the talisman.

Vlad stretched and shifted in front of the fire.

"How can you be cold? Weren't you whelped in Siberia?"

He rolled onto his side, moving his feet closer to the iron box.

A moth fluttered across the back of the chimney. I waved the poker at it, but it settled on the iron hook used to suspend pots over the range rather than fly away.

"How are we going to get Bill's picture-stone away from Glenn?"

Vlad cooed, a happy gurgled noise, which was not any help, and shifted closer to the warmth.

"Beggin' your pardon mistress—I can't help noticing you are sorely vexed by your missing item," chirped a high-pitched voice.

I tensed and looked around the room. All my visitors had gone. The door was firmly closed, and although Anthony seemed able to materialise anywhere, it wasn't his voice.

Vlad raised his head, looking at me in confusion as I stood up with the poker in hand. "Who said that?"

"I have startled thee, apologies."

The voice came from the fireplace, but no one should be able to come down the chimney. There was a grate over the top. I peered into the back of the fire, searching the empty darkness, and stepped back, coughing.

"Show yourself!" I wiped soot out of my eye and brandished the poker again.

"I only wanted to offer my aid." The small shape I'd taken to be a moth squeaked and stamped a foot. He had a tiny body with gigantic eyes that curved to the back of his head in an alien way. The things I'd thought to be wings were, in fact, two large leaves attached to his body like a sail.

Marvellous, another bloody mythological creature.

"Who gifts me with this kindness?" I asked. Manners cost nothing and often helped.

"Our name's not important. Do not wait for Anthony. He is tedious. If you need to find things on this estate, you should consult Urisk."

"Urisk?" That was not a family name around here. Blast, it was probably another odd creature. "I do not know this name."

The small creature giggled uncontrollably. "Urisk keeps hidden. He did not want to frighten you."

The little man flew up and did a small acrobatic loop with his glider, landing neatly on a stone ledge. "Urisk is fun, do not be afraid."

"If he hides his face, how can I find him?" Did I want to meet anyone who this pixie considered fun?

"Porridge mistress, with honey." The little man licked his lips.

"I've made porridge with honey many times, yet have had no strange guest at the table. Speak plainly," I said. There had to be more to finding this creature than simply cooking porridge.

The little man hesitated. "He could be anywhere, mistress. Leave one portion under the stairs and take another to the waterfall behind the cottage. He often hides in a little cave under the water."

"Your advice is most welcome. I will remember your aid," I said, being careful to not use the words thank you. Gran had beat the knowledge into me that you never, ever, thank a helpful spirit. Once thanked—they would leave offended, never to return.

"Good luck." He jumped into the updraught of the chimney, circling higher until he disappeared up the stack.

This day was just getting stranger and stranger. "Who'd have believed it, Vlad, a hearth guardian?" I scratched his ears again before going to find oats and honey.

THIRTY-THREE

An hour later, I set a generous bowl of porridge with honey and a small pot of evaporated milk under the stairs. The tinned stuff was not as tasty as real cream, but I had no wish to travel to the shops.

Vlad sprang forward.

"Leave it!"

His ears flattened to his skull, but the hound backed up. This part of the sprite's instructions made no sense. If the Urisk lived under the stairs, surely I would have seen him.

I waited. Nothing happened. I closed the door and pressed my ear to the wood. There were no sounds. Blast. I wrapped the second bowl in an embroidered tea towel and set off.

Vlad and I walked behind the cottage, following a well-worn dirt track. Bright green bracken grew on each side like a prehistoric forest of ferns. I liked to come out here at night. The sound of the water helped me meditate, and it let visitors sleep undisturbed. Even companions used to my nocturnal wanderings tended to be unsettled by it.

Balancing on large rocks, I picked my way out to the middle of the rushing stream. The stones ran out halfway across, and I stepped into the burn. Cold slammed into me, instantly numbing everything below the knee. Fighting against the current, I thrust the bowl through the cascade, splashing down the cliff face. Fur brushed my fingers, taking the bowl out of my hands.

I stumbled backwards. Loose gravel on the stream floor rolled, shifting under my numb, clumsy feet. My wind-milling arms didn't help. Icy water rushed over my head and filled my lungs. The torrent tossed me into a cauldron carved out of the rock under the falls, smashing and tossing me repeatedly into the pit until I had no idea which way was up. I struggled to coordinate my limbs enough to push off the rock and swim.

A large hairy hand grabbed my arm and lifted, tossing me over a shoulder. My nose pressed into fur the colour of burnt toast, and the overpowering smell of damp wool wrapped around me. We crossed the stream in two giant steps. My saviour set me down on the muddy bank opposite where I'd started.

Vlad barked loud enough to wake the next county. Bloody hound. I waved at the frantic dog to signal I was alive, and the creature was not a threat. Vlad stopped barking, but continued to pace and look for ways to cross without swimming. He hated getting wet.

I forced my heart to moderate its tango beat and looked up. If it stood up straight, the creature would easily be eight feet tall, hairy, and lumpy. The fat square nose stretched out enough to give his face the appearance of a goat-like muzzle, and tiny horn buds stood out on the sides of his head above long earlobes that flapped when he moved. No wonder the creature kept out of sight. The thing wasn't pleasant.

His back hunched, and he looked away as if embarrassed. Could he read my thoughts? It would not surprise me after everything else I'd come across in the last two days.

Coughing, I forced my chattering teeth around words. "Thhhhhha..." Realisation slammed into me like a boot to the belly. This creature could be fey. I pressed my blue lips together before starting over. "That was most kind; may I know the name of my benefactor?"

"You may call me Urisk, and the debt is mine. You slipped while bringing me that fine food. I will make a fire to dry your clothes."

I held up a hand to stop him. "Clothes are a minor concern at the moment. A companion of mine is trapped. To free him, I need to find something. I've been told you could help me?"

Urisk wrinkled his muzzle. "The brownie... He delights in sending folk to ask for favours." He shook his fist at the hill, where the top of the cottage's chimney was just visible.

My stomach dropped. I should have known things wouldn't be that easy. What a waste of a day, making porridge and trekking down here for that damn sprite's sense of amusement. I really needed to be more wary of offers of help.

"Forgive my intrusion. I will take my leave."

Urisk's hand settled on my shoulder, preventing me from walking away. "I did not say I could not help, just warning you that house-elf has a cruel humour. What is it you wish to find?"

I looked up at his fuzzy face. Long hair obscured his eyes, yet he watched my every twitch and blink like a dormouse afraid of a broom strike. What could frighten such a beast?

I glanced around. The only sounds were the distant bleat of sheep. Not even the wind stirred the trees.

"I'm searching for a small white stone the size of a quail's egg, transparent with an image of a man made of blue light." My god, that sounded far-fetched.

Rather than laugh, Urisk nodded and scratched at his ear. "I know of these eggs. The wardens make them when they put a soul into stasis."

"You know the wardens?" I hugged myself tightly to hide my shaking hands. Either cold or fear had got to me. How could there be so much to the world I had never seen?

Urisk hunched over further, crouching as if he was trying to shrink into the hillside. "I know of them. I try to ensure they do not have a reason to speak to me."

"Oh... you won't be able to help, then." My head sunk against my chest. Everything felt too heavy. If a giant didn't want to face Glenn, what hope did I have? One more life ensnared and mangled by that bastard. "I regret wasting your time."

Urisk sucked his breath in. "No... you didn't flee at the sight of me." He sighed again and turned away. Fur silhouetted against the dark forest quivered. "No one has spoken to me in a very long time..."

Urisk paused, scratching a pattern in the dirt at his feet, then nodded to himself. "I know of a place where the warden keeps important things."

A butterfly of hope tickled my belly. "Tell me. Anything you know, however small, will be a great aid."

He shook his head. "I cannot speak of it; however, he has not paid me for services rendered. It is my right to seek restitution."

Services rendered to Glenn—by an eight-foot monster. A chill ran up my spine. Had he caused the sticky brown mess at the warehouse? Was that part of the sprite's joke? To watch as Urisk ripped limbs off and devoured them? Stop—my imagination was running wild. That was the road to ruin.

"What did you do?" I asked.

He looked away. "I move things. The fat one cannot travel on the light bridges himself."

"Nothing else?"

Urisk shook his head, and his shoulders slumped. "I did not know they were your friends."

What a relief. At least the giant did not admit to being a thug, and it explained how my companions were transported from America. "There is much worse that the bastard could have requested. I hold you in no contempt."

Urisk turned and smiled. "One moment." He splashed into the stream and disappeared under the waterfall.

Vlad stepped back, then took a flying leap and splashed across the water. He ran up the bank, stopping long enough to shake his long fur hard enough to soak me through a second time.

I tried to pat his head, but shivers shook my hands so much I could not hold them steady. Everything along the bank, absolutely every branch and leaf, was soggy. There was nothing suitable to make a fire with. Surviving in the Scottish weather was never straightforward.

My fingers turned a pale, waxy yellow colour. Not good, not good at all.

I called fire into my hand. The flames settled into a golden ball, cosy and comforting until the acrid stench of charred flesh fouled the air. I slapped my sizzling palm into a puddle. That had proved to be less than helpful. What good was having the means to manipulate the universe if I did not know how to go about it?

Urisk splashed through the waterfall, showering me again.

"Bless me, that was quick."

The edge of his muzzle curled into a grin. "The fat one is powerful, but dull witted." He passed the picture-stone to me.

I cradled the milky sphere in my palm, watching Bill's reclining form. Air faded from my throat. For all that he looked peaceful, it was not restful slumber. "He's still alive," I whispered, stroking the image.

Urisk nodded. "Stasis is quite a safe way to transport criminals. What did your friend do to offend the warden?"

I chuckled. "Nothing. It was a temporary withdrawal from a bigger threat."

Urisk shook his head with a slapping noise as his ears flapped against his neck. "It's not pleasant. I've never heard of anyone but criminals going there."

"It wasn't planned." Or was it? A shark bite of fear ripped through my stomach. Was Anthony trying to control me through my companions? "Tell me what you know of it."

"It is the place of nightmares. When dreams stray there, you wake up before harm. The stone prevents his escape."

Anthony hadn't told me that. What else was he keeping from me? My fingers closed around the stone, along with my resolve. To hell with Anthony and his risks. I'd free Bill myself. "You have given me a grand prize. How shall I repay you?"

"Visit again with the tale of his rescue." Urisk clasped his hand over mine. "It will entertain me for many years."

I bowed to the large man-beast. "Done. I will return with the tale of victory." If I somehow survived, of course.

His lips pulled into his odd misshapen smile. "I will make sure that stupid sprite never forgets this. The Lady chose me to do her favour."

"Why do you call me that?"

Urisk bowed low enough as his forelock touched the ground. "Even if you choose to live in the gatekeeper's cottage and are often absent, I know the Lady of Sir Richard, Lord, and founder of this estate."

I swallowed, forcing the shock back. He could recall Richard? Laid to rest nearly five centuries ago, I hadn't played at being the lady of the manor in nearly as many years. "How long have you lived under these falls?"

He spread his arms wide, his eyes watching things lost in the distant past. "I found this cosy place when the hills were wild and giant deer roamed the lands."

Giant deer? Those had been extinct for thousands of years. I blinked several times. His millennium made me look like a grade school child. How could I have missed him?

"Grandfather, I'm honoured that you remember me. Until we meet again, go in peace." I bowed before starting up the hill with Vlad.

Urisk stood waving until we disappeared over the crest, but his revelations would never leave my mind. Older than me, older than the wardens, older than any living creature on the planet. Where did he come from?

THIRTY-FOUR

After Urisk's warning about the house sprite, the forest felt safer than my cottage. I returned to the spot Anthony and I had strolled through last night. It was quiet. None of the estate staff had any reason to come here and no tourist would bother scrambling through the bracken since there were no landmarks in sight.

However, even the safest location was better with an alarm. I knelt by Vlad.

"Keep watch." I said and pointed in the cottage's direction.

He arranged himself facing the building, alert and braced, then still as a statue. He wouldn't disturb me unless a threat arrived, but could I hear him in another dimension? For that matter, would I even be able to get out in a hurry? There was still so much I didn't understand.

The picture stone rested warmly in one hand. I stood and shook myself, banishing the doubts. Now was not the time to think—it was time to act.

Images of the dull murk of the crossroads filled my mind, and I stepped forward. A faint blue glow led to the violet patch of fog lingering from our last trip. The blue line was dim, but appeared more substantial if I peered at it out of the corner of my eye.

Perverse world.

I set off walking with Bill's image firmly in my mind, looking at things sideways. The fog felt cloying and sticky. I coughed, forcing a breath in through the suffocating murk. It hadn't been like that last night.

I marched on. I finally had a way to rescue Bill. The discomfort didn't matter.

After just ten steps, the line had dimmed so much it was nearly impossible to detect it in the murky fog. I stopped and turned my head. Crud-buckets, it really was getting fainter.

I broke into a jog, then a run.

Something brushed my arm. My heart leaped into my throat. Invisible fingers clasped my sleeve, pulling me away from the trail. Fear slammed into my gut. The line was so faint, I could hardly see it.

I planted my feet and jerked my arm. The unseen force pulled again. I stumbled to one knee. Teeth snapped and chattered in the mist. What the hell was that?

I pulled out my dagger and swiped at the noise. It felt reassuringly solid in this land of nothing and the blade parted the fog long enough to see large things with too many legs and mandibles instead of jaws surrounding me. The fog closed in again, returning the fake comfort of solitude. My knees trembled, and I forced a breath. Would cold steel cut here? Urisk called this the land of nightmares. The gargantuan insects may have no more substance than what my mind gave them.

I stood and turned my back on the noise. The chittering grew louder.

Do not look. Do not.

I marched away, retracing my steps and following the faint life line. The noises faded into chirping. After a few more heartbeats, the blue line, as pale as the watery November sky, melted into the fog.

"NO! No, no, no—Not again!" I shouted and sprinted toward anything that looked slightly more bluish than the murk.

I stumbled but didn't stop. The ground fell out under me. Sliding, twisting, falling.

I shifted my weight, scrambling to keep my feet under me. Where was I?

Blue light reflected off the fog all around me. I turned in a circle. There he was. I'd found him—without Anthony.

I dropped to my knees and ran a hand down the side of Bill's cheek. A shaky laugh bubbled up. Anthony's help wasn't needed. I'd done this all by myself.

My giggle faded into the gloom as if the mist wanted to stifle all mirth.

"Time to go home," I said.

Bill's eyes opened briefly, then he shuddered and squeezed them closed again.

"Can you get up?" I asked. He didn't respond.

I draped one of Bill's arms over my shoulder and stood with his six-foot frame leaning against me. Just. Bill looked like a hologram. How could he weigh so much?

Damn, this is where Anthony would have been useful. I took a step forward. Bill didn't. It was like dancing with a stone doll. Oh, hell!

I knelt back down, slid more of Bill's weight across my back, then fought to stand again. A fireman's carry was easier, but the leaden weight would be impossible to move far. I inched forward with a step.

There was no rattle of chains. I took more steps, just plodding with one foot in front of another. Was I still on course?

I glanced up. My heart somersaulted. There was no line, no trace of blue anywhere.

Confound it!

I should have left a better trail.

I slid Bill to the ground and patted the marshy surface for any trace of colour. It was completely gone. I peered into the mist, then kicked at it, stomping a circle. All remained a formless, uniform violet mist. Chattering noises clicked in the fog.

I turned around. Where was Bill? Feck-Feck-Feck. My heart thundered in my ears. Had those bugs taken him?

After pacing back, I counted my steps and tripped on something soft. I sank to my knees and pulled the obstacle up. Bill's toe poked through the mist.

I fought the urge to kiss it. Thank the heavens, my luck must not have run out completely. I patted along the length of him until I found an arm, then pulled Bill into a sitting position. I'd drag him home if I had to, but for the first time in centuries, I had no idea where to go.

I hugged Bill's unconscious form, seeing my own arms on the other side of his blue shape. Good gods, that was odd. Damn it, everything about this was odd and now I'd lost the trail.

Feculence!

Gallows humour perchance, but the church's ancient requiem rose to my lips. Dies irae, dies illa, Solvet saeclum in favilla: Day of wrath and doom, Heaven and earth in ashes unending… Was this the last judgement? Was I one of the saved or had I already been cast down?

A claw swiped out of the gloom, slicing across my face and ripping me out of my melancholic musing. More razor-sharp claws appeared, slashing without aim, connecting only by chance.

Anger coursed through my tired limbs. There were too many for one knife, but—by all the saints—I'd make them regret attacking us. I leaped up, dagger out. "Foul pestilence! Meet the bringer of war!"

My knife whipped and cut, matching every movement with sudden steel. The things didn't squeal, didn't bleed, didn't even seem to notice the amputations. Every damaged insect disappeared into the gloom, only to be replaced with another. To keep him safe, I straddled Bill's unconscious form, which limited my attack, but I kept one foot touching him, anyway. After all I'd been through, I would not lose him again.

The chittering never stopped, and the fog didn't lift. There was no way to tell if I was making any progress. I hacked and slashed with pure fury as my only fuel. Of late, there were too many problems with no solution. Simply keeping the blade moving at least required no thought. It felt good. The talisman flashed in my pocket, burning my leg. Damn, I wish we could simply step back to the cross-roads. I lopped off another long claw coming for my knee and dodged a swipe at my shoulder. A pile of iridescent black claws grew at my feet.

I grabbed a claw and stabbed the next bug betwixt its six eyes. It juddered, and the edges of its form blinked in and out of sight as if being erased from a canvas. Grabbing another claw, I stabbed it again. A slow vibration rocked the cylindrical body. All colour drew into the wound. The bug became a colourless shell with no more substance than the fog. The thing waved its antennae as if trying to scent the air.

The chittering stopped. I drew back, pulling Bill with me. It seemed to be blinded.

The beast rumbled away, the thousands of feet sinking into the marshmallow ground with dull echoing thuds as it trundled. No new insects took its place.

Were they all gone? Did they have homes to go to? Home. Would I ever see it again?

A thought surfaced. It was so simple. I could not return by following Bill's lifeline because he was here. I needed to call up one already at home.

There was no one I knew better than Vlad. Hopefully, a dog qualified for a lifeline. I pictured him sitting in the forest, heard his furious barking on the river bank, smelled his stinking liver breath in my face, felt his wiry fur under my hand. When all these were anchored firmly in my mind, a pink line tinted with gold appeared. It glowed and shimmered the same way he bounced when he was happy.

It was beautiful.

Anthony had returned to the cross-roads quickly. Could I do the same? Dragging Bill upright, I held the amulet with one hand and struggled forward without looking back. The violet mist faded into the ghosted outline of the forest. We'd made it back to the between zone.

I stumbled through to our reality and slid Bill's blue form to the ground. It weighed almost nothing here. Vlad leaped up, nosing my hands, then sneezing heavily. I dropped the picture stone. It'd done its job and was empty now, but still warm. I patted Vlad's head.

"Probably best you don't lick me. Bug juice tastes foul."

Now what? Bill was still just a hologram. When I'd rescued Marcus, all I had to do was nudge him into his body, but Bill did not have a body.

Vlad walked around, sniffing. He whined and scratched at the ground near Bill's head, his paw visible through the pale blue outline. Could my hound see the shape? Vlad licked the picture stone, then whined at me.

I picked it up and glared at the rock. "Wake up Idiot."

The translucent stone grew. It became the size of a melon in a matter of seconds. A heavy melon made of lead. I set it down and backed up. It continued to grow. The sleeping holograph reached out to the growing white stone. Vlad nosed the stone, pushing it closer to the light form. The two merged.

Stone filled with the colours of life, transforming from translucent white into a living, breathing companion.

Bill coughed.

I helped Bill sit up. "I thought I'd lost you."

His head snapped around, eyes darting left and right. "Where are we?"

"We're in the thicket near the cottage." I ran my hand down his naked back. A shiver racked his shoulders. He needed to warm up, yet there was nothing to wrap him in, and the ground was too damp for a fire.

A faint chittering noise echoed through the trees. Confound it! Had something followed us? The sooner we could move, the better.

"Can you stand?"

He jerked, looking behind him, then at me. "Aye, there's bracken in my crack."

I helped him up, and we set off. By the blessing of the fates, the cottage was not far away. It'd do him no good to wander the Scottish highlands naked.

Bill limped along, kicking pine cones out of his way. "What—the fuck—was all that back there? I could hear things, feel them brush against me, but couldnae move."

I rubbed his arms as we walked, trying to get some warmth back in them. "Apparently you were in stasis. It kept you alive, but I don't know why you were put there."

He squeezed my hand. "I saw you. Was it real?"

"I came last night, but Glenn had locked your form."

"I've nae idea what that means, but you came. I'd almost given up."

It took twice as long as normal to get back to the cottage. The sun was low on the horizon when we rounded the last corner, but the building was still silent. Thankfully, the rest of my mismatched crew were still shopping.

I opened the door to the cottage and let Vlad trot in before us, then twisted to the side to help Bill in. It was so good to feel him again. I didn't want to let go, but forced myself to step back once he was inside. He took a seat by the fire.

"Wrap up in that blanket," I said as he sank into the frayed cushions of the armchair.

"Aye, that's better. Wee Billy had nearly retreated into my bawbag." He grinned at me and flashed the covers open.

As nice as it was to hear him joke again, the rest of the group would be back soon. I snatched a decorative kilt off the wall and threw it at him.

"Put that on, little man."

"Who you call'en little?"

I stirred at the coals and didn't answer. My limbs felt like sticks of wood. Did I have the energy to make a fire? I pictured a cosy hearth on a wet winter's night. The fire stuttered to life with a feeble flicker. Good, all it needed now was a little extra fuel. I still felt like I was dragging lead weights instead of arms. This needed a gallon or two of coffee. I turned, Bill slouched in the large chair.

"You look like you could do with a drink. Whisky or tea?"

He smiled at me. "I've just survived the most traumatic event of my life. What do you think?"

I patted his hand and pulled down the kettle. "Tea it is then."

"Aye, Hen. Tea it is."

THIRTY-FIVE

The cottage door opened, and high-pitched giggling filled the room.

"You bastard!" Bill shouted over the sound of his seat crashing to the floor.

I dropped the kettle and spun round. Bill's fist lashed out like a viper, sending Marcus sprawling to the floor before I could get anywhere near them.

Tatya screamed, dropping to her knees like a ballerina instead of a grandmother. "What are you doing?" she leaned over Marcus, scrabbling to find a tissue for the blood.

Nigel flung a hand to his nephew's chest. "Easy Bill. There's no need for fists."

Marcus blinked and held his nose. "Let me explain," he gasped.

Bill nudged his uncle to the side. "Out of my way. I dinnae want to hurt ye."

He grabbed Marcus by the ear, lifting him to his feet one handed and pulled back for another swing. Marcus scrambled to get his feet under his weight and kicked a boot into Bill's stomach. Bill grunted, twisting his grip on Marcus' ear.

"GENTLEMEN, take it outside," I shouted, pointing to the door.

Bill let go of Marcus and, not so gently, prodded him to the door.

Tatya watched them leave, then shouted at me. "What kind of barbarians do you keep around here?"

Stalking toward the door, I glared at her. "Honourable ones—like your husband. Don't forget that."

Jamie stood just inside the door with her mouth open slightly, halfway through the joke she had started but now forgotten. I patted her shoulder on my way out. "Put the kettle on, dear. This won't take more than a few minutes."

She nodded and looked as if she was going to ask something, so I quickly pulled the door closed behind me.

Outside, the two men stared at each other. Bill squared his shoulders, flexing his fist repeatedly while Marcus stammered gibberish. Moving between them, I laid a hand on Bill's arm. "He's a bastard granted, but currently he's our bastard."

His seething eyes hardened. "You do not know—"

"What it felt like? Bill, stop and think for a moment. I have a pretty good understanding of captivity and the terror it creates. I also know beating the snot out of Marcus will change nothing."

"That cock-womble intended to kill me! I'm gonna tear his head off," he said, his tone low. The menace hung in the air.

Marcus' face drained of even more colour. He held up both hands. "Bill, I wasn't in my right mind. Let me explain."

I squeezed Bill's arm. He didn't even glance at me. His fist clenched in time with the pulse throbbing along his temple.

"Bill, I won't order you to stay your hand. A brother tried to kill you in cold blood, you have his life as forfeit if you want it. What I will caution is that you are not, at this moment, in your right mind. Think before you act."

Bill yanked his arm back, shaking off my hand. The fury in his eye dared me to step in his way. "Hen, he pulled the trigger. I dinnae want to see his face, let alone have it named brother."

I stared back into the depths of Bill's icy, unblinking eyes. "But brother, he is, regardless. Your fury doesn't change the fact."

Bill narrowed his eyes and spit on the floor. "Nae brother of mine. I dinnae want that shite-bag guarding my back."

I glanced at Marcus. "True. Nothing restores innocence lost."

Marcus threw up his hands. "None of you ever trusted me. And you won't listen this time either. Probably best if I just disappear. Easier for everybody that way." He turned with slumped shoulders. "

I slammed the heel of my boot into the ground. The crack on stone echoed off the eves. "Marcus! You told me you were tired of running." I pointed at the patio chairs. "Now, both of you, sit down!"

Marcus slid into the closest chair, hanging over the left side as far as possible, while Bill perched on the edge of his ready to spring up again. I took a breath to settle my voice into a calmer tone. Why did so many of my companion's arguments feel like squabbling chickens? Couldn't they see we had bigger problems?

"There was a spring day, about twenty years ago… when a rather younger set of the two of you sat like this outside my lodge in Yorkshire. I think it was Bill's second or third gather?"

Bill nodded, dropping his head as pink rose to his cheeks.

I gazed at him, letting the flush bloom. "You remember how Marc took the blame for you that day? Was that something a coward would have done? You were such a gangly youth it wasn't surprising you regularly broke things, but the wilful vandalism... that was beyond compare."

Bill smirked, his lip twisting into a half smile. "You've nae been to Glasgow after an old firm match."

"And how about the time you decided my curfew was just too early? That there was much more fun to be had in the pubs down the road. How Marcus tried to keep me occupied the next morning to cover up the fact that you were still so drunk you couldn't walk. Doesn't sound like a coward or runaway to me..."

Bill slammed the heel of his palm onto the table. "Fucking ancient history. Nae of that measures up to murder."

"Remember when you told falsehoods? Made it sound as if everything was Marcus' idea. You poured on the charm thick enough I almost believed it. That day, you monumentally erred, and Marcus had every right to beat you for your deception. He refrained."

Marcus shrugged. "You were a kid who didn't know any better." He turned to Bill. "That day in the warehouse, it was like a different person was at the wheel. It was me, but it wasn't. Life sucked, nothing mattered, there was no way to fix it..." He hung his head, muttering, "It was complete bollocks."

"You have your head on straight now?" Bill asked through clenched teeth.

"I don't know. This is the clearest I've been in years..., but it always comes and goes in waves."

Had the odorous soil-stain addled his mind with too many recreational drugs? Perhaps I should have dropped him off the cliff when I had the opportunity. I couldn't have a mad dog inside my pack.

The sun slipped below the horizon. The gravel driveway behind me crunched.

"Anthony, punctual as usual," I said.

His measured steps stopped at my elbow. "I see you've been impetuous again."

Bill sprang to his feet, pounding his fist into his palm, and stepped too close to Anthony. "You! You put me in that shite-hole."

Anthony raised one eyebrow, but remained at my side like a statue.

I lay a hand on Bill's shoulder, pushing him back toward his seat. "Save your energy. Fists won't have any effect. Besides, sending you to that place saved your life, however unpleasant it proved to be."

He gave Anthony a look of loathing, but returned to the cast iron chair. He stood next to it and ran his hands over the back, testing to see if it was weighted correctly to throw or swing.

Anthony traced a circle in the air. "They are quick to action."

"It's a human response. You wouldn't understand."

"No, I don't. I also don't understand why you seem so keen to do the same. I advised you not to approach Glenn again."

"I did not need to. The stone came to me."

He tilted his head a fraction of an inch and peered at me. "How? I'm fairly sure you have not mastered trans-location to that degree."

"You shall have to be kept in suspense about that." It was nice to have the upper hand for once.

"As you wish, you have proved surprising about many things. However, do you know if this really is Bill?"

"Who else would it be? I followed a blue line through the dimension the same as when I went with you." I crossed my arms. The trip to recover Bill was definitely more difficult, but I was not going to admit that to this infuriating creature.

"As I told you, the first time you ventured into the unknown by yourself, there is much you cannot see or hear. Much as an infant can see no reason to avoid eating a dishwasher tablet that looks like his favourite treat; all he sees is that they are soft and gummy. He does not understand they have the potential to kill." He frowned at me. "You were supposed to wait."

"Bill had lingered in that abyss long enough. Once I had the stone, there was no reason to delay."

"No reason?"

Anthony's shoulders dropped. Pausing for several seconds, he just stared at me with sad eyes that bored into me, drilling to my core. It was worse than any inquisitor's knife. Why was he taking such an affront that I had acted independently?

"You do not know the hazards." His barely audible words filled the still night.

I swept my arm out across the horizon of my damp glen, devoid of any monster other than Anthony. "We returned safe. Neither of us perished. One must take risks or accomplish nothing." I suppressed a cringe. Marcus had used those very words to goad me into action a few days ago.

"You are not dead but as for damaged... that might take a while to be apparent."

"Damaged...?" Cold gripped my core. Why did Anthony drip feed information? Was he my ally, or was I an expendable peasant?

"For a start, I would like to check you are free of unauthorised entities. You could have brought back a hitch-hiker."

I couldn't help smirking. "I hope it doesn't take as long as the virus scans Carl does on all the computers."

"This is more like a tick check after you have taken a walk in the forest. There are many things that like to feed on the tasty flow of a human mind. You are a delicacy in many dimensions."

I fought to stop myself from scratching involuntarily. Why the hell hadn't he told me that earlier? "Oh, well... that would be appreciated. Next time we go walking in the woods, give me the entire story."

Anthony took his amulet out of his pocket with an air of calm serenity. "My dear, if I told you all the horrors you cannot see, I'm not sure you would ever get out of bed again."

Great. Absolutely great. Stupid rock was bringing even more nightmares into my life.

Anthony held the stone over my feet. It glowed red, a red so deep it was only a shade away from black, translucent and shiny; it pulsated slowly. As he moved the stone up my body, it occasionally flashed gold so bright it blinded before the stone returned to its original colour.

"Interesting," he murmured, looking at the stone.

"Interesting how? What did you find?"

Distracted, he glanced up. "Nothing to worry about. You are clean." He then turned to Bill. "Stand please."

Bill got to his feet and held out his arms, making a T shape. "Time to delouse the dogs."

Anthony started with the stone over Bill's feet. It glowed with a sparkling bright turquoise blue of the sea on a sunny day. As he moved it up, the blue occasionally had flecks of gold, but the colour remained blue throughout.

Bill dropped his arms. "So—any wee beasties?"

"No, you are clean," replied Anthony, still staring at his amulet. "That is what worries me. These reading show an unauthorised presence, but it is not on either of you." He jerked to look at me with suspicion. "Did anyone else go with you?"

"Of course not. I don't even know how to do that. Maybe your readings are confused." I kept my voice light and unconcerned, despite the hammering of my heart. Crud buckets. If he poked too deeply, he might find Urisk. That would be a very poor way to repay the creature's aid.

Anthony looked at Marcus. "Stand please."

Marcus flinched. "What? I didn't go with her. I was playing tour guide all day."

"Nevertheless, you need to be checked," Anthony replied.

He stood reluctantly with his arm out. "Fine, do your chakra scan. Can't see what you expect to find. That old charity shop was full of dirt and spiders, but I doubt it had anything else living there."

When Anthony held the stone over Marcus' feet, it glowed with a dark midnight blue writhing with streaks of purple. As Anthony moved the stone up, there were the occasional gold flecks on him as well, but at Marcus' neck the colour became heavy purple streaked with red. Anthony halted. His amulet pulsated quickly, flashing between the purple and red. Eventually he continued to the top of Marcus' head, where the colours returned to blue.

Anthony's whole body sagged while he looked at the colours flashing in his amulet. "If you did not accompany Anna into the abyss today, when did you cross the border?"

Marcus' eyes widened. "I've been to England a few times. What the hell does that have to do with this?" His voice rose to a squeak.

"My apologies. I was not referring to a land border. I have found a creature that should never see the light of your sun. It is an abomination. Though how it made you its host is still a mystery." Anthony circled Marcus, waving his stone up and down as he walked. "When the amulet was in your possession, did you ever do anything with it? Perhaps fall asleep and have an unusually vivid dream?"

"No, I found it in a bothy chimney, thought it looked cool, carried it around for a few days before posting it to Geoffrey... No dreams, no unexplained out-of-body experience, none of that airy fairy shit."

"Glenn put it there," I said.

"It could be; however, we only have circumstantial evidence. I refuse to believe he would put one of those in a human."

"One of what?" I asked, exasperated with his vagueness.

"It is a creature that lives at the base of the spinal cord. It sends out tentacles that grow into the brain's cortex, feeding from the energy generated there. As it grows, the creature learns what creates the most energy, stimulating those areas more and more. Fear is the first sign, anxiety attacks usually. As it grows, the creature discovers anger, then sadness. Causing more and more irrational behaviour as it matures."

"If they're forbidden to this world, how do you know so much about how they feed?"

Anthony grimaced. "There was a time when travellers could bring them across as an amusement. It was fashionable to grow up suitable trophies and stage tournaments," he replied.

Bill's face twisted like he'd just been offered turd canapés. "And you call humans barbaric."

Anthony looked at the floor as if the tall man wished he could shrink inside his own skin. "There is much my people have done that I'm not proud of."

Marcus tapped his head. "Uh Hello? Man with brain bug here! What are you going to do about this thing?"

"I will attempt to remove it if you wish," Anthony said.

Marcus flung his hand out before slapping his chest. "If I wish? Uh… FUCK YEAH! You think I want this thing messing with me?" he shouted.

Anthony resumed his impassive statue stance. "It is a delicate procedure. Please calm yourself."

Marcus paced between the chairs. "Calm? You expect me to be calm? You've just said I have a thing eating my brain. That's not the sort of news you take casually."

Anthony brought his fingers together and slowly tapped them, one after another. "I really do need you to be absolutely motionless."

Marcus snorted and stomped back to the garden wall. "Get fucked! I'll say whatever I want! Just get the thing out, NOW!"

Bill looked at me with one question on his mind. When I nodded slightly, he stepped forward with a smirk.

Bill's lightning fast right jab smashed into Marcus' chin. Marcus stumbled, eyes rolling back, then slumped to the paving slabs with a sickening crack of bone on concrete. Anthony watched Marcus fall. He was fast enough. He could have stopped Bill, but he remained motionless. Only after Marcus' head hit the pavement did Anthony turn to Bill.

"Was that necessary?" Anthony asked.

"He's calm and quiet," Bill replied. "You did nae say awake."

"Indeed... I will have to be careful how I word things around children. It would have been useful to have him coherent. There is less chance of permanent brain damage."

Kneeling down next to Marcus, Anthony gently rolled him onto his side and placed one hand on the back of his neck, supporting his head with his other hand.

The hand on the back of Marcus' neck became very pale, merging with the skin before ponderously proceeding. Anthony flexed his arm slightly, small, subtle shifts in position until we heard a soft squelching pop from somewhere inside Marcus' head.

My stomach flip-flopped, but morbid fascination kept me from turning away as Anthony removed his hand. Something writhed and squirmed, emitting a high-pitched shriek as it was exposed to the air. The blood covered thing didn't appear to have any eyes or mouth, just a tubular body ending with long tentacles that whipped about wildly.

"Poor Mr Marcus. He did well to keep any of his senses with this size intruder. It is fully mature. He must have suffered for many years."

Festering bunions of filth, Glenn had corrupted Marcus years ago, maybe decades.

Bill leaned forward, peering at the squealing thing.

Anthony held up his hand. "Keep your distance. This creature is hungry and desperate." He took something that looked like a fancy cigar box out of his jacket. When he opened it, there were no sides or bottom to the box, just the starry night. Anthony popped the creature in the box and snapped the lid closed.

I clutched at my skirts, wrapping my hands in the folds to conceal my trembling. Those stars were not in any sky over earth. There were no constellations I recognised.

"Did ya get it all?" Bill asked, wiping his hands on his kilt.

Anthony frowned and looked pointedly at Bill. "Most likely, although I will need him to regain his faculties to prove it."

"Smelt fucking rank, nae wonder his head was rotten," Bill said.

Anthony's frown grew. "I have things I need to attend to. I must go."

"What do we do with Marcus?"

Anthony stood up. "You are a doctor, are you not? Treat him for his head wound. I will be back after I have delivered the creature to its rightful home." His image shimmered, then faded to grey before disappearing completely.

Bill snorted. "Rude cock-splat."

"Anthony doesn't seem to understand polite. That's as good as you're going to get from him."

I knelt down and hooked one of Marcus' arms over my neck. "Come on, we'd better get him inside."

Bill took the other arm, lifting with more care than I'd expected. A thin red line pulsed on the back of Marcus' neck. The only evidence of his recent cure. Rousing slightly, Marcus blinked a few times, and although his head slumped back toward his chest, his legs held.

We stumbled to the door. "You know Tatya is going to have you on her shit list after this," I said.

Bill shrugged the shoulder not supporting Marcus. "Not my problem, but I'll do my best to be charming."

Damn it, he was good at charming, but Tatya excelled at vinegar. "I do so love these quiet family weekends."

Bill chuckled. "How would you ever survive the boredom without us?"

He had a point. As aggravating as life was at the moment, it certainly wasn't dull.

The moment the door creaked, Tatya jumped up, shooing Bill out of the way to lift Marcus' head.

"He has a concussion. Are you happy?" She peered at me with an unblinking stare. "Letting them brawl like school yard brats. What kind of woman lets folk behave like that?"

I pasted on a smile. "A woman who learned long ago men are men and no one can change that."

She shook her head. "Give him to me. You have a habit of getting people beaten." She glared at me, drawing out the words as she spoke, making sure she pronounced each one loudly and clearly.

Marcus blinked again and moved to the edge of the sofa, gingerly feeling the back of his neck. "Is it gone?"

I nodded, but didn't really know. I certainly hoped it was. Damn it, why had Anthony run off rather than make sure?

Tatya bustled back from the hall, pushing by me with a first aid kit and a glass of water. "Take these." She held out two white tablets then put bandages, that really weren't needed, on his nose. "That will have to do. I'll make some tea to help with the nausea." She patted his shoulder as she got up, stalking out of the room without asking if anyone else would like a drink.

As the evening wore on, Marcus continued to improve. Before long, was chatting like the others. Although he looked shaken and tired, there was no irrationality or missing language skills. That was a relief.

Slipping out of the room, I went into the kitchen. I needed a celebratory coffee.

Stefan tiptoed in behind me. "What happened?" he whispered excitedly.

I tried to hide my smile. His youthful eagerness made a refreshing change of pace. "Bill and Marcus worked out their problem." I didn't want to explain the whole brain-sucking squid story.

He made a long face, pulling his hands across his cheeks. "Did you see how he laid into Marcus? I know Bill should be pissed, but he was always so cool. Is he really OK?"

I set a hand on Stefan's shoulder and turned him to look at me. "Remember, what you see isn't ever the complete story. Bill is one of the most amicable men on this planet, but if you do step over the line—you'd better be good at running."

I looked through the doorway at Bill, casually telling one of his famous stories. His charm had obviously worked on Jamie. She leaned so close she just about hung off his arm. Tatya remained slightly stiffer, sitting protectively close to Marcus, but she was smiling.

Warmth flooded my whole body.

The enforcer—my wolf in sheep's clothing—was back. Damn, that felt good.

"I have got to get him to show me how to do that." Stefan swung an awkward punch in the air.

Without thinking, my hand snapped out and blocked his sloppy missile. "My little grasshopper, who do you think taught Bill?" I folded my hands and bowed slightly.

He scrunched up his nose. "Seriously? You?"

"Six hundred years of practice… imparts a level of skill there are no words for." I whipped my dagger out and held it a hair's breath from his eye before he could move. "I never intended to learn so many ways to maim, restrain, and terminate, but it is useful."

He stared at me, ashen faced. "Good thing you're on our side."

Tremors squeezed my gut as I sheathed the blade. I was the only thing protecting this mismatched crew, yet none of my skills would stop Glenn for long.

THIRTY-SIX

Eventually, the house settled into the stillness of night. Everyone had wanted to speak late into the evening and only reluctantly sought a bed when eyes refused to remain open. Vlad sat next to me in front of the fire while I poked the embers and mulled actions into plots that would not work. I knew they wouldn't. There were too many facts missing to begin an effective campaign. Unfortunately, inaction wasn't an option either.

The gist of the problem was that Glenn wanted the amulet and my demise. Secondly, he was immortal, so my usual methods were less than useless.

"Mistress, you still look sorely vexed. Did you have no luck finding your item today?" asked a high-pitched voice, his amusement barely contained.

Damn, the bloody trickster was back. "Quite the contrary. My quest was successful."

The pixie fluttered out of the chimney and perched on the mantle. "Oh... that is good." The sprite sounded disappointed.

If he enjoyed tricks, I couldn't let him get the better of me again. "Yes, your advice proved to be most wise. Truly, you are a useful ally."

The little man puffed himself up. "We are full of knowledge. Do you have more questions?"

I had to tread carefully here. Clearly, this creature knew of worlds within worlds. If I could tease the substance from the chaff, even his tricks and jokes may offer insight. It was worth asking.

"What do you know of the wardens?"

He flew a small circle, landing on my shoulder. "Quiet mistress. We mustn't speak of them. We mustn't bring his wrath here."

"Dear sprite, is it possible to track a warden? To capture one?"

He flitted about, looked left and right before landing in my ear. "Look at the spin."

I was about to ask more when a loud scream followed by a thud made me jump. The sprite flew up off my shoulder, zigzagging to the back of the hearth, where he perched on an obscure ledge in the stonework, watching with wide eyes.

Marcus snorted, then rolled to his side on the sofa. A few moments later, Bill walked unsteadily down the hall. Bare chested, clad only in a pair of black tracksuit bottoms, he flopped into the chair next to me. Without looking up, he stared into the golden glow of the fire. For a man who'd been to hell and back, he looked amazing. My hunger growled.

Sadly, we'd already had too many feeds this week. I continued to poke the embers, putting on another log.

After a few moments of silence, I asked, "Nightmares?"

He nodded once. "Aye... dinnae think I'm going to sleep for a long time." He rubbed his arms, but I knew he wasn't cold.

"Bill, it will get better."

He looked up, his eyes damp. "Nae... I don't think it will. I dinnae want to be alone in my bed, and there's no one who will share it." He shuddered, whispering, "We all die alone."

I knew that feeling all too well. Facing the final curtain call in solitude raised a primal terror in the soul. I leaned over and wrapped an arm around him. "It's not much, but I'm here now."

He clutched tightly, burying his face in my shoulder. "That'll do."

Shame I could not simply move in with him until these fears eased. But even without the fact that it would kill him, we were too different. For heaven's sake, he didn't even remember the great war, or a time without electricity, much less a time before printed paper. Good God... one of the few things we had in common was the loneliness.

As his arms loosened, I patted his back. "Come on, a bit of night air will do us both some good." After wiggling free, I walked to the door and threw a coat at him. He shrugged into it while hopping around putting on a pair of boots. Vlad nipped at the flapping fabric before dashing out the door.

The weather had shifted again, and the night was cool for this time of year. Icy puddles on the path reflected the moon as we walked. Bill strolled along, scuffing his feet to toss sticks ahead for Vlad to chase.

"Nigel wouldn't admit it, but he was getting tired. Thanks for getting him out of here."

I shrugged my shoulders. "Somebody needed to meet Carl at the airport. I'd like to get the twins and Tatya somewhere safe as well, but I don't know if there is such a thing anymore."

Bill picked up a bigger stick and tossed it into the shrubs. Vlad leaped the bracken, bounding into the undergrowth after it.

"Tricky that. If you send them away, that nut bar could just nab them again. Might as well keep them somewhere close enough to watch."

"That's what I'd thought, but it's going to get messy. Maybe I should've sent them with Nigel."

"You never second guess yourself. What's up?"

"I've no idea how to handle dimensional beings. Anthony's given me a few clues, but they're not much help."

Bill scowled, throwing a stone along the path. "You think he's on our side?"

I shrugged. "I don't know, but what else do we have to work with?"

He stopped, grabbing my arm to spin me round to face him. "Not a lot, but that arse made my life a nightmare. No pun intended. That place he left me in was hell."

I stroked his cheek with the back of my hand. "I know, Bill, but I've seen where the other option would have left you. That's a one-way trip, my dear. At least you woke up from the nightmare, and I didn't have to say goodbye yet."

He lent forward, pulling me close. His lips pressed hard on mine, desperate. I stiffened for a moment before returning the kiss, holding him tight. Who knows, maybe this was the endgame. Would it even matter tomorrow?

Vlad crashed back through the bracken, knocking into the back of my leg with the stick. My beloved pet had awful timing.

I leaned down, grabbing the stick with one hand without letting go of Bill's waist. Vlad tugged back, breaking our embrace.

"Not now. Find someone else to play with."

Vlad growled, glaring back at me while scratching at a dark patch of ground.

Bill knelt down to examine the path. "It's blood." He looked up at me. "A lot of it."

"I thought this night couldn't get any worse." I looked at the dog. "Well, you found it. Where does it go?"

He woofed and dived into the undergrowth again. Wrinkling my nose, I picked up my skirt to follow him.

The trail wove over and under things rather than going in a straight line. It gave me the impression of someone trying to hide, not a creature fleeing in panic. A shaggy brown shape darted into a bramble thicket in front of us. It was the size of Urisk, but was it him or were there others of his species out here?

Bill grabbed my arm, holding me back. "What the hell was that?"

"I think it's a friend."

Bill shook his head. "Like hell. I know these woods. There nae animals that big here."

I patted his arm. "That fellow maybe the reason some sheep won't go in the field at the end of the cottage. I passed by his home for hundreds of years and didn't know about him until yesterday."

Bill narrowed his eyes. "Go slow. Anything in pain can be dangerous."

I waved at the figure. "Urisk, may I have a word?"

There was no answer. Not an enormous surprise, since he wasn't used to visitors.

Stomping aside some thorn branches, I edged closer. "Are you well? Do you need help?"

The bedraggled and tangled brown lump was motionless. Although I paused between each step to give him time to say something, he remained mute. My hand settled on his shoulder. "Urisk?"

"You mustn't go back, m'lady." He ducked his head, which seemed even more misshapen than the last time.

"Mustn't go where?" I asked.

"The cottage. Oh, how I've dishonoured you."

His eyes darted left and right. The moon glinted off something... tears, perhaps?

He hunched over further, pulling his arms close around himself like a fur blanket. "The trap's been set, but you mustn't walk into it."

Bill edged through the bracken, fist poised to strike. "What is happening?"

Urisk hung his head, a shudder shaking his whole body. "I should have held my tongue, but he is so…"

I ran my hand down his shoulder. "Turn around... please."

The large man-beast shuffled around, hesitating before taking each step, as if he were loath to lift his feet. When he faced me, I could see why. Each toe twisted at a sharp angle to where it should be.

"Sit." I pointed to a large tree stump.

Bill clenched his fist again. "That's gotta hurt," he whispered.

I inspected the cuts, bruises, and multiple broken things. My heart sunk into a pit of black contempt.

"This is not just a beating, Urisk. These injuries amount to torture. Did Glenn do this?"

He was the only person I knew of that would want information about me that badly.

Urisk bit his lip, but didn't deny the accusation. Stinking crud buckets. What next?

"I've got a small first aid kit in the Rover. You want it?" Bill said.

"There are a few plants growing here that will offer some relief." I wasn't sure if human herbalism would work on this creature, but it was better than nothing and quicker than running two miles back to base. "Bill, look for some of these." I showed him the rounded leaf and began trudging through the thorn bushes to the water.

Anger powered each jerk of my hand, ripping leaves from stems. Just how many more injuries—how many deaths?

Instinctively, I reached out for Mine. Marcus was asleep. Had he been drugged or was Urisk mistaken about the siege? I tried to reach Stefan and Jamie. They were only vague flickers that showed life—nothing more—but at least they were alive.

Returning from the water's edge, I separated the leaves into type.

Urisk's furry hand brushed mine. "Miss, I know of these things. You must not waste time on me. The cottage will be overrun. You must escape. Flee into the hills," Urisk waved his hands at the rocky crags, "or back into the between land. He cannot find you there."

A small flicker of panic nibbled my stomach, urging me to follow that advice, but I remained kneeling at his feet. "Nonsense. I never leave a friend in trouble."

Bill set his pile of herbs next to mine. He lingered, laying a hand on my shoulder with a gentle squeeze. "Never."

Urisk hiccuped. "That makes my deed ever more vile. I can never repay you, miss."

I patted a damp leaf over a broken toe. "Shh Grandfather. Do not trouble yourself with worry over who owes who. That line of thought often brings argument. Instead, tell me why Glenn would not find me in the between land."

Urisk sneered. "He's grown too..." A hiss seethed through his teeth when I got too close to a missing toenail, cutting off his words for a moment. "Glenn is too rotund to travel."

That information could be very useful, more so than poor Urisk realised. If I could travel places Glenn couldn't, perhaps I could use that to ensnare him.

I patted another leaf around the next swollen toe, being mindful of where I placed my fingers. "But if he cannot jump, how did he corner you? I saw you disappear into the between lands when you retrieved the picture stone."

Urisk slumped even further, looking at the ground. "I was just doing my tasks. I have obligations of service to him," he replied, dispirited. "He tricked me into leaving the water."

Bill slouched to the ground in between us, scratching Vlad's ear. "Obligations? That sounds dodgy."

Urisk's ear twitched and flattened to the base of his skull. "He said I will be deported if I do not do these things. This is my home now; I have no wish to begin aimless wandering again at my age."

The pieces clicked into place. That must be the real reason he kept his face hidden.

While wrapping lengths of soft moss along the cuts and open wounds, my mind drifted back to the other part of his advice. "You mentioned a choice, that I could flee to the hills. Why?"

His ears twitched forward. "The hills are alive, miss. Find the circles. Speak to the stones, they know the places." He drew his breath in with a wheeze. "I'm not educated, miss, but I know the land. The circles are loops. Once you go inside, it's different from outside."

His advice made no sense. Perhaps the pain had addled his brain. "Can you walk?"

With a groan he stood, then wobbled enough it looked like he was going to land on Vlad.

Bill scrambled to his feet, wrapping an arm around the furry torso to steady him. "Don't need another casualty. Let's get you home."

The brown giant, looming almost three feet over the top of Bill, patted him on the head. "Ah, good boy. That would be very kind."

Bill caught my eye as he brushed a tendril of fur away from his nose. I bit my lip to stifle a laugh. Poor dear. First trapped in a nightmare, now treated like a favourite pet.

The four of us lurched back to Urisk's watery lair with no further interruptions, where we left him to recuperate in safety.

Bill climbed up the bank of the stream after me, looking at the waterfall with a strange twist of a smile. "You tell no one about that. I'm nae good-boy." He nodded up at the chimney of my cottage. "What do you make of his warning? Think there really is a trap?"

I pursed my lips. "He hasn't lied to me yet, but he was acting befuddled."

Bill grinned, poking my arm. "So you're not planning on running off into the hills to hide, then?"

I smiled and slapped his hand. "What, and miss all the fun?"

THIRTY-SEVEN

We set off through the forest, avoiding the known paths to the hilltop by following wild animal tracks. The sun just nudged the horizon when we got to a flat spot overlooking the garden patio of the cottage. The back of my neck prickled. While the dim pink glow cast over the quiet building was pretty, something wasn't right. A shadow hung over the kitchen, which should have been getting the first of the morning light. Great, fecking great.

Bill sank to the ground next to me, propping himself up on his elbows just as unrecognised voices whispered in the dawn shadows below us.

"Och… get a move on. It's freezing out here."

"On yer bike. G said wait. I'm waiting."

"Dinnae be a poof."

Vlad sprang up. My hand darted out without thinking, hooking his collar as he tried to bolt.

He froze with his hackles up, lower lip curled into a vicious snarl.

The voices continued to bicker in the gloom. The cottage was under siege, with at least four entities waiting somewhere in the twilight. They were most likely outside the kitchen door, but were they waiting for me or a sign from Glenn?

Bill leaned close, his breath tickling my ear as he whispered. "Outnumbered two to one. Not great, but could be worse."

"There's something else down there. Not human and definitely big."

He peered at the building. "I dinnae see it. You sure?"

"It's casting a shadow over the entire kitchen. I think it's pretty safe to assume it's not the cleaning lady."

Bill drummed his fingers on the ground. "Rather storm the place than wait about. Had enough of that in Perth."

My stomach tensed into a ball of iron. Whatever caused that shadow would not be friendly. "You're right, we can't wait. Death before arrest," I said flatly.

Bill jerked as if he'd been slapped, rolling on his side to look at me. "Fuck-sake, you cannae be serious. That's only for oath-brothers."

"What other choice do we have? We've seen the way Glenn plays." There was no way I'd let any more innocents suffer that abuse. A clean death was at least quick.

Bill shook his head. "No way. You got me out. Surely you can get them out?"

It'd nearly killed me jumping with Jamie and Marcus. Could I even make four jumps with passengers? Bowing my head, I sighed. They were unpledged souls that had fed me. I owed them. "It's worth a try."

"Right, that's settled." Bill slapped the ground. "Anything's better than having to bump off Tatya and her bairns."

I hid my grin. He didn't seem too worried about Marcus' fate. "Bill, I'm going to need a diversion while I get them out."

He nodded, cracking his knuckles. "Nae problem. Trouble's what I'm good at."

I ran one hand through Vlad's coarse neck ruff and leaned down to press my face close to his ear, taking a deep breath to savour his earthy smell. "Attention."

The dog's focus snapped, every muscle quivering with his eyes focused on mine. I pointed to the cottage. "Follow Bill."

The deep amber eyes blinked and turned to watch Bill.

I took two steps back into the forest, didn't need to, of course, but old habits were hard to change, then ran at the cottage and flung myself off the hilltop. I plunged toward the ground, biting back my battle cry, and focused on all the warmth and protection of the cottage in my mind's eye. A doorway through the dimensions opened, and I landed on the floor of the smallest bedroom, rolling to one side with my dagger out.

Stefan bolted upright in his bunk at the sound of my landing. I motioned for him to follow me. He hesitated, holding the sheets close to his chest.

"Get up!"

"I don't have any clothes on," he said with a flush.

I threw a pair of trousers at him. "Hurry."

He pulled them under the blanket to put them on without exposing any skin.

I snarled and yanked the covers back. "For God's sake! I've seen hundreds of winkies." As he struggled to fasten the snap, I reached out for the crossroads. The grey space was easier to find this time. I jumped into the between land with no warning.

He stumbled as we landed, trying to do his fly one handed, then looked around startled. "Where are we?"

"Sorry, no time to explain. Got to get your Gran and Sister. Don't wander off." Reaching out to the cottage's other bedroom, I misplaced the jump slightly and landed in the hall. Thankfully, it was quiet and dark.

The faint sound of throaty growls followed by screams penetrated the stone wall. Bill's diversion had started. It wouldn't last long, though. Running across the hall, I flung open the door to the second bedroom and nearly crashed into Tatya, putting on a robe.

Jamie sat up, blinking. "What's all the noise?"

I shook my head. "Trouble. I need to get you out," I said, pushing back a few bits of furniture and pointing to the clearing. "Over here"

Tatya wrinkled her brow, turning away from me. "We need a window or door to escape."

Boots pounded and crashed just a few feet away. I wrenched the old woman's elbow close to me. "Step forward!" I commanded, reaching for the grey space and jumped.

Tatya stumbled once, her face pale as alabaster, speechless for the first time since I'd met her.

"Stef, your Gran's in shock. Look after her while I get Jamie," I said, thrusting Tatya's bony arm at him.

The jumps between the cottage and the grey zone were more reflexive now. I just thought of the bedroom and squeezed my mind's eye like some sort of mental blink to shift back.

Jamie clapped as I arrived in the room, bouncing on her toes. "How did you disappear with Gran? It was so cool!"

Confound it! She thinks this is a game. Marcus' medication was working a bit too well on her.

Outside, dark shadows moved quickly across the window. Too fast and too damned close to the unprotected glass.

"Jamie, take my hand," I shouted, grabbing her the moment she was close enough, and jumped into the grey land.

In the earth realm, the bedroom window exploded inwards with a shower of glass as my dimensional doorway faded. Two henchmen jumped through the broken pane, stopping long enough to rip the sheets from the bed before storming into the hall.

My throat clenched, stopping all breath. Bill couldn't hold them all on his own. Even with Vlad, he was badly outnumbered.

I let go of Jamie's hand. "You should be safe enough for now. Don't move until I get back." I turned to go, but the life force I had sensed by the patio doors oozed into the grey zone from the cottage.

It had no obvious substance. It was just a charcoal cloud with two darker dots near the top that could be eyes. Malice seeped from it. It was trying to outflank us.

"Jamie, get behind me," I said steadily, turning to keep between it and my group. The void darkened when it moved. The thing writhed, growing to two yards wide, then shrinking down to one at random.

Jamie peeked over my shoulder. "Ooh, a brollachan. Awesome."

I jerked to a halt. Did she still think this was a game? Had the torture fractured her mind that badly or were Marcus' analgesics clouding her thoughts?

The brollachan shifted to the left, taking advantage of my momentary distraction. I sidestepped, blocking it again, but the eyes were close enough to touch now. "Did your book say how to get rid of it?"

She squeezed my shoulder. "Oh yeah, fireworks!"

Of course—nothing subtle. I drew up the forces of light and heat, directing them into tiny pinpricks of light, exploding them in a dazzling array of colours inches from my nose.

Jamie clapped her hands once and punched the sky. I heard Tatya gasp, but she held her ground. Unfortunately, so did the brollachan. It hadn't even flinched at the display.

Crud buckets. I'd have to turn up the intensity. Pouring heat and light into one dense sphere, I let the pressure build above its head before finally pulling away my containment. The cannon ball exploded with a thundering boom and blinding flash of light.

The dark cloud shrank in on itself, fading back towards Earth.

"That was sooo cool," Jamie said. "Can you teach me to do that?"

"Maybe later." I smiled weakly. Exhaustion threatened to pull my leaden limbs to the floor, but I pushed it to the back of my mind. "We need to get you somewhere safe. Take my hands." I pictured my mountain bothy, a haven of security. I focused on the feel of rough wood and the smell of peaty smoke. Once they had formed a ragged circle, I jumped.

Calling it a jump would be an exaggeration. It was more like a drunken lumber. We lurched sideways with a stomach dropping intensity before landing in a clump. Each one of us floundered to stay upright, and the circle broke.

Stunned and dressed in nightclothes, they were completely unprepared to be here. Had I just taken them out of the pan and into the fire?

"You should be safe here." I nodded at Stefan and Jamie. "Think of it as your first field assignment. I'll get someone to come for you as soon as I can."

Jamie took a deep breath, tapping Stefan's arm. "I was a girl scout, we'll be fine." She kept smiling, but Stefan looked worried.

I jumped back before Tatya could begin an argument. I didn't have time for answers.

Guttural roars and heavy slams emanated from the lounge when I landed in the cottage hallway. Outside, the loud bang of gunfire echoed. This was quickly sliding from bad to complete excrement. I sprinted down the corridor. Marcus had his back to a corner, flanked by two thugs. They wielded long blades, doing their best to finish him, but he blocked each swing with a broom handle. A third man lay on the floor with a field knife sticking out of his neck.

Credit where it's due. Marcus hadn't lost his touch after all the years of exile.

The element of surprise would only work once. I aimed a lightning fast kick to the knee of the closest thug. As he fell, I grabbed his head with both hands and snapped sideways. He dropped without a cry.

The remaining man looked between Marcus and me before throwing up his hands. "Fuck this. He ain't paying enough. We's just supposed to surround you's. Not get killed."

I shook my head. "Easy enough instructions, even for you. So why exactly are you inside?"

He pointed to the first corpse. "Eejit said he heard something. Thought we should check it out."

"Congratulations, you've checked it out. Not going to look good to your boss, though. Most of the residents are gone," I said.

He flinched at that, glancing around to see if Glenn had turned up already.

I moved closer. "Now then, since you've broken into my home, shall we have a little chat?"

My little sprite flitted out of the fireplace, buzzing past my ear. "The fat warden approaches!"

The thug jerked back, but Marcus hovered behind him, prodding with the broom handle.

I pulled the criminal close enough to meet his eye. "Shady jobs never pay well enough, dear boy. I'm sorry." I snapped his neck with a quick wrench before he could reply. Shame to end such a young life, but the creep had taken up with a monster and tried to kill my family. "Well done Marcus. You managed fine without me."

"I'm not dead yet, if that's what you mean. Battered and bruised to hell and back, but not dead. Damnation, where were you? I heard Vladimir barking ten minutes ago." Marcus kicked at a piece of litter.

The sprite's eyes darted to the cottage door, and he zipped back to the hearth, clinging to a sooty brick the furthest away from the light.

My heart jumped. This could be my chance. "Marcus, quit grizzling. Come with me."

I hurried into the kitchen, fishing out the spare propane tanks from the back of a cupboard. There were only three, but it would probably be enough. I opened the tap on one. "Put those two in the lounge with the taps open."

"You do understand we're surrounded and this will turn the room into a gas chamber?"

"You worry too much. I don't plan on being here long."

He took a cylinder, grumbling under his breath, and we returned to the lounge.

I leaned inside the fireplace again. "I must ask a boon, you who are master of this hearth."

The sprite swelled and flew down to the front. "Master? You called me Master! What is the favour?"

"Torch it." I said the words quietly, for they tore a hole in my heart. Hundreds of nights. Hundreds of golden memories soon to be lost—all because of one bastard.

The sprite flew in a small circle. "Burn it down? It is my home." His circles decreased in small spirals to land on my shoulder.

"You love a mischief, do you not? This will catch the warden in a fine jest." I said, stroking the little man's head with a finger. Another stab of loss threatened to change my mind, but the promise of catching Glenn in the blast was greater. "Once we're gone, wait for the fat man to open the door, then light the largest fire you can." It might not kill the bastard, but it should slow him down.

The sprite's green eyes flew open, twinkling like emeralds. He set off around the room, emitting little sparks from his abdomen. I lunged and caught him gently in between my hands.

"That's a fine display, sir, but you must wait until we're gone."

Marcus stopped in the doorway with a second tank. "Did I just see a moth emit sparks?"

"Show some respect. He's doing us a large favour." I opened my hand to let the sprite out. "I promise, little one. Once you do this, I will rebuild the cottage and there will be porridge with honey every day for a year."

The sprite grinned and flew off with another spark and puff of smoke.

"Marcus? Take my hand."

Marcus raised an eyebrow but held out his hand. I felt the familiar grey of the between land, pulled it closer to me, then leaped through the crossroads and over to the forest in one enormous rush. It felt like I was dragging heavy bags of sand with me. Things ached that I didn't have words for.

I fell to the ground, heaving in a long, slow breath. I wouldn't be able to do that again until I'd fed, but at least we were out.

Marcus gulped and wiped a hand over his brow. He had the travel sick look I'd seen on Stefan a few moments ago.

"I guess you don't remember your first jump."

He rubbed his mouth and swallowed. "The first time? No, all I remember about that was being scared to death, literally." He managed a small grin. "You really should warn people about that first step. It's quite a drop."

I rolled onto my knees and crawled the last few feet toward where Bill crouched with a pile of pebbles and an improvised slingshot. He rolled a round stone between two fingers, watching the cottage so intently he didn't hear us. Then the earth shook. A wave of heat washed over my shoulder with the deafening boom. Good God—That was magnificent. The wee man packed quite a punch.

Bill leaped out of his hiding place with an ashen face.

"For fuck's sake! What the?"

I stood up. Vlad looked at me and thumped the ground with his tail, but didn't get up. He panted heavily, and blood covered his fur. Bill broke into a huge grin. He stepped over the bracken, scooped me up, and swung me high into the air, before planting a firm kiss on my lips.

"Fucking know how to scare a man!"

"How fare thee?"

"Aye, we're surviving. A few wee bumps for me, but our mate here got a kicking." He rubbed Vlad's shoulder affectionately. "Took that nasty shite out, though. Didn't you?"

Vlad's tail thumped the ground harder, and he grinned his tongue-out doggie smile.

I knelt down, tapping the ground. "Forever the hero, aren't you?"

My hound recognised he was going to get a treat and shifted closer with a slow three-legged limp, but his tail never stopped wagging. He wolfed down all the snacks I had with me and sniffed my pockets for more. I ruffled his ears, then stood up, but he continued to snuffle around, checking that I wasn't hiding anything.

"You can't be hurt that badly if your stomach's the top priority." I rubbed his ears again. He was putting on a show, but the poor guy had a laceration from shoulder to rib on his right side. It would take a while to repair that much damage.

Bill nodded toward the cottage. "What happened? Who blew the house?"

My stomach fell into my boots. How could the sprite have mistimed the blast? "You didn't see Glenn go in?"

Bill shook his head. "Didn't see him, but we were watching the back. He could have been on the other side."

Surely the sprite wouldn't destroy our home without the quarry in sight.

Confound it, the wee folk had a twisted sense of humour. Had he warped my words? "We'll have to check once the fire's out." My legs trembled with fatigue. "The twins and Tatya are at the bothy. They're going to need supplies and a guide to get back." I sighed and sunk to the ground. "And of course, there's the small matter of getting rid of the big Glenn permanently."

Bill grinned and clapped my shoulder. "So, not a lot then. You could be free by teatime."

He consistently tried, but the joke couldn't even lift my eyebrow, let alone my spirit.

Marcus spun round. "Chaps, you're not going to like this," he called in a shaky voice. "Bloody hell, what is that thing made of?"

THIRTY-EIGHT

Glenn's rotund figure lumbered from the still blazing cottage, smoke rising from his shoulders as he looked up the hill and pointed directly at me.

Crud! Fetid Brown Crusty Crud! Adrenalin spiked a sharp lance through my stomach, quickly replacing my fatigue. What next? That direct explosion should have bought us a few days at least. What would it take to stop the bastard? Hell's inferno?

I jerked my head toward the forest. "Get to the top of the ridge. You remember the old mourners-way up the back?"

Bill nodded.

"Take Vlad. I'm going up the high road."

Bill grabbed my arm. "We have no ropes."

I grinned at him and shook off his hand, sprinting from the cover of the foliage. "That's why I'm not asking you to do it."

Vlad and I had hunted here for hundreds of years. The deer trails never really changed, so we reached the top of the hill easily.

Unfortunately, Glenn crashed along not far behind us. The higher we climbed, the closer he seemed to get. How was that even possible? Urisk said his size was a problem, but it didn't seem to hold him back now.

The track levelled out where steep cliffs encircled a flat grassy patch the size of a small tennis court. Hidden to the right of the rough stone wall was a path that zigzagged to the top.

I nodded to the easier route. "The sooner you get around the bend, the less likely fat-boy will see where you've gone."

Marcus and Vlad carried on running, but Bill hesitated, lingering by my side.

I pushed him toward the faint trail. "I know already. Don't worry, I'll be careful."

He clenched his jaw, muttering about infuriating, daft, old-birds, without using any term nearly that polite, and sprinted to catch up with the other two.

Glenn stomped into the opening with a purple face and heaving chest. He pointed at me. "Ya! Thieving Bitch! Give me the stone."

I took the amulet out of my pocket, brushing dog biscuit crumbs off it. "All this effort for a chunk of old rock?"

"Give it back, we go easy." He paused, and a manic gleam passed through his eye. "Don't give it back—I have fun."

I nodded. "I've seen the effects of your fun. You've obviously had plenty of practice… Toes are an unusual choice."

Glenn grinned. "Fur ball had it coming."

"For what? Doing your bidding for centuries?"

Glenn laughed hard enough to turn a darker shade of purple, slapping his leg to get a breath in. "Shaggy bastard's fun. Moron was here before wardens. Can't deport 'em unless he screws up, but he still jumps when I bark."

Glenn circled closer. I backed up toward the cliff, trying to avoid the smell of tobacco heaving on his breath.

"Ya! But you... you have my property. I can do as I like. I should submit you to my pets."

A shudder pinched my stomach. Memories flipped between the tank in his flat, and the shrieking bloody squid in Anthony's hand. Pets indeed! "You gave up any rights to the amulet when you began mistreating humans and ignoring your duties."

He smirked and shook his head. "So you think you know my job? I don't keep nut bars out. I'm here to keep the nuts in." A gleam twinkled in his eye. "And I really like my job."

Was he telling the truth? Were they really here to keep human prisoners? I took another step back. "You and Anthony seem to have very different ideas about your job description."

"Two sides, one coin. Enough talk. Stone back—Now." Glenn held his hand out.

I closed my fingers around the amulet, waving it at him. "No, a friend gave it to me. This stone is MINE now."

A warm glow radiated up my arm. The stone flickered red and gold between my fingers before returning to its normal dull grey. I'd never seen it do that before, but really didn't have time to question it now.

He sprang forward. "Good, we get to play."

He was big, but not terribly clever. I ducked and spun under his arm, dancing away. He tried to grab a second time, but I twisted again, putting my foot in front of his and using his own momentum to send him sprawling on the ground. Out of habit, I suppose, I stepped forward to kick him in the temple, but he grabbed my foot, lifting and sending me sailing into the rock wall with an explosion of blue electricity.

Wheezing my breath back, I jumped as high as I could. Thank the saints, I'd climbed this in the dark. My hands landed on the hold I knew was there. I pulled up sharply to keep my momentum, getting my foot out of his reach and kicked against the wall to stop the agonizing tingle from the electric jolt.

After scrambling up the next two moves, I was a good ten feet above Glenn's head when the rocks started pelting me. I hadn't thought of that. He may not be able to climb up after me but smeared out on this wall, I was doomed if he hit my hands.

Just look at where you need to go, hand-foot, hand-foot, repeat. I chanted the mantra to myself while I climbed.

The missiles pummelled my body like a piece of laundry being beaten clean, but nothing hit my hands. The further up the wall I got, the less severe the pelting. Even Glenn must have a limit on how far he could throw a rock.

When the assault stopped altogether, I risked a moment to look down. My heart back flipped. A lackey straddling a roaring ATV swerved through the trees and spun to a stop next to Glenn. There was a lot of shouting and waving before Glenn pulled the man off and tore up the path to the right. The lackey stomped uselessly, then started up the rock face behind me.

Crud.

The guy below raced up the easy climb, jumping between holds like an acrobat. The searing ache of fatigue burned through my arm as I scrambled up two more big reaches. My elbow shook as I pulled up. I had to climb quicker. I had to get to the top before Glenn, but if anything, trying to stretch to bigger moves was slowing me down.

There was a small crack slanting off to the left that led directly to the top. I could be there in half the time if I skipped the logical, safe path and followed that. Tremors shivered through my knees. This was unfamiliar territory. I did not know if the finger wide gap could hold my weight. Any loose rock would send me plummeting to the ground, but I could hear the lackey heaving now. His fingers clutched a rocky shelf only a hand-span below my foot.

Mother of all—have mercy on your wayward kin.

I jumped.

Arms stretched and eyes focused on a flat square of rock near the start of the crack. My fingers slapped the cold damp stone, wrapping tight. I kicked my feet against the wall, toes scrambled across the sheer face, but only found air.

While clutching the frigid stone with one hand, the other slid over the rocks, searching. My balance shifted. Fie! Where was that blasted crack? If I moved my head to look, I'd be a messy splat in a moment.

I pushed my shoulder into the wall; my arm slid another inch. One finger wound into a tiny crack. It was just big enough to wedge the digit in, but that was enough. My balance stabilised. Inching my feet up the smooth surface, something caught my shoe.

I glanced down and quickly closed my eyes. A quarter of an inch of stone was all that kept me from plunging to the boulder strewn clearing below.

When I tilted my head, I saw Bill and Marcus at the top, but more importantly, I spied a space to wedge a hand into the crack. The edges caught the back of my fist. Red drops welled up, but be damned if it was going to slow me down now. Twisting my fist sideways, it locked into the wedge, and I swung up another three feet like an ape. Thrusting one mangled, bloody hand over the other into the narrow gap, I quickly gained height.

Thankfully, my pursuer hadn't had my courage or desperation. He was a good five feet to the side, and almost ten feet below me since he'd chosen to stay on the safe path of large holds in the middle of the wall.

Five moves, three, one.

At last, I pushed up with both arms and something wet smacked into my cheek. With a stomach-dropping lurch, my balance shifted. Scrambling, my hands slapped against the rock. It was too smooth to grip. Time slowed. My weight tilted. Panic shot through my core.

Marcus grabbed my shoulder, digging his fingers into my shirt. "Steady on Vlad. What's the matter with you? She almost fell."

I rolled over the ledge, and Vlad pressed his nose into my cheek again with a worried whine. I tried to brush him away, but might as well have been shooing away an elephant. My arms were as useless as overcooked spaghetti and everything shook.

I'd made it to the top, but we weren't safe. The narrow ridge extending out along the cliff top that I hoped would be too much for the lumbering giant now just seemed like a dead end.

"Our ploy didn't work. Glenn's on his way."

Bill frowned, grinding his toe into the rocky turf. "Fuck. That man's becoming a pest."

Marcus shrugged. "No help for it. Sooner we get started, the more distance between us and them."

Marcus and Bill took the lead, but neither attempted to sprint. Vlad limped along with a three-legged lope in front of me. Each time he miss-stepped, small stones rattled down the edge of the cliff, dropping long enough I couldn't hear the impact.

My stomach wound itself tighter. Although Marcus was right, running an exhausted, wounded party wasn't much of an escape plan.

The trail narrowed until it was just wide enough for single file travel, with a dizzying drop on the right and a sheer rock cliff on the left. That would stop the ATV, at least. Glenn was going to have to divert to the dirt track further down or get off and use his feet.

A hundred paces onto the ridge, there was a bend in the path. Marcus flung up his hand, motioning for us to stop. As I drew up behind him, it was obvious why. The path ahead lay under a mound of loose shale chips that disappeared over the side of the cliff.

Bill grimaced. "THAT was'nae here the last time I stalked deer."

Although the rock looked unstable, there were footsteps visible in the pebbles. Someone had crossed it.

"Is there any way we could cause it to slide intentionally? Maybe use the obstacle to our advantage?"

Marcus hooked his thumb across his neck. "There is every chance that if we tried, it will take one of us as much as them. We'll have to cross one at a time."

Behind us, the ATV roared like a hungry lion. Feculence. I glanced over my shoulder. Glenn and the lackey were arguing at the fork in the path. The beast of diesel roared again and Glenn pointed the cart down to the lower track. His guard sprinted toward us.

"Get moving. I'll be rear guard." I nodded toward the rapidly approaching figure on the ridge.

Both Bill and Marcus were mountain-savvy, but the trail blazer had a tricky job. He would need to find safe footing for the rest of us to follow.

Marcus stepped forward. "I'll go. It's just another day at the office for me." He nudged Bill as he shifted by. "Do try to keep up, kid."

As he set his foot on the grey pile, the whole mass shifted slightly before settling under his weight. He carried on with a slow steady rhythm, placing each foot, letting the rock shift and settle, then repeating. I bit my lip. I wanted to urge him to hurry, but it was too dangerous to move any faster.

Suddenly the rocks shifted, sliding sideways like a silver wave. My leg twitched to jump forward, but what could I do? Going out on the rock would only make the slide worse.

Marcus crouched, riding the wave toward the cliff like a bizarre surfer.

The rocks slowed, rolling to a stop inches from the edge. Marcus waited for them to settle, then carried on unperturbed. His whole crossing probably took less than a minute, but it felt like a century.

As soon as Marcus was on solid ground, Bill stepped out.

By using the tracks Marcus had made, Bill crossed in half the time, but Glenn's goon was only a few yards away now. I patted Vlad's neck and pointed to the far side. "Follow!"

We might still make it if he could cross as quick as Bill had.

Vlad set off with a cheerful, if lopsided, trot. His enormous paws sank into the rocks without making them move.

I clenched my hands, whispering, "Hurry up."

He bunched up his quarters and took a massive leap, clearing the last of the rock easily. He must have heard me, but his speed had obscured Marcus' careful footprints.

I'd find my own path. The heavy gasps of Glenn's flunky were loud enough to spur me on without caution. I leaped out, landing in a sickening slide that oozed toward the precipice.

A hand grabbed my neck from behind, pressing my face onto the ground. The shards cut my cheek. The man shook me, sending scree pebbles bouncing out of sight to the glen below. Either he was monstrously brave or ignorant.

He leaned close to my ear. "You better be worth this..."

I looked over the edge, swallowed, and forced the sight of the jagged rocks out of my mind. Could I jump to the between land? No... I could hardly stand.

"Up!" He shouted, yanking the bun at the back of my head.

Pain shot through my scalp. I liked to respond to gross violence with elegance whenever possible. It tends to confuse them. I unfolded from my prone position in a smooth glide.

He grabbed my arm and walked backward off the scree slope. "G said you were crazy. I thought he made that up."

The Hunger growled. His touch was intoxicating. My senses extended to the pulse thundering in his neck after the run.

When we got to solid ground, I spun round to face my captor. He was young and fit, but not attractive.

Stroking his cheek, I smiled. His life force was so strong, I could taste it without drawing blood. A second life force hovered inside him, inches from my fingers, pulsating and quivering. He was infected.

He tried to back away. I grabbed his throat where the vein pulsed and life flowed. My fingers tingled, and the Hunger took a deep drink. The man's steps faltered as the energy flowed up my arm. My tired limbs pulled the essence in.

The man sank to his knees. A soft moan escaped his lips. The Hunger roared again.

I ripped my hand away from his neck, letting him fall forward. I'd never been able to do that before.

He lay on the ground at the edge of the scree.

Without Anthony's surgical skill, I couldn't remove the parasite, but leaving him here was a distasteful option. There might be another way, though. The Hunger roared its approval.

I place my hand back on the man's neck and traced the second being lurking at the base of his skull. It had a sour edge, like biting a lemon, but the more I drank, the more appealing it became. The man's body writhed, twisting like a live fish on a spear. I sank down on one knee, pinning him to the ground, drinking in the energy until no parasitic life remained.

I could continue. Vibrancy surged through me. The world had such clarity now. I could do anything. I could take all of him...

Flinging myself back, I clutched my hand to my chest. Good God. What was I doing?

The man cringed away, curling into a protective ball.

I tapped his cheek. "Think about your life choices. I rarely give second chances."

He blinked with a very slight nod.

I leaped up and jumped to the golden glow on the scree field. Then another and another. Each faded as I stepped onto it, only to be replaced with more glowing in the distance.

"Don't be so bolshie!" shouted Marcus, alarmed by what must have looked like reckless abandon.

I threw my arms wide and ran faster. No way was I slowing down. I could do anything now.

At the far side, the bright glow continued along the rock strewn ridge.

"Follow me," I shouted as I ran.

Out of the corner of my eye, I saw Marcus throw his hands up in disgust and Bill shrug, but both scrambled up to the pinnacle of the ridge after me. At the top, I teetered over a narrow spine before lowering myself down to a ledge. The golden glow jumped to another ledge, and another, working its way down a hundred feet. The large blocks were firm and dry, but the route would not have been obvious without the lights. Vlad jumped between each large ledge, landing with a soft huff of a whine. His tail thumped, and his tongue hung out in an odd combination of pain and pleasure. He loved scrambling, but his side must still hurt.

The will-o'-wisp led to a grassy slope where the rocks were less numerous. I waved at Bill and Marcus to hurry, but the distance between us increased with each step I took. Hopefully, this illusion wouldn't end in a bog. Glenn's ATV was not in earshot, but it wouldn't be long before he picked up our trail again.

The glow flitted along the valley for several minutes, then dropped over the edge of a ravine. I scrambled down the slippery mud wall, grabbing at heather roots to slow my descent, but ended in a splash, anyway. Although damp, it was as good a place as any to wait for the others.

A few moments later, Vlad leaped into the burn and Bill slid down the bank, joining me in the ankle deep water. His colour was paler than normal, and he leaned heavily against the dirt wall. Then Marcus stumbled down the slope. They all looked shattered. They couldn't keep running.

"You three remain here. The gully isn't visible from above. I'll lay a trail away so you can rest."

"No." Bill barely whispered it, but the words bristled with defiance.

"Excuse me?"

"Glenn could follow you, then circle back for us. Nae-one will come out of that well. We face him together."

Marcus straightened up. "Much as I'm loath to admit it, Bill's correct. Occult things happen when we're with you. We might even survive this madness."

I sighed, shaking my head. "Very well." A rock to my left patiently glowed, waiting for me to follow it again.

After splashing along the stream, the glowing rocks continued for several feet until the banks dropped on one side to a wide, muddy shore. The glow faded into the mud.

We slogged into the knee-deep mess and squelched our way up the bank to a clearing with more lights than I had seen anywhere leading up to this. Following the line a few feet, I realized we were surrounded. The lights formed a circle of evenly spaced glittering spheres; the only gap was where we'd entered.

I kicked at the overgrown bracken near the gap. "Where is it? It should be here."

"What the hell are you talking about, Anna?" asked Bill and Marcus almost in unison.

I dropped to my knees, patting at the ground. "There's a stone missing. It has to be around here somewhere."

Bill looked at the path leading out of the glen. "There's nae cover here. Shouldn't we be moving?"

Exasperated, I snapped. "I gave you the chance to hide. You wanted to stay with me—now look for the damn stone. It should be rough cut, about an arm-span wide."

A few feet away, Vlad barked, his tail wagging furiously as he sniffed at a large mossy rock.

I hurried over to the hound. His nose pressed against the same speckled grey as the rest of the stone circle. I ripped away last year's bracken, uncovering more and more cream colour with every handful. In the end, there were almost six feet of granite, half of which was buried.

Marcus sagged as the size became apparent. "Jolly good, but what are you proposing to do with it?" His eyes drooped, fatigue wearing on him despite the day's excitement.

I patted his arm. "A friend told me we could seek refuge in the circles. I have no reason to doubt his sincerity. Once this stone is in place, the ring will be complete. We can rest."

"It'll nae move on its own. We need a crowbar." Bill glanced around slowly.

There were no trees in the valley. No debris. Nothing of any use as a tool. I clenched my fist. We were so close. By God's teeth, everyone was exhausted, and we had no tools. There must be a way.

I took out my talisman.

If I could make the boulder float, the men could push it into place. Nothing happened. Stinking cow plop! My thoughts rolled and skittered, refusing to focus on the rock in my palm. No, we were so close—I could not fail now. I pictured a cork in the sea and focused on the buried rock. It shifted a fraction of an inch. I dived deeper into its particles, slowing the spin of the ones at the bottom. The stone rocked a little. I reached into the ground, feeling its nature and aligning the stone as the opposite. It lifted, hovering over the hole left behind.

It reminded me of the night Geoffrey had become so excited about magnetic energy, he'd waxed lyrical about it all evening and put the rest of the companions to sleep.

While concentrating on keeping the particle spins in the right directions, I tilted my head toward the circle. "One of you—give it a push, please?"

Bill nudged it with his foot and gave a satisfied nod as it slid away. I followed close behind until it was at the edge of the circle, then checked that it was an equal distance from the others, before releasing the particles. Although I tried to let go one at a time, halfway through, the weight of the stone took over. It crashed to the ground.

I sunk to my knees. I felt like I'd been towing a lorry. Every bone ached, every muscle screamed in protest. Moving something that heavy was harder than it looked.

All around us, a wall of gold rose as soon as the stone touched the earth. It was so thick and bright, I could see little on the other side. Hopefully, it worked the same in both directions.

Bill glanced around with a worried frown. "So now what?"

"With any luck, we're safe."

"How's that work? All I see is open hillside."

"The circle's so bright. How can you miss it? The will-o'-wisp took us straight to it."

He shook his head. "Dinnae see any of that. No will-o'-wisp either. Nae idea what'd got into you. All I did was try to keep up."

All those perilous jumps and scrambles and all they saw was me running like a loon? I shook my head in disbelief. "It must have looked insane."

"Nothing unusual about that," Marcus grumbled.

A loud splash mixed with the whine of an ATV made me freeze. "If this doesn't work, run. Do not hesitate. Don't even try to help me. Get up to the bothy and get the rest of the crew out of here."

Bill helped me to my feet and squeezed my hand, reluctant to let go. Marcus reached for my other hand. Vlad, being Vlad, just sat by my side intent, but not really all that concerned. All of us watched the stream bank, waiting for the storm to break.

Soon the ATV roared out in a spray of muddy water. The machine tilted on the sloppy bank, sinking in on one side.

Glenn lost his balance and fell, sliding along the muddy bank head first. He looked like a grotesque mud gargoyle when he got up. I bit my lip, fighting to keep the giggles contained. He stomped back to the ATV, kicked at the machine furiously while rocking it, and got two tires free of the mud.

The ATV revved several times before thundering up the path we had left in the bracken. Glenn stopped a few feet from us, got off, and stomped around the valley floor, kicking at the bracken again. My heart thudded in my ears. Thankfully, he gave no sign he could see us.

"Ya! I know you're here. I'm coming for you."

I held my breath. He came within inches of our circle; however, did not actually cross it.

He planted his feet, hands on hips, and scanned the horizon. He stared at the exact spot where I stood. My heart froze. A moment later, he turned to stomp back to his vehicle without recognition.

Vlad sneezed.

Glenn whipped back, staring straight at us.

"They can't hide forever," he seethed and got back on the ATV, roaring a few more yards along the valley before stopping to kick ineffectually at the bracken. He continued to stomp and swear his way up the glen until he eventually disappeared over the horizon.

After he had gone, I let out my breath.

Bill rolled his shoulders again. "Thank fuck for that, nearly pissed myself."

Marcus nodded at the horizon. "How long do you think that will fool him?"

I shook my head. "No idea. I thought our trail was obvious."

What would have happened if he had tried to cross the boundary? Was it just an illusion or was it a real barrier? I walked up to the wall, holding my hand out. It was warm and made my fingers tingle. Tentatively, I reached out. A sharp shock raced up my arm to my shoulder. I snatched my hand away, rubbing as I came back into the centre of the circle.

"We should be safe. Whatever it's powered by just gave me one hell of a belt."

"Good, I don't think I could move another step," Marcus said as he sank down.

Bill and I joined him sitting on the damp ground, too tired to care that we were all getting soaked. Vlad put his head in my lap, tongue out, panting.

It was out of character for my hell-hound to get winded by a romp in the hills. He even closed his eyes to sleep. A real sleep, not the napping he normally did out of habit. Damn it, that was worrying. What if he died? I didn't think I could survive on my own.

I clasped him tight and put the thought of losing my oldest friend out of my mind. He would be fine in a few moments. He simply needed a little rest.

THIRTY-NINE

"I hate to bring it up, but we are rather exposed out here. Looks like some weather's coming," Marcus said.

I nodded, still stroking Vlad's shaggy head. He lay motionless in my lap, his breath hardly lifted his chest. Shallow breath was a terrible sign. He desperately needed a feeding.

I surveyed the countryside for life signs and found a robust young stag on the side of the ridge we'd run through earlier. After clearing my mind of distracting emotions, I called to the animal. My mind's eye saw his head lift. He'd heard me, but would he come? The antlers silhouetted against the sky for a moment, before the creature leaped forward.

I directed him down the valley with my thoughts. Damnation, it was so easy. I felt like the witch with a gingerbread cottage. I nudged a stone out of place as he neared us. The creature sailed over the golden wall with fluid grace and landed in the centre of the circle. I returned the stone, and the wall sprang up to full height.

The stag paced, looking for a way out, his eyes wide with fear. I whistled to wake Vlad. It wasn't nice. So many of life's practicalities weren't.

Vlad climbed to his feet. His attention snapped to his prey as the hunting instinct took over. He, at least, was properly equipped for our brutal life.

As Vlad's enormous canines tore at the flesh, I turned away to watch the clouds race across the sky. The wind was picking up. A storm was on the way.

Bill laid a hand on my shoulder. "You okay?"

I flinched away, hanging my head. There was nothing I could say. The enormity of what I had just done washed over me in a wave. All our life Vlad and I had hunted and killed for our survival, but only after a fair chase. All the violence of the last two days played back in my head.

Marcus joined us. "One assumes you had something to do with that animal's sacrifice?"

"Am I becoming as sick and twisted as Glenn?" I asked, hardly able to speak for fear the answer was something I didn't want to hear.

Marcus stood at my side with his hands behind his back, watching the clouds. "You are ruthless and difficult, but fair. You don't take delight in it."

I hunched my shoulders and looked at the ground. He didn't know how much I'd enjoyed the attack on the ridge. The ecstasy I'd felt after feeding on the parasite.

We stood with the wind ripping at us until Vlad trotted over. He thrust his shaggy head into my hip, shook once, and bounced, tugging at my sleeve for a game of tag.

"My apologies, games must wait." I untangled the fabric from his teeth and ruffled his ears.

It was time to go. Vlad was restored, and the weather was not improving.

Turning to the capstone, I shifted the particles just enough to lift it inside the circle, and the wall of light sank back into the ground. I drifted the tip of a finger across the stone as we left, whispering, "Thank you."

I might have been mistaken, but a very faint warmth flowed up to my hand. It was the same sort of feeling as when a friend smiles.

An unrelenting drizzle started. The damp worked its way through every layer of clothing in moments, but the morning's run had been strenuous enough the men didn't have the energy to walk any faster. It was good enough to be moving without the sound of pursuit, despite the soaking.

"Bill, you live here. Any emergency supplies in this part of the estate?" I asked as we trudged up the hill. "The folks at the bothy are all in their nightclothes—no shoes, even. They won't be able to go very far like that."

He thought about it for a minute. "The estate has a cache for mountain rescue at the base of Cat Gully, but the village shop is only an hour's walk. I could get some stuff there if you wanted."

"The strongbox is closer. Get what you can carry and meet us at the bothy. We'll decide what, if any, supplies are needed once everyone has warmed up."

"Nae bother." He changed his path to head higher up the hillside, while Marcus and I continued to the bothy.

About a half hour later, smoke whipped by my face, then the chimney of a little stone building came into view as we rounded the top of the slope.

Vlad charged ahead and Marcus' strides lengthened, but I wasn't in a hurry. The impending onslaught of questions wouldn't be nice. I lingered by a rough wall that used to be sheep pens. They almost formed a defensive barricade around the front of the building, but stones had fallen out and half were missing. Almost would not be good enough. If we had time, perhaps Marcus and I could rebuild some of it. Anything would be better than sitting around with Tatya.

The smell of peat and mildew overwhelmed me as I stepped into the building. Better appointed than a typical bothy. It had two rooms. One contained a wooden table with a stack of chairs and an iron range, the other had wooden sleeping platforms, two small cupboards and the necessary shovel for toilet duty.

Tatya and Jamie sat by the window watching the rain, while Stefan tended something on the range. One of them must have figured out how to snare some wildfowl. Lord knows there were so many hares on the hill's, it was hard not to trip over the blasted things.

Jamie jumped as the door banged shut. "Jesus... you look awful. What happened?"

Tatya shuffled over, her slippers making scuffing noises as she walked. The belt on her robe dragged behind her like a fluffy pink slug, leaving a trail in the dust.

"You are dripping all over the floor. Have you no manners?" She glared at us.

"For goodness' sake, give a man a chance," Marcus grumbled, shrugging out of his shirt.

I peeled my wet jacket off and held it in front of Vlad. True to form, he started shaking violently, showering everything in his path.

"Horrible habit. Never been able to break him of it." I apologised, but was grateful for something normal to discuss.

Tatya peered at me with hands on hips. "Explanations! What are we doing here?" Her words clipped precisely.

"I'm sorry."

That was an understatement. I was sorry she was here and sorry I had to talk to her.

"There are things I can't tell you and others you wouldn't believe even if I did," I said.

She folded her arms. "Try me. I've raised three children and nine grandchildren. I know hogwash when I hear it." She lifted her chin to stare me in the eye.

I hesitated, not knowing how to start. Which bits were believable enough to even try?

"Anna, you need people you can trust. To do that, you have to talk to her." Marcus smiled at me.

So many worries fought for my attention I could not begin to identify them. He was right, though. As much as it was against my nature, I had to trust them. This was too big to conquer on my own.

I sank into the chair by the window where rain slid down the glass like thick slime. "Sit down Tatya. Just promise me that what you hear today goes no further than this room. You will hold my existence in your hands after this."

She perched on a chair with tight lips. "I promise nothing."

After closing my eyes to block out the faces watching me, I forced my lips to move. "Although I was born a human, something changed my body many years ago. It's not anaemia. I simple don't make any blood, age, get sick, or die. With help from my companions, the sun has risen and fell over me for six hundred years."

The fire crackled in the corner. It sounded ludicrous, but I continued. "It has become more complicated recently. Beings from somewhere else have become involved."

"Aliens?" Jamie asked with wide eyes. "I knew it. Do they have big grey heads?"

Stefan drummed his fingers on the table. "Jamie!? Did she say aliens? Let her finish."

I held up my hand to calm both of them. "I don't think they're aliens. Glenn's one and Anthony is another. I don't know how many more there might be... Glenn wants something I have. Clearly I will not give it to him, so he's making our life difficult."

Tatya leaned back in her chair, arms folded again. "If any of that is true, show me this thing that's causing all our trouble."

I removed the amulet from my pocket and laid it on the table in front of her. It shimmered in the firelight.

Tatya reached out to turn the stone over, but Stefan grabbed her hand. "Don't touch it. It stings."

Tatya smiled at him. The first warmth I'd seen from her all day. "It's okay dear, I've held it before." She picked up the foil wrapper, gently stroking the stone. A faint sky blue colour flickered over the surface. "I'd wondered where this had gone." She handed it back to me, reluctant to let go.

My heart skipped a beat. "You've seen this before?"

"Of course, my husband told me most things." She smiled ruefully. "Geoffrey was trying to find if it had any value."

The door to the bothy slammed open as a gust of wind caught it and Bill staggered in, dropping a large rucksack on the floor with a thump, before kicking the door shut behind him. "I come bearing gifts," he joked, but his voice sounded weary.

"Any trouble?" I asked.

He shrugged. "A bit of surveillance, but nothing a decent mountain man cannae outsmart."

"Jolly good, they've followed you straight here, then," countered Marcus drily.

"Gentlemen, truce?" I looked pointedly at both of them until Marcus turned to the fire.

Bill opened the rucksack, and we spread the contents on the floor. It was all essentials, a few tins of food, firelighters, water purification tablets, spare fleece, waterproofs, but sadly, no weapons. I was beginning to feel very underdressed with just a couple of hairpins and a small dagger.

Bill separated out all the clothing and passed it to Tatya. "See what fits."

While the girls and Stefan traded clothes, I stacked the first aid and survival items into a pile and tossed the bag of tea to Marcus, since he was closest to the fire. The rest was a strange assortment of noodles, soup, and tinned meat.

When Tatya and the twins returned, she had a pair of waterproof trousers tied tight with a belt to hold them up and the hems rolled over three times, combined with a baggy purple fleece and woollen socks inside her slippers. Jamie had been wearing tracksuit bottoms and a tee shirt, and now had another fleece over the top.

Similarly, Stefan had on the trousers I'd thrown him, now combined with an overcoat that would have swamped his smaller relatives.

I waved at the provisions. "Tatya, if you wouldn't mind, can you organise this mess? There should be enough for everyone with a creative cook at the helm."

Stefan snickered, nudging his sister with a knowing look. "I'll do it, Anna. Gran is a terrible cook. If Jamie can catch us some more of those funny brown birds, we'll have a feast."

Blast it. Hares were vermin, but I'd have to replace the grouse once this was all over. No matter, we had bigger problems than a few lost game birds at the moment. Socks and slippers would not get them far outside the bothy. We needed footwear and weapons. I knew of a place that had everything… if I had the energy for one more jump.

Bill and Marcus were in no shape to ask for another donation, and the energy I'd received from the bug had been drained by sealing the circle. My stomach fluttered. What would happen if I jumped and couldn't come back?

Only one way to find out.

I turned to the two men sitting on opposite sides of the fire. "If I get you something more dangerous than a rock, will you know who to point it at?"

Bill laughed, while tracing his gaze down to where my soggy skirt clung to my hip. "Darling, I always know where to point my sword."

Hiding my smile, I raised an eyebrow. "That's not quite what I asked."

"We will play nice, miss." Marcus saluted. "Scouts honour. What do you have that's more dangerous than a rock?"

"If you were a scout, I'm a horned toad," muttered Bill.

"You said it," Marcus spat back.

I slapped my hands together with a loud crack. "Desist your squabbling, or I will treat you like school boys having tantrums."

Marcus leaned back with a shrug. Bill's jaw clenched. It had to be difficult to keep his retort under his tongue, but he said nothing further.

I pulled the amulet out of my pocket. "I'm going to the bunker. Have you any requests?"

Marcus straightened up with a jerk. "The bunker? That was under the cottage. Which, if I'm not mistaken, has burnt to the ground. Wouldn't the police or fire brigade have it cordoned off by now?"

"Probably, but I have an alternative mode of travel now." I waved the stone.

Bill scowled at me. "You look like death warmed up. I thought you said you didn't have the energy for another jump."

"Not sure I do, but have you got any other ideas? I'm feeling particularly under dressed without a sword, and these three haven't even got shoes."

"You're insane." Bill stood up. "But I'm going with you."

I pushed him back. "Jumping two bodies is twice as hard. I can do this myself."

"Maybe, but that would require a couple of trips to carry everything. Wouldn't it be easier to make one trip with two people?"

The truth was, I didn't really know what would be harder. I also didn't know what state the room would be in after the explosion above it. The stone walls and roof should have survived, but anything could have fallen down.

"Very well, let's move," I said.

Marcus smirked. "Watch that first step," he said with a laugh.

FORTY

Bill frowned, but I took his hand in mine before he had a chance to respond. Picturing the bunker in my head and focusing on the smell of musty air and oilskin, the feel of damp, and the dark, I stepped out into the between-zone. We flashed through the crossroads in a second before putting my foot down on the packed dirt floor.

It was pitch black, and a metronome drip splashed somewhere behind me. Somehow the fire brigade must have got an engine all the way up the overgrown, rutted lane outside.

Something moved in the gloom, followed by a moan and the clinking sound of armour.

I froze. There shouldn't be anything down here. A vision of Urisk's bloody toes flashed behind my eyes, quickly followed by the image of the shadowy brollachan. A shiver twisted down my back. God knows what else Glenn could have conjured up.

I called the light of fire into my hand.

Bill stood nearby with one hand over his mouth. "That was awful. Dinnae want to do that again." He paused. "Och no, gonna have to if I want to go home."

"Sorry, I'm new at this." Pain shot up my fingers as the heat of my impromptu light scorched them. "Can you remember where the candles were?" I shook my hand, trying to keep the urgency out of my voice.

He passed me a couple, which I lit with relief, and tucked into the wall holders around the room.

The small room had suffered. Water leaked through the sagging ceiling beams, gathering in uneven puddles under all the equipment. Dirt and loose rock from a collapsed wall buried the firearms, but the older weapons were all safe.

I lovingly unwrapped my Italian long sword, its hilt worn smooth from years of service, and ran a finger over the quillons, tracing letters that looked random. The pang of loss stabbed as fresh as the day I'd etched those initials into the metal. So many companions—vibrant, alive one minute, gone the next—so many snuffed out all at once. Forcing the thought out of my head, I buckled the belt, cradling the faceted pommel in the palm of my hand. Heaven, lend me your aid and guide my arm. I have no wish to repeat that massacre.

Bill picked up a hand and half sword, rolling it between his palms to gauge the weight. "Pity the ceiling buried the shooters. Swords will do for Marc and me, but for the rest..."

"Stef and the girls need to retreat. I don't want them fighting."

Bill kicked the edge of a trunk. "They may have to. Marcus and I cannae stop a horde. From the look of you, I'd be surprised if we actually get back. You're certainly not going to be jumping any more people today."

My the devil's tail, he was right. They deserved the chance to survive if things went arsy-varsy. I could hardly stand, let alone contemplate another jump.

Bill walked along the shelves, peeling back cloth as he went. "Axes messy, but easy to use... Pole arms and staves—take too much space... Bingo—crossbows. Anyone who can point and shoot should be sorted."

I threw some boots and linen tunics into the centre of the room, then went to a large wooden chest with carved doors tucked in a corner.

The key to it dangled from my sword belt, protecting the unwary. There were a couple of bottles in this cabinet even I wouldn't touch without gloves. The old iron lock creaked before clicking open. Carefully moving bottles, I sorted through the overstuffed shelves, hovering over king cobra venom before plucking out a yellow and blue ring-spotted bottle. That would do nicely. I'd been saving the octopus toxin for a strong opponent. Nothing would be bigger than Glenn. I slipped the poison into a leather pouch on my belt before locking the cabinet again.

A buzz flicked by my ear. I jumped, fumbling the key, nearly dropping it in the puddle at my feet.

"Mistress, I thought I heard you," panted the house sprite. "I did your favour. As you can see, the house is no more." He flew in small circles, then landed on my hand. He was thinner than this morning, and his hair looked frazzled.

I patted a finger over his tiny foot. "It was remarkable. Are you injured?"

He sighed. "It is a trifle. The lack of a hearth saps my strength. I will be restored once the cottage is rebuilt."

Bill leaned close, his brow creased into a worried furrow. "Who are you talking to?"

I lifted the sprite to Bill. "A brave warrior who's been injured covering our retreat this morning."

The sprite pulled himself up and flapped his wing to look impressive but just fell off his perch, spiralling toward the floor.

I caught him before he hit and set him on a shelf next to me. "I can take you to another hearth. It won't be used as often as this cottage was, but it is alight at the moment."

He straightened. "Where? I cannot travel far."

"If you agree, I'll take you there."

The sprite nodded, wobbling on the shelf again.

"Can you think of anything else?" I asked Bill.

Bill hoisted the improvised bag he'd made of the tunics to hold the gear. "Got all we came for and then some." He looked at the little sprite.

It was quite a lot of stuff. Tentatively, I lifted a tunic-bag. This was going to be my heaviest jump ever. What would happen if I didn't have the strength?

I pushed the memory of the dead peace lily out of my mind.

"If you would be so kind, please climb on my shoulder. Do you have the strength to hold on?"

He flew up from the shelf, circled once, and planted himself firmly against my ear. "I'm secure, mistress," he wheezed, clutching a fold of my collar.

I clasped Bill's hand and gave him a lopsided grin. "You ready?"

"Just a Sunday stroll." He smiled, but clutched my hand in a death grip.

I took one last look round the room before extinguishing the candles with a thought. Would I be able to come back? My stomach clenched. To rebuild it, I had to survive.

I pushed the worry and doubt aside, picturing the bothy, warm and snug, full of people talking and cooking, the smell of wood smoke, crowded but for the moment safe. The feeling settled in my mind, and I stepped into the between-zone.

There was a lurch, then a slow time-delayed falling sensation that lasted until my stomach flipped over, before we tumbled into the grey copy of the world in the between-zone.

I let go of Bill's hand. "Wasn't so bad, was it?"

His face was white, but he managed a small smile and a slight nod. "Aye, just getting my guts back."

The extra equipment had been harder to move than I'd expected. The bothy was visible in the distance, but only barely. There was no way I could move us back into reality without getting closer. "Seems we have a bit of a trek ahead of us. Plenty of time to settle your stomach before the next jump."

I lifted my foot, but as I put it down, blackness engulfed me. My field of vision shrank to a pinpoint, then nothingness. My body pitched forward, but I never felt the ground.

The next thing I knew, blinding light filled my eyes. Anthony called my name. Crystalline rainbows bounced off things, but I couldn't see what. It was so bright, all I could make out were the colours.

I blinked back tears caused by the dazzle. "Where are the others?"

Anthony frowned. "You have done too much, too quickly." His frown grew, forming wrinkles at the edge of his chin. "Again, you have ignored my advice. It is good you live so long. You are a very slow learner."

I let his remark sink away. I didn't have the energy to remonstrate.

"I'm not surprised you're exhausted, but I will never stop being amazed at what you are capable of. How did you manage it?"

"What are you talking about?" My head felt full of wool. So many strange things had happened in the last few days. Which one was he getting excited about now?

He laughed a light chuckle. "The stone circle you hid from Glenn in. I did not think it was even possible for a human to make a fairy ring, let alone make one so quickly."

"Glenn didn't leave me with a lot of choice," I mumbled.

He drew his breath over his teeth. "Glenn has been troublesome lately."

I lifted an eyelid. "Troublesome? That's the understatement of the century. I'm just glad it worked. We needed somewhere safe, somewhere quiet."

Anthony smiled. "Well, you have that now. It is your ring. The stones will only obey you."

"Anthony, I'm so tired I can't think straight. Can this wait? I need a little rest."

His frown deepened. "If you do not return now, your friends will be trapped."

My eyelids fell shut again. "Five minutes. That will be enough."

He shook me. "There is no time. Your spirit has fled your body! I've sent someone to assist, but you must promise me this will be your last dimensional activity until you are fully restored."

"Not much of a promise. I don't think I could take another step, let alone jump."

My shoulder shook again. I glanced up, but Anthony sat an arm's length away with rainbows spinning around his head like lazy pin-wheels.

A vicious slap rocked me onto my side. "ANNA! Wake up!"

I blinked. The world was grey again. A hand whistled toward me.

I caught it before the second impact. "Thank you, Bill. That is sufficient."

He had the good grace to flush. "Anna, you scared me."

"No, 'tis I who should beg forgiveness. Carrying so much was more tiring than I expected."

A wet patch soaked my skirt near my hip. Damn. I pulled the bottle of poison from the leather pouch. The wax seal had cracked, but if I didn't bump it too much, the rest of the liquid should make it back to the bothy. I'd have to be careful no one else touched the bag.

The little sprite buzzed over to sniff at the bottle. At least I hadn't fallen on him or any of the weapons in the bag.

"Something's coming." The sprite squeaked and flew away.

I shoved the bottle back and got up just as Urisk's head popped over the twilight coloured bank behind the ghost image of my wrecked cottage. The herbs must have helped his feet. He clambered up the last few yards easily.

Was this the help that Anthony had promised? If so, Urisk really had nothing to fear.

The sprite laughed a cold mocking tone. "You must be feeling brave today. People are going to LOOK at you," he taunted.

"My lady, I had a dream you needed my assistance." Urisk came close to speak to me, pointedly ignoring the sprite.

I waved at the little building on the horizon. "Are you well enough to help us to the bothy?"

He nodded and lifted a bag, shaking the sprite off. "The Lady has my favour, not you. Don't forget it, little one."

As Urisk turned his back, the sprite stuck his tongue out, wagging it up and down like he was licking a dessert.

"Your little face is no threat to me," Urisk replied calmly, without stopping.

The sprite landed on Urisk's head, pulling clumps of hair out.

Urisk swatted at the little man. "If you persist, I will leave you in the bog."

I looked at Bill. He shrugged, picking up his bag and offering me his arm. "Best friend or most annoying roommate ever?"

It really was hard to tell which was more accurate with the sprite. We set off walking toward the horizon. As we moved, a plan formed. Urisk reached the bothy first and opened a dimensional doorway directly into the sitting area. The sprite zoomed to the fireplace, making another face at Urisk before disappearing up the back of the chimney. The smell of roasting meat and some kind of pudding wafted out. Bill's stomach rumbled.

I pushed him toward the warmth. "Go on, I want to ask Urisk about the circle we found this morning."

Bill scowled at me. "Anna, you were out of it a minute ago. Can it nae wait?"

"This is too big to handle without help. Urisk has proved his worth several times."

Urisk lay a shaggy hand on my shoulder. "Have no fear Sir knight. I will protect m'lady until she is in your care again."

"She's nae-in-the-mood to listen." He clapped the larger man's furry shoulder. "Good luck."

When Bill stepped into the bothy, Tatya and Jamie jumped up, but Urisk closed the portal before I could hear their questions.

"Can you jump to a place if I describe it?" I asked.

"If there is water near."

"That will not be a problem."

Drawing the feeling of damp wind along with the smell of heather into my mind, we jumped from the grey land to the muddy burn near the open circle. Watery sun peeked between the clouds. It might be false hope, but the change in weather lifted my mood, and my limbs felt lighter.

I pointed to the stones. "They protected us this morning."

Urisk looked around, wrinkling his nose. "The fat warden has been here."

"If we trick him inside, could it contain him?"

Urisk backed up. "No one can trap a warden." The grey between-zone flickered behind him. "It is fraught with danger. He will be angry when he finds out."

I grabbed Urisk's hand. "It is your choice, but he lied to you. You settled on Earth before the wardens were appointed. They can't make you leave."

Urisk stopped pacing, standing motionless before turning back to me. "I don't have to hide? I can walk this land without fear?"

I shook my head. "As long as you don't cause any trouble, Anthony has no reason to bother you."

Standing up straight, his beard trembled, and he pounded his hairy chest. "A gracious gift, my lady. Thank you. A thousand time over, thank you. What can I do to repay this kindness?"

"Tell me how the circles work."

Urisk walked clockwise, tracing the outline of each stone with his finger. "These were not carved by human hand. These bones of the earth were spewed up. It took aeons for the stones to walk to this spot."

"They walked?"

His head tilted like a curious child. "They do not hurry, you see. Only the very patient have ever noticed."

My heart sank. "Is that how all circles are formed?"

Urisk jerked to a halt, looking at me over his shoulder. His lip raised in an odd approximation of a grin. "No. The humans built many circles in these hills. They hold little."

"If I made one around the bothy, would it keep them safe for the night?"

Urisk shook his head, his ears slapping in time to the movement. "It may turn a human eye, but not the warden's."

Not good, but better to know. The small spurt of energy my hope had unleashed faded into the ground. Every part of me felt too heavy. I needed to rest.

Urisk stepped into a slow moving burn that fed the main stream. It was little more than a trickle, but as soon as the water covered his toes, a door to the grey zone opened. I took his hand, and we returned to the ridge next to the bothy.

"You have been most helpful. Will you join me for the evening meal?" I asked.

"Your guests will not enjoy my company." A breath sighed out, heavy enough to make his shoulders slump. "I will keep watch."

"Once they are safe, we shall feast together. All of us, my friend."

A small twitch curved his upper lip.

It could have been a smirk, a grin, or a sneeze. I did not have enough experience to tell, but with luck it was good humour. I had enough enemies.

Urisk climbed to the top of the hill and settled on his haunches, blending into the colour of the heather and bracken perfectly.

One on watch.

One loyal to this land through ages longer than mine. A warm glow tingled my core. So much experience… knowledge… life. We had a great deal to discuss. If I survived, of course.

FORTY-ONE

I walked to the bothy. Warm light glowed from the tiny windows, inviting me into its shelter, but the sanctuary was only skin deep.

Out here, a madman terrorised the world. All humanity over six centuries had not cost me as much as this one being. He could attack again at any time, and the only protection we had were a few crossbows and three swords. Please let it be enough.

Vlad jumped up from the fire as soon as the door opened, barrelling into my chest and knocking me to the floor. Sitting on top of me, he held me prisoner while licking my face.

"Get off, foolish hound."

I wriggled to the side, but Bill moved to my shoulder, holding Vlad in place, so I couldn't sit up.

He cracked a grin as he looked down at me. "Vlad's our only hope of keeping you in sight. We can't keep having you disappear on us all the time."

I glowered at the dog. "I'm not amused. Move!"

Vlad woofed and jumped to the side, nosing under my arm to see if I was hiding anything.

Bill's smile disappeared faster than unattended food around my hound. "Not funny from my side, either. You vanished—again. Don't keep doing that." He took my hand in his, his tone growing softer. "Please?"

I patted his hand. "You should be able to sleep safe tonight. Urisk is on watch."

"Sleep's going to be in short supply, whatever happens, but thank you for trying," Marcus said from one side of a small semicircle of people huddled around the fire.

They all looked weary, but no one seemed inclined to replace the security of the hearth with the cold and dark of the sleeping room. Jamie and Stefan reclined on the floor, leaning against Tatya's chair with coats rolled up for pillows in between crossbows and swords.

"Marcus, when you shot me—"

"Which time would that be?" Bill thumped onto a bench and glowered at Marcus over his sword.

I flashed a grimace at Bill, and he turned his attention to his blade. His sniping was worrying. We were critically wounded from the inside out if my men would not trust each other.

I turned back to Marcus. "At the Cairnpapple, you had a weapon that nearly destroyed Anthony. Where did you get it?"

Marcus let his eyelids sink closed, blotting out the sight of me. His finger tapped at his leg like a rabbit looking for a hole to hide in.

"Think Glenn gave me the pistol, but can't recall when."

"Think harder. I need to know what was on it."

He shrugged. "Remember, it was bloody heavy. My wrist hurt for days."

Heavy? Could lead be the secret? No... ordinary bullets had lead tips and were useless... Anthony mentioned gravity linked every dimension together... Could gravity be attached to a weapon?

Stefan dropped his phone onto his lap. "Dead as anything."

Jamie slapped his shoulder. "What did you expect? No signal up here anyway."

"So? Would have been nice to have some tunes."

"Stefan, give me your device."

If I could light candles, why not charge a battery? Holding the phone, I sank my awareness into its case. The plastic and glass lump had a flicker of electrons, but no steady movement. I pictured the phone blinking and chirping like I'd seen it do so many times in Stefan's hands. It was too complicated to trace exact circuits. The electrons flowed faster, yet the appliance did not light up. I pulled energy from the fire, channelling it up my arm and trickled it into the solid storage mass.

The phone flashed to life with a tinny rendition of Mozart.

Marcus shuddered, grabbing the arms of his chair. "Blast, that's a bad rendition," then relaxed and nodded his head to the beat. "I've not been able to listen for such a long time—play it again."

Bill frowned. "What are you wittering about?"

"Mozart. I used to love listening to his work, but that damned thing in my head made me ill every time I played it. Feels good to hear him again, even if it is a substandard recording."

Stefan tapped the phone, and the measure repeated. It was a terrible recording, but then again, Mozart was so modern to me I was not sure what the fuss was about, anyway. A good bard with a lute was my preference.

The door rattled with a loud knock. I jerked upright, fear rocketing through my stomach. Marcus slapped one hand over the phone's speaker before setting a crossbow to his shoulder. Jamie leaned closer to her Gran, her fingers white on a crossbow as well, while Bill and I edged toward the door.

Tatya stroked Jamie's hair. "Thugs don't knock. Just open it."

She spoke with calm authority, as if she'd been witness to many midnight raids, but I would rather not walk into any more traps. I held my sword ready while nodding for Bill to stand opposite the door and swung it wide.

"Good evening." Anthony lowered his hand mid knock and looked between Bill and me. "This is a custom I am unfamiliar with. Do I need a metal bar as well?"

"Bollocks, it's you again," Bill said through clenched teeth, sliding his sword back into its scabbard.

I thumped my sword pommel into the door frame an inch from Anthony's nose. "What were you thinking, frightening the wits out of us?"

Anthony tilted his head a fraction of an inch. "Is a knock not the way to request entrance to a building?"

"You've never even tried to be polite before. Seems a bit late to start now." I waved him inside and peered into the night. The mountain side appeared quiet, but I shut the door and slid the bolt through the latch. It would not stop much.

When Anthony's scarecrow shape stepped into the light enough to be recognised, Stefan's head snapped up. "What are you doing here?"

I stood up straighter, crossing my arms. "That is an excellent question."

"I wanted to verify you and your companions are well."

"See if we are well? Jamie's been tortured, Marcus had a thing in his head, Bill is still haunted by the nightmare you subjected him to, and now everyone is hiding in a mountain hut because we've had to burn my home! We are not WELL!" I threw my sword onto the table with a bang. Empty tins of soup scattered and crashed to the floor.

Anthony bowed his head. "It is regrettable what has occurred."

"Be useful or be gone." Marcus pointed to the door with the crossbow.

"Glenn has disrupted your lives unacceptably. Restraint has proven to be less than satisfactory. Perhaps confinement would allow him time to pause for reflection on his actions," Anthony said.

Bill tapped his fingers on his sword hilt. "Aye right. We've just watched him walk out of a burning building. How can you lock that up?"

Anthony closed his eyes. "I should not say, but I am an oath-breaker already." Turning to me, he leaned close, whispering, "When corporeal is transformed into vapour, it distils into its essence. A chemically inert, perfect sphere will contain this."

I could not believe my ears. Why was he worried about saying that nonsense out loud? "What a load of tripe. How does that help?"

Bill edged closer to Anthony, cracking his knuckles. "I've been on the receiving end of his help. You want me to get rid of the time waster?"

Anthony held up his hands. "I have given you the means to trap my species. That is not a waste."

"What?" Stefan perked up, glancing between Anthony, Bill, and me. "How?"

I waved my hand in the air. "Senseless rubbish—corporeal essence contained in an inert sphere."

Jamie's eyes widened as thoughts spun into place and blossomed like a sunflower. "A genie in a bottle!"

For the love of all the saints, how had she worked that out? Bloody myth and legend were coming to life again.

"Cinema has lost most of the truth, but that will do." Anthony clasped his hands together, bowing his head. He hesitated and looked away. "It is a last resort. I must speak with him again. The disassociation may not be necessary. It can be hazardous to all parties."

Bill scoffed. "Hazardous?! Mate, everything we do is hazardous!"

Anthony turned to me. "I'm sure you remember the upheaval at the Cairnpapple? That will be mild compared to Glenn's disruption. You hold his amulet. Please refrain from further rash actions until my return."

My stomach sank. If we got this wrong—we'd destroy the world. Oh, hell.

Anthony walked to the door, but disappeared before opening it.

"Well, that was abrupt." Marcus said.

"Aye, rude bastard," Bill said.

"He's difficult, to be sure." I sank onto a bench.

Bill perched on the edge close to me, laying a hand on my shoulder. "You make any sense out of that?"

Tatya snorted. "Clean your ears, Bill. We've been shown a weakness. One is all you need to crack the strongest lock."

"Anthony never speaks plainly. All we know is there might be a way to trap Glenn and there are risks." Shivers swept through my core. Risk sounded so mild. One mistake would be the end of the world, possibly the end of the galaxy. Making that choice was too big a responsibility for the likes of us. "We can't do anything at the moment."

Tatya's eyes blazed. "He stole Geoffrey. We were going to the Caribbean when we retired. Instead, I've had a trip to hell." She brushed back a tear and stood up to pace the room.

"Anna, we cannot carry on hiding forever. Unless you wish to hand each one of us to the slaughterhouse, we should take action," Marcus said.

Did my personal feelings for my oddball family overrule the needs of thousands? "You have no idea what you are asking. If we make a mistake—"

Stefan kicked my shin. "IF." He stared at me, cutting through the paralysis the demons of fear cast over my mind. "Don't make choices on ifs. What's the best that could happen?"

The young soul had fought enough mental battles to have splendid weapons. His words framed the problem better, but did not reduce the weight on my heart.

"Aye. What's one more scuffle?" Bill said.

"A mistake doing this and everything—each and every particle that makes up our galaxy—will unravel," I said.

"Will it be quick?" Jamie poked at the fire. "If there's no pain, maybe ending it all would be best..."

"Are you suggesting suicide?" Tatya paused mid-stride.

"No, but have you seen what the world looks like now? Maybe it's time to wipe the slate clean." Jamie set her gaze on the flames.

Stefan knocked his sister's shoulder. "Or—we get rid of that monster and things get better."

Bill lay a hand on my knee. "I agree with them. Either we die trying or live well."

Marcus nodded. "Win or lose, there is no draw."

The people had spoken. Even if it was a tiny group, it was unanimous. "Very well. We try to capture G."

Now the question was—How? What kind of weapon would dissolve Glenn's form? Physics had only played a cursory role in my research for a reason behind immortality, since biology and chemistry had seemed so much more relevant. More fool me. I knew precious little of particles and forces.

"Marcus, give me the bolt from your crossbow."

It was sharp and flew accurately. It had a metal body. All that seemed reasonable for attracting gravity. I dropped it. Metal echoed off the bare plank floor.

I scooped it up, pushed thoughts of lead cannon balls into the bolt, and dropped it again. It did not appear to fall any faster, but I didn't have a way to measure the descent.

I added elephants and steam locomotives to my thoughts, pushed that into the bolt, then dropped it a third time.

Tatya snapped the projectile off the floor. "Stop that racket!" She held a hand to her head.

I snatched the bolt back. "Mrs Briggs... I am attempting to make a weapon to kill the unstoppable. Excuse me if discovering how to attach gravity to a weapon is noisy."

She snorted. "You can't attach gravity to a thing. If gravitons even exist, they have no mass."

"Graviton? What is that?"

"A theoretical particle that, much like the rest of this week, should not, and has never been proven to, exist."

Theory. Myth. Could it be real? Recent events would suggest it was entirely possible.

"What else do you know about them?"

She crossed her arms and peered at me. "Gravity is not used therapeutically."

The pieces clicked. Carl had told me her specialism, but I'd been engaged since. "You must have read something while qualifying? Nuclear medicine can't exist without physics."

She glared at me. "That was a long time ago. I only vaguely recall string theory."

"That's more than we have at the moment," Marcus said.

She sighed. The weight of her grief, fear, and frustration pulled the air out of her like a slow tooth extraction, but it loosened her tongue.

"The formula is hazy… something like…"

Tatya took a sooty stick from the fire and started sketching numbers and figures on the floorboards. The sprite flitted to the front of the fireplace, watching the stick move. He nodded a few times and fluttered to my shoulder.

"She knows the way of it, miss," he whispered and darted back to the fire.

"As I recall, gravitons were proposed to be mass-less bosons spinning in a certain way. When they encountered something with the opposite spin, it was shown, theoretically mind you, to give rise to a field exhibiting properties similar to gravity."

The figures and letters made no sense to me. My interest in physics had started and ended with Sir Isaac, but her description of opposite spins corresponded to Anthony's instructions.

"My thanks, Tatya." What was mass-less and had a spin opposite Glenn? It was still confusing, but at least I had something to tease sense out of.

Light had no mass, but how did I look for a spin? All Anthony had taught was lighting a candle. That was not dealing directly with the pure wave form. I bowed my head. There was still so much I did not understand, yet all our lives depended on this.

I crossed my arms, leaning back. "You're all tired. That's asking for mistakes. You should be to your beds."

Bill shook his head. "Exhausted is a better word, but I doubt anyone is going to sleep tonight, hen."

"All we can do at the moment is speculate. I can do that while you at least attempt to rest."

It was like telling school children to go to sleep before Christmas. No one moved an inch.

"How about we make a list… what we need, what we have, and what we're going to do with it," Bill said.

"We need a container. If we find the Jinn before the art dealer returns, we must be prepared," Tatya said and returned to pacing.

The only bottle in the room was half full of whisky. I pulled out the stopper.

Marcus snatched but was too slow, twisting his fingers into my sleeve instead. "What are you doing?"

I shook him off and tipped the bottle into the fire. The flare set my sleeve alight. The sprite jumped at the back of the hearth, then settled again and stretched his legs out, toasting his toes in the extra flames.

"One inert vessel." I said, patting at the steaming fabric on my arm.

Would a squat cylinder hold him? Short of a chemistry lab, I'd never seen a complete sphere made of glass.

Bill tapped his fingers on his sword. "Glenn won't travel alone."

"Some of his men were infected by those parasites. Marcus, do you think others would share your aversion to Mozart?" I asked.

Marcus shrugged. "It's possible. I certainly heard no classics while in their company."

Stefan tapped the phone. "There's enough battery for a few hours. Won't be hard to set it to loop."

I nodded. "Good. There's a place where the path narrows to a small gap in the ridge. That would probably be the best place to discourage the infected."

Jamie ran a hand across her bruised cheek. "I've been cooped up in here all day. Let me have a chance to get back at that creep." She took the phone from her brother and stood up.

This was only a diversion. It should be safe enough. "Very well, but you must be careful. The paths are slippery after heavy rain."

Stefan slipped his new boots on and scrambled to join her. "I'll feel better knowing we won't have any more of those things sneaking up on us."

Bill lurched to his feet. "Wouldn't want the junior rangers on the wrong path," he said with a grin that concealed his fatigue from those who didn't know him.

Jamie set her jaw back with mock indignation. "Junior Ranger? Wrong path? We're not that stupid."

Bill tugged on her ponytail gently as they walked to the door. Vlad jumped up and slipped outside the moment it opened.

"Dinnae say stupid, hen. If you'd like a nickname, that could be arranged. How about..." He paused, grinning even more as he watched her fidget.

She slapped his shoulder. "I don't think so."

They headed out into the night, bantering about nicknames. Tatya stopped pacing and sat down by the hearth again, twisting the simple gold wedding band around her finger while staring at the door.

Marcus patted her knee. "We will get these ruffians."

She nodded, but her eyes were vacant until he put an arm around her shoulder. Life sparked in that instant. She slapped him away. "Keep your hands to yourself, or I will deal with the ruffian in this room."

Watching them glare at each other, it was obvious they needed to say things that didn't require my ears. Also, to determine how to disassociate Glenn, I needed quiet. The way would present itself once I had enough time and space to study the problem.

"I'm going to get a bit of fresh air. Call me if you need me." Neither even turned to look as I walked to the door, picking up my sword on the way and slid it into its sheath.

The moon illuminated the small clearing around the bothy. A few random stones caught the light, glowing faintly and casting a feeling of calm around the small building.

I sat on the closest rock and wrapped my fingers around the crossbow quarrel. Particles, waves, photons... All were unknown things, but it had to be the opposite of Glenn. Did that mean... the opposite of me?

Would I be able to touch it once I made the thing?

Who knew?

I thought of everything I loved and pictured the reverse, casting that into the crossbow bolt. It did not appear to have any effect.

I sank my awareness into myself. Flecks of gold surrounded by red so dark it was almost black pooled around my body. The same colours that had flashed when Anthony checked for the parasitic infection.

The gold flecks bobbed and circled, as if fencing against the red. I dived deeper into the colours. The red pulsated slowly and felt hot, like molten steel. The gold was neither hot nor cold, and its movements were as light and quick as a butterfly.

If one of these was Glenn's influence, the black was more likely, but there was so much of it. Horror seeped into my thoughts. Was I a mouse stuck in a tar pit?

I sank into the red, letting it wash over my conscious. It moulded around me like an old shoe. Everything about it felt right. I backed away. How could I be so much like him? I reached for the gold flecks. They darted away. Each time I tried to touch one, it flitted to the side at the last moment. My stomach twisted. Had my humanity rejected me already?

I reached out again, changed my mind at the last second, and snatched the opposite side.

Gold sizzled my mind. Fiery agony seared every sense. The worlds spun away—earth, the between-zone, the ghost's realm—everything blurred and went fuzzy.

The stone underneath me bucked. I fell to the wet earth. The trance broke as I landed. Breath came in short fast heaves. My hands burrowed into the coarse heather, clenching tight to the woody stems, clutching at reality, feeling the universe as it should be.

The ground stabilised. The alternative realms returned to their place in the back of my mind.

It made no sense. The gold flecks tore holes in my mind and threatened to disrupt reality, but they were part of me. Why did something fundamentally part of me cause so much destruction when I touched it? I didn't have the time or resources to experiment. It fit no models I was aware of. Damn!

More importantly, if these light bodies had the same effect on Glenn, would it be enough to trap him? It probably wasn't gravity, but seemed powerful.

Sitting up cross-legged on the damp earth, I leaned against the stone and let my awareness sink into the crossbow bolt.

Its dull surface melted away, revealing cuboid patterns of molecules arranged in a lattice.

I extended my awareness, looking for the colours that swirled around me. The pool of red and gold followed my thoughts a short distance, stopping at the edge of the weapon.

I poured energy into my fingertips, extending the tones around my hands. Layer by layer, my colours soaked into the pattern of the metal like bunting hung from chain link armour.

The quarrel grew hot in my hand. Every scrap of metal in the area rattled. The vibrating increased until every void, every space I could find inside the pattern, was full of my colours. I opened my eyes.

The four sharp ridges down the side of the bolt head glinted pale gold in the moonlight. That was pleasing. It had not been my imagination. Something had changed inside the quarrel, but would it have the right effect?

Vlad jumped over the boulder, landing at my feet, accompanied by the sound of footsteps pounding up the path. Jamie limped badly, but kept up with the other two as they cleared the rise of the hill.

"Arseholes are on to us!" Bill shouted as he ran.

I followed the threesome to the bothy.

Tatya jerked up from her seat. "What's happened?"

Jamie heaved a fresh breath. "We got to the pass, but men were already there. We left the phone and ran."

I leaned against the door. Damn, damn, damn... Where was Anthony when you needed him?

"We only have one chance. Bill, Marcus—hold out your hands. I need to know who's steady enough to hit first time." I would have liked to do the honours, but I had to be free to contain Glenn the second his essence shifted.

"Give it to me," Tatya snapped. "The mountain men are tired."

Bloody woman, we did not have time for this. "Tatya, I realise you're upset, but Marcus and Bill are excellent marksmen. They will not miss."

She spun to face me. "Neither will I."

Stefan tapped my arm. "Anna, it wasn't Papa that taught us to shoot. It was Gran. She's fantastic."

"Can you hit the head of a running deer at five hundred yards? Bill has. Can you hit the eye of an enraged gorilla swinging out of a tree behind you? Marcus has."

"I have killed an entire squad of police holding a family hostage, then shot the politicians who organised it while hiding on a roof top six storeys above them. All that and more horror than I ever want to remember. I will NOT miss."

The pieces of her puzzle fell into place. It was against my nature to trust her, but the wretched woman had more in common with me than most. May the gods pity her soul. I held out the quarrel. "I'm assuming Marcus showed you how to use a crossbow?"

Her hand fell to the floor as she took the bolt. She stumbled and righted herself. "I've trained with all weapons. Historical or modern makes no difference to me, but I will have to make some adjustments for the weight."

I gave each of the twins a crossbow. Jamie grabbed hers, stroking the stock as if it were a pet. "This is going to feel so good."

"Take Vlad and get in the back room."

She kept stroking the weapon without stirring.

"Move."

"It's payback time," Jamie shouted and ran outside.

Shit was piling up faster than a town infected with cholera. Having her in the open wasn't great, but she would be mobile. The bothy was a bottleneck with only one door and two small windows... No escape if things got bad.

"Stephan and Bill—get that crazy girl and bed in on top of the rise behind the bothy. And don't shoot Urisk. Drop anything else that gets inside the sheep fence. You don't have to kill, just slow them down."

Bill narrowed his eyes, obviously not happy at being sent away to bodyguard the youngsters, but didn't oppose me.

I pointed to the dark doorway of the second room. "Tatya, I want you over there. Hopefully, fat-boy won't notice you in the shadows."

I passed Marcus the amulet. "Desperate times need desperate acts. When Glenn arrives, lay it on thick. We need to give Tatya a chance to get a clear shot."

Thuds and screams mixed with manic barking erupted outside. The sharp rattle of automatic gunfire sounded. Feculent, liver-less cur were using weapons that killed without discrimination, without effort, without honour. By the devil's tail—let this end.

I knelt on the floor at Marcus' feet with the empty bottle hidden under my skirt. He held the tip of a field knife pricked against my spine. Cold wormed down my back, but I didn't flinch. I had to trust his mind had healed.

A bolt thudded into the front of the building, followed by the sound of a body landing heavily.

"Ya! Damn apes!"

My stomach somersaulted at the sound of his voice. Across the room, Tatya settled her shoulders and raised the bow.

A boot kicked the door open. It slammed against the wall. The rotund figure outlined by moonlight threw the useless missile across the room, clapped his hands together, and stepped in with a bounce.

"Marc? You're still alive! What you got for me?"

Marcus pressed his blade into my neck. "Took long enough, but I got that necklace you fancied." He waved the amulet.

I glanced up. It was impossible to tell he was on our side. His lips pressed tight to his teeth, like a hungry beast cornering a rabbit. He pressed the blade tighter. Something wet ran down my neck.

Bill peered around the cottage door. "God Dammit! I knew we couldn't trust you."

I glared at Bill, willing him to leave before he ruined everything. Why had he ignored my instructions to go to the top of the hill?

Glenn spun and flung a hand out, catching Bill on the side of his temple. Blue sparks exploded. Bill flew backward, landing in a twisted heap.

Glenn stalked out, and more sparks flew. Bill convulsed.

Crud buckets! I'd seen Glenn kill like this before. I had to get him away from Bill.

"Lost interest in your toys already?" I asked.

"Ya! Be with you in a moment," he sneered, watching with glee as Bill's body twitched.

I plucked the amulet back from Marcus, focusing on Glenn, and yanked him into the bothy. He landed with a thud that rocked the floor.

"Pick on someone your own size... Oh!... there isn't anyone your size."

Glenn got to his feet, glaring at me. "You need to respect your betters. Pain should sort that."

He stepped closer. The fire cast an orange glow over his boot. One more step and Tatya could see her target clearly.

"I doubt it. I've never held respect for tyrants."

He smiled, his tongue ran over his lips anticipating his grim games.

Tatya sighed. If I hadn't known she was there, I wouldn't have noticed the sound. I stepped back. The bow string released. Glenn flew forward. Into me.

We fell. The end of the crossbow bolt stuck out of him, pinning the beast on top of me and both of us to the floor.

I held the amulet over my head. His arm flapped at it, but the fat sausage couldn't reach. A gaping hole grew in his back around the bolt. He flailed for the stone again, but only knocked my hand further away.

Swirling colours floated out of Glenn like funfair pinwheels.

The ground under us heaved.

"The bottle!" I screamed. "For God's sake, get the bottle, Marcus."

I envisioned a heavy blanket draping over Glenn and myself. It kept the swirling rainbows hovering over his body, bobbing and shifting with each breath I took.

Tatya scrambled to where I lay. "You knew I was shooting. Why didn't you move?"

The ground heaved again. Cups fell off the table as it tipped and crashed to the ground.

"Where do you want this?" Marcus held the bottle over my head.

"Hold it still." I folded the energy blanket into a funnel, gently pushing the coloured rainbows into the vessel. Glenn's form shrank in on itself like a pool with the plug pulled. His struggles grew more feeble as his size diminished. The quivering ground under us reduced to shivers, then stopped.

The last spinning rainbow disappeared into the bottle and his shell of a body burst, covering me with a thick slimy goo.

"Get the stopper in it," I panted.

Marcus looked around in a panic, slapping his thumb over the top. "It must have rolled away in the quake."

Tatya jumped up, throwing weapons and clothes around the room as the bottle shook violently in Marcus' hand. Rolling over, I realized the bolt had not actually caught me. It was just my tunic pinned to the floor. I ripped the fabric free.

Tatya leaped up. "I found it!" She raced over to wedge the stopper in the bottle's top, hugging Marcus in the process.

I took the bottle from Marcus, holding the top down as it continued to wiggle and shift. "This shall not hold him long. Once he's out, he'll be livid."

"Perhaps we could fasten the lid, like a champagne bottle," Marcus said.

"Doubt that would be enough, but I have an idea."

I turned and paused at the door. Bill lay on the dirt with his knee twisted to the point his foot appeared to be attached backwards. His chest rose and fell. Other than that, he didn't stir as I stepped over him. Bloody, infuriating, lovable idiot. When would he accept I didn't need a chaperone?

"Tatya, assess the ox-headed lug for injuries. Marcus, make sure the twins don't get into too much trouble while I'm gone," I said before ducking out the front door. I needed a better cage for the beast before he escaped.

FORTY-TWO

Outside, several thugs crouched behind the scant shelter of the sheep pen. One leaned out, aiming at my head. Bullets whizzed by with a strange insect like noise as they zipped by my ears. I sprinted forward, flinching as more winged by. That was close, too close. Glenn would be out in an instant if I fell over now.

A crossbow bolt spun through the air, knocking the shooter on his back.

I flashed a thumbs-up at the twins on the hilltop and sped up, leaping over the wall. One thug got brave and moved to block my path. Vlad charged into him, sinking his canines into loose flesh and jerking sideways. Screams behind me faded as I galloped down the trail, leaping over loose rocks the size of house bricks. Discarded weapon littered the route so the bad Mozart must have had some effect.

Over the top of the first rise, I met the welcome sight of a small troop led by Carl and Nigel.

I slowed enough to shout, "Bothy's surrounded. One down. Take charge of the mess."

"Thought we heard gunfire." Carl waved at the rest to get weapons ready.

Over the next rise, Urisk stepped into the path. "My Lady, where are you going in such haste?"

I stopped only because he obscured the entire path. "The old stone circle." The bottle jumped in my hand. Glenn hadn't liked the sound of that. The stopper wiggled. I slapped a second hand over my thumb and lunged to the side of Urisk. I had no time to waste on conversation.

Urisk scooped me into his enormous arms, then took a few running steps and leaped into a small burn trickling down the side of the hill. Colours flashed by, then settled at the muddy stream edge of the circle. The bottle shook and jumped again as Glenn lunged at the amulet from inside his prison. I held the bottle up, and the colours condensed. A humanoid shape swirled in the mist.

"Not this time, mister."

I threw the bottle into the circle and focused on the stone I'd shifted yesterday. The stopper popped out almost as soon as my fingers let go. An arm grew from the opening, grabbing me as the stone moved back to complete the ring. The inertia knocked me off my feet. My face slammed into the ground inside the circle.

Mist condensed out of the bottle, and a much thinner Glenn stood up. "Ya! I needed to slim, but not like that." He stalked up to me. Electric blue flew from his hand.

I wasn't prepared. The agony raced across my body, locking every muscle for what felt like an eternity. Eventually, I remembered how to control the electrons and funnelled them deep into the ground, all the way down to the solid granite and iron ore below.

As I wheezed a breath in, Glenn lashed out with a boot, catching me in the ribs. Bones cracked, and the air left my lung with a whoosh.

Stuff this. I rolled sideways, escaping the ring before he could catch me again, and raised the circle.

A golden wall sprang up from the bracken. His boot hit the edge and there was a loud cracking noise. His limbs flailed as he jerked back, the boot trembling in the air. He paced two steps sideways and tried again, getting a second shock.

Good God—It worked!

He stopped moving, and calm settled over his face. "You know too much. Anthony's soft for you." He snapped his fingers. "Urisk, my sword!"

The air rippled. Urisk reached into the between lands, fetching a large black sword out of the air. It pulled in all the surrounding light, the black not a colour but an absence.

Urisk brandished the sword at Glenn. "False filth. Carry your own rubbish."

"Behave yourself." Glenn snapped his fingers again.

Urisk rolled his shoulders, making the fur on his arms flap, then leaned back and flung the weapon over his head. It somersaulted in a long arc punctuated by a splash as it sunk into the bog. "You have no power over me, liar. I know the truth."

Glenn sneered. "Truth? From a mortal?"

Urisk scooped a hand under my shoulder, helping me up. "She knows loyalty and love. All you know is pain."

"What use is that?" Glenn shouted, battering at the circle with his fist. The light slipped, the gold dimming to yellow.

Urisk's hand tightened on my shoulder. "He is escaping. We need the other warden." He leaped into the grey zone and beckoned to me. "Come quickly."

A small voice urged me to follow to safety, but a much louder voice REMEMBERED. Even if I wanted to, I could never forget the blood, the bruises, the pain this thing had caused. "Go, find Anthony. I shall slow Glenn down."

I flicked my hand. The air rippled again, taking away my only escape. My heart slammed into my chest, pounding a manic beat as the door disappeared. At least Glenn could not slip into the crossroads.

I slapped a hand on the nearest rock and poured my strength into the circle. The golden glow continued to fade. Glenn's manic grin grew wider as the light dimmed. What was I doing wrong?

When the light dropped to knee level, he stepped over the faltering wall with a casual stride. "Shoddy work, as expected from a half-arsed ape."

I stared at the rough shaped stones and trampled bracken feeling betrayed. Anthony said they would obey me.

Glenn raised a hand, and the black sword flew out of the bog, trailing moss.

Putrid donkey piss. He should not be able to do that. I drew my long sword, just getting the blade over my head before his thundered down.

His blows came more swiftly than a mortal could deliver. It was only centuries of practice that allowed me to keep my head. Well-trained muscles remembered how to block and parry faster than thoughts.

After several rounds, he paused to gauge my stance for an opening. "You're too good at this," he muttered.

"I have you to thank for that."

He wrinkled his brow. "All I have for you is a hard shag." He thrust his groin out.

Welcoming the respite, I stepped further out of his reach. "Think back to Ravenser. You tried to pillage the Barber Surgeon's apothecary."

He shook his head and lunged.

I danced backwards, catching his blade and twisting my own to the side. "'Twas early autumn."

Flipping my blade to the side, I threw a slice toward his head. He bent backwards, his head almost touching the ground before he snapped upright again.

"We had a bushel of newly harvested apples behind the counter. I've not been able to stomach the smell of one since."

He looked bemused. "I've not been anywhere near the sea this year."

I circled left, changing my guard as I stepped. "Try six hundred."

His mouth opened and closed. "Years? Humans don't live that long."

"No, we shouldn't." I laughed, a high-pitched giggle. "It tends to make us slightly insane or, so I've been told."

"You're lying."

I feigned a stab, then sidestepped to strike, but he didn't fall for the trick and circled round with me. He swung a sharp slice toward my face.

My blade twisted, catching his on the cross guard. "Why would I? What could I possibly gain by making that up?"

"No matter, you're guilty." Striking faster than an adder, his blade lifted off mine and swung again.

I mistimed my block, and he nicked my arm as I parried too slowly. A drop fell to the ground, and the circle flickered.

Blood! If my hands weren't already occupied, I would have slapped my forehead.

In the distance, I heard footsteps and voices.

"How could you let her do this?" Anthony said.

"Let her? Let her? How could I have stopped her?" Marcus shouted.

Glenn glanced over his shoulder, then leaned toward me with a grin. "Anthony's pissed. How did you get under his skin? He's never sullied with a mortal before."

It was all just background noise. There was no chance I'd take my attention off Glenn now that I knew what was needed.

I worked round in a slow circle. Each step led Glenn to the stone ring like a dog following a biscuit.

"Anthony's been nagging me to police this planet more…" He lifted his sword.

My shoulder hit one of the standing stones. I'd made it. We were inside the ring.

"You've got nowhere to run, and nowhere to hide," he sneered.

"I've no intention of doing either." I drew my sword across my wrist. Blood poured onto the ground, splashing the stones. Glenn was so entranced by me, he didn't notice the glow gathering around his feet. Instead, he raised the pitilessly black sword that pulled light from the sky.

"Stupid girl. I know that's just a flesh wound, but this—" He lunged, thrusting straight for my heart with lightning speed. There was no time to block it.

If life flashed before your eyes at death, I would have had a welcome rest, but searing pain split me instantly, knocking me backward. The hilt of the pitch black sword protruded from my chest, the blade buried in the ground.

I didn't even have the energy to flinch when Glenn wrenched the blade, shredding the tissues of my lungs. Then he leaned down like a lover, his mouth hovering over mine before yanking the thong of the amulet off my neck. My head cracked against the ground as the leather snapped.

A thump, followed by a growl, then Vlad's stinky breath crossed my cheek in a hot wave. I struggled to open an eye. My hound lunged across the open ground, positioning himself between Glenn and me. I twitched one finger to stroke his paw, the only part I could reach, then let my lids sink closed again and slapped a hand against the closest stone, smearing a crimson hand print across the rough granite.

"Rise."

The earth sent up the wall again. This time, no light penetrated through our prison of solid gold. If the light couldn't get through, Glenn wasn't going anywhere.

A small sigh escaped my lip. It was all I could do anymore. As life slipped away, a warm blackness engulfed me. Glenn was in prison now. If the stones only obeyed me, I would not let him out. EVER.

Geoffrey's form flickered next to me; his translucent hand patted mine. "Hold on! It's not your time yet."

However, there wasn't anything left to hold on to. Dimly I heard Glenn yelp and lifted one eyelid. He seemed to be dancing around, juggling hot potatoes. It was not my problem anymore. I let my eye drift closed.

More of my warriors appeared.

At least I wouldn't be alone anymore. I let myself drift, settling into warmth as comfortable as a soft bed at the end of a long campaign, and slipped from my body.

Once free of my shell, I saw all of my warriors clearly. They stood shoulder to shoulder, four rows deep, with drawn blades that glowed like captured stars. Hundreds of pin-points of golden light knitted together all around me.

I stepped toward them, then stumbled to one knee as agony ripped through my chest. Feculence. Pain was supposed to end after death.

The searing intensified. I snapped back into my body. Anthony stood over me with the black sword in his hand, glaring at Glenn. Struggling for breath, I clamped my teeth together to refrain from screaming. Vlad licked the gaping hole in my chest. His tail beat a cheerful tune on the blood-soaked ground. Anthony stalked over to Glenn, hopping around on the far side of the circle.

Anthony raised the black menace, and his voice rang across the valley. "The enabler has chosen a new carrier. If you had shown even one act of kindness, one act of contrition, I would have spared you this." The blade swung downwards, cutting through Glenn's centre.

Glenn split in half. The corporeal fell to the ground with a wet splat as multicoloured gases swirled out from his shell in spiral patterns.

I've seen pictures from the Hubble telescope; the horse-head nebula was nothing compared to this. Infinite galaxies welled out, swirling multicoloured kaleidoscopes of particles. Far more than had at the bothy. My army parted, and the cavalry charged in. Each rider scooped up a piece of the vortex and galloped into the sky. Ghostly equines leaped and soared, charging into the blue until they were too tiny to see.

Next, the men on foot collected their pieces, each heading in a different direction. Some blinking out into the between land, some dropped into the ground, some simply walked over the hills. The last was Geoffrey.

He paused with a bittersweet twist of a smile under his moustache. "Tell Tatya I'm happy she will not be lonely." He collected his piece and vanished.

One last bit remained, slowly swirling in the breeze. I held up the poison bottle, gently coaxing the breeze to push the particle into it. Capping the lid, I whispered, "You're one of Mine now."

Anthony bent down slowly, picking the amulet out of the goo glistening on the ground and held it out. "Whether or not you meant to, it has chosen you as its keeper," he said sadly.

"Is Glenn gone now?" I croaked, taking back the amulet. It hummed, and a comfortable warmth flowed up my arm, much like a welcome home hug after a long journey.

The side that had been cracked before was now complete. Runes ran in an uninterrupted line down the side.

"It chose you. Glenn was no longer required. It was time to end this," Anthony said.

I stared at him, too weary to shout. "What? Just like that —it's time to end this? You stood there and watched him pin me to the floor, then suddenly decided enough was enough?"

"Your execution was his job. Until the amulet refused his touch, I could not interfere."

FORTY-THREE

I slapped the ground. "Just doing his JOB?! For heaven's sake. Remind me to never ask you for a favour."

He bowed his head. "On the contrary, you will probably need quite a lot of my attention over the next few years."

I stiffened. "Why? Is Glenn coming back?"

Anthony tilted his head. "Of course, but I expect you will know how to deal with him in a few millennia."

Cold settled over me, nailing me to the ground. "Millennia? I will still be here?" Oh, God, you cruel demon, how was that a fitting reward for my deeds?

"Certainly." He blinked twice. "I did say the amulet chose you." He paused, peering at me. "I thought you knew what that meant. You are a warden."

I stared at Anthony, the world around me fading to nothing. A warden? What the hell did that mean?

Vlad pawed at the ground, bumping my arm repeatedly. I shook my head, coming back to my senses. He woofed and bounced across the stone ring, scratching at the ground again.

On the other side, my troop gathered in a ragged cluster. Marcus and Nigel held Bill up, Jamie and Stefan leaned on each other, and Tatya twisted her hands with a tired expression.

Getting to my knees, I crawled to the edge of the circle and touched the stone. "My thanks."

The wall of gold fell back to the ground. Marcus set Bill down next to me and Tatya dropped to my other side.

"Do you need medical care?" She checked for my pulse and dropped my arm with a look of disgust when she didn't find any.

"Thank you for your concern. I am as well as possible, Tatya, but how is Bill?"

He lifted his head, laying a hand on mine. "All's peachy now you're moving."

Anthony hovered just outside our group, watching me intently. The twins limped closer.

"And what happened to you two?" I asked.

"Someone had to cover your escape," Jamie said.

Stefan shrugged. "Gran reckons I'll be all right with a few of these butterfly strips." He sank to the ground, holding his arm. "But sure does hurt."

I looked round the circle of weary faces. "Nigel, can we open the medieval hall tonight?"

"Aye, why?"

I reached up and squeezed his hand. "You deserve a celebration."

Carl and the rest of my brethren walked into the far side of the valley. They moved slowly, carrying several odd shapes. I glanced over my shoulder to see if the enigmatic warden was still with us.

"Anthony, can you open a doorway to the bottom of the ocean?"

"I could, but you would not like what came out." He tilted his head at Carl's group. "I am assuming you want an obscure place to put things. May I suggest a cave? I know of one a thousand feet below the earth. There are some fascinating creatures that dwell at those depths that will not like it, but it might suffice?"

"Give us the biology lesson later. Just open the door, please."

Anthony inclined his head, and the air rippled, revealing a very black space that smelled of wet clay. I pointed to the twins. "Crossbows, if you don't mind." The rest threw their weapons in without prompting.

Carl heaved a large lumpy sack with a grunt. "One of these magic pits would be mighty handy up at the bothy," He drawled. "This is just the start of the clean-up. It's gonna be a bureaucratic pile up if we don't get a move on. Better to have a few missing walkers than the remains of a gunfight. If anyone bothers to report those guys missing."

I looked over my shoulder. "Anthony, would you be willing to help?"

He stood immobile, looking down at me. "It is against my nature, but if I do not, you will. You are in no state to open dimensional doorways at the moment."

I stood up, swayed slightly, then planted my feet. "Damn straight I would. So, thank you for not making me."

He bowed, waving his hand in the air. The world shifted, and the black pit became the grey crossroads. "This way, Mr Carl." Anthony held out his hand.

Carl stepped across, waving at us from the other side. He did not appear at all travel sick. Anthony was going to have to teach me how to carry passengers more smoothly.

After the shimmer shrank into itself, Marcus offered me his shoulder since one of the younger companions had stepped in to help Nigel with Bill. We began the trip back. Limping down the track took four hours, but the injured couldn't move any faster and everyone was exhausted.

A square tower of solid granite stood at the edge of the river guarding the estate at the only pass between two rows of mountains as ragged as shark teeth. My manor, my refuge, the offer of rest and safety for my troops. The grimy stone, imposing towers and thick walls had never looked so good.

We stumbled into the courtyard. We were safe again. No siege had ever breached these fortifications. Economics was a different matter, though. Tourists from one of the many buses parked on the cobbles veered to the side, whispering excitedly as our group staggered in.

I wasn't a fan of the idea of opening my estate to the public, but had agreed to grant a few special dates each year. My luck… this was one of those weekends.

A stout, middle-age woman with her hair tied up in a neat bun at the back of her head and a phone in one hand bustled out of a side door.

She waved at the tour operator. "What's the problem?"

She saw us and nearly dropped her phone as she ran over.

"Oh, my God! Mr Kirkwood, I've been trying to call you for days. What happened?"

Bill lifted his head, the edges of his eyelids crinkling as he smiled. "Ah, Sally… mah phone died. That's all. We're fine. Just a wee spot of bother up on the ridge. Should have looked where I was putting my feet."

"Sir, the gamekeeper's cottage was torched. Police think it was arson," she said in a rush, the words tumbling out.

He patted her arm. "Nae worry Sally. I'll see to it."

She followed us to the manager's office, her eyes never leaving Bill while Nigel eased him down to a sofa. She hovered just behind them, plumping a cushion to put under his swollen leg.

Nigel stepped back to let her fuss. "We need the medieval wing open tonight. The board of trustees will be staying. Need to discuss the fire damage."

Sally looked nervously between the current and the retired managers.

Bill nodded at her. "He's right. Cannae leave the trustees out in the cold."

"Of course. Is there anything else?" She asked, her hand lingering on his. "Do you need me to call a doctor?"

"Naw, but a couple of paracetamol would go down a treat."

"Consider it done." She stroked his arm once, before turning with her phone to her ear. "Kelly, it's me... got a last-minute request... need to open the medieval wing. Aye, get the girls back—it'll need a bit of a clean..." her voice echoed down the hall as she disappeared further into the building.

Nigel waved at the window showing our dirt streaked group in the courtyard. "I'll get them some brekkie. Going to take Sally and her mob an hour or so to get the barracks ready." He nodded at his nephew as he left. "You get some kip and stay off that leg."

I sat down next to Bill, holding his hand after everyone had left, enjoying the peace of the room, content to watch the rise and fall of his chest. No one was shooting at us or trying to torture anyone. It was bliss.

"You should see more of her," I said after several minutes of silence.

He blinked, his breath catching. "You what?"

"Sally. It will do you good."

"Thank you, but I dinnae need a matchmaker."

Heels clicked in the hall outside Bill's office.

"You know I can't be anything more than I am." I squeezed his hand and stood. "Hope the tablets help."

I went outside without looking back. Second thoughts were a luxury I could not afford.

Around the corner of the building, a small crowd grew in front of the café. Vlad balanced a stone on his nose before flipping it into a puddle and getting lots of snacks for his effort. He never passed up an opportunity to scrounge.

Inside the café, the smell of bacon, eggs, and coffee mixed with damp stone. No amount of heat ever drove out the mustiness of the centuries-old carriage hall. Voices echoed off the flagstone floor. A lot of voices. Most of the tourists lingered over their finished plates, gawking at us. Presumptions flew thick in hushed whispers, trying to guess what we were filming.

My troop had pushed together several pale oak tables to make one long rectangle down the centre of the room. I made my way along it, greeting each man who had come to my aid with a kiss.

"Not sure you still need this but..." Nigel handed me a mug of coffee.

My beloved... My elixir.

I took a sip. The divine aroma followed the warm liquid, wrapping comfort around me like a blanket. "Cheers." I raised it to the table. "Good Health."

Ten men raised their drinks.

I carried on down the table, clasping shoulders and offering my thanks until I reached the end. Marcus, Tatya, Stephan, and Jamie sat in a tight cluster separate from the primary group. It was only a few inches of table space, but enough to be a worry. I needed to integrate them or risk splintering the entire troop. I pulled an empty chair over to sit next to the twins.

"There are several things we need to arrange." My words carried more bravado than they should. My future was uncertain. How could I arrange anything for these two?

Tatya dropped her head into her hands. Her shoulders quivered and Jamie put a hand on her back.

"If... and it is by no means certain, but if you two would like to start your training, I suggest you do so individually."

Stephan wrinkled his brow. "What?"

"You need to toughen up, my boy. I'd like you to stay here. Bill and Nigel can teach you a thing or two. Jamie—where do I start? You've got more on your plate than most your age. Familiar surroundings will help, as will familiar faces, so you need to go back to Maple Grove."

She kicked at the table leg. "Just like that? I'm back-benched. Why do the boys get to do the exciting stuff?"

Stephan wrapped his arms around his waist. "You want to stay here, be my guest."

I tapped a finger on my mug. "Going back to Maple Grove won't be dull. Quite the contrary. I'm sending Marcus with you. Trouble will probably come to you."

Marcus' body tightened ramrod straight. "ME? I've not practised in years."

"Considering how much you seem to remember, I think it just proves you'll be perfect. Also, both of you can clean up together."

Marcus frowned.

I leaned closer and lowered my voice enough it didn't carry to the rest of the table. "Intoxicating substances... You both seem to be enthusiasts... but it's not the best frame of mind to be in right now."

Jamie folded her arms and looked away. "I'm not an addict."

"But you do have issues with authority, family groups, trust... The two of you share more traits than I have time to list."

She turned to look at me. "I. Don't. Need. Help."

Tatya raised her head and looked at me with a face set like stone. "She's wrong. We do. We need... something."

Good, Tatya was tough enough to know when to accept a truce.

Marcus toyed with his fork, tracing the wood grain, so he didn't have to look at me. "First no family, now a squabbling flock. You do not make life easy, Anna."

"Thanks Marcus, never said I would." I leaned over and kissed his cheek. "Welcome back."

FORTY-FOUR

I left the others to their morning meal and walked back to the cottage. The coffee had restored my limbs, if not my mood. Vlad trotted next to me, sniffing at every stalk of grass. His eyes darted back and forth, then glanced at me every few feet. Poor fellow. Recent events had unnerved even his steady countenance.

The narrow trail had two deep ruts cut into the dirt. Multiple times, the track turned into a mire of sludge where the fire engine had fouled on the soft track and been forced through with the pure stubbornness of the crew. I shall have to send them a gift. They'd worked hard to save my home. Pity I'd worked harder to make sure it was destroyed.

At the top of the lane, three walls and part of the garden enclosure were all that remained of the old cottage. Yellow police tape fluttered from the door frame. Traces of smoke floated in the air, stirring bittersweet memories. Even the best restoration would never return the feeling of safety. The security, the familiarity, all that and more was gone…

Slow, ponderous steps shuffled through the grass behind me.

"Good morrow, I trust you are well, m'lady?" Urisk inclined his head.

"Urisk, I hold no authority over you. Call me cousin."

His beard trembled. "Truly?"

"Who else in this earthy realm knows the world as you do?" I reached out, holding his large fur covered hand in mine. "There is no other I would rather have as a confidant."

He tilted his head. "In spite of devastation, a blessing has grown. That is a most welcome occurrence."

I paused. Had this goat-man just spouted philosophy? Why not? Shape did not illustrate knowledge or intentions. There was much I could learn from him. "There is to be a gathering at the Hall this evening. I would be honoured if you would attend." Urisk deserved the reward as much as any of my companions.

He hunched his shoulders and looked away. "My thanks, but I will frighten the others."

"Would it please you to sit with me in private? I shall regale you with fine wine, and we can share tales in warmth and comfort."

The balcony was near enough to watch the celebrations without being observed. I preferred the distance. It was exhausting being amongst a crowd of youngsters for too long, but I loved hearing their joy and excitement. Urisk still looked worried.

"If I leave a tub of water out, you could jump from the between-zone," I said.

Urisk giggled. "I have never tried wine. You are sure no one will be frightened?"

I clasped his hand harder. "I am. Only my companions have access to the gallery."

Urisk's ears lifted. "Am I to be a companion?"

I froze. I'd never considered my words would appear to grant that favour. Part of me seized on the thoughts of what delights this majestic specimen of masculinity could grant. Another part of me cowered in fear. He wasn't even human. Rationality overruled both. I could not condemn any more souls to eternal, ghostly bondage. It was one thing to do it out of ignorance, but not intentionally.

"Since I do not know what it will mean to be a warden, I may have to…" Regret closed my throat. The words would not come. How would I remain sane without my companions? How would I keep any of my humanity?

Urisk pulled me into a bear hug. "I will not fail you."

Oh, dear… that wasn't quite what I meant…

Later that evening, the wind played with my hair as I sat on the rooftop listening to music and laughter tumble out of the hall. Sally and her team had done a wonderful job. From the number of people milling about, it seemed most of the village had been invited.

I smiled. Never hurt to ensure the goodwill of the locals.

Vlad sat down, then stood up, then down again, leaning hard against me. He watched my every move, uncertain if he liked this height. The only perk of the new job, as far as I could see, was that he could go everywhere I did now. However, what did it mean to be a warden? Unease settled in my stomach like a greasy lump of meat.

A stir of air announced Anthony's arrival.

"You pick very strange places to enjoy the night air." He sat down beside Vlad.

"Before I knew you, 'twas a quiet place for solitude. People down there know my secrets and are not oath bound.

That is a bit of a problem. I would appreciate some time to think about it."

"They are not a problem. No human will ever be able to incarcerate you now. Your secret is meaningless," he said.

"Perhaps, but 'tis never good to leave loose lips." I paused, bitterness flooded my heart. "Do you think the ghosts are suffering?"

He shrugged. "They seemed content, but I cannot know. You realise wardens have no power in the shadow realm. I was surprised you could even see them, let alone talk to them."

I played back what Geoffrey had said to me. He hadn't sounded aggrieved about his situation. "Perhaps their afterlife is not worse, simply different from most?"

Anthony shrugged again. "From my limited understanding, yes."

Perhaps I'd misread the situation, but it was still too early to decide. I looked at the night sky. The image of the guard chasing me on the ridge flitted through my mind. "I don't need them—do I?"

He glanced up at the crystal black expanse above us, then back at me. "No, it was never blood that you needed. It was the essence of life. You can drink that from anything. Remember I told you to walk in the sunshine? That is an excellent source of nutrition." He stood up, patting Vlad's back. "I will leave you to enjoy your celebrations. We will speak more tomorrow."

Anthony disappeared, leaving Vlad and me alone under the twinkling stars.

Some things changed, but others stayed the same. Tomorrow's problems were for tomorrow. All of Mine were safe and well for now. I hugged my hound tight and listened to the laughter, breathing deep to savour the night air.

Books in this series

Out of Time
Out of Step
Out of Control

If you'd like to know more about the start of Anna's unusual life try
1392 Into the Storm

Farewell

Thank you for visiting my story land. I hope you've enjoyed your adventure. In a world where thousands of books are written every day, finding the gems is a needle-in-a-haystack task. Please help me, and other readers, by leaving a review either on the site you purchased this from or a review site such as goodreads.com or bookbub.com. Every review is an enormous boost to emerging authors. Thanks for your support.

Also, if you'd like to keep up with all the latest news, as well as bonus material, back stories and insiders peek-behind-the-scenes, please take a moment to sign up for my newsletter. Details can be found at dragonlime.com.

You can leave comments on the website too. If I know which bits of my stories grab my reader's interest, I'll probably add more scenes and characters like that in future books.

About the author

Cherie grew up in rural Iowa; however, she currently calls England home. On this wet and windy island, she's learned to sculpt glass, climb mountains, run ultra-marathons and swing a long sword. In between all that activity, she carves out time to walk her dog and write.

You can keep up with all her endeavours at

dragonlime.com

and

facebook@CherieBakerAuthor

Acknowledgements

I would like to thank:

My parents for instilling my love of books and stories from a young age.

Alex for the plotting meetings, sympathy, and endless cups of coffee.

My advanced readers for casting their eyes over this work and offering suggestions for improvement.

The West Lothian Writers for your patience, laughter, and suggestions.

Thank you one and all.

Glossary

Arse — Bum.
Aye — Yes.
Bawbag — Scrotum or testicle, also used as an insult.
Bin it — To throw away or dispose of trash.
Bevy — Alcoholic drink.
Blether — Talking, sometimes rambling long-winded speeches.
Blighty — Britain.
Bolshie — Brash or aggressive actions.
Brekkie — Breakfast.
Brollachan — A bad-tempered, spiteful, shapeless entity from Scottish Gaelic mythology.
Burn — River or stream.
Cannae — Can't.
Cheers — Thanks or good bye.
Cludgies — Toilet.
Coo — Cows.
Cuppa — Warm drink, usually tea.
Dinnae — Didn't.
Dreich — Soaked. Heavy rain. Dreary atmosphere. Constant damp weather.

Eejit — Idiot.
Fancy a brew — Would you like a cup of tea?
Feart — Afraid.
Glen — Valley.
Greetin' — Crying or wailing.
Gubbed — Exhausted, ill, not thinking clearly, broken.
Hen — A word used to address females.
Jakey — Alcoholic, drug addict, or unsavoury person.
Juice — Fizzy soft drink.
Jolly — A frivolous trip. Can also mean very – as in jolly good.
Keep the heid — Calm down, act rationally.
Kelpies — Mythological horse that lives in the sea and steals children.
Kip — Sleep.
Knackered — Very tired or broken.
Nae — No, naw, or not.
Nowt — Nothing.
On yer bike — I don't believe you. Shut up. Go away.
Och — A sound made when exasperated or sympathetic.
Plod — Police.
Sarnies — Sandwiches.
Shite — Excrement. Pronounced like kite.
Snitch — Informant, tattle tail.
Ta — Short for thank you.
Telt — Told you.
Twat — Derogatory insult.
Wee — Something that is small or a young.
Wheesht — Be quiet.
Zeds — Sleep, have a nap.

Printed in Great Britain
by Amazon